PRIVATE PLEASURES

She studied Rafe Stewart's solid frame—powerful legs planted defiantly wide beneath a broad, unyielding chest. At the thought of his insolent vigor, she felt her pulse race as she groped down the maple tree to the ground.

The summer sun—oh, surely it was the summer sun—warmed her cheeks to a flaming peach color.

"Dare I ask why you found refuge in a tree, my lady?"

"I . . . I am not your lady." She took a step closer to Stewart, without knowing why.

He stared intently into her eyes and Sukey felt reason abandon her. "I loved climbing trees as a girl. For a brief while, I longed to relive my childhood and enjoy that pleasure again." She edged forward one more step.

Stewart's voice rumbled low in his chest. "What else do you long for, Mrs. Howard?" With one hand, strong yet gentle, he tilted her face up toward his. His fingers caressed the curve of her cheek.

Other Zebra Books by Marilyn Herr

WHERE THE HEART LEADS

SILK AND DENIM

SUMMER SWEET

LOOKING GOOD

FOR SUSANNAH

Marilyn Herr

ZEBRA BOOKS
Kensington Publishing Corp.
http://www.kensingtonbooks.com

ZEBRA BOOKS are published by

Kensington Publishing Corp.
850 Third Avenue
New York, NY 10022

PROM
Herr

All Kensington titles, imprints and distributed lines are available at special quantity discounts for bulk purchases for sales promotion, premiums, fund-raising, educational or institutional use.

Special book excerpts or customized printings can also be created to fit specific needs. For details, write or phone the office of the Kensington Special Sales Manager: Kensington Publishing Corp., 850 Third Avenue, New York, NY 10022. Attn. Special Sales Department. Phone: 1-800-221-2647.

Zebra and the Z logo Reg. U.S. Pat. & TM Off.

First Printing: May 2004
10 9 8 7 6 5 4 3 2 1

Printed in the United States of America

For my sisters in spirit:
Fran, Helena, Norma, and Ruth

Thanks, also, to Katie and William S.
for their kind assistance

Chapter One

Pennsylvania, 1755

"Damn George's deceit!"

Sukey Howard pinched brocade draperies back from her front parlor window and scowled at torrential April rains pounding her elegant Lancaster home.

"Tsk! Must not speak ill of the dead, cousin," Lettie Morris chided, peering anxiously over her shoulder. "Even . . . even if he was your husband."

"Men are not be trusted, Lettie. George tricked me into marrying him with false words of love. I assure you, I shall never marry again. Never!"

Six months of mourning, complete with smothering black garments and tiresomely drawn faces, bored Susannah Whitfield Howard. After all, George Howard, twenty-two years her senior, had never been a loving husband.

"Sukey! At twenty-nine, how can you say such a thing?" Lettie glanced round the expensively furnished parlor as she sipped from a porcelain tea cup. "George did provide many fine material possessions."

"Ah, but he never touched me! Not in the vigorous way a husband is supposed to touch his wife."

"Oh, mercy, Sukey!" Lettie clutched her chest. "I . . . I fear we ladies should not speak of such sensual matters." Hot fuchsia circles flamed Lettie's scrawny cheeks.

"George, it seems, wanted me only as a young decoration for his political and business soireés."

"Nothing more?"

"Not through our entire ten-year marriage, Lettie. And I shall tell you a secret, cousin. Expensive clothes and trinkets can never fill the hollow, loveless ache in a woman's life."

"Ma'am?"

"Yes, Anna?" Sukey turned to acknowledge her maid.

"A message just now arrived from your sister, ma'am."

Lettie Morris abruptly set down her tea cup. "I must dash off, Sukey. Do remember, you promised to attend our soireé tonight. I beg of you, dear, help me amuse Archie's out-of-town guests. You know how painfully shy I am around strangers. But Sukey . . . ?"

"Yes, dear?"

Lettie twisted her fingers anxiously. "You *will* behave yourself, will you not? Widows in Lancaster are expected to be—well, that is, can you conceal your natural ebullience just for one evening?"

A mischievous smile corrupted Sukey's lips. "I shall try my utmost, Lettie dear. For your sake. But the strangers?"

"A very fine gentleman and his aunt, according to Archie. His name is Sir Edward Knowles, I believe. Who knows, Sukey?" Lettie tittered into her gloved hand. "You might find the gentleman enchanting. Though . . . though, of course I know you are still in deep mourning and must therefore—"

"Yes. Of course," Sukey said dryly. "I shall come, Lettie. But only for your sake. Faith! Never again shall I crawl in bed with a 'very fine gentleman.' "

"Sukey! You must not say such scandalous . . . oh,

mercy!" Clasping her hands in horror, Lettie bolted out the front door and scuttled down Lime Street.

Sukey eagerly opened the red wax seal of her sister's letter. "Ah, Rachel! How I envy you!" Sukey murmured, as she read on.

Rachel, who lived with her husband near the Allegheny River, was now pregnant with their first child. The couple shared a trading enterprise with Sukey's father and brother.

Suddenly Sukey brightened. "The perfect escape!" she said, clapping her hands so abruptly it startled a soot-colored cat sleeping at Sukey's feet.

Excitement, sense of purpose, an element of danger? Oh, quite!

In one fell swoop, she would be liberated. She could assist Rachel in childbirth, pursue adventure on the Allegheny frontier, shed her tiresome black mourning clothes—all at the same time! Praise be! Sweet precious freedom, with no man to dominate her, as cunning George Howard had.

Sukey dimpled at the thought of her scheme. Who could possibly question a "sad widow" who desired to rejoin her family?

But how?

"No woman can travel all that distance alone," she whispered. Crossing Pennsylvania's endless mountains seemed a formidable challenge. No stagecoaches journeyed that far west.

Still pondering her dilemma that evening, Sukey walked two blocks to the brick home of Lettie and Archie Morris, then winced at the idea of the company there. "A tedious assemblage of self-important men lamenting about politics!" she muttered in disgust as she hoisted her skirts to ascend the front steps. With an annoyed sigh, Sukey adjusted her plain black bonnet before entering the drawing room.

"Cousin Sukey!" Reaching for her hand, Archie Morris emerged from a circle of merchants. "Susannah Howard, may I present Sir Edward Knowles? Sir Edward and his aunt just arrived in our fair city after an arduous journey from Philadelphia."

Though tall, with large hands, Sir Edward Knowles struck Sukey as an excessively adorned peacock.

She disliked him at once.

His cambric neck cloth topped a ruffled shirt of fine linen. An abundance of silver braid trimmed his silk vest. He wore not just one, but two pocket watches with tasseled fobs, and clocked silk stockings.

Guardedly extending her right hand, Sukey addressed the stranger in cool, clipped tones. "Welcome, Sir Edward," she said. Mentally dismissing the man as a trivial fop, she turned away.

Knowles, however, kept her hand firmly in his grasp. "Mrs. Howard, I beg of you, allow me to extend my condolences on the recent tragic loss of your husband."

" 'Twas six months ago, sir."

"Six months ago," he repeated.

Those twinkling blue eyes behind Knowles's spectacles made Sukey uneasy. An intense shade of blue were those eyes, the color of exuberant autumn skies just before an onrushing storm. They shone with a mysterious sense of comprehension, as well.

Almost . . . almost as if the stranger could read her mind.

Mercy!

Perhaps he understood Sukey's secret wish to be liberated from all this dreadful black crepe and bombazine mourning attire—something she had not confided to one living soul other than Lettie. She needed to escape this odious man's prying eyes at once!

"Your kind expression of sympathy warms my heart, Sir Edward. Now I feel certain you long to discuss politics with the gentlemen, so I shall not detain you one moment longer."

He lingered. "Mrs. Howard, I wonder if I might beg a favor of you—most certainly a gentle woman of a deeply sensitive, compassionate nature."

Her eyebrow rose. Sukey resented Knowles's wry expression as he described her character.

"The favor, Mrs. Howard, concerns my aunt, Regina Ramsey. At the moment, she appears to be alone. And being new in town, Aunt would relish meeting a woman as gracious as yourself."

"Of course, Sir Edward," Sukey replied, eager to flee this alarming gentleman's amused gaze.

"Especially since we shall be leaving town shortly to travel west," Knowles finished.

Sukey froze in her tracks. She turned back to face Knowles. "West? Did you say, 'west,' Sir Edward?"

"Indeed, madam. Business interests near the Allegheny River compel us to travel west almost at once."

"You . . . and your aunt, sir?"

"And of course my servant, Fitch. A guide will escort all three of us. Though, indeed, I do so fear the hazards it entails." Pursing his lips in fitful agitation, Knowles flicked his wrist with alarm.

Despite her repugnance—this tall, dandified coward had a face troweled with a thick layer of white powder and rouge—Sukey fought back a self-satisfied grin. "Why, how very exciting, Sir Edward! Indeed, I shall be pleased to make your aunt's acquaintance this very minute. I should not want her believing Lancaster to be an inhospitable town."

"Most kind of you, Mrs. Howard. I knew the moment I saw you that your character was indeed noble."

Knowles's puzzling tone irritated Sukey as she searched out Regina Ramsey. Foppish Sir Edward's voice continued to say one thing . . . while his probing blue eyes flashed quite another. Sukey found pudgy Regina Ramsey, a middle-aged woman with soft, kind eyes, stranded near a side table of refreshments.

"My name is Susannah Howard, madam, though everyone calls me Sukey. Do come join me for some cake, Mrs., uh, Miss . . ."

"I respond most warmly to plain 'Regina,' Mrs. Howard. And I am delighted to make your acquaintance."

Sukey found Regina Ramsey instantly amiable. Seated beside Knowles's aunt on a maple settee, she asked, "Will you find it dreadfully inconvenient—to travel all that distance on horseback, Regina?"

The older woman smiled merrily. "Not a bit of it, Sukey! I was born with a desire to travel, you see. Always needing to discover what lies beyond the horizon. And dear Edward, my nephew, is quite solicitous of my welfare at all times."

Sukey swallowed a bite of walnut cake. "Your . . . nephew, Regina. Is he stalwart enough for such an arduous journey? He . . . he seems . . ." She stumbled over an appropriate choice of words.

"Edward? Well, I grant you he has great fondness for personal fashion, powder, and paint. But beneath all that lace and adornment lies a valiant spirit." She dropped her gaze. "At least, one hopes."

"Indeed," Sukey murmured, scarcely believing a word of it as she savored another cake crumb. Her glance shifted to Knowles, who stood amidst a clutch of worried men huddled over whiskey and clay pipes.

"I tell you, gentlemen," insisted a squat, bow-legged

Lancaster banker, "that Mohawk bolted down the Susque-hanna quick as he could to spread the news! Says a whole detachment of French have left Montreal for the Ohio Valley . . . with more detachments to follow!"

A white-haired German farrier shook his head. "Ach, there will be hell to pay before this is over."

"Who, I ask you, will stop the French?" a worried shopkeeper fretted, pounding his fist into his palm.

Sir Edward Knowles, Sukey noticed, shifted rest-lessly from one foot to another. Quite as she suspected. Danger made this overdecorated dandy ill at ease. Dressed in abundant frills and lace, brawny but skittish Sir Edward Knowles seemed more harmless than a frightened kitten.

Divinely perfect for her purposes, she thought, sup-pressing a sly smile as Knowles suddenly came to her side.

"Aunt, I fear our departure for the Alleghenies must be delayed for a day, at our guide's insistence."

Sukey straightened. "Then you and your aunt must dine tomorrow at my house, Sir Edward! My cook's chicken-corn soup is superlative. You must come sam-ple it."

Knowles squinted through his spectacles at Sukey's abrupt shift in disposition.

"Charming!" Regina exclaimed. "Ah, Edward, we shall be delighted, shall we not? Edward?"

After a studied moment, Knowles adjusted his spec-tacles. A keen sparkle returned to his vivid blue eyes. "Indeed," Knowles replied, delicately moistening his lips with his tongue.

Sukey watched impatiently, next afternoon, as her two guests relished savory bowls of soup ladled from a tureen. After daintily wiping her mouth with a pale linen napkin, she cleared her throat.

"Dear Regina and Sir Edward," she began in honeyed tones, "for I now think of you as my dear friends. It occurs to me that we three have a common goal. For different reasons, of course. Your critical business interests along the Allegheny River require your immediate attention."

Sukey paused.

Knowles studied her expression. "Go on, Mrs. Howard," he urged cautiously, neatening his shirt ruffles.

"I have family out there, you see. Father, brother, sister, and her husband—together they operate a trading post on Turtle Creek." Sukey dabbed theatrically at her dry eyes with a handkerchief, as if to dispel tears. "In my lonely widowed state, dear friends, I feel a momentous longing to rejoin my adored family."

A muscle twitched in Knowles's firm jaw as he followed Sukey's drama.

"But thus far, I simply have not been able to secure a respectable guide. Nor chaperone." Sukey swept the handkerchief across her eyes once more for effect.

"Sukey, my dear!" Regina cried. "Distress yourself no longer! You shall travel with us! Your company would enchant us, would it not, Edward?"

Sukey shifted uncomfortably in her chair. Knowles's piercing blue eyes, even through his spectacles, unnerved her. She evaded his stare.

"Why, you mean . . . you mean you would permit me to travel along with you?" Sukey feigned astonishment. "Oh, dear friends! I must give this matter deep thought. What a fascinating suggestion on your part!"

With a sly smile, Knowles lowered his spoon to the table. "Mrs. Howard, dare we hope?" he gushed, gaily waving his lace-trimmed wrists. "Might you consider travelling with our humble group? Truly a more merry band of compatriots I simply could not imagine! Though, of course—"

"Yes?" Abruptly, Sukey dropped her handkerchief to stare at Knowles's thickly rouged and powdered face.

"We shall, I fear, require the consent of our guide. A Lenape chap named Red Hawk. Determined sort of fellow. A bit, well, ferocious, actually." Knowles shuddered, as if ferocity frightened him.

Leaning toward Knowles, Sukey patted his hand in a calming gesture. "Fret not, Sir Edward. I am a strong and fearless woman, as you shall shortly discover. I shall not burden Red Hawk with any superficial requirements."

"No? A strong and fearless woman, you say?" He seemed to be hiding a smile.

"In fact, you shall most likely find my courage an asset on our westward journey."

"An asset, you say? Hmm. You mount a most convincing argument for travel, Mrs. Howard." His bushy dark eyebrows swooped low over his twinkling eyes as he cradled his jaw in the palm of one large fist. "But would it be proper for us to snatch you away from Lancaster, you being in . . . deep mourning?"

Avoiding Knowles's acute gaze, Sukey coughed quietly. "I am stalwart, sir. I shall cope."

"My dear Susannah!" Regina burbled. "You would be such delightful feminine company for me! In return, we could properly chaperone and escort you."

Exactly the response Sukey Howard sought. She lowered her gaze to conceal her pleasure.

And to heighten drama.

"How can I possibly thank you two sufficiently for your kindness?" she murmured, affecting feigned teary tenderness with downswept eyelashes.

"There, there now, dear Mrs. Howard," Knowles

replied, bowing. "Rest assured, the joy you will bring to us shall far outweigh our humble efforts."

Unpleasant heat flamed Sukey's cheeks as Knowles's gaze lingered on her bosom.

"We shall seek Red Hawk's approval this very afternoon, Mrs. Howard. But heed this, dear lady—I fear the menacing chap's word must determine our actions."

"No!" Knowles bellowed, stripping off his satin waistcoat in his rented room. "Bloody hell! A high-spirited woman like Susannah Howard can only complicate our plans. The wench has danger written all over her!"

Hands on hips, Regina Ramsey glared at her nephew. "Do be reasonable, Edward! Sukey would be the perfect foil for our activities."

Knowles yanked impatiently at his cambric neck cloth. "Foil? God's blood, Aunt! Scheming Mrs. Howard is more devious than any backroom full of London politicians. And with her pretense at mourning, about as safe as a coiled rattlesnake."

"But with her sparkling green eyes and fetching dimples, Edward, far prettier than a snake."

Knowles snorted. "Aunt, your transparent efforts at matchmaking will do no good. Hell! Are all women devious?"

Regina gently rested her hand on his arm. "Dear boy, not all women are like Isabel, I assure you. But more to the point, French officers will never suspect our intentions with the amusing 'Widow Howard' along to distract them. I recommend we take her with us, Edward."

Listening to their conversation, Fitch glowered as he carefully folded Knowles's frock coat. "Keeping an adventure-seeking widow out of trouble . . . and our hair . . . will likely prove to be . . . "

"Irksome!" Knowles exploded, tugging off his silk stockings. "Especially when she meets up with Rafe Stewart."

"Now, Edward!" Regina hid a conspiratorial smile. "Do be brave. Surely Susannah Howard is a person that you—or Rafe Stewart—can easily handle."

Stripped down to her cotton shift, that night Sukey brushed her loose auburn tresses with long, pensive strokes. Something indefinable disturbed her about Sir Edward Knowles—a man impossibly vain in his attention to speech and personal adornment.

"An absurd dandy!" she muttered between clenched teeth. "A fool! Near effeminate, truly, with his painted face and fancy clothes!" Oddly, though, beneath Knowles's exquisite satin garments, there seemed to be . . . well, a lean-muscled man of vigor.

"Impossible!" she cried aloud, resuming her brushing in short angry bursts. Surely she was mistaken. The man possessed not one jot of masculine strength. Not one!

Why, then, that curious, unsettling gleam in Knowles's eyes whenever he beheld Sukey? Disturbing eyes, actually, more intensely blue than a whole field of flax flowers shimmering under a summer sun.

Sukey shivered.

No matter. Tall but prissy Sir Edward Knowles was harmless. He and his aunt would liberate Sukey from her Lancaster "prison" and her mourning.

Sukey stared into the mirror at her melancholy expression. Though nearly thirty, she had never truly been loved by a man. Never known the arousing touch of a passionate husband still in his prime who could make her feel . . .

Dear God, what was it she yearned to feel?

Still almost virginal, Susannah Whitfield Howard scarcely knew.

Two days later, she questioned her sanity as insects stung her flesh and damp river air filled her nostrils. She jounced on horseback over low, rolling hills that tipped down toward the wide Susquehanna River.

Descending the last rise, Sukey discreetly studied her four new "travelling companions." An effeminate, spineless man, an amiable but equally useless woman in the face of probable disaster, a dour-faced servant, a sullen Indian guide.

"A madwoman, am I!" she muttered under her breath as her horse sidestepped a treacherous hole. "Surely my teeth and bones shall rattle loose from days of riding!"

The wisdom of undertaking this westward adventure began to elude Sukey.

"Exquisite scenery, Mrs. Howard," Sir Edward called to her, as they halted at Harris's Ferry. "But these gnats are an abomination!" he whimpered, dabbing at dust on his brocaded frock coat.

Rafting the mile's distance across the Susquehanna, Sukey bit her cheek and prayed for patience. To escape the prying eyes of Lancaster and seek adventure, she had to pay a steep price . . . the grating companionship of Sir Edward Knowles.

Sukey grimaced at the thought. "How long might our journey take, Sir Edward?" she asked, thin-lipped and tense.

"Perhaps seven days or so, depending on the weather." Knowles gestured toward the dour Lenape standing at the raft's fore. "Red Hawk will make haste, since he knows how eager we are to reach the Allegheny River."

The strength in Knowles's hands and arms astonished

Sukey, as he helped her disembark from the ferry. Surely her overzealous imagination played tricks on her. Any fool could see, by Sir Edward's limp demeanor, that even the weariest of women had greater strength than he.

While the men shared a brief smoke with the ferry-man, Sukey tarried alongside Knowles' aunt.

"A lovely locket you wear, Regina."

The older woman opened it to reveal miniatures of two children. "My angels."

"You never mentioned your children. Where do they live?"

"In Heaven, surely," Regina answered simply. "My darlings were carried off by putrid fever many years ago."

"And . . . your husband?" Sukey asked, tentatively.

"Killed by the French, one tragic day, eight years ago. Edward is the only family I have left. The dear boy is like my own child, and most accommodating to my needs."

The very mention of family made Sukey long for the sight of her own. Rachel, a carefree but loving sister, and her husband, Jonah Butler. Zeb Whitfield, a strapping brother with a talent for fixing almost anything, especially guns. And Pa—Eli Whitfield—an irascible widower, devoted to his adult children.

Regina mistook Sukey's silence for introspective sorrow. Tenderly, she patted Sukey's arm. "Susannah, my dear, I know you still feel great sadness at the untimely loss of your husband. But perhaps one day, when your heart mends, you will marry again."

Sukey jerked her head up. "Never!" she said.

"Oh, I know how you feel, dear. But . . ." Regina cast a sideways glance at Sir Edward, as if linking him to their conversation.

Sukey detected that curious glance. Did Regina, even for a moment, entertain the notion that Sukey might consider bloodless Sir Edward Knowles as a potential husband? Never, Sukey thought with a shudder! Marriage had proved to be a hollow disappointment. Nothing more than a prison for unloved women. A prison for which she had no use. Did Regina think she was grieving for George Howard?

Sukey knew otherwise.

Men dressed in wigs and silks and ruffles—men absorbed by politics and business—made poor lovers and husbands. What good was a dull husband? She intended to carve out her own fate without any man to interfere. If ever she took another man into her bed—an unlikely occurrence—it would certainly not be weak, frivolous Sir Edward Knowles, who tended his fine clothes and face with absurd self-absorption.

He bowed low when she and Regina rejoined the men.

"Ladies, a small repast before we depart for Carlisle," Fitch announced, setting out some cheese, cold meats, and bread.

Regina daintily sidestepped, leaving Knowles next to Sukey.

Tiny prickles traced Sukey's spine. This will not do! she thought. That ominous twinkle in Knowles's blue eyes whenever he beheld her? Surely it did not mean the man had designs on her affections?

Once in Carlisle, Knowles politely excused himself. "Fitch and I shall arrange for new horses while you ladies, ah, freshen your attire.

A curl of smoke rose from his pipe as he engaged fresh mounts in the livery stable.

"I see how you watch the Howard woman," Fitch scolded, with a click of his tongue. "She tempts you, my boy. But nothing is allowed to disrupt our mission. Not even a luscious little crumpet like Mrs. Howard. Else, all may be lost."

Knowles snorted at the insinuation. "My passions, Fitch? You fret over nothing. My . . . appetites remain under complete control. Mrs. Howard is merely another pretty lass, no more. Like all the others I have bedded."

"Like all the others, eh?" Fitch asked skeptically. "Be certain your mask does not slip, even for a pretty lass. Else you might lose your life . . . and ours, as well."

Knowles's levity vanished. "My reasons for this trip are too powerful, Fitch, for me to be distracted by a bored little widow in search of adventure. When have you ever seen me lose sight of a military goal because of a woman?"

"Well . . . never," the older man replied, dragging out his response dubiously.

"Exactly. And this occasion, you shall see, is no different."

But was it?

Adjusting the queue of his stylish white wig, Sir Edward watched stable hands groom a nervous mare. Susannah Howard, Knowles reminded himself, aroused nothing more in him than a scant *frisson* of curiosity. If that.

A bored, frisky wench who played a less-than-convincing young widow in mourning. Much like the edgy mare he continued to study, Susannah Howard needed the strong hands of a determined man all over her to calm her down.

He smiled at what that challenge might present.

The wench was up to something, all right. But what? Knowles drew on his pipe as Sukey Howard and Regina emerged from the tavern door.

Fitch was right, of course. France and England intended to batter each other in the backwoods of Pennsylvania. Much was at stake, in the next few weeks. Knowles needed to keep his hands off the tempting Mrs. Howard.

He shrugged.

Even so, over his shoulder, he watched her rearrange a black shawl around her comely shoulders. A brief gesture, yet something in that graceful motion heightened Sukey Howard's feminine curves. Her breasts, hips, arms, even her peach-colored cheeks with those saucy dimples, displayed an enticing roundness that begged to be touched. Under all that black cloth Sukey Howard wore was pale white satin skin that he . . .

Knowles felt blood rush to lower portions of his own body. He muttered a curse.

Maybe Fitch was right. Even thinking about the lovely Mrs. Howard's body might sabotage Knowles's critical reconnaissance mission.

To stay alive, and fulfill his orders from Whitehall, somehow he had to keep his hands off this one particularly tempting wench. Not easy, considering his lusty sexual appetites.

Only one way to carry it off.

Susannah Howard flinched at Knowles's foppish antics. Perfect. He must exaggerate "Sir Edward's" mannerisms even further—to fool suspicious Frenchmen and repel this dimpled widow. In a few days, mischievous little Susannah Howard would disappear from his life forever.

"Not a day too soon," he muttered, before rejoining the two women.

"My dears," Knowles began, feigning flustered agitation, "Red Hawk assures me the mounts he procured are suitable for our journey across the mountains. But merciful heavens! They seem far too nervous for my liking."

Sukey studied the horses. "Quite likely animals, Sir Edward. I should think they will serve beautifully. Calm yourself with the notion that Regina and I shall be riding close by in case you need assistance." She flashed him a condescending smile as she clicked her tongue at his inadequacy.

That tongue-click nearly undid Knowles.

Mrs. Howard's sweet pink mouth . . . and that pert tongue. Lord! Knowles ached to pull Susannah into his arms and show her what sort of man he actually was.

Precisely what he must never do.

Until, that is, he completed the job London had assigned him. By then, tempting Susannah Howard would be long out of his sight. He need only hold off for six or seven more days . . .

For England, and Thomas, he reminded himself with tensed muscles.

They rode single file down the twisting valley of Conodoguinet Creek that April afternoon. The bright sun cast sparkles along banks of pale bluets and shone emerald green in soggy marshes thick with huge skunk cabbage leaves.

When Red Hawk paused, to allow his party a brief rest, Regina pointed out a mallard drake swimming close to his mud-brown hen. "How romantic!" she purred. "Even ducks and birds know 'tis spring. See how they all settle into cozy pairs? Love is so delightful!"

Sukey scampered onto a round boulder for better observation.

Ignoring his aunt's pointed comments, Knowles was about to turn aside when a chilling pattern suddenly caught his eye. On the boulder, a coiled rattlesnake lay poised ready to strike Sukey's stockinged ankle. With only a split second to respond, Knowles pulled his concealed knife and hurled it at the creature.

At the commotion, Sukey spun around. She gaped, speechless, at the snake and the knife protruding from its body, only inches from her foot. Then at Fitch and Knowles standing close by.

"My dear Mrs. Howard!" Knowles spluttered, with an unseen nudge to his male companion, "I do believe Fitch has just saved your life!"

"How very quick-witted and brave of you, Fitch!" Sukey exclaimed, finally able to breathe once more. "Sir Edward is indeed most fortunate to have a clever servant such as yourself."

"Quite!" agreed sly Regina, who had seen the entire episode.

Knowles fanned himself excessively with his hand. "Oh, mercy! I fear this means we must scrutinize every rock and path for viperous attackers! Dear me! Vigilance shall be the order of the day from here to journey's end, must it not? Oh, I do hope I can bear up!" Turning away from Sukey, he winked knowingly at Fitch.

But from that moment on, Knowles knew he must keep a watchful eye on Sukey Howard till journey's end. "Only for the wench's safety," he muttered to himself, scowling.

When Knowles nicked his finger that night at their campsite west of Shippensburg, Sukey snatched up a large mullein leaf to bind his wound. "Bear up, Sir Edward!" she chided, watching his jaw tense as she gently bandaged his hand. "You must learn to be brave, like your servant, Fitch. Surely the pain cannot be so great?"

Knowles stared hard at Sukey's slender fingers wrapped around his own hand. "Oh, my dear . . . you have no idea." His mouth quirked at one corner. "Would that I could be courageous like Fitch. My fondest hope, you see."

"Your signet ring bears a trace of blood, Sir Edward."

Still holding Knowles's right hand, she dabbed at the ring's elegant blue stone, which featured a prominent swirling letter "K". "As well, you have bloodied your fine satin jacket, sir. Hand it to me. I shall clean it as best I can."

He removed it, keeping his shirt on. Curious, Sukey thought, looking away from Knowles's obviously muscular chest and broad back, how such a large man could have matured into a . . . well, an emasculate coward.

No matter.

Sir Edward Knowles's predicament was none of her concern. Riding toward the western frontier, Sukey anticipated sweet liberation from society's constraints. Delicious freedom flooded every inch of her body.

No man would ever steal this glorious freedom from her again.

Chapter Two

Sukey felt her saddle press into her backside as she followed Red Hawk and Fitch through a gap in Blue Mountain, then over a washboard of low mountains. They labored across Kittatinny Mountain, Tuscarora Mountain, and through Shade Gap.

At the narrows cut by a creek through Blacklog Mountain, a drastic storm forced Red Hawk to halt. Huddled beneath a root-laced overhang, Sukey wrapped herself in her blanket and hunkered before their campfire.

Knowles contemplated rainwater gushing down the mountainside near Sukey's soaked and shivering figure. He pulled a blanket from his own shoulders.

"Mrs. Howard," he began, "my blanket warms me to excess. Please accept—"

Suddenly Knowles heard the crack of torn roots and a boulder on the move above Sukey as thunder exploded near by. Seizing her, he shoved Sukey aside.

"Really, Sir Edward! Entirely too rough of you! Indeed, you nearly knocked me down this hillside!"

"Pray, forgive me, Mrs. Howard!" he begged with exaggerated sighs, glancing at the rock tumbling on down the steep slope. "But that last thunderclap simply undid my resolve to be brave. I fear I must have clutched at you in an impulsive, frightened gesture."

"Bravery, Sir Edward, is a characteristic you might

surely develop if you tried. One's attitude makes all the difference. Why, I feel near-fearless every day."

"My dear Mrs. Howard! I do so marvel at your splendid courage." Knowles cocked one bushy black eyebrow.

"Breathe deeply, sir, then straighten your spine and remind yourself that nothing out there is more cunning or ferocious than you."

"Sage advice, indeed, Mrs. Howard." Knowles readjusted his tipped wig. "When the next fearsome situation arises, I shall attempt to follow your clever wisdom."

He exchanged a silent glance with Regina and Fitch.

"Apparently, Sir Edward, you are more at ease in a town drawing room than traversing the wilderness," Sukey noted.

He fanned out wrist ruffles on his white linen shirt to hasten drying. "Mercy, yes, Mrs. Howard! Decidedly so."

"Then why have you elected to cross this rugged frontier? Surely you could have sent a trusted servant to do your bidding? Well, could you not?"

Knowles hesitated. "The lure of new business, madam, raises a gentleman's blood. I eagerly anticipate . . . arranging judicious trade bargains with natives along the Allegheny frontier."

"But, sir, with your . . . your nervous sensitivity, do you not fear threats from encroaching French soldiers? I hear they can be brutal to British traders."

"French soldiers?" Knowles waved his fingers in a show of nonchalance. "French officers at Fort Duquesne are likely true gentlemen, madam. I look forward to exchanging pleasantries with them."

Sukey gasped. "Your naiveté appalls me, sir! How could you possibly think—? Do you speak French?"

"Fluently, madam," he replied, his voice somber.

Sukey found Knowles's tone and facial expression altogether odd, while discussing Fort Duquesne.

When the storm abated that evening, Sukey took her sewing from her reticule and reviewed Knowles's puzzling demeanor. She detested a fainthearted coward, to be sure. So unlike a real man! Yet, by virtue of his accidental touches, she discovered that beneath Knowles' gaudy silken attire was the rock-hard body of a strong man. His eyes—at times a plum-blue, the shade of distant mountains—pierced his surroundings with hawklike sharpness.

As if he was perpetually vigilant.

Yet he tittered often, indicating that serious thoughts rarely entered his well-coiffed head.

Did she tend to see mystery where none existed? Likely so, Sukey thought, dismissing her concerns as she resumed stitching.

Fording Aughwick Creek, next day, they rode through an afternoon squall with high winds. The scent of damp sphagnum filled the air as dead limbs from overhead trees crashed to the forest floor.

"Best be vigilant," Fitch growled. "This howling wilderness spooks our horses."

Sukey sensed a tense unease grow among horses and riders alike.

Knowles edged his gelding close beside her piebald mare. "Forgive me, Mrs. Howard, but in anxious moments, I feel more secure in your brave shadow."

She resented his clinging, pathetic inadequacy while she struggled with a nervous horse. Sukey's mount whinnied in shrill plaints. Feeling the horse tremble beneath her, Sukey clutched at the reins.

"Sir Edward!" she burst out impatiently. "How many times need I remind you that—"

With an ear-splitting crash, a huge limb plunged to the

ground just to their left. At the sound, Sukey's terrified mare reared, pawing at invisible demons in the air with its front legs.

Sukey screamed as she began sliding from her saddle.

A strong invisible hand seized Sukey's reins and steadied her horse. Regina closed in from the right.

Gasping for breath, as Sukey stared at her panicked horse's mane, she failed to notice which hand had steadied her mount.

"Ah, Regina! How quick-witted and clever you are!" she exclaimed, while Knowles edged away. "Did you see that, Sir Edward? Your aunt heroically calmed my horse. You might certainly learn a lesson in bravery from her!"

"Quite!" he answered in a quavering voice that bespoke awe. "Reluctantly, however, I fear Aunt has inherited the family's entire share of courage."

They followed Aughwick Creek and reached Standing Stone at dusk. The men tended horses while Sukey admired the sunset's beauty from the edge of a high rise.

"Look at the sky, Regina! Such magnificent clouds and brilliant colors!"

"'Twould be hard to imagine a lovelier sight," the older woman agreed. "Red Hawk says we must be nearly halfway across these endless mountains."

"I feel enlivened since we left Lancaster, Regina. This crisp air exhilarates me."

"Quite a contrast to your gracious Lancaster home, Sukey. Will you be content to stay in the wilds of the Ohio Valley? Even in the midst of your family?"

Sukey stretched out her arms to the sunset's blazing orange and lavender rays. "I feel convinced, somehow, that a spirited adventure awaits me along the Allegheny River. That my life will never again be the same. Oh, Regina, you cannot imagine how I long for excitement!"

"Your . . . marriage, Sukey. Not a happy one, I surmise?"

Plucking a tightly coiled fern crozier from its slender stalk, Sukey stared ahead through a maze of walnut trees. "A decoration for drawing room soireés, Regina. 'Twas all George Howard wanted from me—though I had no way of knowing it till after he married me."

"A passionless marriage," Regina commented with a knowing nod. "Lacking in love."

"I have never known the touch of a strong man who loves me, Regina. No matter how desperate my circumstances, never again shall I marry a man who fails to engage my emotion."

A merry twinkle enlivened Regina's hazel eyes. "Take heart, my dear. Perhaps just west of the Allegheny Mountains, a rugged suitor capable of great tenderness eagerly awaits your ardor."

"Hmph! Likely no such man exists, Regina. It matters not. Adventure is what I crave, not love. How long do you suppose business will detain you and Sir Edward on the frontier?"

Regina's blithe expression vanished. "As you so accurately commented, Sukey, one never knows these things. I . . . I can only hope Edward will complete his business in short order. I have friends in Philadelphia whom I long to see again."

Sukey patted the pudgy woman's hand. "Poor Regina. Never fear. I shall be your friend while you linger on the Allegheny. You shan't perish with loneliness if I can help it."

"Dear Sukey! You have a kind disposition. Now, enjoy the sunset while I step behind the bushes a moment."

Ever curious, Sukey edged closer to the plateau's rim. Far below, cool white mists lingered in a steep, boulder-strewn gorge. Rain-soaked soft earth crumbled beneath

Sukey's foot as a red-tailed hawk drifted in lazy circles over the abyss.

Caught up in splendid sunset tranquility, Sukey leaned closer to the rim. Suddenly the moist earth yielded beneath her feet! Certain she would tumble down the gorge, Sukey screamed and flailed the air for a branch to grasp . . . and felt strong hands clasp her waist.

"Sir Edward!" she cried, glancing back over her shoulder. "I never heard you! I . . ."

He held her briefly till her breathing slowed. "Mrs. Howard, you do seem to have a penchant for disaster. I, uh, did call to you, but you failed to hear my approach."

His voice rumbled deeper than usual.

Allowing her tension to ease, Sukey realized she had lingered within the tender circle of Knowles's arms. She abruptly pushed away from his embrace.

"Thank you, Sir Edward," she sniffed, brushing off her flowing black sleeves, "but I am quite capable of caring for myself."

He released her. Slowly.

"Of course you are, madam. I only wish I possessed a fraction of your unbounded courage." He rearranged crumpled ruffles adorning his shirt and smiled wryly at her.

That smile disturbed Sukey.

In fact, Knowles's entire manner unnerved her. His eyebrows formed sardonic wings above his nose as he . . . was that a smirk he wore? And his voice sounded almost . . . husky.

Merciful heavens! Was this repulsive, lace-clad fop falling in love with her? Out here in the middle of Pennsylvania's mountains, where escape was not a possibility? She would have none of it! Or him!

"I heard a commotion! Sukey, did you scream?" Busily rearranging her skirts, Regina hastened back from her brief absence. "Edward, what has happened?" Puzzled, she looked from one party to the other.

Sukey's chin shot defiantly into the air. "I merely slipped, Regina. Sir Edward happened upon the scene. Ever the perfect gentleman, he . . . he assisted me."

As if suddenly comprehending the situation, Regina grinned. "You naughty rascal!" she exclaimed, shaking a forefinger at Knowles. "Can I not let you out of my sight, Edward? Even for a moment? I promised dear Sukey I would chaperone her, but indeed you are proving a challenge!"

"Aunt! You embarrass us both with your sensational accusations. Can you not see the blush claiming my cheeks?" He simpered in mock shame.

"Repast is prepared, sir!" Fitch called from the campfire.

Grateful for Fitch's intervening summons, Sukey edged toward the welcoming odor of broiled meat.

As Regina read her Bible that night, and Knowles labored over his journal by firelight, Sukey settled against a broad maple trunk and contemplated her present situation.

She was about to craft a brand new life.

Marriage, thankfully, would not be a part of it! Not marriage to a timid fool like Sir Edward Knowles, who giggled and preened to wretched excess. The thought of coupling with such a man revolted Sukey. How she longed for the lusty ardor of a vigorous man who would sweep her into his arms, cover her with passionate kisses, and pledge his true love!

Sukey exhaled.

Was that ecstatic euphoria only a dream? Never to happen in her life? Perhaps. But she would never again marry a man she did not love with her whole heart and soul.

Branches rustled in the darkness several yards beyond

their campfire. Leaves crunched, as if something—or someone—trod nearby in the black of night.

Sukey swallowed hard. Glancing up, she saw Sir Edward Knowles staring at her over the pages of his journal.

"Strange noises can be so frightening in the woods. Especially at night," he whimpered. "Do night noises fill you with dread as well, Mrs. Howard?"

Had she been too harsh with Knowles? Possessed of a delicate nature easily bruised, the skittish fellow seemed entirely lacking in rugged bravado—despite his brawny frame. Might a few kind words from her soothe his nocturnal panic? She could spare that much compassion.

Seated on the ground, she slid closer to him.

"You must not allow fear to consume you, Sir Edward. Night noises are simply sighs of the forest. Nothing more. Especially when we bolster one another with our companionship."

"Oh, Mrs. Howard! You invariably say the precise thing to calm my various frights. Could you . . . could you sit a bit closer, madam? Oh, I do feel ever so much calmer when you comfort me with your brave words."

Reluctantly, Sukey leaned close enough to feel Knowles's warmth.

"I notice, Sir Edward, that as we approach the Ohio Valley, you labor in greater detail over your journal."

His startled, unusually somber response jolted Sukey.

"I, uh, suppose the area's stupendous physical beauty charms more words from my pen, Mrs. Howard."

"Are we now quite close to the Allegheny River?"

"Red Hawk assures me, based on his previous experience, that two more days of hearty travel should place us within sight of the Ohio Forks. Did you not say your sister lives thereabouts?"

"Yes, according to her letters."

Regina lowered her Bible. "How pleased she will be for your assistance in her labor, Sukey."

"And where will your business take you, Regina?"

The plump woman's eyes shifted abruptly. "I scarcely know about these things, my dear, being only a mere woman. I must defer to my nephew. Where will we be staying, Edward?"

"By a delightful whim of circumstance, Aunt, our trading affairs take us to a humble lodge . . . also not far from the Ohio Forks."

Regina clapped her hands with joy. "Indeed! Do you hear that, dear Sukey! Perhaps we shall see one another again."

"I could not be happier, Regina," Sukey replied, praying silently that Sir Edward would not be part of the bargain. "No doubt your trade affairs will completely occupy your time," she directed at Knowles.

"Not entirely, Mrs. Howard. I . . . look forward to congenial socializing with the French officers of Fort Duquesne. All fine gentlemen, I have been informed."

Red Hawk scowled. "Some's fair enough, all right. But their commander, Captain Charlevoix Mouceau . . ." Red Hawk paused long enough to spit a tobacco-laced stream into the fire. "Mouceau has the eyes and manner of a scheming rattlesnake."

Regina flashed her nephew a warning glance. "Dear me! The man sounds positively ominous. You will be careful, Edward?"

Knowles lay down his quill. "I have not come here to threaten anyone, Aunt. Surely all manner of men can readily judge that by my benign appearance." His fingers traced the silver threads edging his brocaded vest. "I feel certain those French gentlemen will respond to my civilized entreaties with matching kindness of their own."

"You mean, trade agreements?" Sukey asked.

Shifting his long legs, Knowles hesitated. "Possibly, Mrs. Howard."

She studied his face, then Regina's and Fitch's. Some imperceptible silent message seemed to pass between those three, she noticed. What was it? Why did Sir Edward seem, at rare times, grim-faced and solemn? As if he were deeply concerned about some grave issue?

No matter.

Sukey had little interest in the twinned demands of politics and business—concerns that sapped all of a man's passion, leaving him none for the woman who loved him. George Howard had made that lesson abundantly clear.

In search of the night noises, Sukey followed Fitch and Red Hawk into the darkness. A blazing pineknot torch revealed their procession. Regina Ramsey chose the moment to corner her nephew.

"Edward! Naughty beyond belief is what you are, taunting poor Sukey so."

Stroking his stubbled jaw with his fist, Knowles bit back a grin. "Poor? Aunt, that scheming wench deserves a comeuppance. She's up to something. I intend to give Mrs. Howard some of that frontier adventure she so ardently seeks."

"Edward! Impossible to believe I raised you!"

Knowles snorted. "I learned all my devious tricks from you, Aunt."

"Hmph! I shall ignore your jibe, Edward, however true. But regarding Sukey Howard, you err. Sukey is simply a woman in search of love . . . from the right man. Though I doubt she realizes it."

"Love?" Knowles's face darkened.

Regina tenderly grasped her nephew's arm. "Dear boy, you must leave Isabel's memory behind. 'Tis not such an impossible concept, you know. A man and woman loving each other . . . forever."

A swell of thunder and lightning flashed through Knowles's eyes. " 'Tis impossible for me, Aunt. Mrs. Howard plays games with us. I shall amuse myself by playing games with her. Love enters into it not at all."

"And once you reach the Allegheny River?"

"I shall be hard at work and never see the wench again."

Regina smiled slyly. "As you say, Edward," she finished, beaming suspiciously at her nephew. "Ah, Sukey has returned!"

"Yes. Red Hawk and I checked the area with torches, Regina. Nothing threatening within sight. So now, Sir Edward, tucked inside your blanket, you may sleep at peace with your surroundings."

Ruffles at Knowles's wrists fluttered as he bowed. "Kind, thoughtful Mrs. Howard! Once again you bring me serenity and comfort."

Knowles seemed a bit too merry for Sukey's serenity and comfort. Was he about to kiss her hand in gratitude? She shuddered. Tucking her hands deep within her thick, black skirt folds—out of Knowles's reach—she yawned.

"I shall retire for the night," she announced, eager to avoid Knowles's fawning attention.

Wrapped in her coarse blanket on a bed of fragrant pine needles that night, Sukey listened to wind shift across countless evergreen branches. Like a thousand gentle sighs, that lullaby soothed her as she drifted toward sleep. Excitement . . . adventure. That was how one escaped from empty solitude, was it not? With mounting certainty, Sukey knew the adventure she sought awaited her somewhere beyond these endless mountains.

She fell asleep that moonless night with a smile of anticipation on her lips.

Cold drizzle soaked her, next morning, as they set out on a narrow trader's trail overhung with mammoth sycamores. Riding single file with Regina and Knowles, Sukey shivered in the rain.

Knowles nudged his horse forward.

"Mrs. Howard," he called to her, "Fitch and Red Hawk require an additional pair of hands to retighten their loads. I fear I might soil my frock coat. Would you do me the honor of draping it round your shoulders . . . to protect it for me? Thank you so much. I shall most likely be of little use to Fitch, but I must try, to keep the dear boy cheerful."

Overlooking her skepticism, she accepted his offer.

"One does what one can, Sir Edward," she replied, raising an eyebrow quizzically. Perverse gratitude swept her as she snuggled into the massive coat's smooth, protective depths. A masculine aroma, not unpleasant and subtle, arose from its long folds.

"Curious," she muttered to herself after he rode ahead, "that a man so inadequate as Sir Edward Knowles would require such a voluminous coat."

Coatless in the rain, Knowles's broad shoulders and thick upper arms bulged under his white linen shirt as he labored. He tightened cinches skillfully, quickly, uncomplaining.

Open-mouthed, Sukey watched him. Was there more to Sir Edward Knowles than she perceived? It seemed almost as if . . .

No matter.

Sukey shook off her suspicions. They would part company in only a day or two—forever, she hoped, eager to be rid of Knowles's irritating mannerisms. Sir Edward would busy himself with trading concerns and fraternize among Fort Duquesne's French "gentlemen."

"Hmm."

"Did you say something, Sukey?"

"Just pondering the 'French gentlemen,' at Fort Duquesne, Regina. Sir Edward thinks highly of them. Red Hawk, and the townsmen of Lancaster, perceive them as villains. Am I to view the French along the frontier as friendly . . . or dangerous?"

Regina blinked repeatedly. "I cannot answer that for you, my dear. Though I suggest you treat them with caution. Not that you will have much opportunity to meet the French. Your family will surely keep you occupied. Ah, Rachel will be thrilled to see you, with her child imminent."

"And I, her, as well as all my family."

In one of April's quirks, the day's damp gloom warmed, by evening, to a clear pleasant air sweet with the scent of emerging ferns. Red Hawk set up camp high above water, to avoid morning fog.

"I have kept your coat quite safe, today, Sir Edward," Sukey commented, sliding it from her shoulders and handing it back to him.

With a flourish, he bowed low. "I cherish your compassion, Mrs. Howard. Soiling my fine garments distresses me so!"

Repulsed by his gush of gratitude, Sukey turned and groped for a large linen sack tied to her horse. "My own garments remain soaked from this afternoon's rain. This seems an excellent opportunity to . . . to freshen up. You will excuse me, sir?"

Knowles watched Sukey carefully pick her way down root-studded paths toward a stream. Her figure, a swaying feminine form swathed from head to toe in dull black cloth, caught Knowles's interest.

"Damn," he muttered. He knew better than to tempt fate in this manner.

Still watching her, he draped his coat loosely over his arm. A strange animal urge made him smell the garment—the same cloth which enrobed her body for hours. A delicate hint of perfume emerged from the cloth folds—a hint of the nosegay of wildflowers Sukey had tucked into her bodice.

His pulse throbbed.

Only a fool would seek her, he knew that. Soon, he would be free of Sukey Howard's meddling intrigues forever. "Good riddance!" he grunted. The wench would only corrupt his desperate mission.

His mutinous feet started him down Sukey's path. He would follow at a distance—only to protect her from danger, he assured himself.

But who might protect her from him?

Against his better judgment, Knowles discreetly leaned against a hickory tree. Peering between dense grapevines, he watched Sukey Howard.

With astonishing speed, Sukey stripped off her black mourning clothes. She undid the hooks and eyes of her caracul jacket, shucked off her cap, and stepped out of her dull black petticoat.

Clad only in her white shift and brocaded corset, she moistened her cheeks and forehead with cool spring water. Then she loosened the bodice drawstrings of her shift.

Knowles squeezed his eyes shut against the temptation . . . but quickly opened them.

Sukey dabbed cool water over her throat and across the gentle rise of her full breasts.

Knowles groaned.

This sacrifice he was making for England seemed almost too great for a man to bear. He ached to enfold Susannah Howard in his arms, to throw off his charade and show her how a real man made love to a woman. But doing so would surely risk his life . . . and hundreds of others as well.

Whatever else happened, Knowles knew, the cunning Mrs. Howard must not learn of his true identity or audacious mission, a dangerous challenge that excited him.

Unfortunately he had not calculated on encountering the charms of shapely Susannah Howard.

Long auburn-colored tendrils, escaping her pinned hair, dangled low over Sukey's shoulders as she trickled stream water over her bared wrists. Sunlight sparkled across the rich brown of her hair. In slow, undulating motions, she relaxed her shoulders and massaged her weary back. Hoisting her shift a trifle, Sukey examined her stockinged ankles to remove burrs.

Knowles felt his mouth run dry.

His strong hands gripped a branch of the hickory tree where he leaned. Two minutes—all that he would need to dash to Sukey's side and clasp her in his arms. An aroused man in a hurry could easily breach that distance in two minutes.

And Knowles was definitely a man in a hurry.

Abruptly, thoughts flashed through his mind of British and colonial soldiers—thousands of them—dying in Pennsylvania's back woods because he had failed to complete his reconnaissance mission. Knowles gripped the hickory branch till his knuckles bleached white. His muscles tensed at the very sight of luscious Susannah Howard in partial undress.

Gone were her former dull black, high-necked mourning clothes, which Sukey had stuffed into her satchel. She slipped into a silk gown shimmering with pink and green roses on a coral background. White lace flounces peeped from her sleeves. She finished by tying a white lawn apron over her gown, and clamped a straw hat trimmed with a pink ribbon over her white lace cap.

"A magical transformation, Mrs. Howard," Knowles whispered under his breath.

Clearly, the better his disguise as prissy Sir Edward Knowles, the more he repulsed her. Despite the wench's tempting appearance, now was not the time to lower his guard with Sukey Howard.

Even so . . . perhaps he might yet find a way to taste her sweet lips.

Knowles massaged a sinister grin from his powdered jaw. "Do not assume, my fetching Mrs. Howard," he muttered under his breath, "that you are the lone schemer on this devilish journey."

Chapter Three

Hemlock needles, sweet-spicy in fragrance, carpeted damp forest lowland as Sukey approached Laurel Hill. Cool shade from giant evergreens blotted out sparse undergrowth plants.

Clutching her reins, as she rode up from the lowlands behind Regina, Sukey smelled a change in scenery. Soaring oaks and poplars replaced hemlocks. Mountain laurel branches, swollen with spring buds, jutted at odd angles across the narrow trail. Noisy blue jays squawked their displeasure at intruders.

"Rest the horses here," Red Hawk ordered, halfway up Laurel Hill alongside a narrow ravine moist with past rain.

Regina tugged at Sukey's hand. "Come share the view with me, my dear," she called, tiptoeing onto a jagged limestone ledge facing east.

"Ah, Regina, the lovely sounds fill my soul!" Sukey cocked one ear to listen.

Amorous toads trilled their spring songs across forested hills lush with new greens. Somewhere close by, water cascaded downhill over half-submerged rocks, while songbirds high overhead warbled exuberantly to one another.

Sukey sidestepped fragrant arbutus peeping from

shale outcroppings. "Never have I seen such spectacular views as these, Regina!"

Rearranging her skirt folds, the older woman smiled. " 'Tis lovely, indeed, though it means we near the close of our journey. I shall miss your company, my dear." Regina lowered her voice. "I feel certain Edward shares quite the same emotion."

She cast a furtive glance at Sukey.

"Regina, 'tis useless, you know. Your endeavors are in vain." Sukey patted Regina's pudgy hand. "Marriage and men sorely disappoint me. I shall never again allow a man to deceive me. Or, yes, entrap me in some dull, lifeless marriage."

Regina blinked. Her gaze shifted awkwardly. "But, dear Sukey, not all men are, as you put it, deceptive."

"Was your husband?"

"My Rupert? Bless him, he was a wondrous man!" Regina laughed, recalling her deceased spouse's personality. "Naughty in trivial ways, perhaps, but nothing that ever mattered. A brave, noble man devoted to his family and country. How I miss his tender companionship!" Regina stared off into space a silent moment before addressing Sukey once more. "In many ways, Edward reminds me of Rupert."

Sukey gulped, to suppress her laughter. "Sir Edward? Noble perhaps, but . . . but brave?"

"Bravery manifests itself in various fashions, my dear. A truth you will better understand with the passage of time."

Sukey tapped her foot impatiently. "I seek adventure now, Regina. Not some irksome man to imprison me in a loveless marriage. I shall remain free to do exactly as I choose, without the smothering hindrance of some tedious man. My sister needs me, at least for now."

"Of course she does, my dear."

Fragments of Fitch's conversation with Red Hawk floated back toward them. "Soon . . . Rafe . . . by God!"

Catching Regina by the sleeve, Sukey leaned close to whisper. "This . . . this Rafe Stewart that I sometimes hear the men mention, Regina, do you know of him?"

Regina turned sideways and busied herself with a spray of wild phlox. "No, my dear. Other than that he is the sort proper ladies must take care to avoid. Oh, do look! Fitch summons us at once." She eluded Sukey's arm and scuttled back toward her servant.

Descending Laurel Hill's boulder-strewn west slope on horseback, Sukey studied Knowles's grim countenance. Had the sight of such rugged trails plunged the fragile-natured Englishman into gloomy despair?

"I can afford compassion for the poor wretch's downtrodden spirits," she murmured, nose held high. After all, their trip neared its conclusion. Knowles would soon vanish from her life forever.

Cheered immensely by this thought, Sukey smiled. She edged her horse alongside Knowles's gray mount.

"Granted, the profusion of rocks in this area truly stuns my comprehension, Sir Edward. But you must not allow these laurel-entangled boulders to distress you so." Her appearance at Knowles's side coaxed a faint smile from his craggy face. His lips, more sensuously full and commanding than she recalled, framed his perfectly proportioned white teeth.

Sukey forced her gaze away from Knowles's mouth.

What did it matter if the man sported a beguiling smile? Such trivial information concerned her not a whit! His spectacles and askew wig framed a male face layered with ridiculous amounts of white powder and thick rouge. Foppish Knowles could never excite Sukey's passions. Not for a marital lifetime, not for a day . . . not even for one tempestuous hour.

"Distress me? Ah, Mrs. Howard, kind of you to heed my distress," he replied. "Oh, would that I could face tribulation with your courageous spirit! Indeed, your sterling example inspires us all."

As their horses plodded around the thickly-set boulders, Knowles's renewed smile gave Sukey caution. And what of that curious sparkle in his shaded eyes? Almost as if a glimmer of mischief lurked in those infinite blue depths. Surely she was mistaken. If ever a man were found completely incapable of deception, that man had to be Sir Edward Knowles.

Shifting in her saddle, Sukey dismissed her suspicions.

"Alas, Sir Edward, try to be brave. Together, our stalwart party shall be watchful for danger. Remember, on the occasion that you need me, I shall be riding close at hand."

"*Need* you? Ah, Mrs. Howard, your merciful disposition touches my very soul. How comforting to know that when I . . . need you, you shall be close by." Knowles's voice dropped to a low gravel at those last words.

Uneasy prickles traced a path down Sukey's spine. Something about this broad-shouldered, silver-bedecked peacock alerted her sense of danger.

Absurd! Dandified Knowles, she felt certain as they crossed the steep rib of Chestnut Ridge, possessed not one devious bone in his body.

Pink and white dogwood blossoms fluttered in April breezes rich with the husky scent of anemones, and gray foxes yipped at encroaching dusk, that night, as Red Hawk brought the company to a small abandoned Indian hut on the Loyalhanna Creek. Devoid of any furniture, the plank-floored cabin nevertheless seemed inviting to Sukey. Vibrant sunset hues splashed across

the walls and warmed the bare floor, where she sat huddled between Fitch and Regina Ramsey.

"It appears, Sir Edward," Sukey commented, glancing up from her needlework, "that writing in your
journal helps calm your insecurities."

He glared at Sukey over his spectacles. "Clever of
you to take note, madam."

"As we approach the Ohio forks, Sir Edward, I also
notice that you labor in greater detail over your writing.
Have you a purpose?"

Her direct question startled him.

"Birds, of course, Mrs. Howard," he responded, after
a moment's hesitation.

"I beg your pardon?"

"The preponderance of wild creatures and wild plant
material, in these *endless mountains*, madam, captivates
my imagination. I must commit my observations to paper,
the better to relate them when I revisit Philadelphia."

"Indeed," she responded flatly, tapping her fingers
against the bare plank floor with impatience.

"I ask you, madam, can anything be more exquisite
than a yellow-bellied sapsucker in graceful repose?"

"Likely not, Sir Edward. Well, you will forgive me
if I—"

Horses tied outside the cabin abruptly whinnied in
terror. Fitch and Red Hawk, shouldering their rifles,
cautiously stepped outside to investigate.

"A bear prowls nearby," Fitch soon reported, before
rejoining Red Hawk.

"A bear?" Sukey's eyes widened to near-circles with
fright.

Knowles watched her intently for a moment.

"Dear me, how distressing!" he exclaimed suddenly,
glancing sidewise at Regina, then back to Sukey. "Ah,
Mrs. Howard, how is it you habitually manage to remain

bravely calm under duress? Pray, come sit by me and impart your much-longed-for wisdom."

Instantly, she slid over to his side.

"You must not fear, Sir Edward," she whispered, her own voice bristling with dread. "Fitch and . . . and Red Hawk will surely protect our interests outside this shelter. And . . . and I am close at your side to . . . to guard you." Slipping her hand inside the crook of Knowles's elbow, she snuggled closer.

He leaned toward her. "Compassionate of you, Mrs. Howard, to reassure me. When you hold on to me, I no longer tremble. But pray, do not leave my side till this matter is resolved, else I might relapse."

"You have my assurance, Sir Edward," she replied, drawing courage from her proximity to a man so large.

Strangely enough, as her desperate fingers clung to his arm, she became aware of oaken musculature inside Knowles' sleeve. Surely she only imagined that hardened male strength. Knowles was nothing but a weak, ineffective man fearful of his own shadow.

Stranger still, she drew a measure of comfort snuggled close to his side.

Absurd! Utterly impossible. Sukey dismissed the entire notion with a sniff. Surely she would have been calmed by any close, warm body at this point.

That night, while Red Hawk and Fitch dressed out bear meat, Sukey fell into a deep sleep from her day's rigors.

Glancing up from his journal, Knowles watched her graceful sleeping form curved in front of the fireplace. Far longer than he wished, he visually feasted on her languorous beauty.

Stray curls tumbled from the confines of Sukey's muslin cap. White lace sleeve-flounces dangled casually across her slender arms. Her coral silk gown, with its shiny profusion of pink and green roses, draped Sukey's seductive feminine curves.

Knowles felt his mouth run dry.

Like a famished man hungering for . . .

Knowles shook his head and tried to look away. Susannah Howard meant nothing but trouble for him. A reckless, conniving woman who made a habit of dashing into the jaws of disaster, and just as often, requiring a hasty rescue.

He scowled.

Sukey Howard would soon need more rescues. Lots of them, no doubt.

England and France were about to wage desperate war over rights to the Ohio Valley—a vital trade link between Canada and New Orleans. At this very moment, a major British offensive was organizing in Maryland. Their target? French-owned Fort Duquesne.

Precisely the area where Susannah Howard was headed.

Knowles shuddered.

With her blithe crusade for adventure, the curvaceous Widow Howard would land in one calamity after another. Of that, Knowles felt certain. Who, then, would rescue her once they parted?

Damn.

The foolish little witch was no concern of his. Women meant nothing to Knowles. Except his aunt, of course. A British undercover agent more shrewd than most, Regina Ramsey could cleverly extract information from even the most suspicious Frenchman.

Knowles had a dangerous job to perform. Whitehall demanded reconnaissance information for General Braddock's summer offensive against Fort Duquesne. Every detail, no matter how picayune, mattered to a British army unfamiliar with western Pennsylvania's rugged terrain.

No area roads existed. Knowles had to draw maps of possible approaches, mountain passes, rivers . . . and ultimately, the interior of Fort Duquesne, itself.

Only then could Fitch relay Knowles's written reconnaissance details to General Braddock.

Saving his own neck, these next few months, would require all Knowles' concentration. No time in this frenzied plan to guard a giddy, duplicitous woman itching to escape her widow's weeds.

None at all.

Stirring in her sleep just then, Sukey Howard murmured delicate whimpers before settling into deep slumber.

Hearing that sweet seductive purr made Knowles profoundly uncomfortable. He watched fading fireglow bathe Sukey Howard's face and arms in a rich golden glow. He recalled how, earlier, she had curled soft and warm against his own male hardness.

Knowles liked that arousing sensation.

"Entirely too much," he muttered.

War made no allowance for personal pleasures, he grimly reminded himself. No time for playful dalliances with doe-eyed women.

Or the escapades of roving Susannah Howard.

One more day. Just one more! Finally he would be free of her tormenting touch. Forever. With a grunt, Knowles tore his gaze from her enticing feminine contours and resumed laboring over his journal.

"Smoke ahead, Sukey! Do you see?" Regina shouted excitedly over her shoulder as her sturdy mare clopped along the twisting path. "From Red Hawk's description, that must be the Monongahela. And perhaps even your sister's own cabin!"

A pair of mongrels barked at their approach. From a doorway of the cabin, a pregnant woman walked out to investigate.

"Is it she? Oh, Regina! I cannot be certain! 'Tis nearly two years since I last saw Rachel!" Sukey waved furiously to attract the woman's attention.

Knowles eyed Sukey's precarious lean from her mount. "Mrs. Howard, in your euphoria I fear you might unhorse yourself."

"You need not trouble yourself, Sir Edward. I am an excellent horsewoman. And . . . oh! 'Tis Rachel! I feel certain!"

Knowles shook his head. No, he thought, the wench was not his responsibility. Never had been. The quicker he abandoned her, the better. He would lift her down from her horse one last time. Then never again would he clasp her waist in his hands.

"Madam," he said, watching her flinch in disgust at his touch as he slowly lowered her to the ground, "I shall miss the hint of lavender you wear."

"Then here," Sukey replied impatiently. She plucked a miniature grey-green bundle of dried lavender from a fold of her skirt and handed it to Knowles. "A memento of me, Sir Edward. Something to stimulate your courage when you feel it lacking."

"Stimulate . . . my courage?" Knowles's mouth twitched.

A relief, he reminded himself, to be liberated from the burdensome company of this ridiculous, irresponsible woman whose taunting dimples framed her full pink lips. Finally he was free to concentrate wholly on his mission.

Still, he sniffed the tiny lavender packet before wedging it into his waistcoat buttonhole.

* * *

"Did you see the look on Pa's face? Did you see it, when he first caught sight of Sukey?" Rachel Butler purred with delight as she fetched her guests another plate of warm biscuits.

Regina Ramsey hugged Sukey. "Indeed! It made our entire journey worthwhile. I shall miss your company, my dear," she said, preparing to depart.

"Then stay here with us," Rachel insisted. " 'Tis obvious Pa and the men delight in your company."

Regina took a welcome swallow of cool water. "Bless you for your kindness, Rachel, but truly," she lowered her voice to a whisper, "I must watch over poor dear Edward."

"Indeed!" Sukey agreed, nodding in the direction of Knowles, absorbed in properly readjusting his wig. "Poor frightened Sir Edward *always* needs someone to calm him."

A sudden loud voice from Jonah Butler's gunsmith shop alerted them all.

"An altercation, madam?" Sir Edward timidly inquired.

"Pay no attention, sir," Rachel replied. " 'Tis only Michel Margry, a French trader who camps just outside of Fort Duquesne. Now and again he drinks more rum than he ought. Michel's tongue loosens with a torrent of boasts that no one seriously believes."

Knowles's eyes narrowed.

"We must be on our way, sir," Fitch insisted. "Red Hawk insists we require daylight to locate our lodge."

Waving off his servant's advice, Knowles blithely strolled toward the smithy.

Sukey tugged at Fitch's linen sleeve. "I fear your master may stumble upon a French ruffian with evil intent, Fitch. Please, spare a moment to extricate him from the smithy before he endangers himself. You know how helpless is poor Sir Edward!"

Clucking her tongue at Knowles's inadequate prowess, Sukey hastened back into Rachel's kitchen to bid Regina farewell.

Lowered eyelids shielded Knowles's wary eyes as he approached the dimly-lit smithy. Concealing his presence, he listened carefully to Michel Margry's inebriated taunts.

"This land, all of it, belongs to the French!" Margry ranted through slurred speech. "Soon . . . soon, I tell you, French soldiers shall push British settlers clear back to Philadelphia! Perhaps even to the Atlantic Ocean."

Jonah Butler handed Margry his repaired rifle. "My friend, when you drink, you spout foolish things. Go home and sleep well."

"Foolish? Monsieur Butler, you do not believe me? I tell you, the commander of Fort Duquesne is a personal friend of mine. A close and trusted friend! Captain Charlevoix Mouceau and I grew up in the same beautiful Norman village. So lovely . . ." Margry choked back homesick sobs. "I tell you, one Frenchman is the equal of five . . . no, six English men! The French who live on the Ohio have nothing to fear from Englishmen."

Knowles sauntered inside the hot, shadowy world of Jonah Butler's smithy.

"A personal friend of Captain Mouceau, the commander of Fort Duquesne, himself, eh? Impressive, *mon ami*! Permit me to introduce myself." With a flourish of his lace-edged sleeves, Knowles bowed low. "Monsieur, I am Sir Edward Knowles, newly arrived from Philadelphia to ponder trade possibilities with frontier savages. Regretfully, it has been many months since I had the opportunity to converse with French gentlemen. I pray you will do me the honor of introducing Captain Mouceau one day very soon."

The buckskin-clad *coureur de bois* disdainfully sized up Knowles. "Monsieur, Captain Mouceau is a busy man," he sniffed. "With serious military responsibilities. However, on occasion he entertains visiting ladies and gentlemen. I . . . might see what I can do."

Knowles patted Margry's shoulder. "Capital, my fine fellow! I shall look forward to seeing you again one day quite soon at Fort Duquesne."

Inside the Butler cabin, Regina Ramsey beamed fondly at her pregnant hostess. "Such a delight, Rachel, to have met you at last! I shall be comforted knowing that you two wonderful sisters are now in each other's company. Though, of course, I shall miss Sukey dreadfully."

"Then you must come visit her here, Regina, whenever you like," Rachel insisted, clasping the stout woman's hand. "Women are all too scarce out here on the frontier. We shall sip mint tea and gossip over our spinning."

"And perhaps you will allow me a turn rocking your precious baby—which by the looks of your belly will join us quite soon."

"To be sure, Regina. Oh, Sir Edward beckons you."

Standing beside her sister, Rachel Butler waved to Knowles's party as they rode off. She swiveled her gaze from the departing Knowles to her older sister. "Sir Edward is . . . is a fine looking man, Sukey. You rode with him all the way from Lancaster?"

Affectionately linking arms with her sister, Sukey breathed out a huge sigh. "I sense conniving thoughts galloping through your head, Rachel, dear. For naught, mind you. I have no interest in vain, overdressed Sir Edward Knowles."

Together they strolled toward the kitchen door.

"Pray, dear sister, be honest with me. From your melancholy letters these past few years, I understood that George Howard functioned more like a pretend husband than a real one."

"I was nothing more than his parlor ornament, Rachel. George misled me into marriage. Foolishly, I . . . I thought he loved me."

"How dreadful for you. You mean he never—?"

"Only a few times in the beginning. Then he seemed uninterested." Sukey raised her chin defiantly. "Those lonely years in a loveless marriage . . . ? Ah, Rachel! Never again shall I yoke myself to a man who fails to love me."

"Which . . . brings us back to Sir Edward."

"Which does *not* bring us back to Sir Edward!"

"Well, say what you like, Sukey, but there was something charming about the way he gazed at you. A flush to his cheeks, a special shine in his eyes as you walked past. Hmm?" Rachel dimpled coyly at her sister.

Annoyed, Sukey shook her head. "Say no more about that pathetic imitation of a real man, Rachel. Now, I want to know all about your pregnancy. In exquisite detail. What does it feel like to carry a child inside your belly?"

"Divine, Sukey. As if I was sharing in a miracle with my beloved Jonah!" Resting both her hands on her swollen abdomen, Rachel scrutinized her sister. "Plenty of time to discuss that later. For now, we must change your appearance. A lovely silk gown simply will not do. Not out here on a frontier trading post. I have just the thing for you."

Later, Sukey patted the muslin apron which covered her borrowed striped cotton sacque and dark wool skirt. "Before you stands a woman prepared to meet the wild frontier."

Rachel frowned. "No. Not yet." She studied her sister for another moment before darting into her own bedroom. "No. You need two more items to complete your attire." She emerged from the bedroom holding a necklace and a knife.

Sukey gaped at the two shiny articles.

Rachel tied a leather string, holding an etched silver pendant, around her sister's pale throat. "This pendant will save your life someday, Sukey, as it did mine and every other person ever to wear it. 'Twas given to me by Old Eliza, a trader's wife who moved further west."

"Superstitious nonsense, Rachel!"

"Hush, dear. Wear it always, promise me. The wearer's life may be saved once somehow by the pendant, then it must be passed on to someone else. 'Tis your turn now."

Sukey clicked her tongue in disbelief. "If you insist, Rachel. I shall wear it only to humor you. But . . . but the knife?"

Rachel smiled. "I shall show you how to tie its sheath round your thigh for concealment. Someday it, too, will likely save your life. And Sukey . . . be certain you do not fear using it."

Clutching a leather bucket, Sukey clambered alone up a steep hickory-clad rise east of the Monongahela River.

"I shall not fail you, Rachel!" she whispered, fighting to ignore her mounting concerns over Rachel's imminent labor. No other women lived close by to assist with the delivery. And women often died in childbirth.

"I shall not fail you," she whispered again into the moist May breeze as she searched for childbirth herbs. "Not if I can help it."

Agitated birds, squawking overhead, led Sukey toward a thorny rose patch studded with faded red hips. She was about to pluck a few hips somehow overlooked by birds, when a horse's snort startled her.

Sukey spun around.

Before her, a lone man, tall in the saddle, sat astride

his shining black gelding. A magnificent man, with shoulders so broad they blotted out the warm sun. Fringed leather buckskins hugged his husky frame. A long rifle dangled across his saddle. May breezes ruffled the stranger's lustrous dark hair. Splendid hair, Sukey noticed. Not the dull, pasty color of a fashionable gentleman's wig, but dark and dangerous like scorched earth before it erupted with exciting new life.

Fear crept along Sukey's limbs. She had no intention of showing it. Her chin jutted forward.

"I do not appreciate strangers sneaking up behind me, sir," she commented, mindful of the man's size, unsmiling demeanor . . . and gun.

"No? Well, my dear lady, then you best not leave your back unguarded. Not here in the wilderness, where wild animals might assault you on a moment's notice."

She sniffed. "I am not your 'dear lady,' sir! And you may rest assured, I do not fear wild animals." A lie, she well knew, but Sukey hoped nevertheless to dupe this horse-bound, swarthy stranger towering above her.

"I laud your courage, madam. But keep in mind, wild animals come in both four-legged and two-legged varieties."

He smiled menacingly.

She did not care for the man's insinuation. Watching him casually swing his leg over the saddle to dismount, she felt unease prickle her spine. Sukey took a step backwards.

"What are you doing?" she asked.

The lank stranger glared at her. "Guarding your back, madam," he answered lazily. Legs spread apart, he planted his feet in a frankly masculine gesture of conquest. Fringes on his leather shirt and breeches shimmered at his slightest movement.

"Guarding my back . . . ? See here, you need not trouble yourself, sir. I am not your responsibility. Or any man's, for that matter!"

A slight smile played across the stranger's full carmine lips. "Oh, I can see that." His languid response came slow and deep, though his fierce blue eyes flashed. His large hands wrapped easily around his gun barrel.

Watching the stranger's intense expression, Sukey nervously gnawed the inside of her cheek. She should not have divulged her manless state to a male so blatantly predatory.

She parried.

"Do not assume I am a helpless female, sir. I am quite capable of defending myself. In addition, my father labors with a well-sharpened axe just . . . just beyond that next hill."

"No, he does not."

Her fists clenched. "How do you know?" she demanded.

"I make it my business to know everything that happens around here, madam. Who moves where . . . and when." He took a step closer to Sukey. "For instance, two Frenchmen and an Ottawa passed by here only moments before you began collecting herbs. Judging from their conversation, they would have been . . . delighted to meet up with a lone woman in the bushes."

Sukey gulped.

Unobtrusively, through her soft petticoat folds, she fingered the small knife strapped to her leg. Rachel had insisted she go nowhere without the modest but lethal weapon. Studying this stranger's broad chest as he advanced toward her, Sukey wondered if she could find the fatal mark with one knife thrust. One chance. All that a man this powerful would ever allow her.

Propping his rifle against a beech tree, the strange ruffian reached for Sukey with one hand.

Eyes widened, nostrils flaring, left hand patting the concealed knife, she lurched backward.

He shook his head in disgust. "Your bucket, woman! Give me your pail."

A curious twist, she thought. A rogue who pillaged, not women's bodies, but their collection of rosehips? Doubtless a hungry villain. Maybe he stole a woman's food first . . . then her body! She had to make a stand. Not yield one inch to the ogre. Stubbornly, Sukey clung to the bucket handle.

Shaking his head, the stranger easily pried the handle loose from Sukey's clenched fingers. Protected by his buckskin breeches, he leaned through menacing brambles to harvest the bright red hips missed by winter birds.

She stared at the man, now encased in a cage of thorny stems. An evil smile curved her lips.

"I suppose 'tis my turn to watch your back now," she offered aloud, while nibbling on a crisp new mint leaf.

Sukey scrutinized her would-be assistant. The tall, muscular man was everything George Howard had never been. Yes, and lace-clad Sir Edward Knowles, as well! Clearly a man of the outdoors. His dark hair fluttered wild and free in the summer wind without the confines of any powdered, pompadoured wig. No ruffles or gilt or silver adorned his primitive clothing.

He wore leather and bare skin with astonishing vigor.

Watching him, Sukey involuntarily moistened her lips. When he returned to her side again, she did not flinch.

"If you like, madam, I will hold the bucket while we pick hips and herbs, so thieving birds cannot make off with your spoils."

We? She liked the sound of that entwined word. More than she cared to admit. "Thank you, sir. I appreciate your kindness, though of course we shall divide the booty between us when we finish. Uh, you have not mentioned your name, sir."

His lips parted into a sly smile. "True. I have not, Mrs. Howard."

She gasped. "You know my name! But how?"

He slipped a furred new mint leaf into his mouth. "Remember, madam, I make it a point to know everything—and everyone—in this area. With war brewing between the English and French at Fort Duquesne, only a fool shutters his eyes."

She liked the way his mouth curved sensuously as he spoke. His strong, white teeth sparkled in the May sun. Flashes of granite and royal purple colored his intense, deep-blue eyes. Her gaze returned to his full-lipped mouth.

"You have me at an unfair advantage, sir." She tapped her foot in annoyance.

His unflinching sidewise stare bore into Sukey's features as he contemplated her words. One corner of his mouth tugged into a reluctant grin. "I suspect, Mrs. Howard, that no man could ever have you at an unfair advantage."

"Your name, sir!" she demanded in a huff. "Who are you?"

A sharp, sudden whistle from a distant rise distracted the male intruder. His eyes widened at the signal. "Let us just say I am a man of the mountains, Mrs. Howard. Here to watch over innocents like you."

"Like me?"

In anger, Sukey's hand fluttered to her bosom. "Sir, I most certainly do not require the services of you, or any other primitive bodyguard!"

"No? Before this war is over, Mrs. Howard, you might be surprised at just whose services you require."

In a hasty gesture, the stranger seized Sukey by the

shoulders and kissed her mouth. She felt the flames of that impulsive kiss fan from her lips to every forbidden inch of her body. When finally the rogue released Sukey, she reared her hand back to slap his arrogant face.

But like a ghost, he blended into the wooded hills in an instant. Listening to the diminishing rustle of his horse's gallop, Sukey breathed furiously. Her chest heaved with rage.

"The nerve!" she said. "That impudent beast had appalling nerve!" Never, she thought, had she ever . . . !

Though her breathing slowed, Sukey's blood still pounded with arousing friction across her limbs. Deep inside her womb she felt a compelling warmth that craved satisfaction. With the back of her hand, she salved her bruised lips.

A thrush, high up in a huge old sycamore, sang of beauty and grace. Emerging fern croziers filled the air with a subtle woods' aroma, and pale pink spring-beauties lined the slope where Sukey stood.

Was this how it felt to be kissed by a real man?

Never in her life had Susannah Whitfield Howard experienced such rousing heat, such sizzling passion. Never! George Howard, after a few limp efforts, had quickly lost interest in love-making with his young wife, leaving Sukey to yearn for what could never be.

She rearranged the wrinkled bodice of her cotton sacque. Cloth crumpled by the stranger's bold embrace.

How dare that rogue!

Yet somehow, his stolen kiss had wakened every beseeching fiber in Sukey Howard's body. A foolish wish rose from somewhere deep within her breast. A dangerous wish. Sukey yearned to see the handsome ruffian again. She ached to feel his strong arms and rousing kiss once more.

Just once more.

But who was he? And why did he seem to avoid her probing gaze?

No matter.

With her new-born reckless cravings, Sukey understood only one thing for certain. It would be most unwise for her to ever be alone with the lusty stranger again.

Praying that she would never see him again—yet curiously bereft at the thought—Sukey hoisted her leather bucket and trudged back toward her father's trading post.

Chapter Four

"Sukey?"

Startled, she jerked upright from hoeing the kitchen garden. "Zeb! You startled me. I never heard your approach."

Zeb Whitfield leaned his gangling frame against a split-rail fence and frowned. "Best pay closer attention to sounds, Sukey," he warned his sister, "now that Frenchmen skulk around these mountains."

"The French! Bah! That's all Englishmen speak of, these days. I refuse to fear any man, Zeb. I have my own means of protecting myself."

Zeb, she felt certain, would never understand her true feelings. The smothering chains of a dull, restrictive marriage? This, Sukey feared far worse than any glib-talking Frenchman enamored with the sound of his own boasts.

Zeb shook his head. His scowl deepened. "Someday you may rue those words, Sukey. Right now, though, something troubles me more than the accursed French."

Breathing in the scent of fresh sweet loam, Sukey trifled with a sprig of yellow mustard blossoms and listened to a veery's flute-like trill. "You look dreadfully somber, Zeb. What is it?"

"I have no knowledge of women, Sukey, and . . . and what happens when they bear children. None at all. Except I know they oft die. I fear for Rachel. When she thinks no one sees, she lapses into a weary expression. Her face and hands look swollen. Ah, Sukey, I am powerfully glad you came! Rachel needs your help."

"Rest assured, Zeb, we shall not lose Rachel now, or any time soon." Her troubled brother needed to hear those soothing words from his elder sister. Sukey needed to believe them, herself. "Now, return to Pa's storehouse at once or . . . or I shall seize you by the ear and force you to visit industrious weeding upon this garden. It simply will not do, having you lie indolently about the place."

Zeb grinned. Sukey's scolding fell like light-hearted music on his ears. "I am glad you decided to come, Sukey."

She lunged playfully toward her brother. "You will not be so grateful, Zeb Whitfield, when I box your lazy ears!"

Dodging her feint, Zeb ambled back toward his father's storehouse where trade goods demanded his precise accounting.

Sukey watched the concern melt from her brother's face. A result, likely, of her convincing tone. Men could be so easy at times. Women, too, she supposed. A firm voice uttering positive words—hollow though those words might be—apparently mollified the most worried or angry of listeners.

"Hmm," she muttered, putting aside her hoe. "Perhaps that curious knowledge might prove useful some future day."

Bearing an armful of lustrous blue forget-me-nots, Sukey crossed the courtyard which separated her father's lodge from Rachel and Jonah Butler's cabin.

"Sit down, Rachel! At once!" Sukey insisted, seizing

a stirring spoon from her sister's hand at the huge walk-in fireplace. "I do swear, your child appears ready to be born any minute now. With your round belly, I fear you might lose your balance and tumble into the fire."

Rachel massaged her bulging abdomen. "Dearest Sukey! My saucy big sister," she commented with a laugh. "Always watching over me from the time we were mischievous little girls. We were naughty, were we not?"

Sukey laughed. "We did manage to keep Pa guessing with our antics."

"Oh, Sukey!" Rachel reached for her sister's hand. "I rejoice so that you travelled all the way out here in time for the birth. Pa and Jonah and Zeb are happier, too, since you arrived. Your life with George Howard distressed you so. Perhaps . . . perhaps somehow we can give back your kindness by making your life happier as well."

Sukey studied her sister.

"That conniving look on your face, Rachel . . . hmm. I well remember that expression from our earlier days. Pray tell me, what does it mean this time?"

Eyes widened, Rachel feigned utter innocence. Her hand fluttered to her swollen bosom. "Why, Sukey, dear, I cannot imagine what you mean!"

Sukey squinted at her sister.

Rachel squirmed uneasily in her ladderback chair. "Well, you see, since tomorrow is the Sabbath, I thought it might be quite jolly if we invited Regina Ramsey round for a visit."

"Regina." Sukey assented with a nod. "I see."

"Well, she is a delightful soul, Sukey. You said so yourself."

"I cherish Regina's merry company. But Regina is not the reason why you smile so impishly, is it, sister dear?" Hands on hips, Sukey squarely faced down her sister.

Rachel coughed quietly. "Well, of course, it would be

rude to invite Regina without including Sir Edward. And Fitch, naturally."

Through pinched-thin lips, Sukey groaned, "I sense a conspiracy here."

Rising from her chair, Rachel said. "Now, Sukey, do be gentle with the dear man. After all, he is kind, and elegant, and handsome. Well, is he not? And . . . and you are now alone in this vexing world."

"Whatever else he may be, Rachel Butler, Sir Edward Knowles is incurably bloodless. Not to my liking at all. And I am neither alone, nor vexed by this world. Only by marriage to a cold, dry cod of an uninterested 'gentleman.'"

"But you will be polite to Sir Edward?"

"Only if you promise to sit down for the remainder of this evening, Rachel, while I prepare the food. It simply will not do, having you worked to exhaustion when your labor is nigh."

Watching her rough-mannered father, brother, and brother-in-law warmly greet Sir Edward, next day, Sukey pondered what her boisterous male relatives could possibly find to discuss with the gaudy Englishman.

Politics, of course. She quickly discovered that over the steak pie and roasted hare she served for their noon meal.

Jonah Butler, Rachel's lusty husband, pounded the table between bites of gravy-soaked beef. "Rumor has it that thousands of French troops have converged on Fort Duquesne. As many as 12,000 men, perhaps!"

"Indians, too many to count, have joined them," Eli Whitfield insisted. "Ojibway, Pottawattamie, Shawnee and Delaware from the Ohio, Ottawa from Detroit. Likely others, as well."

"All of them committed to defending the Ohio River

for France," Zeb insisted, with a worried look. "England must send troops at once, or . . ."

"Or Englishmen will find themselves driven all the way back to Philadelphia?" Knowles finished for Zeb.

"Well, yes, by God!" Jonah shouted, "if French claims can be given any credence."

Knowles assumed a curiously sober countenance when speaking of Franco-British politics, Sukey noticed. Even his eyelids narrowed. Only her imagination? Knowles appeared to sit up straighter, smile less often, and stare intently when discussing the defense of Ohio.

Watching Knowles's mysterious transformation, she stirred uneasily on her wooden bench.

"Mind you, busy as I am establishing trade links, I have yet to make the acquaintance of French officials at Fort Duquesne," Knowles began, daintily wiping his mouth. "But from what I've . . . overheard, the French believe there's little chance of English soldiers crossing the Alleghenies to Fort Duquesne this entire year."

A bolder expression. A distinct change in posture. A subtle trolling for information from others! Sukey noticed these signs each time Sir Edward spoke of the tense Ohio situation. She grew suspicious. Was she mad to entertain such a bizarre theory? Could it be possible? Was Sir Edward Knowles, a man fluent in the French language who had declared his eagerness to meet with the officers in Fort Duquesne, actually a French spy acting under the guise of an Englishman?

Merciful heavens!

"Sukey? Are you all right?" Rachel asked her open-mouthed sister.

"I . . . I am fine," Sukey answered dully.

Fluttering his lace cuffs, Knowles offered an apology. "I fear we men are boring the ladies. Perhaps even frightening the poor creatures. My dear Mrs. Butler!" Knowles exclaimed as he polished off a second helping of meat. "Truly I have never tasted more delicious roasted hare in even the finest establishments of Philadelphia."

Rachel beamed. "Thank you, Sir Edward. But truly, the honor belongs entirely to my sister. Sukey, alone, baked everything you eat today."

"Ah. Dear Mrs. Howard," Knowles acknowledged, with a sardonic half-smile in Sukey's direction. "Is there no end to your extensive talents?"

Jonah Butler suddenly mopped his forehead with a broad handkerchief. "A perniciously warm day indeed for May in these mountains," he grumbled. "Too hot to stay inside. Fitch, I have a harness fitting that I think you could use."

Eli and Zeb Whitfield followed the two men outside.

Almost as if on signal, Rachel rose from the oblong kitchen table as quickly as her maternal bulk would allow. "Regina, I am entirely perplexed by unmatched seams in a baby quilt I am making. Perhaps you might share your wisdom with me? Oh dear, I almost forgot . . . how thoughtless of me! Sir Edward, might you consider helping Sukey carry food back to the springhouse? The crock is altogether too heavy for me to carry these days."

Rachel's treacly smile conveyed touching innocence.

Knowles bowed in her direction. "I shall be only too happy to assist Mrs. Howard, madam." His voice dropped low. "Any way I can."

Tugging Regina by the arm, Rachel abruptly disappeared into her cramped bedroom.

Sukey felt suddenly abandoned. No, trapped! Alone in the kitchen with Knowles, she busied herself to avoid his penetrating stare. Despite Sir Edward's plethora of lace and ruffles, something in his intense blue eyes spoke of masculine want. And need.

He leveled his gaze directly at her.

"Mrs. Howard, I find these long dark nights much more intimidating without your brave consoling presence at my side."

She hated his cowardice. And his scrutiny. Swatting at flies, she busily wiped crumbs from the table. "Chin up, Sir Edward! You are a man, after all, with most likely a host of hidden talents and strength to sustain you."

Fingering the silver buttons of his embroidered velvet coat, he leaned closer to her. "Truly? You feel I might possess hidden strengths? Oh, Mrs. Howard, your confidence emboldens me. If only you were still by my side, each night, I feel certain I would no longer fear the dark."

"The dark . . . ? See here, Sir Edward! Our nights together are finished, do you understand? Never shall we sleep together again."

His eyebrow twitched as he appeared crestfallen. "Never sleep together again? Oh, Mrs. Howard, how will I manage my fearful needs?"

She gasped for breath. "Sleep together? Dear me, no! No, those were not the words I intended. I mean, we shall not lie near one another in the dark ever . . . ! Oh! At times, Sir Edward, I feel you are quite hopeless! You have Fitch and Regina with you to stave off the goblins of night. You do not need me."

He took another step closer. "Do not underestimate the empowerment of your tender touch, madam. I shall always need you."

His curious crooked smile . . . what did it mean? As if he knew some tawdry secret about Sukey Howard of which even she was unaware! She had to distance herself from this helpless wretch.

"Forgive my sister, Sir Edward," she muttered through clenched teeth. "She forgets this is women's work. Off you go, sir, with the menfolk." She furiously wiped the table with the damp cloth.

"Mrs. Howard," he began, his voice echoing deep within his broad chest, "I find it most gratifying to see you once again."

Mercy! What did the man have on his mind? Truly, she would rather not know! Backing away from him, she clamped a lid on an earthenware crock. "And I, you, sir. But on such a warm day, I dare not keep you from mentalk out in the fresh summer air."

The dark blue velvet of Knowles's frock coat spanned tight between exceptionally wide-set shoulders. Sukey had even discovered accidentally, on their journey west across Pennsylvania, that Knowles's frilly lace shirt concealed solid-muscled arms.

But Knowles was an irritating fop. A spineless, weak-intentioned, self-absorbed fool, which he demonstrated at every available opportunity. To make matters worse, Sukey felt a gnawing suspicion he might also be a wicked French spy as well!

His vibrant blue eyes sparkled now as he extended his arms toward Sukey. "Perhaps," he began, "I may be so bold as to—"

"Sir Edward! Really!"

"Madam! Have I offended you? I was merely about to reach for the meat crock." His bushy black eyebrow arched. "Surely you did not imagine that I . . . that I . . ."

She straightened her spine in angry defiance. Knowles wore a look of mirth. Somehow, this man was playing with her. His words conveyed one meaning—that of innocent naiveté. His dancing blue eyes flashed quite another. Surely she had not mistaken his intent.

Or had she?

Troubled by her burden of suspicions, Sukey noisily rattled dishes.

"Sir Edward, you have always been a perfect gentleman in my presence," she snapped. "In the future, as well, I shall count on you to behave with complete decorum. Now, if you will carry that crock to the springhouse for me . . ." Reaching for the dish Sukey held, Knowles's hands brushed her own. He leaned close to her, as if he longed to convey some unspoken meaning.

Unthinkable!

Sukey would have none of it. Bothersome Sir Edward Knowles no more inflamed her passions than had George Howard at his most uninterested ebb.

But, oh, the wild guardian of the mountains who stole her heart with one rousing kiss in the forest? Sukey could still feel the warm imprint of his magnificent embrace. If only he were near! She longed to feel his strong arms draw her close against his rugged male body, once more. Just . . . just once more.

"Thank you for your assistance, Sir Edward," she directed with frosty indifference. "Here is your burden. I shall carry a pitcher. After we set them in the springhouse, you can rejoin the menfolk, as I feel certain you are anxious to do."

"My burden, Mrs. Howard?"

She felt it again. Knowles's unspoken sultry message couched in a puzzling half-grin. Had she chosen inappropriate words? Hardly! No matter how she phrased replies, Knowles veered the conversation toward . . . toward . . . well, just what did that upraised bushy black eyebrow of his indicate?

"Do be careful, however. 'Twould be most unfortunate if you spilled meat juice on your elegant waistcoat."

He bowed low before her. "My dear Mrs. Howard, nothing you ever ask of me would be construed as a burden. Though sadly I might lack swaggering bravado, my great honor will ever be to serve you in whatever capacity I am able."

She hated him. Despite the man's size, his pathetic

male inadequacies annoyed Sukey. And why the perpetual twinkle in those glowing blue eyes of his?

"Then carry the food to the springhouse and be done with it, sir. We shall speak no more of your questionable honor."

"Or yours, madam."

Balling her fists, Sukey tensed. Truly, no man ever irritated her more than Sir Edward Knowles. She jammed the crock into his outstretched hands and stamped out the kitchen door.

Late that Sunday afternoon, Eli Whitfield cornered his elder daughter in the courtyard. With his clay pipe, he gestured toward Knowles, engaged in political talk with Jonah Butler and Zeb.

"Sir Edward is a fine man, Sukey. Intelligent, noble, well-intentioned."

"As well as weak and shallow."

"Sukey! 'Tis shamefully unkind of you. Especially from a young widow living in the wilderness in need of a husband."

"Pa! I am not in need of a husband! Now, or ever again!" Glancing around her, Sukey quieted her voice, that no one might overhear. "My marriage to George Howard was a dismal sham. Those were the loneliest years of my life, Pa. Never again will I marry for security, or to 'have a husband,' no matter what dangers I encounter. For love, Pa. 'Tis the only reason I shall ever contemplate marriage again."

"Bah!" he exclaimed, waving his pipe. "Love? That has nothing to do with survival on the frontier."

"No? You need only observe the deep affection Rachel and Jonah share with one another to know that is not true.

Besides, Pa, I came here to help Rachel, not seek out another husband."

Eli Whitfield scrutinized the face of his unruly elder daughter—a girl-child he could never tame despite his most sober efforts. "I have seen that dangerous look on your face before, Sukey, my girl. And your dubious words sound suspicious to me. What might you be up to?"

She brushed an imaginary speck from her sleeve. "I have no ulterior motives. Not out here on the frontier, for goodness' sake, where our every thought is simply for survival. I only wish to help Rachel in her time of need."

Eli's eyebrow quirked. "Nothing you ever did was that uncomplicated, my girl. But mind, this is not the time for one of your high-spirited schemes. Not with war brooding just over the next mountain."

Sukey blinked with contrived innocence. "Of course, Pa. I could not agree more." She watched her skeptical father trudge off to feed his livestock.

She sighed, recalling how her Lancaster "mourning" had nearly smothered her every breath. Rachel's pregnancy supplied the perfect escape from Sukey's bored state of misery. Ah, precious freedom! Pa thought she ought, out of desperation, marry prissy Sir Edward Knowles?

"Hah!" Sukey exclaimed aloud.

She could no more love Sir Edward than love a warty frog from yonder pond. Her heart belonged to the forest rogue whose kiss made her feel like a woman for the first time ever. Sukey shivered at the memory of that vigorous mountain man. His gentle but rough-skinned touch drove her into a fine madness of sweet passion.

But if Sir Edward did not quench her thirst for love, he did spark her lust for adventure . . . in a strange new way.

Indifferent to politics, Sukey cared not why France and England squabbled of late. But adventure for its own sake? There, indeed, was a thrilling animal of an entirely different stripe!

Knowles, she began to suspect, was more than a preening, lace-encrusted nobleman. Quite possibly he was a sinister French spy who posed as an inept Englishman to gather vital information. Such as . . . ? Sukey did not know. She intended to find out. Without telling a soul, of course. Pa would only scold her intentions. But if she could unveil an evil French spy, everyone would applaud her valiant maneuver.

That evening, Sukey lit the wick of a Betty lamp and congratulated herself on her own brilliance.

Next morning, she frowned at the deepened circles rimming Rachel's eyes. "A bad night?" she asked her sister.

"The birth is imminent, Sukey, 'tis all. You must stop fretting over me."

No-see-ums tormented Sukey's skin, that hot May afternoon, when she prowled the forest in search of birthing herbs. Thrashing at the insects, she accidentally brushed against stinging nettle.

"My skin is afire!" she cried, dashing for the soothing mud of the nearby creek. Raised on the Conestoga River banks, near Lancaster, Sukey felt confident in stream water. She glanced, now, at the surrounding hills.

No sign of any humans.

Seeking relief from sticky heat and pesky insects, Sukey stripped off her apron, skirt, and sacque. Clad only in her chemise, she glided into water up to her shoulders.

"Ah! I feel revived," she murmured, languishing in the cool river. She trickled water along one arm, all the way to her shoulder, then the opposite arm. Blissfully, she closed her eyes to savor the moment. When she re-opened them, a man stood before her.

Sukey blinked in horror.

The thick-muscled frontiersman, tall and dark-haired, leaned against a gnarled chestnut tree. The same mountain ruffian who had earlier kissed her. He stared hard at Sukey.

She crossed her scantily-clad bosom with her bare arms.

"Sir!" she burst out indignantly. "How long have you been watching me?"

"Not long enough," he drawled.

She sucked in a nervous breath. "Most unkind of you, sir. Gentlemen do not stare at ladies who think they are alone."

He sidestepped tall fern plumes and edged closer. His long black hair glistened loose and free under the morning sun. His snug leather pants and linen shirt clung to the hardened contours of his powerful frame.

"Ladies who swim near-naked in rising water need to be watched by a man," he said defiantly. "And for your information, Mrs. Howard," he added, "no one ever labeled me a gentleman." He took another step closer.

"Stay back!" she demanded. "I do not require your assistance. Nor do I need to be . . . to be watched by you, or any man, like some sort of careless child."

He walked directly to her pile of clothes.

Her eyes bulged. "Sir! What are you doing?"

He offered her a twisted grin. "Why, madam, your apparel is fast growing moist from morning damp. Including your knife. I shall move it to a safe and dry location."

He now stood between Sukey and her clothes.

Mercy! She had nothing but her fists and feet to defend her. In a careless moment, she had even unstrapped the small sheathed dagger from her thigh. A treacherous-looking knobbed hickory branch lay wedged beside a boulder. Hoping the defiant stranger did not guess her intention, Sukey edged toward the potential weapon. And squatted in swirling river waters to conceal her undressed form.

"You have me at a disadvantage, sir," she murmured, trying to disguise her plan to reach the potential weapon.

"Mrs. Howard, I suspect no man ever had you at a disadvantage." He stomped the branch to bits before stripping off his shirt and trousers.

She gasped. "What are you doing?" she demanded once more.

"Why, joining you, of course. How can I save you from treacherous waters and your own careless actions if I stand thirty feet away?"

Her jaw sagged. The mountain ruffian now stood arrogantly before her dressed in nothing but a leather breech clout. Thick muscles and a dusting of black hair defined the villain's arms, legs, and broad naked chest. Little of his rugged anatomy was left to Sukey's imagination. She stared in horror as he stepped into the river.

"Get away from me!" she shouted, furiously backpaddling.

"Mrs. Howard, I have no intention of harming you. And though it would appear you might benefit from manly guidance, I do not even intend to scold you for this careless swim. But this river conceals treacherous sinkholes, madam. One more backstep and I fear you might disappear forever."

He reached his bare arms toward her.

"Nonsense! You are attempting to trick me, sir, but I am neither gullible, nor in need of your ridiculous rescue attempts." She continued to tiptoe backwards through soft river-bottom mud, away from this scheming, near-naked rogue.

Suddenly, in a vortex of swirling water, Sukey felt the river bottom give way into a fierce, boulder-strewn sinkhole that threatened to engulf her. In that same precise moment, she felt strong hands seize her by the arms and drag her to safer waters.

Muddy brown waters concealed all but the rogue's head and shoulders. "Truly, Mrs. Howard, I think you enjoy living dangerously," he said, still clutching Sukey's arms as he stared into her eyes.

Cool waters failed to calm her racing heartbeat. This vulgar primitive man excited Sukey more than had any man in her entire life. But his taunts were far too impertinent. She yearned to slap his leering face. If only she still had her knife within reach! She would teach the ogre a much-needed lesson in humility. He would suffer penance under her sharp blade.

No man alive could overpower her fierce will.

The rogue's blue-eyed gaze locked on Sukey's face as he gripped her by the arms. She drew her knee back to smash his most vulnerable area.

Her gaze fell on the play of muddy water against his black chest curls. Muscles on his naked arms flexed and formed a sheltered welcoming cove. Sukey allowed her knee to relax. A curious urge, devilishly unharnessed, made her reach up to trace the moist patterns in his chest hair. Her index fingers twirled inside those coarse black curls. Sukey's palms flattened against his shoulders. A compelling primitive urge demanded that she reach up to explore the darkness of the stranger's stubbled jaw.

His hands prowled across Sukey's back. He was pulling her close. In those silken umber waters, she felt pleasurably caressed by man and river. Sharing a watery embrace, like two undulating denizens of the deep, she drifted along the swollen river with this haunting stranger. At his touch, a thrill of glorious excitement rippled through her entire body.

He kissed her. A gentle taste, at first, then more fierce.

A conquering gesture. His mouth pressed her lips with a bruising kiss that seemed unwilling to end. Sukey prayed it never would. This bold rapscallion with piercing indigo eyes and wind-blown dark hair—a man Sukey barely knew—now led her toward a place where she had never been. A vibrantly exciting realm of racing hearts, unexplained desires, soaring passion.

"Sir," she pleaded, her arms still clinging round his shoulders as he kissed her throat, "I do not even know your name."

"'Tis Rafe, my lovely. Rafe Stewart."

Against every danger signal screaming in her head, Sukey allowed him to pull her closer still. Locked inside Rafe Stewart's strong bare arms, Sukey responded with twisting beseeching motions of her own. Feeling Stewart's aroused manhood press against her belly, Sukey freed the needy, desperate woman trapped within her.

She kissed Rafe Stewart with an insatiable hunger forbidden to her for so very long.

He led her toward the river bank. Toward a plush, mossy knoll beneath a widespread maple tree. His look spoke to Sukey of an equally insatiable hunger. Watching the water drip from her pale shift, Stewart silently appreciated Sukey's feminine form. Wet ivory cloth clung to her full breasts, rosebud nipples, rounded hips, and the dark mound between her thighs.

On that soft emerald cushion of moss, he pulled her into his arms and kissed her. His fingers loosened the drawstring of her chemise as his mouth explored her delicate throat. In his strong hand, he cradled her breast.

"Sukey, my love," he rasped, voice husky with desire. "I have waited . . ." His mouth sought hers once more. She felt his tongue mate with hers in a sensual dance of hungering passion. He kissed her cheek, her pale pink earlobe, then trailed his kisses down along her shoulder.

"Rafe, never have I—"

Suddenly a sharp whistle echoed off a shielding hill. With a muttered curse, Rafe released Sukey.

"What is it?" she asked.

"I must go. At once." He kissed her quick and hard, then lunged for his clothes.

No! He was about to leave, and take her heart with him. "But when will I see you again?" she cried.

Mercy! Was she begging? Where was the haughty pride she once displayed in her lavish Lancaster parlor? Clothed now only in her wet chemise, was she actually groveling before a lusty, half-naked mountain man?

Yes.

With one hand Stewart fastened his leather belt over his trousered hips. With the other hand, he cupped Sukey's petulant face. "One day I will find you again in these woods, my beautiful Mrs. Howard. But right now there is work I must do. An ugly war between France and England may soon erupt."

"Be careful, Rafe!" she pleaded.

"Your life might be in equal danger, Mrs. Howard. French scouts continually prowl these hills. Take no chances. Guard your back at all times . . . till the day I return to kiss it for you."

Like a predator on the wing, he instantly vanished through the trees.

Chapter Five

"The news is not good, Edward. Most alarming, indeed," Regina Ramsey declared, struggling to neaten a black solitaire over her nephew's stiff cambric neckcloth.

"What I find 'most alarming,' Aunt, is the manner in which you seem determined to strangle me."

"Oh, do be serious, Edward!" Regina exclaimed, swatting his arm. "You know very well to what I refer. The colonies appear reluctant to undertake their own defense. I feel sorely vexed."

Knowles's lazy smile faded from his tanned face. "A pair of Mingo runners arrived here from Cumberland, just after breakfast. They confirmed that General Braddock and his army have indeed safely arrived there from England."

"Hah!" Regina exclaimed. "Little does the brash general know! His perilous voyage across the Atlantic cannot compare to the dangers awaiting him enroute to Duquesne."

"'Tis our job to warn him of those pitfalls," Fitch insisted, "with the most detailed reconnaisance information we can gather about these treacherous Pennsylvania back hills."

"And the internal layout of Fort Duquesne." With that thought, Regina clucked her tongue impatiently. "If only

Braddock could have begun his campaign against Duquesne earlier this spring. A mere six or eight weeks would have made a vital difference. Fort Duquesne would have been his for the asking, so poorly supplied had it then been. Now . . ." Anxiously she twiddled with the folds of her apron.

Knowles grimaced at the job ahead. "Now Braddock will have to mount a major assault against Fort Duquesne with every hearty man he can muster. Somehow, the poor beggar must move all his men, horses, and cannon across the Alleghenies . . . beseiged by French and Indian scouts every step of the way."

"Promises, promises!" Regina burst out, pacing the bare plank floor. "Colonists pledged horses, wagons— yes, and food!—for Braddock's army, but failed to deliver. Oh, the poor soldiers! Arduously hacking a road through the wilderness while barely existing on rattlesnake meat and wild game! Ugh!"

Knowles adjusted his powdered wig over his own dark hair. "Several hundred wagons apparently did reach Fort Cumberland, though, thanks to Ben Franklin's prodding. Braddock's army will soon be on the move. That makes our mission more urgent than ever."

"And fraught with danger!" Fitch growled. "French scouts will watch us as closely as they monitor General Braddock." He eyed Knowles somberly. "No distractions now from our job, else it might prove fatal . . . for all three of us."

Regina detected silent tension between the two men. "Fitch? What hidden meaning lies buried within your admonition? No, do not withdraw into sullen silence. Out with it! I insist!" she demanded.

"Rafe Stewart's fascination with Mrs. Howard."

A gentle smile wreathed Regina's broad-cheeked face. "Sukey? Edward, you naughty boy! What have you been up to? And how could Susannah Howard endanger any of us?"

"I have no qualms about the woman," Fitch added quickly. "That is, when she remains safely tucked back east in her elegant Lancaster drawing room. But out here, where the threat of death lurks behind every mountain tree, Mrs. Howard's insatiable curiosity—and her lust for adventure—can only provoke disaster. Especially when Rafe Stewart throws all caution to the winds and enjoys a private swim with the spirited Mrs. Howard."

"A private swim?" Regina's hazel eyes fairly danced.

Knowles cleared his throat. "Banish the twinkle from your eyes, Aunt. Mrs. Howard and I remained . . . clothed."

"Just barely!" Fitch exploded.

"How delicious, Edward! Indeed, I am quite fond of Sukey. She would make a lovely bride for you. But you must contain your passion for her until after our work is done. Fitch is quite correct. She might inadvertently unveil your secret identity to the French. That would indeed prove perilous for us all."

"And for General Braddock and his entire army!" Fitch growled.

Knowles waved his hands. "I assure you both, my 'passions' remain under meticulous control. Aunt, you well know I have not the slightest interest in making any woman my bride. Neither Susannah Howard, nor any other giddy, foolish vixen who tries to imprison a man with matrimony. Besides, she detests Sir Edward Knowles. I feel certain we have nothing to fear from Mrs. Howard. 'Sir Edward's' presence will not alarm her senses."

Knowles tugged impatiently at his ruffled cuffs. Had

he truly convinced his two copatriots that his interest in Sukey Howard was under rigid control?

Perhaps.

Now . . . if he could only convince himself.

Sukey smoothed the dainty buffon which encircled her shoulders, as the bay mare she rode cantered toward Sir Edward Knowles's lodge.

Business, she reminded herself haughtily, glancing over at her father and Zeb, also on horseback. Sukey agreed to make this jaunt principally to bolster trading prospects for Eli Whitfield's trading establishment. The three rode in response to Regina Ramsey's carefully worded invitation.

An afternoon with Sir Edward and his French guests? Surely a tribulation, Sukey thought, fanning herself in tense little arcs. How that fanciful man could irritate Sukey's delicate instincts!

But her family seemed unusually tense, of late, over the fate of their livelihood. Politics, threats of war, foreign soldiers clustered in hastily erected backwoods forts along the Allegheny River—none of it mattered a whit to Sukey. Apparently, however, those issues mattered a great deal to her menfolk. Their worried looks raised the nub of her bored sensibilities. For their sakes, she would behave this afternoon as a gracious guest. Visiting with Regina Ramsey, of course, would be a treat.

And Sir Edward?

A sly smile tipped Sukey's carmine lips.

Though the idea near repulsed her, she would watch him like a hawk scrutinizes its prey. Adventure? Was that not one of her motives for abandoning her sedate Lancaster home to journey west?

Of course.

And to unveil a duplicitous British spy? Surely that was the pinnacle of all adventures!

She released a delicious little giggle to the June breezes as she rode up in sight of a waving Regina Ramsey.

"My dear Sukey!" Regina called out excitedly. "So good of you and your family to come!"

Knowles planted himself squarely at the left side of Sukey's horse. "Mrs. Howard," he said with a droll expression as he stared up at her, "our every hour apart from you has been diminished by your absence."

There it was again! A look on Knowles's face that fairly drove Sukey mad with irritation. A sparkle in Sir Edward's indigo eyes, a crooked, inscrutable grin, a mask . . . aha! Yes! As if Knowles wore a mask that concealed his true inner thoughts. As if he knew far more about Sukey Howard than he ought.

As if he was *not* the man he portrayed himself to be.

Of course! It had to be so! Surely the cowardly-appearing Knowles was a nefarious spy laboring undercover to discern British troop movement approaching Fort Duquesne.

"Pray allow me to help you dismount, Mrs. Howard."

Mercy! She could not escape his determined presence . . . or his outstretched arms. Squeezing her eyes closed to avoid seeing Knowles's odious embrace, Sukey slid from her horse into his waiting grasp. His strong arms lingered a tad longer around her waist than she felt necessary.

Strong?

A mistaken impression, surely. Sir Edward had not one strong fiber in his entire body. Or did he?

"Rachel, I regret, was not up to the ride, Regina. Jonah remained at home with her. They both send you and Sir Edward their felicitations."

Regina clasped her hands together. "Pray, Sukey, tell me Rachel is well."

Nervously fingering the edge of her fan, Sukey pondered the entreaty. "I want to believe that, Regina. Truly I do."

"Something troubles you, my dear."

"My sister seems quite puffed about her face and ankles. And so fatigued. I shall be most grateful to see Rachel delivered of her child and vigorous once more."

"Of course you shall. Oh, upon my word, our French guests from Fort Duquesne have arrived!"

Michel Margry led two French officers and a shy woman to Knowles's front door.

"*Enchanté,* Madame Howard," Sergeant Nicolet said, bowing low after Margry introduced everyone. "My wife, Jardine," he added, indicating a plain, square-bodied woman.

The three Frenchmen mingled with Eli and Zeb Whitfield as Knowles fluttered about. Sergeant Nicolet seemed almost courtly in his manner, Sukey thought. Hardly the villain so avidly described by local English traders. She did wonder, however, about the unchecked manner in which Corporal Allouez's dark eyes flickered over her figure.

Well, she was now a secret spy for England—though of course, no British officials were yet aware of her vital role—and certainly every spy lived with an element of risk.

Ah, yes, adventure! Precisely what Sukey Howard craved.

"Madame Howard?"

Sukey spun around to face Jardine Nicolet.

"It pleases me to make your acquaintance, Madame Howard. And that of Madame Ramsey's, as well. I relish an opportunity to speak English with other women."

"Your . . . your English, Madame Nicolet? 'Tis quite excellent."

Jardine smiled. "Most kind of you, *mon amie*. My mother was English, my father, French. Mama died many years ago, and I find that English words fade from my memory if I do not use them."

Regina caught the arm of her French guest to escort her indoors. "Then, Madame Nicolet, you must chat at great length with Sukey and me. Truly, a noble excuse for women to visit one another."

Jardine Nicolet hesitated. "Your papa, Madame Howard . . . Michel led us to believe he would bring a satchel of trade items with him today. We . . . we are in desperate need. Supply lines from Montreal have been—"

Jardine paused, fearful of carelessly betraying information about Fort Duquesne's current status.

"Indeed," Sukey responded, sensing the French-woman's unease. "Pa and Zeb brought two saddle bags filled with all sorts of things. Sacks of flour, cloth, needles."

"My husband fetched lustrous pelts," Jardine added hastily, before relaxing her tense shoulders. "Surely the men will arrange a judicious exchange."

Knowles, Sukey noticed, frequently spoke French to his guests. Her eyes narrowed. Ah, if only she could speak fluent French! She understood a mere handful of words, scarcely enough to make even casual conversation. Still, Sir Edward's actions spoke volumes—surely the behavior of a spy, Sukey felt.

"Monsieur Whitfield," Sergeant Nicolet began, after plunking his cider cup back on the table, "I have need of your services at Fort Duquesne."

Suddenly, Knowles ceased speaking to Zeb and Michel.

The room grew eerily quiet.

"Our most knowledgeable gunsmith lies ill with the bloody flux. I should like you to visit Duquesne with your tools. You would, of course, be recompensed with valuable peltries for your trouble."

A dubious Eli Whitfield chewed over the invitation.

Gesturing effusively, Knowles broke the awkward silence with a level stare at the elder Whitfield. "Eli, my dear fellow, I cannot imagine a more cordial convocation! Fitch and I shall accompany you to Duquesne and make ourselves useful. That is, if Sergeant Nicolet permits. Fitch is blessedly handy at fixing guns, you see."

"And you, Monsieur?" Standing sideways, Michel squinted over his shoulder skeptically at Knowles.

"Ah, *mon ami*, I regret my hopeless inadequacies but—" Knowles broke off his words for a paroxysm of coughing. "The knowledge of gun repairs, and all manner of mending, I fear, tends to elude me. Indeed, though, I relish the opportunity of meeting your commander, whom I hear is quite the well-born gentleman." He delicately sniffed the crocheted edges of his linen handkerchief.

Jardine Nicolet smiled shyly. "Perhaps Madame Howard and Madame Ramsey would accompany the men? I would welcome feminine company."

Knowles's eyelids flew open. "But—!" He searched for words of protest.

Not quickly enough, however.

"Madame Nicolet," Sukey burst in, "I should love the opportunity to visit with you again! A more delicious adventure I simply could not imagine! Never before in my entire life have I been inside an actual fort. And Fort Duquesne? Ah, it sounds quite exciting!"

A dangerous sparkle lit her eyes as she grinned defiantly.

Sukey watched Knowles exchange silent alarmed glances with Fitch. Just as she suspected! They feared her vigilant presence at the fort, knowing full well she might detect their backstabbing brand of skullduggery. They desired few witnesses, least of all an observant woman such as herself.

Jardine Nicolet eagerly accompanied the three Frenchmen to a lean-to filled with Eli Whitfield's trade goods.

Fanning herself beneath the shade of a split sycamore tree, Sukey suddenly saw Knowles' approaching shadow cross her shoulder.

"Mrs. Howard," he began cautiously, waving his lace trimmed wrist in the May air, "forgive my impertinence, born indeed of concern for your tender well-being. But my senses warn me it might be . . . unwise for you to journey inside Fort Duquesne."

With chin thrust upward, Sukey accelerated her fanning. And ignored his piercing stare. "Thank you for your kind attention to my welfare, Sir Edward. But after traversing nearly the entire width of Pennsylvania, under primitive conditions at best, I hardly see where my brief jaunt to Fort Duquesne should be of any concern to you, or anyone else."

Fanning herself, she stamped off toward a shady grove of locust trees.

He followed, blocking her retreat with the crook of his arm.

"Dear Mrs. Howard, at the risk of offending your delicate sensibilities, I must remind you that lounging inside that French fort are hordes of . . . ravenous soldiers whose spirits may be even more primitive than the forest wilderness you so bravely traversed. Men who have not seen a beautiful, sophisticated Englishwoman, such as yourself, in a very long while."

He glared at her.

Shaking her finger, Sukey wheeled on him. "See here, Sir Edward, are you questioning my morals?"

Knowles's eyebrow lifted. "Dear lady, indeed not! At no time would I ever contemplate such a vile act!"

She hated his perpetual smirk. "Good. Then may I remind you that my sensibilities are neither delicate nor tender. I shall travel to Fort Duquesne in the company of my father . . . whenever I choose. And I am quite capable of fending for myself, as you might recall from our recent journey."

Ignoring his reproach, she dashed back to Regina Ramsey's protective company.

Rachel Butler worked around the bulge of her advanced pregnancy. With care, she fanned flax fibers across her lap in preparation for spinning.

"Silly goose, Zeb! You mistake my . . . my moderation for fatigue. All your fretful concern is for naught. This early June heat is what slows me a bit. That, and my concern in not wasting any flax. You simply are unfamiliar with the sight of a woman nearing childbirth, so you imagine I must be unwell."

Frowning, Zeb Whitfield studied his sister's swollen hands. "Call me what you will, Rachel. Still, your appearance troubles me."

She pressed her index finger to her lips. "Hush, Zeb. Promise you will not alarm Jonah and the others. All will be well, you shall soon see, when you behold my darling new infant."

"Alarm, Rachel?" Sukey questioned, sweeping into the kitchen from the courtyard which separated Rachel's cabin from Eli Whitfield's lodge. "Did you scold Zeb for his alarm just now?"

"Nonsense, Sukey!" Rachel exclaimed, with an annoyed click of her tongue. "I spoke just now of our 'barn' to Zeb, not an 'alarm.' Did I not, Zeb?" Rachel shot her brother a warning glance.

Scowling, Zeb shuffled back toward the smithy.

Sukey shoved a stool alongside her spinning wheel. She dipped the fingers of her right hand in a small bowl of water, then moistened the flax. All the while, she scrutinized her pregnant sister. The dark circles rimming Rachel's eyes seemed to deepen with every passing day.

"Now, Sukey, you must tell me all the fascinating details about your visit with dear Regina and Sir Edward," Rachel begged, as she wound flax fibers onto a distaff.

"And the pompous French, Rachel. One cannot forget them even for a moment. Oh, I do wish you would lie down to rest! Your hands are never idle, even for a moment. Rachel, I insist that you halt at once."

"Despair not, dear Sukey. Seated here beside you as you spin and tell stories is such a pleasant pastime for me. You have no idea how much I cherish your companionship. And your bravery, heaven's sake! Crossing Pennsylvania's 'endless mountains' with little more than dashing Sir Edward as your protector? Ah . . ." A coy smile teased Rachel's lips. "Reminds me of when my darling Jonah did the same for me. And we all know where that led!" she said, massaging her protuberant abdomen. "Surely, dear sister, you have many tales to tell about your journey with such a sophisticated man of the world. Eh?"

In a whirl of smooth motion, Sukey's left hand stopped the yarn from going up into the distaff while her right hand cleared flax knots and pulled out thick threads. "Sir Edward? That mewling imitation of manhood?" Pounding the spinning wheel treadle with her foot, Sukey snorted. "Truth be told, Rachel, he had far more need of my protection, than I of his."

"But he is debonair, Sukey. You must admit that

much. And, well . . . rather handsome." A twinkle illuminated her weary soft green eyes.

"Rachel! Stop, at once! For some mysterious reason, you and Pa seem to think I must be immediately paired with another man." Sukey's foot resumed pounding the spinning wheel treadle with impatient force.

Clutching a handful of flax, Rachel paused. "George Howard did you a dreadful injustice, Sukey, despite all his money. You rebel against marriage because George left you untouched . . . and unloved."

A flax line tickled the soft pads of Sukey's thumb and finger as she continued to spin. Her mouth tensed. "I have no need for the touch of any fool man. Or the smothering confines of marriage. I am a free woman, now, Rachel. Truly an enviable state. And I intend to stay that way."

Sukey's spinning wheel whistled faster as she defiantly labored on.

"Free? Sukey, a woman without love is cold and hungry and empty. A passionate husband fills her with his tender warmth. He brings her to a paradise she can never realize on her own. He . . . oh!"

Rachel suddenly pressed her belly with both hands.

"Dear sister!" Sukey cried. "What is it? Oh, Rachel, sweet, you must not excite yourself over my situation. Is it . . . ? Are you . . . ?"

Sukey clambered up a steep slope edging away from Turtle Creek. Drifts of white locust blossoms perfumed the air and coated the path where Sukey trod. Her breath came in short gasps as she accelerated her pace. She had to find them at once . . . the healing herbs so vital to Rachel's imminent labor.

"Trust me, dear Rachel," she murmured aloud in solitude to the four winds. "I shall not let you die. Not while I have an ounce of strength in my own body."

Abruptly, to the right, she heard a chilling sound. Mens' voices—loud at first, quickly escalating to anger. French accents choked with hate. Peering between tangled laurel, Sukey caught sight of two French soldiers badgering a third man who, even from a distance, looked vaguely familiar.

One of their compatriots, perhaps?

They dismounted from their horses. Only then did Sukey get a better look at that restless third man.

"'Tis Rafe!" she gasped, watching the unfolding scene in horror.

Yet another Frenchman, knife upraised, crept out from a dense labyrinth of viburnums. With his back to the sinister-looking man, Rafe seemed unaware of the intruder's approach.

Merciful heavens!

A screamed warning from her lips would serve no useful purpose. She had to alert Stewart! But how, without exposing herself to danger? The only weapon she bore was the knife strapped to her leg. From this distance, she had no assurance of hitting the interloper.

Heart pounding furiously as she leaned from her overhead rocky perch, Sukey hurled a small triangular stone with all her might at the furtive Frenchman.

"Ughh!" he cried, alerting Rafe to his presence as the stone struck his forhead.

On guard now, Rafe backed up to keep all three Frenchmen in his field of vision.

Sukey dashed downhill through underbrush toward the skirmish. When she emerged at a partial clearing close to the men, the first two French soldiers attacked Stewart with upraised fists.

"Look at him!" Sukey whispered, marvelling at how

adroitly the brave Stewart held his own. At last, the first
Frenchman dropped under Stewart's fists.

A metal glint in the morning sun caught Sukey's eye
as the third Frenchman again flashed his knife. No time
to scream! Grasping her own knife from under her skirt,
Sukey hurled it at the stealthy Frenchman. The knife
whistled past his nose and landed near Rafe.

Crouching, the attacker pivoted, spied Sukey, and
scrambled toward her.

The second Frenchman fell under Stewart's fist at the
same moment. Stewart dashed to Sukey's rescue. He
wrestled with the third man.

"Rafe's winning!" Sukey whispered, till suddenly she
saw the Frenchman slice at Stewart's arm. A swift punch
from Stewart knocked the knife from his attacker's
hand, while the two men continued thrashing one another with fists. Edging closer to his grounded weapon,
the Frenchman knelt and retrieved his knife.

Stewart drew his own dagger, and with his back to
Sukey, plunged the weapon into his attacker. An ominous red smear spread across Stewart's sleeve.

"Rafe is wounded!" Sukey murmured. "Perhaps
weakening!"

Dashing toward Stewart's horse, Sukey grabbed its
reins, scooped up her own knife, leapt into the saddle,
and rode to Stewart's side.

"Get on!" she shouted to him.

He glared first at the lumpish assaulters sprawled on
the ground, then at Sukey. "A difficult choice, Mrs.
Howard. Drunken, belligerent Frenchmen . . . or you,
possessed of knives and stones." His bushy eyebrows
twitched. "Which is more formidable?"

"Mule-headed man! Deliberate, if you like, till the
cows come home, Mr. Stewart. But mount your horse at

once. Blood stains your sleeve. We must tend to your wound immediately."

In one careful upswing, Stewart mounted his horse behind Sukey.

Stewart's muscular warmth surrounded Sukey. His chest pressed close to her back. His arms reach around her waist as he clutched the pommel for support. His long legs grazed her own.

Rafe Stewart's nearness excited Sukey far beyond what she considered wise. Or safe. Sukey felt her will-power slip a notch. Clinging to the worn leather reins, she reminded herself that no man would ever dominate her life again.

"One can only pray," Stewart's voice rasped in her ear, "that your nursing skills surpass your battle skills."

She sniffed. "I was quite brave, Mr. Stewart, if you took time to notice."

Again that deep voice growled in her ear. "What I noticed, madam, was the manner in which your knife parted the hairs on my cheek as it whistled past my face."

"All part of my skilled precision, Mr. Stewart," she insisted, as they rode past a huge Jack-in-the pulpit jutting from a shallow stream. "Besides, you exaggerate. My knife accurately found its mark on that sullen Frenchman. Quite likely I . . . I saved your life." Even as she boasted, she marveled at how fiercely Stewart fought in the face of overwhelming danger. So unlike cowardly Sir Edward Knowles!

Or frigid George Howard.

A sea of pink geraniums reached toward sunlight motes piercing the forest. A woodpecker assaulted decaying logs in a symphony of staccato echoes.

Stewart's arms tightened around Sukey's waist. She feared the weakness of her own foolish passions. "Mr.

Stewart, I understand your concerns, but you need not cling to me quite so firmly. I feel certain, at this slow gait, that you will not be unseated from your horse."

"Under normal conditions, Mrs. Howard? Yes. But . . . my head grows somewhat woozy from the pain. In my weakened condition, I might tumble from the horse were it not for the security of your waist. Surely you would not condemn me to yet another tragedy this fine day."

A smile! Sukey swore she heard traces of mirth in Stewart's low voice buzzing in her ear. What perplexing sort of man was this semi-savage? Perhaps a blackguard who preyed on unsuspecting innocent women?

Stewart's hands inched further around her mid-section. His fingers interlaced at her front till they formed a snug corset over Sukey's apron.

She glanced down at those strong hands and arms which near-imprisoned her. She could tell no one just how much Rafe Stewart excited her. Least of all brash Stewart, himself! How deliciously easy it would be to unleash all her inhibitions. Just lean back into the cove of Stewart's broad chest, and allow him free rein to do what he obviously desired.

Sukey had no intention of granting the ruffian that much liberty with her passions.

She cleared her throat. "Dizzy, sir?" she asked. "Then we must locate a place of repose for you at once. Ah, this will serve our purposes. A stream, some shelter, a carpet of soft moss. This should do nicely," she commented, halting the horse. "You first, Mr. Stewart."

He took his time dismounting.

His arms lingered firmly around Sukey's torso. His breath warmed her nape as his stubbled jaw tickled her pale skin.

Sukey's heart raced till she thought it might leap from her chest. For one brief moment, he kissed her throat. A moment that made her breathing halt, her blood pound, her heart sing with exuberance. Sukey closed her eyes.

Then he swung free and once more stood on the ground.

She fought to breathe normally. 'Twould never do, letting this ruffian know he ignited her womanly desires, that he shredded her resolve to determine her own destiny. Never again, never, would she yield control of her life—or her passions—to any man. Misery would be the inevitable result of such weakness.

And Sukey Howard was not weak.

Ignoring Stewart's outstretched arms, she dismounted on her own and slung the reins over a hickory limb.

"Settle yourself on that moss by the stream, Mr. Stewart, and I shall cleanse and bind your wound."

Stewart propped himself against a boulder. His eyes closed as he grimaced.

"Aha! You are in pain, Mr. Stewart, are you not?" Sukey deftly tore back his ripped sleeve to expose the angry wound.

"Nonsense," he mumbled, his eyes remaining closed. "Pain is for cowards. Men my size are brave, and bold, and . . ."

"They lie, Mr. Stewart. As you are doing now."

Sukey dipped a moss plug in the rippling stream, then used the moistened ball to cleanse oozing blood from Stewart's arm. Gently she dabbed at the pouting lips of his jagged wound.

He opened his eyes just as she yanked the kerchief from her shoulders. "You are disrobing for my pleasure, madam. What more could a wounded man possibly ask?"

Sukey tore a long strip from her kerchief and clicked her tongue in disgust. "You, sir, are a vile, unprincipled man. I should just leave you out here in the woods to bleed to death."

Binding his biceps with her torn garment, she ignored his unflinching stare. And those curved lips that seemed so perilously close to her own.

With his good hand, Stewart caught Sukey's arm and held her fast. "But you would not, would you, Mrs. Howard?"

At that precise moment, a thousand leaves sighed in the June breeze, rich with the perfume of rose petals.

Sukey's breathing escaped her control. Watching Stewart's tongue moisten his lips, she felt the unwelcome heat of desire warm her body. Those eyes of Stewart's—quite the unusual shade of blue, more vibrantly intense, even, than the first and purest flax flowers of summer. Where had she seen those same eyes before? And why was Stewart's gaze now inching down her throat . . . to her bosom?

"Mrs. Howard?" He warmed her arm with his slow-moving hand.

"Mercy!" she exclaimed, clutching at her exposed cleavage and the silver pendant dangling from her throat. "I . . . I did not realize . . . when I stripped off my kerchief, that . . ."

"I am grateful, madam, for your extreme compassion in tending my wound. Please, let me express my gratitude."

Delicately, as if he feared crushing them, he kissed the fingers of her right hand, which still covered her cleavage. Each individual finger.

Orioles and thrushes sang sweeter than Sukey ever remembered.

She found it difficult to muster sufficient breath. "Mr . . . Mr. Stewart, really. 'Twas . . . mere common charity."

He lifted the trembling fingers covering her bosom.

"I need also proffer my apologies for soiling your

garment with my blood." Stewart gently kissed the naked rising hills of Sukey's breasts.

On her knees before him, she felt her legs grow limp. Damp need moistened the cleft above her thighs. Never had she known a man like Rafe Stewart. The ruffian drove Sukey mad with unfamiliar desires. But she had to remember her vow—never again to allow any man access to her heart—to guard her cherished new freedom.

"My clothes will sweeten when properly exposed to the sun," she insisted weakly, knowing she must push free from Stewart, yet lacking the strength to do so.

"Everything sweetens when properly exposed to the sun, Mrs. Howard," he rasped. "Even a man and a woman." He drew her into his arms and kissed her mouth, tentatively at first, in an exploration of her trembling lips. Then full and firm, possessively.

Her arms slid up over the bulge of Stewart's shoulders as she wilted onto his lap. He kissed her greedily. She longed to express her own ardor. Feeling Stewart's hungry mouth move down her throat . . . down, down toward her breasts, made Sukey stir restlessly in his arms. But when his hand slid inside her chemise and cupped her breast, Sukey suddenly cried out.

"My sister!" she blurted.

Stewart hesitated. "I beg your pardon?"

"Dear Heaven! How careless of me! Rachel needs help. In the excitement of your conflict, I nearly forgot my reason for being out today."

He released her. "What has happened to your sister?"

"Her time is near. I fear—our entire family fears—Rachel is not doing well, sir. Her face, the swelling of her limbs . . . Oh, I must find herbs at once, Mr. Stewart, or . . . or . . ."

Sukey could not complete the terrifying thought.

Chapter Six

Captain Charlevoix Mouceau, unsmiling, elbowed his way through a sea of French soldiers and militia inside Fort Duquesne. Sunlight cast a sheen over their pearl-grey coats. Striding across the dusty central parade, Mouceau winced at dense throngs of backwoodsmen and Indians lounging near the flagpole. Corporal Allouez followed close at Mouceau's heels. Overhead, the fleur-de-lis fluttered in a steady afternoon breeze.

"Crowding brings epidemics of disease, Corporal Allouez. We need every man, yet this crowding is intolerable." Mouceau passed a row of low huts jammed into one of Fort Duquesne's bastions. He pressed his hands against the notched oak logs and grunted in dismay. Wiping his perspiring brow, he viewed Sergeant Nicolet's approach.

"Your scowl, Sergeant Nicolet, bodes ill for us. Am I correct?"

"*Oui, mon Capitaine*. The half dozen cannon sent from France appear quite rusty."

Mouceau spat contemptuously. "More refuse from the King's arsenal, no doubt! But the *bateaux* that just arrived from Fort Presqu'Isle? Surely . . ."

"Laden with flour, salt pork, dried peas, brandy."

"Ahh! *Magnifique*! Surely that will erase your displeasure, Sergeant Nicolet."

Nicolet kicked at the soft earth with the toe of his worn leather boot. "An insufficient amount, sir, for the enormity of our needs."

Mouceau's pock-scarred face flushed crimson with anger. "Rusted artillery, jammed rifles, our most experienced gunsmith near death with the bloody flux!" Mouceau uttered a series of profane oaths.

Corporal Allouez emerged from the shadows of his superior officers. "Michel Margry, sir, has discovered a source of assistance in our dilemma."

"Eh?" Mouceau's eyes narrowed.

"An English trader, apparently eager to do business with us."

"Absurd, Allouez! No right-thinking Englishman will barter with us just as their general begins a march across the mountains toward our fort."

Sergeant Nicolet intervened. "This particular Englishman is . . . well, perhaps not right-thinking. Certainly less than clever. An inordinate fool, even. He seems eager to meet with you 'as one gentleman to another,' while building his fortune out here along the frontier."

A twisted smile crimped Mouceau's parched lips. "A fool, you say? Easy to manipulate for our purposes?" His gray eyes glittered in the June sunlight.

Allouez concurred. "Sir Edward Knowles is weaker than the most compliant woman you could ever imagine, *Capitaine*."

"Then we must quickly meet your new friend, Allouez, to determine his worth for us. And if you are mistaken . . ."

"You mean, if Knowles is not the fool he appears to be?"

Mouceau's gnarled hand touched the sword dangling across his left hip. "Then, messieurs, we will . . . dispatch the would-be British spy in our own unique fashion."

* * *

"A distinct treat awaits you this afternoon, Sukey," Rachel Butler announced, a coy smile tugging her lips as she peered out her kitchen window.

"Indeed, Rachel," Sukey replied, slipping a silver thimble onto her middle finger. "If, that is, you esteem darning as an afternoon of pleasure."

"Oh, dear sister, you shall do far better than that! Sir Edward Knowles approaches our front door even as we speak."

"Sir Edward?" The needle in Sukey's hands dropped to her lap. "Mercy! Whatever can that annoying, misplaced sophisticate be up to now?"

"You puzzle me, Sukey. Sir Edward is really quite a pleasant man."

Sukey scowled at her sister.

"No, truly, Sukey. And with his tall, debonair manner and dress, he cuts a handsome figure. Surely you cannot argue with me on that."

"Argue with you, Rachel? Can, and shall. All your attempts to convince me of Sir Edward's magnificent good traits must surely fail. The man is nothing more than a front parlor dandy. Every bit as bereft of real manhood as . . ."

"Sukey! Knowles is not George Howard, and he never will be. Oh, if only that odious man had not tormented you so! Wait! Where are you going?"

"Out the back door. The treat this afternoon shall be entirely yours, Rachel, my dear. Not mine. A perfect opportunity for you to rest and sip tea with Sir Edward while I hoe the kitchen garden."

Sukey stamped outside to avoid Knowles. Seizing a wooden-handled hoe, she flailed away at soft earth lining a row of cabbage seedlings. In her zeal, auburn-colored tendrils escaped her mobcap and dangled informally across her throat, where the silver pendant sparkled. Warm June breezes, fragrant with lilac, whipped at her homespun apron.

Sir Edward Knowles and his absurd vanity revolted Sukey. "So unmanly!" she muttered, striking away at aggressive weeds. And so unlike audacious Rafe Stewart. The thought of Rafe—brash, courageous, strong—made all Sukey's strung-tight fibers relax.

A sudden noise behind her brought Sukey to instant alert. A wolf? A bear, perhaps? She whirled with hoe upraised.

"A novel greeting, Mrs. Howard, even for a frontier woman. Begging your pardon if I frightened you."

She lowered the hoe and exhaled. "Have you forgotten, Sir Edward? Nothing frightens me."

"But of course, Mrs. Howard. I remain in awe of your bravery on our recent sojourn across Pennsylvania. A more courageous woman I simply could not imagine." A smile played at the corner of Knowles's mouth.

She despised that knowing smile.

Dozens of times since their departure from Lancaster, Knowles pondered Sukey in that same guileful manner. As if Sir Edward could see straight through to her soul and read her unsavory thoughts . . . about men and marriage and her secret longing to be seized by virile Rafe Stewart.

Damn Knowles! A study in lace-covered vexation, if ever there was one! His signet ring glittered in the afternoon sun as he waved his hands.

"Most kind of you to cheer my sister with your presence, sir. I could not, in good conscience, further detain you from such a noble mission." Turning away, she whacked her hoe at weeds encroaching on the herb garden.

He ducked, to avoid her lethal swing. His thumb rubbed small arcs over his watch fob. All the while, his droll smile persisted.

"I came to see you as well, Mrs. Howard." He seized her hoe to command her attention.

No! She would not have it! If Sir Edward craved a limp-wristed damsel to share his life—and his bed—he would most definitely have to look elsewhere.

Still clutching the hoe, Sukey glared at Knowles. "Hearty greetings and salutations to you, sir. Now, if you will kindly release my tool, I shall resume my . . ."

"Sukey!" Rachel called from the front door. "Do pause a moment to share a cup of mint tea with Sir Edward and me."

"But I—"

"Come now, Sukey. It would do us all a world of good. Everyone knows that good company over a cup of tea enormously benefits one's constitution."

Sukey's glance swung from Knowles's dapper countenance to her sister's wan features. Unwilling to upset Rachel, she complied with a protracted sigh.

Seated in a Windsor chair by the kitchen fire, Knowles stirred his tea in delicate little circles. "Regina sends her warmest regards to you both," he announced, brushing crumbs from his brocaded waistcoat. "Unfortunately, Fitch required her presence at home today to organize several housekeeping details."

"Regina sent more than just her kind regards, Sukey. She had Sir Edward fetch me a large bunch of herbs for my labor. Smell the squaw root and butterfly weed? Just inhaling their vibrant aroma tingles all my senses with revived healing."

One look at her swollen-faced pregnant sister told Sukey that statement was far from the truth. "I miss

Regina's pleasant demeanor, Sir Edward. Her daily company on our journey proved such a consolation."

"From the . . . grievous burden of your mourning?" Knowles asked. His eyebrow rose with a hint of disbelief.

Sukey scowled over her teacup at him.

Despite Knowles being a weak-minded fool, he appeared to understand more than he ought. Sukey shifted uneasily on her wooden bench. "Exactly, sir," she answered, fidgeting with her fichu. "No one comprehends the depths of my personal misery. I . . . I keep my feelings to myself."

"Indeed. I observed that, madam. Your tragic fortitude is almost too monumental for one so . . . tenderly feminine."

Only Sukey's imagination? Or was that a grin Knowles smothered as he lowered his head for another sip of mint tea. The wretch! With narrowed eyes she studied Knowles.

"How compassionate of you to discern my sister's feelings, Sir Edward. The more you learn of Sukey, I assure you, the greater your appreciation of her many virtues."

"Indeed, Mrs. Butler." Knowles's voice deepened as he fixed a lazy gaze on Sukey. "Mrs. Howard's abundant virtues are quite remarkable."

Rachel rose awkwardly from her chair.

"What is it, Rachel?" Sukey begged.

"You two must forgive me, but the soothing tea has relaxed me to the point of requiring a nap."

Sukey nodded. "Doubtless Sir Edward will want to . . ."

"Oh, surely not depart, after riding all this way!" Rachel exclaimed. "Sukey will cheerfully entertain you, sir, while I rest in the next room."

"But—!" The exclamation escaped Sukey's open

mouth. She felt trapped, by every definition of the word, she thought in disgust. Her entire family seemed in collusion to unite her with Knowles.

Rachel waved her hand from the bedroom doorway. "Sukey, Sir Edward will surely forgive my tiresome fatigue if you show him the wonderful new cloth and tools a pack train just brought in from Philadelphia. Truly, the finest ever seen in these parts. Now I bid you *adieu*, Sir Edward." She disappeared into the shadows of her cramped bedroom and closed the door.

With mouth set in a prim straight line, Sukey returned her teacup to the kitchen table. A long blue shadow emerged at her side. Sukey's gaze swept up Knowle's broad silver-trimmed waistcoat to his rouged cheeks. An earnest expression shone in those intense blue eyes . . . as if they harbored a message she needed to know.

His eyes lingered on the soft pink curves of Sukey's cheeks. He leaned close. "I have missed our daily afternoon conversations, Mrs. Howard."

Great Heavens! The man still entertained notions of . . . of dallying with her! A silken fop whose limp demeanor could not begin to approach Rafe Stewart's rugged manliness. Sukey moved quickly to elude Knowles's warm proximity.

She reached the door.

"A lovely June day of uncommon beauty, would you not agree, sir?" Gentle breezes ruffled her muslin skirt.

Studying Sukey's bodice and skirt pressed firm against her shapely figure, Knowles nodded in assent. He moistened his lips. "No lovelier than your beauty, madam," he commented, clasping her elbow in his hand as if to guide her.

"The breeze intensifies," Sukey commented, holding

tight to her mob cap as winds ruffled her fichu enough
to expose her cleavage.

"Indeed, madam." Knowles bit back a smile as he
watched her feminine disarray.

In Eli Whitfield's shadowy storeroom, Sukey turned
her back to Knowles and chattered fast to distract his
steady gaze. But when she lifted a fabric sample for
his approval, she felt his hand lightly feather across her
shoulder.

Only her imagination?

She talked more rapidly. And felt it again. And an instant later, the press of his lips against her nape. She
spun around.

"Sir! You—!" she exclaimed.

Ignoring her protestation, he kissed her mouth in a
lingering gesture.

She blinked, then slapped his cheek. "Sir Edward!
Have you lost your mind? What has come over you?"

Knowles breathed deeply. A veil of caution returned
to his face. Stepping back as if to reclaim his self-con-
trol, he spoke now in a higher octave as he waved his
hand with a flourish. "Please accept my apologies, Mrs.
Howard. Surely the sweet-smelling violets momentarily
blotted my sense of reason."

"Have I your assurance it shan't happen again?"

He took another deep breath as a subdued spark returned to his flax-blue eyes. "Oh, never, madam. Unless
. . . unless, of course, you deigned to become my wife."

Sukey gasped audibly. "Sir! We shall not mention the
subject again. Ever!"

Knowles fluttered his lace handkerchief. "Is that
wise, madam? Have I not compromised your reputation
by my rash actions?"

"Your rash—! Sir!" she spluttered again, annoyed
that Knowles would equate his mild kiss and spineless

touch with true inflamed passion. Oh, the overdressed fop would near-faint if he saw Rafe Stewart's unbridled, masculine lust!

Or Sukey's trembling response to Stewart's hunger.

Glaring up at Knowles's sizeable frame, she hoisted one of Eli's dull black hammers in mid-air. "I may be short, compared to your great height, Sir Edward. But I am fierce. You shall not kiss me again, is that understood? Else I shall be forced to . . . to *discipline* you! Have I made myself quite clear?"

At her use of the word, "discipline," she saw Knowles's eyes flash and widen. He gnawed his quivering lips into submission. Almost, she thought, as if he struggled to suppress emotion. Mercy! Had she worded her sentiments too strongly for such a weak-minded soul as Sir Edward?

He shuffled backwards. "Oh, madam, I stand meekly chastened. And in awe of your avowed ferocity, I might add."

She patted his hand gently. "There, there, Sir Edward. You must not fret. We shall speak of this matter to no one. Ah, my father approaches! Remember, Sir Edward, no further kisses shall pass between us. Agreed?"

"I remain grateful, madam, that you have forgiven my impertinence. Despite your compelling beauty, I shall endeavor not to insult you with my kisses again."

No, she wanted to believe, 'twas not a wry expression on Knowles's heavily rouged face.

In his bones, Rafe Stewart felt the dying wails of English ghosts. "A few hundred starving Englishmen, sick and dispirited," he muttered, "including Thomas." From his lofty perch on a spur of Chestnut Ridge, he reined in his horse and glared south.

"They named it Fort Necessity," Red Hawk informed him, about a meager barricade that desperate Englishmen hastily built in a Pennsylvania meadow the previous year.

"As if a name would dignify it," Stewart snorted. "That rain-drenched day, when Frenchmen attacked them . . . Thomas died a miserable death."

"You have come to avenge your brother's death."

Glancing over at the aging Lenape, Stewart nodded. "You read me well, my friend. I must go to that meadow and touch the spot where Thomas and those men died."

Red Hawk shook his head. "A long hard ride, Rafe."

"I have come a long way, Red Hawk. A few more miles cannot trouble me. As I ride, I shall scan the hills for the best possible route for General Braddock's advancing army. I have no right to detain you, Red Hawk. Your kindness in teaching me the spirit of these mountains is more than I can ever repay. Fort Necessity's sorrow is mine, not yours."

"My friend, you shall not lose me that easily. For my own brother, I would do exactly as you are doing. Follow me. I know a direct route to the Great Meadow." Red Hawk nudged his mount into a descent of Chestnut Ridge.

Hours later, entering a low meadow ringed by wooded hills, Rafe confronted the abandoned "Fort Necessity."

"Damn!" he muttered to Red Hawk. "Nothing but one scrawny hut surrounded by a circle of split-oak pickets." He squeezed his husky frame between two tall vertical logs to reach the lone hut inside. Trailing his hands over the shed's crude logs, Stewart peered at motes in sunlight gleaming through a humble roof of bark and animal skins.

"They kept the ammunition here," Red Hawk reminded him.

"And . . . the wounded." Stewart's jaw clenched.

"Charlevoix Mouceau led the assault, Red Hawk. I hold him responsible for my brother's death."

"That was before the French made him commander of Fort Duquesne?"

Stewart nodded. Deep in thought, he chewed on his lower lip. "I will get him, you know. The bastard!"

"Be careful, my friend. Charlevoix Mouceau did not get where he is by being careless."

Stewart's eyes narrowed. "The same could be said of me, Red Hawk," he replied.

"Basket? Sukey, you must not trouble yourself on my account," Rachel insisted, propping her sewing on what remained of her lap.

Sukey pressed a forefinger to her own lips in a secretive gesture. "Hush! Pa must not hear, Rachel. You know how he rants about 'the virtues of hard and constant work.' But I simply must abandon my chores ever so briefly and get outside on this glorious sunny day. If Pa asks my whereabouts, just tell him I search for willow branches to make you a new sewing basket."

"Devious girl! But really, Sukey, you work so hard here. Pa could not possibly fault your labors." Rachel fingered her badly-frayed sewing basket as a sparkle crept into her eyes. "To have a new basket, though . . . indeed, it would be lovely, Sukey."

Cheered by the scent of fresh white viburnum flowers and the whistles of a tiny phoebe, Sukey scampered uphill. She climbed a sprawling maple tree, as she often did in Lancaster as a child. Seated on a sturdy limb, she hugged the main trunk and peered through branches feeling much like a carefree songbird. Studying flexible willow whips which threaded their way between gnarled maple limbs, Sukey reached for the sheathed knife strapped to her calf.

"Peeling off your garments again, Mrs. Howard?"

She jerked her head around in search of the voice's owner. A swarthy, long-legged, leather-clad man wearing a bear's tooth necklace stood directly below her.

"Rafe Stewart! You startled me!" she shouted. "I could have tumbled out of this tree from the shock. I never heard your approach."

He smiled up at her. "No one ever does, Mrs. Howard." Stewart's white teeth flashed in the morning sunlight. Copper highlights danced across his tousled black hair. "Now, methinks I shall climb up there to have a closer look at your fetching thigh."

Suddenly remembering that her skirt dangled high in her fingertips, Sukey shoved the hem down over her legs.

"Indeed you shall not, sir! Else we shall both tumble to our deaths."

He massaged the bristle of his jaw. "Then you had better come down now, Mrs. Howard, for modesty's sake. While you sit perched on your tree limb, I have an astonishing view of your undergarments. Or lack of them."

Her eyes flared. "Sir! You are a depraved monster."

Stewart flexed his chest muscles. "A monster? Nay, Mrs. Howard. But I am a man. Now, are you coming down, or must I climb up there and fetch you?"

She studied Stewart's solid frame—powerful legs planted defiantly wide beneath a broad, unyielding chest. At the thought of his insolent vigor, she felt her pulse race as she groped down the maple tree to the ground.

A curious instinct drew her to stand within Stewart's grasp, though he did not touch her. The summer sun— oh, surely it was the summer sun—warmed her cheeks to a flaming peach color.

"Dare I ask why you found refuge in a tree, my lady?"

"I . . . I am not your lady. And I sought willow whips for basketmaking." She took a step closer to Stewart, without knowing why.

"Though those same whips lay everywhere on the ground?"

When he stared intently into her eyes, as he now did, Sukey felt reason abandon her. "I loved climbing trees as a girl. One of my favorite places to sit, you see. For a brief while, I longed to relive my childhood and enjoy that pleasure again." She edged forward one more step.

Stewart's voice rumbled low in his chest. "What else do you long for, Mrs. Howard?" With one hand, strong yet gentle, he tilted her face up toward his. His fingers caressed the curve of her cheek.

She stood close enough to him now that she could smell the seductive musk of his manliness. "You must not do that, Mr. Stewart," she whispered.

"Pray, why not?" His head leaned nearer her own.

Her voice grew faint. "B-B-Because, Mr. Stewart, then I shall have to do this." Sukey slid her arms up over Rafe's shoulders and kissed him on the lips.

She stepped back.

He eyed her solemnly. "You have never been kissed by a man before, have you, Mrs. Howard?"

"Of course I have. I was a married woman. I . . ."

Seizing her by the arms, he pulled her tight against his chest and kissed her. But this kiss was unlike any absentminded, bloodless token George Howard ever bestowed on her! Stewart's mouth brushed her own repeatedly till Sukey felt herself sag limp in his arms.

Tightening his embrace, Stewart deepened his kiss with demanding friction.

His hunger overwhelmed her. White-hot fires surged through her body, raising restless energy Sukey never knew she possessed. When he released her, she stood with her burning lips parted.

"You are a beautiful woman, Susannah Howard. You deserve far better than you have gotten. Care to see what your husband denied you?"

Her breathing came in irrational gulps. Desire enflamed her lips, her breasts, the dreadful hollowness above her thighs. She closed her eyes in an effort to blot out the craving.

A failed effort.

"Rafe," she whispered. "I have looked for you every day. At dawn, when the sun first brings light to the earth. Just before sunset, when brilliant colors stream across the mountains."

He drew her into his arms and kissed her throat. "Sukey, I need you, too, my love. The waiting is hard on us both."

"But why, Rafe? What is it that keeps us apart?" she begged.

Listening to a thrush warble its joy at living in the forest, Stewart stroked her loosened hair. "Stay safe and well, Sukey. Guard your back at every moment. And know, all the while, that I keep watch over you."

He kissed her lips, then abruptly vanished through the trees.

"Men get their dander up over the silliest nonsense, Pa. Truly! I still find it hard to believe that powerful nations like France and England want to lock horns over a set of backwoods rivers here in Pennsylvania."

Jouncing on horseback, Sukey glanced over at her father and brother as the three rode west toward Fort Duquesne.

Eli Whitfield shook his head. "When we reach that

clearing up ahead, my girl, you shall understand everything."

Emerging from a grove of giant oaks, Sukey felt river-dampened air, thick with hungry insects, moisten her face and arms. Her ears rang with the urgent sounds of water rushing west to an even more primitive frontier.

"Well?" she demanded impatiently. "Here we are, Pa, and all that surrounds us is . . ."

"Sukey," Zeb injected, "can you not see? 'Tis the water!" He swung his arms in an arc that included three rivers bordering French-constructed Fort Duquesne.

Suddenly the mystery dissolved before her eyes. Her lips moved in silent comprehension. The Allegheny River, rolling down from the north, merged with the Monongahela sweeping up from the south to form a vital point, right here in western Pennsylvania.

"Fort Duquesne sits defiantly on that point and guards the Ohio River, formed from those twin rivers," she reasoned. "So . . . the war to come will be fought to control all the trade in this whole new country." Sukey's eyes widened. "Anyone who wishes to trade inland—from whatever European nation—must likely travel down the Ohio River. And France now controls that river!"

"All the way to the Mississippi, and New Orleans," Eli added.

"Mercy!" she murmured.

They rode through a doorway in the picket wall surrounding Fort Duquesne, before dismounting. An unwashed French soldier led them to a row of low log buildings inside the fort.

"Stay close, Sukey," Eli insisted, eyeing dozens of lean-faced, unshaven Frenchmen.

"Pa!" She exclaimed in annoyance, with a click of her tongue. "Have you not noticed? I am no longer a child. I shall inquire as to Madame Nicolet's where-

abouts. Doubtless we ladies shall enjoy a delightful afternoon. Now, you two men go about your business and
fret no more over my well-being."

Unsmiling, Eli Whitfield stomped toward the fort's
smithy.

Sukey waved off buzzing insects as she went in
search of Jardine Nicolet. She swept past clusters of
traders who mingled with hordes of French soldiers and
Indians. Several women busied themselves with cooking and laundry. Jardine Nicolet was not among them.

Approaching a hut that bore an opened door, she suddenly heard Sir Edward Knowles's voice. Knowles sat
huddled in animated conversation with a French officer.
Something about the scene heightened Sukey's suspicions. Leaning against an outside hut wall, she
eavesdropped on Knowles.

The two men conversed solely in French. Struggling
to comprehend, Sukey clicked her tongue in disgust.
She understood only a half dozen French words. If only
she could follow the gist of their conversation.

"Oo, la-la, *mademoiselle*!" Three approaching French
militiamen loudly assessed Sukey's physical attributes.

"*Bonjour*, gentlemen," she responded coldly. Her voice
alerted Knowles and a French officer to her presence.

"Mrs. Howard! Indeed!" Knowles exclaimed.

Sukey cleared her throat to gain time for thought.
"Sir Edward? Indeed, I had no idea. Astonishing to find
you here this morning."

"I might say the same of you, madam." Knowles wif-
fled his ruffle-trimmed sleeve dramatically through the
air. He lowered his voice, for her ears alone. "Though I
am forced to question your safety in such a masculine den
of . . ."

"Iniquity?"

He drew in a deep breath. "One hopes, for your protection, that is not the case."

"Thank you for your concern, Sir Edward. However, I rely on no one for protection but myself."

"Quite. I had . . . nearly forgotten about your prodigious bravery, Mrs. Howard. How I marvel at your sense of courage!"

She struggled to appear self-assured. "Besides, sir, you inspired us all with your talk of the gracious, well-mannered French gentlemen who no doubt reside at Fort Duquesne."

"Quite." Knowles tone had gone flat.

"When my father mentioned that he and Zeb consented to some trading and repair work here in the fort, I insisted on riding along with them for company."

Knowles exaggerated his bow. "Ah, Mrs. Howard. A more delightful companion I simply cannot imagine."

Rising from his camp desk, Charlevoix Mouceau sauntered to Knowles's side. "Monsieur Knowles! What delicious companion have you discovered? A former acquaintance, perhaps?"

Knowles's eyes narrowed. "Madame Susannah Howard, may I present the Commander of Fort Duquesne, Captain Charlevoix Mouceau?"

"*Enchanté*, madame!" Mouceau gushed, reaching for Sukey's hand. Lust sparkled in his cold gray eyes as his parched lips planted a lingering kiss on her fingers.

Sukey detested Mouceau . . . and Sir Edward's fawning attention. She flicked dust from her striped cotton sleeve, and wished she could brush off Knowles as easily. "Gentlemen, you are far too kind," she responded, tight-lipped. "But, indeed, I came as well to visit with charming Madame Nicolet. Perhaps you have . . ."

Suddenly Sukey halted mid-sentence.

"Sir Edward, pray tell, what are *you* doing here inside a French fort?"

Knowles's blue eyes darkened abruptly. "Quite the same as you and your father, Mrs. Howard. I seek an afternoon of trade discussions, and an opportunity to speak French with educated gentlemen."

His choked response troubled Sukey. She filed it away for future reference. "You will forgive me, now, Sir Edward, if I . . . oh, pardon me, monsieur!" she begged, reaching toward a passing French soldier. "Could you direct me to Madame Nicolet's abode, please?"

Watching Sukey's swaying figure as she walked toward Jardine's quarters, Captain Mouceau grinned broadly.

"A beautiful, spirited woman, eh, Monsieur Knowles?" he hissed.

"Quite."

"No doubt a . . . a delightful companion in the dark for some lucky man. Where might her husband be, sir?"

"Dead."

"Dead, you say!" Mouceau's gray eyes flashed with sudden animation. His smile widened as he stroked his unshaven black whiskers with the nubs of his bitten fingernails.

Nudging Mouceau's side, Knowles turned back inside the commander's cramped quarters. "I know you are a busy man, monsieur, so perhaps we should resume discussing your trade needs. I might be able to secure them for you."

Charlevoix Mouceau did not immediately follow Knowles inside. Instead, he leaned against the outer doorway watching Sukey Howard's trim figure till she disappeared inside Jardine's hut.

Chapter Seven

Twisting oak ribs up to frame a second basket, Sukey stole sidewise glances at her sister. "I do wish you would contemplate a lovely rest beneath this shade tree, Rachel."

"Nay. Carding wool is not laborious, Sukey." Rachel replied, dragging a brush over teased locks of wool. "Especially when we sit outdoors in the lovely fresh air. Besides, it comforts me to sit near you as we work. Your stories do so make me laugh. Now tell me more," she begged.

"About Fort Duquesne?"

"Yes! And the fabled 'French gentlemen.' Pa is so taciturn, you know. I could not pry even two sentences from him about the bustling activity of an enemy fort."

Plucking a new oak splint from bundled wood, Sukey clicked her tongue. "Pa thinks women should not trouble their heads about such things, Rachel. He believes 'tis unhealthy for us." She laughed wickedly. "Reading sermons, delivering babies, making food. He limits us to precious few categories."

Rachel giggled. "You do oversimplify, Sukey! But 'tis true. Pa never believed women should concern themselves with matters of war and politics. Now, do go on! What happened when the three of you entered the stockade gateway? Were the men civil to you? Was Madame Nicolet exceedingly overjoyed to see you once more?"

"Well, they made it clear that—" Hands halted in mid-air, Sukey abruptly interrupted her narration and stared off in the distance.

"Sukey? What is it?" She followed the direction of her sister's gaze. "Are we receiving guests! Why . . . 'tis Regina Ramsey!"

"Accompanied by none other than himself, Sir Edward Knowles," Sukey added drolly.

"Sukey! You *will* be civil to the sweet, gentle man!" Rachel demanded in a scolding tone.

"I . . . shall do my best, though one cannot hope for miracles with a man so persistently irritating," Sukey replied, forcing a falsely beatific smile. "I do rejoice at seeing Regina again, though!"

Dropping her oak splints, Sukey dashed to greet her former traveling companion.

"My dears, my dears!" Regina exclaimed, sweeping the two sisters into an enormous hug. "Simply divine, beholding you two precious friends again! How have you been? Rachel, dear, it appears you have not . . . been eating sufficient for two."

"Come inside and restore yourself after your dusty ride, Regina," Sukey urged, seizing Regina by the arm. "We shall have a cup of tea together and—"

Freezing suddenly, Rachel gave a small cry.

"Rachel! What is it?" Sukey begged.

"Nothing, perhaps. But when I stood up just now, a strange chill, and a cramp, rippled across my belly."

"I have assisted in many childbirths," Regina said. "Is this your first inkling, my dear?"

"No," Rachel confessed sheepishly, rubbing the small of her back. "I felt some curious backache, earlier this

morning as Jonah left, but I did not want to trouble anyone. I supposed 'twas nothing but the false labor again."

"We shall help you indoors, dear, and make you comfortable. From all signs, I believe you truly are in labor,"
Regina announced, cradling Rachel's arm in her own as
they strolled together. "I brought along some squaw-
vine leaves," she said, holding up a fistful of withered
herbs. "Red Hawk assured me these would hasten your
labor."

Rising apprehension tensed Sukey's every fiber. This
pregnancy had drained Rachel's health. Their own
mother had died soon after childbirth.

Sukey gripped her sister's hand.

"How fortunate that you happened along at this very
moment, Regina!" she commented.

Most likely, squeamish Sir Edward would be entirely
useless at such a medically momentous event. Fearing
he might even collapse, Sukey glanced back at
Knowles, who trailed the three women through a modest apple orchard near Rachel's cabin.

Clutching her bulging abdomen, Rachel suddenly
moaned once more, just as her knees gave way.

"Edward!" Regina shouted.

In a trice, Knowles scooped Rachel into his arms.
Hoisting her high against his chest, he carried her to the
cabin.

"I feel foolish," Rachel whispered, demanding to be
set down inside her kitchen. "Surely a cup of tea will re-
vive me."

"Where is your husband, madam?" Knowles asked.

"First thing this morning, Pa and Jonah rode to a mill
beyond the next mountain. Zeb labors in the smithy. But
you must not distress them—or yourself, Sir Edward."
Stiffening, she massaged her belly once more. "First babies arrive in no great hurry."

Knowles disappeared outside as Regina busied herself making a tea of the squaw-vine leaves.

"Poor Sir Edward!" Sukey exclaimed with a laugh, while propping her sister up in bed. "Likely we have frightened him off for the day with women-talk."

Handing Rachel a cup of tea, Regina smiled inscrutably. "One never knows, my dear. Edward may yet surprise us by mustering a dollop of manful courage."

When the sun reached Rachel's south cabin window, Sukey noticed their water supply was nearly gone. Rubbing the small of her back, she stepped outside and nearly bumped into Sir Edward Knowles. He dangled a thick wooden pole across his broad shoulders. Water splashed from filled buckets balanced at both pole ends.

"Zeb has gone to fetch Jonah. I thought you ladies might need more water," he said. Setting down the buckets, Knowles seemed more somber than usual. "How is your sister, Mrs. Howard?"

Sukey twisted her fingers nervously. "I yearn for this to be over, Sir Edward. And I want Rachel—and the babe—to be well."

He laid a gentle hand on her shoulder. "Then we shall do all in our power to make it so, madam."

Inside, Rachel insisted on pacing the floor between contractions. "You must allow me these brief strolls, Sukey," she urged, much to her sister's consternation. "They bring me comfort."

"But you wobble so, Rachel. I fear you might stumble on these irregular planked floors," Sukey protested.

Stepping forward, Knowles gallantly offered Rachel his arm. "Allow me the honor of escorting you, madam, thus placating my irascible aunt and your tempestuous sister. I vow, I shall not let you fall."

Astonished, Sukey watched Rachel lean on Knowles for several steps at a time. His patient tenderness with a laboring mother amazed Sukey. With each crescendoed contraction, Rachel blanched as she seized Knowles's arm.

"Thank you kindly, sir," she whispered. "But the pains seem intensified. I shall rest in bed for awhile."

Knowles led Rachel to her rope bed.

Hours later, Jonah Butler burst through the door and kissed his wife as Regina mopped Rachel's perspiring brow.

"Sir Edward vanished," Sukey whispered to Regina. "Perhaps he fainted dead away from Rachel's cries."

The soft tones of a wooden flute suddenly drifted through an open window. Hearing the music, Rachel sighed. "How lovely!" she murmured, before another contraction overtook her.

Sukey stepped outside in search of Knowles's co-matose body. To her surprise, she found him hunched on a tree stump. Breezes inflated his linen sleeves and fluttered the queue of his wig as Knowles played his flute. His signet ring sparkled in fading sunlight.

What sort of man was Sir Edward Knowles? Sukey wondered. Fearful of even the most insignificant insect, yet strong enough to easily lift a pregnant woman about to give birth. Obsessed with each trifling detail of his fine-tailored garments, yet oblivious to that same personal ornamentation when Rachel needed his tender compassion.

She approached him. "Your music calms my anxious sister, Sir Edward. For that, I most humbly thank you."

He studied her. "And you, madam? Does my music calm you as well?" He awaited her response.

She blinked. "I, uh, yes, I . . . Whatever do you mean by that, sir?"

"Music soothes the frightened. It entertains the weary. But . . . my dear Mrs. Howard, Indians use the flute to signal messages of love to their intended." Wig askew, Knowles peered through his spectacles at her.

Sukey nervously fingered her apron gathers, all the while feigning absorption in dramatic cloud formations. This eccentric man before her was likely a French spy, definitely an emasculated fop, and worst of all—apparently falling in love with her.

Could she face a more vexing predicament?

Perhaps.

The elusive Rafe Stewart—handsome, primitive, masculine—roused Sukey's affections in a vibrant new way. Every minute away from him was an agony of longing. But Rafe appeared and vanished from her life like a capricious summer breeze. She needed him, without knowing why. If only she could see him right now, as she wished!

Sukey forced herself to meet the stare of bespectacled, rouged, and powdered Sir Edward Knowles. She would make her opinions clear at once before—

Suddenly a newborn infant wailed its displeasure.

"Oh, thank God!" she exclaimed, dashing back toward Rachel's cabin.

"Women, eh?" Captain Charlevoix Mouceau guffawed. "So . . . General Braddock finds his soldiers waylaid, not by fierce French men and Indians, but by shapely native maidens in the bush! *Mon Dieu*!" He laughed till spittle frothed at the corners of his mouth.

Examining the contents of an ammunition barrel, Sergeant Nicolet leaned forward. "When he finally expelled the Indian women from his camp, *mon Capitaine*, their men went with them. *Monsieur le Général* now foolishly tries to thread his way across the mountains without the guidance of natives who understand this terrain."

Mouceau stroked corners of his unkempt moustache. "Even so, he and his men lug those monstrous guns with them. Ships' cannon, mind you! Have you any idea how much damage those huge brass guns will inflict on Fort Duquesne if Braddock ever reaches us, Sergeant."

Nicolet shrugged to ward off anxiety. "*Oui, mon Capitaine.* Braddock's guns against the fort? 'Twill mean our destruction."

"*Oui.* The end of French control over the Ohio River . . . and the loss of a vital trade route all the way to New Orleans." Mouceau's icy gray eyes narrowed with pure hatred for the English.

"But *mon Capitaine*, have we not heard that many troubles plague his British army? Dysentery, poor food, few Indian allies. Surely hauling all those wagons and horses over mountains he's unfamiliar with will—"

Mouceau held up his hand to silence Nicolet. "Brave men led by a determined *général* can accomplish wondrous deeds, Sergeant. And Braddock is fanatically determined. We, therefore, shall intensify our efforts. We must be absolutely certain that *Général* Braddock's army—and those gigantic guns—never make it across the Alleghenies."

Nicolet scratched his unshaven jaw. "You mean . . . send our own regiments south to block the mountains?"

"Far too direct and costly, Sergeant. I have something more devious in mind. Something that will paralyze those Englishmen with fear. You see, my friend, a terrified soldier is a man unable—and unwilling—to fight." A thin-lipped smile tugged Mouceau's scarred face as he fingered the treacherous dagger at his side. "And my dear Sergeant Nicolet, I know precisely how to terrify men. Listen carefully. Here is what I want you to do."

* * *

Sukey cuddled her two-day old nephew and kissed his rosy cheeks. "Oh, Rachel, he is so beautiful! Truly. Never was a new babe more fair to look upon than your little Adam." She kissed him again and handed the swaddled infant to her sister.

Rachel tucked the infant in front of her partially concealed breast. Listening to Adam's earnest gulping, she relaxed against a feather pillow. "You are older than I, Sukey. Surely all your instincts plead with you to have a child of your own. I know you would make a wonderful mother."

"Hah! Are you not forgetting a vital factor?"

"Sukey, why did you and George never have children?"

"My dear sister! Shall I be blunt with you?"

"George almost never . . . touched you, did he?"

"Touch? In so many ways, George never touched me. Not in the passionate way that men love their wives. Not even in small tender ways like kissing or hugging. Cold and calculating as an ice floe, was George Howard. Oh, if only I had known his true nature before I married him, Rachel! Believe me, I shall never make that same mistake again."

"Oh, Sukey, dear! Not all men are like that. My darling Jonah makes me feel loved and cherished."

"I am filled with joy over your complete happiness, Rachel. A loving husband . . . a perfect new son. But I fear no man lives who can bring me that same happiness." Her voice softened. "Except . . ."

"Sir Edward?"

"Rachel, you jest! Sir Edward is only a poor imitation of rugged manhood."

"But he was so kind to me throughout my labor. He would make a superb husband and father. And have you noticed, Sukey, how the man fairly sparkles whenever you enter the room? Hm?"

"Calm yourself, Rachel. All men are devious, Sir Edward no less than any other."

"Fie! You must not indict all men just because of George Howard's treachery."

"I judge Sir Edward based on his own peculiar perfidy, Rachel. You see, I fear that he . . . oh! He and Regina approach, even as we speak. Now mind, Rachel, promise! Not a word of this subject to our guests."

Over a noon meal of roasted pork and fowl prepared by Sukey, Rachel smiled her gratitude. "No mother could have received better care than you offered, all of you. Thank you, Regina, for the 'milk' herbs you brought me today. And baby Adam thanks you for the darling little embroidered hen."

"True enough, I did the stitching, but Edward contributed the downy milkweed fluff for stuffing."

"Never mind the women's stuff," Zeb insisted, finishing off a large slice of dessert. "I say Regina's custard pie is her best gift."

Knowles, Sukey noted, seemed uncharacteristcally alert when the topic switched to politics . . . or the impending war.

A shiver prickled her spine as she contemplated his thick powder and paint, spectacles, and too-perfect wig. Was he an evil man masquerading as a fop to cover his real intentions? A miscreant in fact hired by the French to spy on British activity?

That would explain his frequent "business" trips inside Fort Duquesne to "enjoy the opportunity to speak French with those gentlemen." And his new-found coziness with Michel Margry and Captain Charlevoix Mouceau.

Of course! It had to be.

Sir Edward Knowles was a conniving French spy in disguise. A malignant truth no one suspected except Sukey Howard. War and politics had never interested her previously. Bored her to shreds, in fact. But had she not left Lancaster to seek adventure, as well as aid Rachel?

This, then, was adventure of the highest order!

Pa had always scorned a woman's place in society other than tending home and hearth and making babies. Well, she would show Pa. And everyone else. A dangerous French spy was about to be unveiled—and by a woman, no less.

By shrewd Susannah Howard.

But mere accusations were not sufficient. She would have to prove Knowles's guilt. Only one way to do that.

She needed to become Sir Edward Knowles's very shadow. Though it might choke her with disgust, she had to remain close at his side. Follow his every move. Eavesdrop on all his conversations. She had to become every bit as devious as Knowles.

Sukey dabbed an impatient finger at her upswept hairdo. "Regina? Sir Edward? May I offer you more pie?" she urged in honeyed tones. The excessive smile permeated every fiber of her voice.

"Oh, my dear! More pie and I shall burst!" Regina confided, laughing. "I do so miss your company, Sukey. How I enjoyed those long lovely chats we shared on our journey."

Sukey tipped her head in acknowledgment. "As did I, Regina. Ah, here is a thought. I could ride to your abode and spend a day with you and Sir Edward."

Regina, she noted, beamed with pleasure.

But Knowles blanched.

He tugged at his high stock as if it suddenly choked his neck. "A perfectly delectable thought, dear lady. But

I fear it would be selfish of us to steal you from your
family . . . especially the needs of your sister."

"Not selfish at all, Sir Edward," Rachel responded,
her eyes twinkling with mirth. "I feel stronger by the
day. Little Adam and I shall enjoy a quiet day of respite
here while Sukey visits Regina to spin and gossip."

Watching Knowles's subtle discomfort, Sukey
smiled.

Spinning wheel strapped to her horse, next day,
Sukey rode to Knowles's humble lodge.

"I am overjoyed at your visit, Sukey!" Regina ex-
ulted.

But Knowles avoided her, even as he and Fitch held
a discreet conversation with a French soldier in their
courtyard. Sukey needed an excuse to eavesdrop. How
could she appear nonchalant and still spy on Knowles?

Flattery.

Every man loved a recitation of his attributes.
Knowles, more vain than most, would certainly tolerate
her proximity if she . . . well, flattered him. Perhaps
even—oh, dear heavens!—flirted with him.

"For England!" she reminded herself, groaning in-
wardly at her noble sacrifice.

When she caught up to him, alone, at the doorway
of his stable, she cleared her throat. "Sir Edward, I must
say, you look extremely smart today. The silver braid
which trims your frock coat is quite elegant."

"Thank you, madam." He studied her approach.

Edging closer, she casually rested a delicate finger
against his chest as she pretended to contemplate his
garment. "And . . . and the fine cut of your coat dis-
tinctly sets off your courtly stature."

Despite the excessive layer of white powder which

covered Knowles's face, Sukey detected a distinct crimson glow rise along his throat. She felt triumphant. But she had to delve deeper, in order to winkle spy information out of the unsuspecting fool.

A small muscle tightened in Knowles's jaw. His arms hung motionless at his sides. "Madam, your compliments are indeed music to my ears. And the lavender water you wear is perfume for my tender soul."

Knowles averted his gaze from the demure woman who now stood only inches from his chest. His hands remained firmly pressed against his legs.

She aimed her sweetest smile at him. "Most kind of you, Sir Edward. Tell me, did you find the French officers of Fort Duquesne hospitable? Were they eager to . . . do business with you?"

As Sukey leaned forward, he took an evasive step backward. "Delicate matters of business require time, madam."

"Then you shall return to the fort again?"

"I . . . have yet to consummate a trade deal."

"Captain Mouceau appears quite the shrewd negotiator. Do you not fear him?"

"I . . . dear me! I do believe Aunt has just called you back to the lodge."

"You are mistaken, Sir Edward. My hearing is splendid and I heard no such thing. Mercy!" she exclaimed suddenly, slyly fingering a silver button on his waistcoat. "It would appear that one of your buttons has loosened to the point of near-loss." She relished his subtle agitation.

"I thank you for your solicitous observation, madam. I shall bring it to Aunt Regina's attention." Aroused navy flecks colored his piercing blue eyes.

"If you like, Sir Edward," she said, in a syrupy voice, "I would be happy to sew it on you . . . while you tell me all about those interesting conversations you shared with the French gentlemen. You can feel free to speak in front of me . . . I being a mere woman."

Sukey offered the bewildered Knowles a wide-eyed gaze.

"Madam, you once graciously reminded me, after I lost my sense of decorum and impetuously kissed you, that an event of that nature must never occur between us again. That you would discipline me—" here, his mouth twitched—"should I e'er stoop to such depths again."

"Poor Sir Edward! I had no intention of frightening you, sir. Merely wanted to restrain your unchecked outburst. After all, you have shown great compassion to my family. I was hoping that, with your prodigious wisdom, you might help a poor simple woman such as myself better understand our current military dilemma."

Clench-jawed, Knowles allowed his bespectacled gaze to drift from Sukey's upturned face to the laces supporting her rounded bodice.

His face reddened.

"My delicate disposition renders me in awe of any woman who threatens me with well-deserved discipline, madam. I suggest we seek the chaperonage of my aunt at once. In fact, since duty and business summon me, I shall remove myself from the premises. You and Aunt Regina can enjoy woman-talk without my witless interference."

Mounting his horse, Knowles abruptly rode off.

A noise . . . in the woods?

Riding home alone on horseback that June evening, Sukey grew intensely aware of every slight rustle. Zephyrs whistled through pine boughs, releasing a spicy scent. Overhead, a wide-winged hawk screamed in search of prey. "Indeed, many creatures live in the woods," she murmured, to calm herself. Those obscure rustling noises? Likely just a squirrel. Maybe a deer.

"Surely . . . surely not a bear," she whispered.

She halted her horse. The noise stopped.

She rode again. The noise resumed.

Sukey's breathing quickened. Something—or someone—was following her! The trading post where her family lived was still two or three miles away. Not a fast or easy ride. A jutting mountain loomed between Sukey and her Pa's refuge. Groping for the knife strapped to her leg, she prayed for bravery.

She jerked her horse to a halt. Turning in her saddle, she scanned the woods. Nothing moved. Yet clearly, something lay hidden behind one of those many bushes. A two-legged varmint rather than four-legged? Perhaps one of those unshaven Frenchmen who had not touched a European woman in months. Or an Indian. Numerous places for a predatory man to hide. There was only one thing to do.

Sukey took a deep breath.

"All right, coward! Out with you!" she barked into the silence. "You have not fooled me! I know you are there."

Nothing moved.

"Show yourself at once, coward! I insist. Or I shall shoot you!" she shouted.

An almost imperceptible movement in thickly tangled wild grape vines. Sukey wheeled to the left.

There sat swarthy Rafe Stewart, astride his horse. Stewart wore a cocksure grin.

"Sorry to disappoint you, ma'am, but I'm no coward," he growled. "Just out of curiosity, Mrs. Howard, what will you shoot me with? Your little finger?" He nudged his horse closer.

She glared back at him. "Count yourself fortunate, Mr. Stewart. Wickedly skulking up behind a woman! For shame! That can be every bit as treacherous as stalking a man. I carry a concealed weapon, you see. I am armed . . . and dangerous."

"Oh, absolutely. I agree wholeheartedly with you, Mrs. Howard," he said, drawing his horse beside Sukey's mount. "You are indeed a dangerous woman. And I?" His carmine-red lips curved into a smile that exposed perfect white teeth. "For your information, Mrs. Howard, I am a wicked man. But tell me, madam, where under your pretty skirt have you concealed a weapon?"

She blinked. "None of your business, sir. And just why were you following me?"

Stewart's smile vanished. "I promised I would watch over you, madam."

"Hah! No need of that, sir." Chin jutting forward, she thrust her face away from his penetrating stare. "I require no man to guard my safety."

With his arched fist, he gently nudged her face toward his. "I am not just any man, Mrs. Howard. And I have missed your tender healing touch."

Reluctantly she met his gaze. Almost fearfully. Something about the wildness in Rafe Stewart's infinite blue eyes, the sheen of his wind-tossed dark hair, the robust hardness of his muscles invariably made Sukey yearn to undo all her clothes and offer him her body.

Every craving feminine inch of it.

Damn Rafe Stewart!

Sukey still cringed from the memory of George Howard's cold arrogance. She would never allow any man to dominate her life again. The door to her heart must forever remain closed.

His hand still resting beneath her chin, he kissed her mouth. Sukey felt the burn of that kiss across her lips . . . felt it ripple through her breasts and probe deep into her womb.

Swinging one long leg over his saddle, Stewart planted his moccasin-clad feet on the ground. "Get down off your horse, Mrs. Howard," he ordered.

She returned his bold stare. "No," she retorted.

His bushy black brows arched. With narrowed eyes, he contemplated her sass. "Do I need to climb up there and get you?"

She knew he would, of course. Savage men never allowed obstacles to interfere with their lustful intentions. But she was the one who remained mounted. The one in control. With a quick, silent gesture she could . . . would goad her horse onward and leave this ruffian standing alone in his forested retreat. Indeed! She would toss her hair back in the wind and laugh uproariously as she galloped away.

But before Sukey could prod a knee into her mare's flank, Stewart seized her reins.

Sullen, she slid off the horse. "Sir, you are a brute. Do not think for one moment that—"

"Have you plans to shoot me, woman?" he taunted.

"N-no."

"Or stab me with that menacing little knife you hide beneath your skirts?"

"No. Though the thought has occurred to me once or twice."

Plaintive now, he stared down at her. "Ah, Susannah Howard, the days and nights are long without your sweet warmth and beauty."

Her resistance withered to naught. "Rafe . . . !" His name escaped her lips on a sigh. Standing on tiptoe, she leaned her hands against his chest and softly returned his kiss.

She felt him stir and warm and harden against her touch.

He drew her close, enduring no distance between their two bodies. His strong arms tightened around Sukey. His mouth covered hers in a kiss of intense beseeching. When his tongue swirled in a mating dance with her own, Sukey felt flames of desire lick through her torso.

"I've missed you so, Rafe. If only . . ." she begged.

"Shh, my love. You are in my thoughts every minute of the day and night." Kissing her cheek, he allowed his tongue to explore the soft skin leading to her ear.

She felt his teeth gently play with her lobe. "Rafe!" she groaned in rapture, "why can we not meet?"

"Trust in me, my love. The day will come. But not . . . not for awhile."

Sliding her arms around Stewart's brawny shoulders, Sukey clutched at his dark hair with an unfamiliar need that astonished her.

"Are you . . . are you a married man? Is that why you are so mysterious?" She feared his answer.

He laughed. "Rafe Stewart? Married? Worry yourself not on that score, my love." Nuzzling lower on her throat, he trailed kisses along her shoulder till he confronted her shift. With the fingers of his right hand, he sought to untie the laces shielding her bosom. " 'Tis a warm day, Mrs. Howard." He kissed her throat, between the cords of her dangling silver pendant. "Would you not fare better without such abundant clothing?"

When his fingers caressed her breast, she blushed. "It . . . it is quite warm." Perspiration moistened her brow. Her breathing came in more rapid gasps.

He deepened his kiss. "You are not accustomed to the touch of a man, Sukey. Why? Did your husband not lavish attention on you?"

Dizzy from Stewart's arousing caress, she struggled for an answer. "George viewed me as a parlor ornament, Rafe. Nothing more."

His tongue explored her throat. "Then you have never been loved by a real man."

His bluntness made her laugh. "A real man? How tremendously humble you are, Rafe Stewart!" She felt his raw power as he tipped her head back.

"You need to feel a real man, Sukey. And I need you." His mouth burned her lips with passionate energy. "Still frightened by my touch?"

She glared at him with false bravado. "I am not afraid of you, Rafe," she replied defiantly.

"No?" His eyebrow arched. A crude smile tugged one corner of Stewart's mouth. The bear's tooth necklace he wore highlighted his wide-slung shoulders. "Maybe you should be."

She ignored his warning. "Indeed, the hot sun beats fiercely this afternoon." Playing at modesty, she loosened the scarf crossed over her bosom.

"Shall I help you, Sukey?"

She spun away from him with her cleavage partially uncovered. Merciful heavens! What had come over her? Rafe Stewart made her lose all sense of propriety. He—

She felt his warm mouth kiss the back of her shoulders. Eager, hungry kisses that wilted her resolve. His arms slid around her waist from the rear. Wanting his kisses never to cease, she sagged against his strong chest. "Rafe," she whispered.

"Turn around, Sukey," he said.

She hesitated. "If I do, then . . ."

He kissed a path across her shoulders. "Then I shall touch you as you need to be touched."

She twirled languidly in his embrace. Sliding her fingers through his thick, wild mane, she seized his hair and kissed him fiercely, exposing her dreadful need. When he pulled her to the earth, she did not resist.

Sliding Sukey's scarf from her shoulders, Stewart kissed her soft cleavage . . . until he heard a rustling sound.

She glanced over his shoulder. "Look, Rafe! 'Tis a darling little bear cub!"

"A darling little—? Sukey, get up at once!" he ordered, leaping up from the ground. "Its mother is likely nearby."

In silence, Stewart escorted Sukey to the Whitfield post, then abruptly vanished once more.

"Rafe Stewart," she murmured, watching twilight settle over the tree-clad mountains after he left, "why must you be so mysterious? And why does my heart ache so when you are gone?"

Chapter Eight

Hunched inside Fort Duquesne's command hut, Michel Margry picked at his teeth with a blood-stained knife. The stub of his partially amputated little finger jutted upward. Captain Charlevoix Mouceau shuddered at the vulgarity of his childhood friend.

"Ah, Charlevoix! Summer days like this make me yearn for our boyhood days in Normandy. Wind whipping across the water, twisting cobbled streets of Honfleur, blood-red poppies picked by fetching maidens. When, *mon ami*, shall we return to France?"

Mouceau shook his head at the insobriety of the uncouth trapper. "We are men, now, Michel, with far more pressing concerns on our minds than childish memories," he replied, waving off his friend's longings. "Urgent orders from Paris demand that we sweep all Englishmen east of the Alleghenies. Michel, *mon ami*! Those orders shall bring unimagined honor and glory to me if we succeed. When we return to France, I shall be venerated as a hero." Contemplating his own future notoriety, Mouceau puffed out his uniform-clad chest.

Margry warily eyed Mouceau. "If, that is, you succeed."

Mouceau scowled. "That wretch, Braddock, and his damned army continue their march over the mountains straight for us, despite my—"

A knock vibrated the door.

"*Entrez!*" Mouceau shouted.

"Sir, two Shawnee scouts have just arrived from the Potomac River," Sergeant Nicolet announced.

"Yes?" Mouceau barked harshly. "What news do the savages bring?"

"Our Indian allies, along with a dozen of our own marauders, have done as you commanded."

Mouceau rubbed his palms together. "Excellent!" His cold gray eyes glittered with delight as he fondled his sword. "And the results?"

"Just as you foresaw, *mon Capitaine*. After random firing and scalping incidents in those dense, gloomy woods, British soldiers are terrified even of their own shadows. They fear the unknown, they fear Indian attacks, they fear wild animals . . ."

Mouceau could scarcely contain his glee. He rocked forward on his toes. "So the British army and those monstrous guns are halted in their tracks!"

Nervously clearing his throat, Sergeant Nicolet shook his head. "I fear not, *mon Capitaine*. Braddock's army continues its northwestward march straight to our door."

Mouceau's leathery face suddenly bloomed with angry purple blotches. His hands balled into tense fists as his breathing rattled. "'Tis not good enough, Sergeant! Do you hear me?" he shouted. "I want more scalping parties dispatched out on that trail till those British soldiers soil their breeches in terror, throw up their weapons, and run straight back to the Atlantic. Is that understood?" he screamed at Nicolet.

"*Oui, mon Capitaine*," the Sergeant assented, backing out of Mouceau's quarters.

Alone again with Margry, Mouceau rubbed at his throbbing temples and groaned.

"Your tension will bring on sickness, Charlevoix. Perhaps even destroy your ability to think clearly."

"Go amuse yourself elsewhere, Michel. Your platitudes nauseate me."

"But *mon ami*, I know how to remedy your situation."

"You? Hah! You are an insolent fool and a drunk, Michel," he growled, shuffling papers on his camp desk.

Margry leaned forward, propping his elbows on Mouceau's desk. "You need a woman, Charlevoix. Not just some cheap camp whore, either. I mean an elegant spitfire." He smiled knowingly.

Mouceau grabbed at the crotch of his uniform trousers. "You . . . have someone particular in mind?"

"The English tart that befriended Madame Nicolet."

"Madame Howard?"

Margry nodded. "Of course, *mon ami*, uh, you would have her first. Then . . . then I shall have my turn, eh?"

"Hmm." Mouceau rubbed the food-stained pewter buttons of his pearl-gray jacket. "Perhaps we could make time to . . . become better acquainted with her family, Michel. Mind you though, spoil things by becoming slovenly drunk again, *mon ami*," he said, nervously tapping his pistol, "and . . . this time I shall have to kill you."

Tiny Adam Butler screamed his need for nourishment post haste.

Sukey handed him back to Rachel, then mingled with Regina's other guests. Her head spun, attempting to spy on nefarious French soldiers and Sir Edward Knowles, all at the same time.

"Madame Howard!" oily-voiced Captain Mouceau

greeted her, "you look enchanting with a babe in your arms. But then, I must confess, you charm us all no matter who rests in your arms."

Sukey felt Mouceau's stale hot breath as he leaned close and brushed his hand against her flowered silk sleeve. She choked back her revulsion. For England, she reminded herself. "Monsieur, your endless responsibilities in running Fort Duquesne fascinate me so. Do tell me about it all."

"Captain Mouceau, my dear fellow!" Knowles suddenly exclaimed, at Sukey's elbow. "Capital of you to visit our humble picnic! Allow me to offer you more cider. Or perhaps . . . something more stimulating?"

Mouceau beamed at Sukey. "Monsieur, your picnic abounds in stimulation."

Fitch approached with a bow. "Gentlemen, I managed to secure some whiskey for your pleasure. If you care to follow me . . ."

Men! If only she could break into their exclusive whiskey and tobacco circle. Alone, now, Sukey cursed under her breath. She longed to eavesdrop on the animated conversation Knowles shared with Mouceau.

Late that afternoon, as Regina's guests departed, Mouceau clutched at Sukey's elbow. "Madame Howard, I wish you to understand that I, er, we welcome the pleasure of your visit at our fort anytime you choose."

"Myself?"

Mouceau coughed abruptly. "Well, you and, uh, your family, of course."

"Splendid idea, good fellow!" Knowles joined in. "Pray, might we all be included in your generous hospitality?"

Mouceau's eyebrows knit together in a brief scowl. He forced a smile. "But . . . but of course, Monsieur Knowles."

* * *

"Well done, you two," Knowles commented to Regina and Fitch, as he labored at unbuttoning his formal silk waistcoat.

"Thank you, Edward." A fleeting smile crossed Regina's lips. "Indeed, I think we achieved a laudable goal this afternoon. Captain Mouceau's boastful companion, Michel, could scarcely keep his mouth closed. Plying him with cider and fresh-baked cookies, I obtained more information than he meant to disclose about Indian reinforcements at Duquesne."

"Ah, Regina, you are a wizard when it comes to winkling information out of unsuspecting men," Fitch agreed, pinching Regina on the bottom.

She squealed with delight. "I shall box your ears, you old rogue!" she said, reaching for his arm.

"Here! None of that nonsense now, you two," Knowles scolded. "Else you might slip out of character and forget the roles you need to play."

Regina's expression suddenly darkened. "Speaking of roles, Edward, I could not fail to notice Captain Mouceau's . . . attention to Sukey Howard today." Her fingers anxiously toyed with the smooth ribbon trim of her sleeve. "Do you not, as a man, er . . . also find this situation alarming?"

Knowles's jaw tensed as he released the buckle of his black stock. "The Captain is a snake, Aunt, as is that scum, Margry. Would that I could run a sword through the both of them! One day soon, I shall. But for Thomas's sake, not because of reckless Mrs. Howard."

Fitch grunted. "Scouts tell us the British army falters on their advance toward Duquesne. Now is not the time to allow any weakness of the heart to muddy our efforts."

Knowles stepped out of his buckled black shoes. "My friend, have you ever before known me to weaken over any woman?"

"Nay. But I ken somehow that for you, Edward, this woman is different."

Knowles shrugged. "No different from any other wench," he growled, lying to himself. "Though perhaps, due to her audacious gullibility, a menace to herself." He reached for a dram of whiskey.

"And to our mission!" Fitch retorted.

Regina paced the floor. "No. No, it need not be so," she asserted suddenly, holding up one hand for attention. "I have a plan whereby all parties can more safely, ah, function."

Dubious, Fitch studied her with cocked eyebrow. "Your clever ideas invariably roil my digestion, Regina," he said, massaging his midsection.

"I shall ignore your impertinence, Fitch. Here is my plan, gentlemen. I think it high time that 'Sir Edward Knowles' asks Sukey Howard to marry him."

"What?" Knowles bellowed.

"Well, not actually, of course. 'Sir Edward' will chivalrously explain to Sukey that he suggests acting out the charade of being her new fiancé only to keep those predatory French vermin at bay."

"Utter lunacy!" Fitch exploded.

"Not quite," Regina continued. "You see, with Sukey Howard on his arm, 'Sir Edward's' persona will exude a greater degree of credibility. Since Sukey is bound and determined to visit Fort Duquesne anyway, Edward can keep a better eye on her if she's close at hand. Safer for all parties, do you not agree?"

Knowles tossed Regina an evil glance over his shoulder. "And pray what, dear Aunt, makes you think I *want* to keep a close watch on Mrs. Howard?" he asked, with a sneer.

"Well, if you do not, Edward, that is even better!" she crowed, clapping her hands exuberantly. "A sophisticated lack of passion on your part for your '*fiancee*' shall only heighten your foppish image. Sukey Howard's charm can deflect French attention from your military activities. Meanwhile, the endlessly curious girl will benefit from your protective proximity. Everyone wins."

Removing his pigtailed wig, Fitch scratched his head. "Claptrap, Regina! I suspect this is merely another of your clumsy matchmaking ploys."

Regina clutched her bosom with mock indignity. "Ah, 'tis hurt, I am, you fiend! You wound me with your criminal assertions, Fitch."

"Sit with me by the fire tonight, my girl, and I shall wound you with—"

"Enough, you two!" Knowles barked.

"Then what do you say to my idea, Edward?"

Knowles wiped his mouth with the back of his hand. "I know better than to underestimate your plots, Regina." A twisted smile crossed Knowles' face as he scrubbed the powder and rouge from his cheeks. "Tomorrow, then, we shall test out your idea on the volatile Mrs. Howard."

"Married? To *you*, Sir Edward?" Sukey exploded, surrounded by her family in Eli Whitfield's kitchen. "Sir! I thought I made it abundantly clear that . . ."

"Madam, indeed, I sympathize with your concerns, but I have already discussed this . . . delicate matter with your father and received his consent."

Spinning in a tight circle, Sukey scarcely knew whom to attack first. "Pa! Shame on you. Nigh on thirty years old, and a widow at that, I no longer require your approval on . . . on personal matters." She wheeled on Knowles. "And as for you, sir——!"

Sensing Sukey's mounting rage, Zeb Whitfield and Jonah Butler slunk out the door toward the trading post storeroom.

"Oh, I quite understand, madam, that I do not find favor in your eyes. But you see, this is not a true matrimonial proposal. I do not actually intend to marry you."

"What?" Sukey shouted, her eyes widening at the fop's insolence.

Sir Edward leaned his broad shoulders back against the Windsor chair in which he sat. His blue eyes sparkled behind his spectacles, as he coughed quietly.

"For shame, Sukey," Eli Whitfield chided. "Your hostile outburst frightens this poor, sensitive-natured gentleman. Hear him out, child."

Knowles twiddled with the lace shirt cuffs dangling beyond his brocade jacket sleeves. "Your father and I share concern over your welfare, madam. French soldiers behold you in a manner we fear bodes ill. For your safety, that is. We thought, madam, if I pretend to serve as your intended, guarding you from danger——"

Surveying Knowles' thickly rouged and powdered face and elaborate clothes, Sukey could scarcely suppress her mirth. "You? Protect me? Sir Edward, your memory deceives you. 'Tis I, if you recall, who frequently protected you on our hazardous journey over the mountains."

Knowles mouth twitched as he gnawed his lower lip. "Quite, madam. And I remain deep in your debt for your compassionate protection of me. But note that I offer only to *pretend* guarding you as your *fiancé*."

Despite his gruff manner, Eli's face shone. "And the pretense should serve just as efficiently as a genuine betrothal. A superb plan, Sukey. 'Tis gallant of Sir Edward to think of your welfare, you must agree."

The chinked log walls of Eli's cabin closed in on Sukey. She sensed a family conspiracy to throw her into the arms of the absurdly foppish Sir Edward Knowles. Intolerable! At once she had to flee the stuffy kitchen for fresh outdoor air. "I do not agree! Not to anything that hints of marriage shackles!" she cried, bolting outside and up a steep, laurel-choked hill.

"What rubbish!" she cried, shoving aside tall stands of jewelweed as she reached a hilltop. Sir Edward . . . her *fiancé*? Absurd. And for the purpose of protecting her? Even more absurd! Why, the man could not even safeguard a fly, so spineless was he. And her own family collabrating against her?

Her bosom rose and fell in furious breaths, as tears moistened her cheeks.

At the sound of rustling underbrush, Sukey spun around to confront her sister.

"Sukey, what is it? I saw you dash up here as if chased by a mountain lion." Rachel patted Sukey's cheek. "And, poor dear, you have been crying."

"Bosh, Rachel. You imagine—"

"I know you better than anyone, Sukey. Now, out with it."

Sweet yellow clover perfumed the air as, overhead, an oriole warbled to its mate. Sukey dabbed at her tear-stained cheeks. "'Tis Pa, Rachel. And that absurd meddling dandy, Sir Edward Knowles."

"A curious duet, indeed. But what did they say to upset you so?"

"Sir Edward proposed to me."

Rachel's eyes bulged. "What?"

"Yes. And Pa, all ham-fisted and red-faced, demanded that I comply."

Adam Butler, whom Rachel toted Indian fashion on her back, interrupted with shrill screams. Rachel nuzzled him against her breast. "Really, Sukey, Sir Edward is such a kind, gentle creature. A more devoted husband I could not imagine—except, of course, for my dear Jonah. And look how you gaze on little Adam! I can tell you yearn to have children of your own."

"With the right man, perhaps." Sukey stirred uncomfortably. Images of rough-featured Rafe Stewart haunted her dreams and her daytime longings. Bold, masculine, wild, Rafe was the only man alive who roused the woman in Sukey. "The proposal is merely a façade, though, Rachel. Knowles and Pa feel I need a protector from supposed carnal French appetites."

"How chivalrous of the dear man! How can you possibly object to such a plan, Sukey, when the men have your best interests at heart?"

"Because, sister, I have seen that look in Pa's eyes before. He will not cease bullying and cajoling till this pretend marriage is a reality. You know Pa, Rachel. His favorite theme is that all women of childbearing age should find husbands, else they commit a heinous offense against society."

Rachel's laughter echoed off the hills. "Forgive my mirth, Sukey. You look so vexed, despite the whole matter sounding positively romantic."

"Romantic?" Sukey shuddered.

"Indeed. Need I remind you that it was Pa who literally tied me to Jonah's side till the two of us realized how much we loved one another? Pa is quite the romantic, Sukey, albeit a . . . a gruff one."

"Rachel! Knowles, a veritable explosion of lace and face powder, possesses not one manly aspect. Never again shall I marry such a man! *Never*! Besides . . ." Sukey hesitated.

"Yes? Tell, tell, you wicked taunter! You know a secret and you dare conceal it from me? Let me guess, 'tis some intriguing tidbit about Sir Edward!" Rachel hoisted the baby over her shoulder for a burp.

Sukey guarded her own suspicions. "Too early for me to confess anything of a certainty. Let me just confide that Knowles is likely not the man he appears to be."

"How very mysterious, Sukey! Has he committed a crime, or—?"

"Hark, Rachel. We have more company." From their hilltop vantage point, Sukey saw men in pearl-gray uniforms, some with blue cuffs, some with red, of French infantrymen.

"More men bringing Jonah their broken guns."

"I fear desperate times are just ahead, Rachel."

Yes, and British troops needed all the help they could get for victory. Not just from men . . . but from women as well. Sukey's chest puffed out with swelling pride. Britain needed the courage and daring intervention of Sukey Howard.

Suddenly a burst of inspiration seized her.

Sir Edward Knowles was quite likely the most despicable of all men—a traitorous British man serving as a French spy. Perhaps his weak nature led him to spy, as a pathetic attempt to redeem his flagging manhood. Whatever his reasons, the traitor had to be stopped at once, before it was too late.

Sukey squared her shoulders.

She, alone, would bravely prove Knowles was a French spy and expose his chicanery. To accomplish that, however, she had to witness his every move. A wicked smile curled her lips. Knowles, she now realized, had foolishly provided her with the precise means to do so.

Pretend to be his fiancée?

Of course!

Shallow, spineless Knowles would never become her husband. She knew that, of a certainty. Pa could shackle her to Knowles's stark naked body if he wished, but she would never change her mind on that score. George Howard's sad marital lessons still lingered far too fresh in her mind to ever allow such a travesty.

And what of robust Rafe Stewart, with his tantalizing, rough masculinity positively daring Sukey to . . .?

She shivered, despite glittering summer sunshine. The coarse mountain man had melted Sukey's resistance with his sizzling kisses. No other man would do, now that she had tasted Stewart's warm lips and felt the friction of his arousing embrace. Yet he continued to slip from her hands quicker than water through a sieve.

"Look, Sukey! Sir Edward went over to greet the Frenchmen."

Mopping her tears and wearing a new-found smile, Sukey understood there was only one way for her to uncover Knowles's chicanery—be at his side every possible moment. Waving off her sister, she scampered downhill to where the three men stood by Eli's storeroom.

"Sir Edward, my dear *fiancé*! Have you neglected to introduce me to your friends?" She slid her hand possessively into the crook of Knowles's elbow.

Caught offguard, he cocked one eyebrow at her abrupt change of attitude. "My . . . dear Sukey," he began, "may I present messieurs Joncaire and Dieskau."

She beamed. "A pleasure, gentlemen. Have you come to us from Fort Duquesne?" she inquired with contrived innocence.

Both men nodded. "*Oui, mademoiselle.*"

Perfect, she thought, clinging even tighter to Knowles's arm. "Pray, do not let me interrupt your conversation, gentlemen." She glanced sweetly at each man. Surely these culprits were passing vital secrets to one another. Feigning innocence, Sukey meant to glean every incriminating tidbit.

But with their guns now repaired, the Frenchmen quickly rode off.

Turning to Sukey, Knowles peered long and hard through his spectacles at her. "My dear Mrs. Howard, your marked change of heart comforts me."

"But does not embolden you." Tapping her foot, she glared at him with a stern reminder.

"Oh, never, madam! Never," he exclaimed, as a tiny muscle tensed along his jaw. "This arrangement is solely for your protection. I should not dream of taking liberties with you. Why, to this very day, I continue to positively tremble in fear at your sense of 'discipline,' madam."

Her gaze swept across Knowles's broad chest, along the wide sweep of his shoulders, up the thickness of his neck to the angle of his jaw where it met his white powdered wig. Somehow, this whole picture seemed absurdly out of balance. Edward Knowles was a sizable man. Even his large-knuckled hands looked powerful.

Could she be mistaken?

The lines of demarcation about Knowles's character, drawn earlier in Sukey's mind, now blurred. If perchance he was not a treacherous French spy, then . . . surely the inadequate wretch needed help fulfilling his . . . his manhood.

She patted his arm gently to reassure him.

"Sir Edward, it pains me to see you apprehensive about so many things in life. Surely you must understand, you are a . . . a large man. And potentially a strong man. You need fear nothing, and no one. Not another man who might attempt to bully you. And certainly not a woman of my size."

Knowles watched the languid movement of her slender fingers along his coat sleeve. His eyes narrowed, as he swallowed hard. "But you are not just any woman, Mrs. Howard. You are strong. And fierce. A force to be reckoned with. And I heartily respect you for that."

She clucked her tongue impatiently. "Really, Sir Edward! Look at your size." Measuring the span of his muscles with her hands, Sukey explored Knowles's arms.

His Adam's apple signified another difficult swallow.

"You see?" Her fingers, trailing across Knowles's chest, continued their leisurely assessment of his brawn. "You are every bit a man, sir. You must remind yourself of that fact each and every day."

"Oh, I do wish I could believe that, Mrs. Howard. Truly." His lips tightened as he contemplated her hand resting against his waistcoat.

"I shall help you become more of a man, Sir Edward," she insisted, clutching his coat lapels with both her hands.

Knowles's tongue moistened his parched lips. "Indeed, Mrs. Howard. Somehow I believe that to be true."

"I shall share my strength and personal courage with you, sir, until you sense bravery pounding through all your veins." She tapped her forefinger against his chest for emphasis.

Perspiration beaded on Knowles's forehead as he readjusted the set of his coat . . . and breeches. "Ah, the very thought of your tender and compassionate mentoring, madam—about making me more of a man, that is—brings a new surge of warmth to my . . . my inner soul." Retrieving a handkerchief from his breeches, he mopped his temples. "I feel stronger already."

"You see? I can help you if we struggle together each day." She smoothed a crease in his coat lapel.

The corner of his mouth quirked. "We shall struggle together . . . every day? Oh, I want to believe you, Mrs. Howard. Truly."

"But our relationship shall continue to be platonic, Sir Edward, even as we masquerade to the world as lovers."

"Quite." He stared down at her through his spectacles.

"In summation, Sir Edward, I shall teach you to become more powerful, you shall appear to be my protector, yet at no time shall you inflict unwelcome liberties upon my person. I think that neatly sums up our arrangement. Remember, sir, I am small compared to you, but when crossed, I become quite nasty. Vicious, even."

Turning abruptly from her, Knowles seemed to choke for a minute. When he gazed back at her, his composure appeared somber once more. "Madam, you are most kind. I shall eagerly anticipate your gracious lessons in manhood."

She nodded decisively. "And while I think you and Pa err about my need for protection from lascivious Frenchmen, I shall play out your false betrothal scheme to keep peace. At least for awhile." Till she discovered for certain whether Knowles was, or was not, a charlatan.

Fitch suddenly appeared at the storeroom doorway. "Sir, have you forgotten? We must be off at once."

"Oh, quite, Fitch. I had nearly forgotten. Until another day, then, Mrs. Howard, I bid you *adieu*."

Mounting his horse, he pulled reins in the direction of the departed Frenchmen. And out of Sukey's prying sight, she quickly realized. "Sir Edward!" she cried, dashing toward him.

In a gesture of respect, Knowles touched the brim of his black tricorne hat. "*Adieu*, madam," he called again, before riding off.

* * *

Crouched on a ridge high above the Monongahela River, Rafe Stewart quietly eased viburnum branches apart to enhance his view.

"There!" he hissed to Red Hawk, pointing toward the Allegheny River. "French *bateaux* fetch supplies downriver from Montreal."

"Food, my friend? Or guns?"

"Wish to hell I knew. I need to get closer."

"Fancy preserving your neck, Rafe?"

Stewart muttered an oath. "I must get back inside the fort again, Red Hawk. 'Tis the only way I can accurately determine what those *bateaux* have fetched. And just how well Duquesne is supplied."

Red Hawk shook his head. "But not as Rafe Stewart, my friend. You know what Mouceau has vowed. He would have you drawn and quartered before your saddle even cooled from the ride."

Stewart's fingers reached for the letter concealed in a pouch beneath his shirt. The last letter he ever received from his brother. Those ink-streaked written words of Thomas Stewart shone nearly as fresh as the day Rafe first read them in Philadelphia a year ago:

Charlevoix Mouceau is the devil's own spawn, Rafe. He means to force all British traders off the Allegheny River. After you left for Philadelphia, he and his accomplices brutally evicted me from our trading post at Venango. When I moved downriver, he sent another host of threats, and the ugly wretch, Michel Margry, after me. Beware, my brother. This much is certain. If Mouceau ever sees either of us again, he will kill us on sight. Now, I am off to help frontiersmen battle the

*French at a tiny redoubt jokingly labeled Fort Ne-
cessity. I send this missive with a friendly native.*

Stewart clenched his jaw. "The man does not live,
Red Hawk, who can boast of killing my brother and not
fear my revenge."

"Charlevoix Mouceau has risen in rank. Now he
commands an army. Each time you ride into that fort,
Rafe, you risk being identified by him."

Stewart grimaced. "For Thomas's sake . . . for the
sake of all those British soldiers now clawing their way
north across the Alleghenies, I must take that risk."

Red Hawk shook his head at his stalwart friend. "Dis-
guised as Knowles?"

Stewart nodded grimly.

In a gesture of skepticism, the Indian spat. "You truly
believe face paint is thick enough to conceal your identity from suspicious eyes? A good hot summer sun can
melt away that disguise."

Studying those approaching French *bateaux*, Stewart
tucked his brother's ominous last letter back inside the
leather pouch. "Face paint, fancy clothes, foppish mannerisms—these are my weapons, Red Hawk. I must
enter the fort again tomorrow morning."

"Beware of the French trapper they call Michel, my
friend. Easy to dismiss him as a fool who drinks too
much and utters false boasts. But when he is even
slightly sober, his eyes move in every direction. The
sign of a dangerous man."

Chapter Nine

Rafe Stewart's neck hair rose in alert, early that same evening. Fighting to stay alive did that to a man. Made him raw-edged and cautious. One false move inside Fort Duquesne, tomorrow, might well prove to be Stewart's last. Charlevoix Mouceau? A cunning, vicious adversary never to be underestimated. Stewart knew Mouceau's cruel reputation better than most. He would need all his wits to avoid detection by Mouceau and that craven henchman, Michel Margry.

Even so, a restless primitive urge compelled Stewart to ride, not toward his own cabin, but to a wooded rise overlooking Eli Whitfield's log house. Smoke ascended, in lazy arcs, from the chimney. Inside Eli's dark cabin, Sukey Howard likely tended that cooking fire.

Stewart's groin throbbed with a surge of unwelcome heat. To his dismay, the same disturbing response occurred every time he saw Sukey. Or even thought of her.

Bloody hell!

He had vital work to do. The future of Britain's role in America might well hinge on how carefully he completed his reconnaissance mission.

Never mind the safety of his own fool neck.

Yet one quick glimpse of Sukey Howard made Stewart's tongue hang out like some crazed buck pawing and sniffing after a doe in heat. Her slightest touch, soft and

Get 4 FREE Books!

We created our convenient Home Subscription Service so you'll be sure to have the hottest new romances delivered each month right to your doorstep—usually before they are available in book stores. Just to show you how convenient the Zebra Home Subscription Service is, we would like to send you 4 FREE Kensington Choice Historical Romances. The books are worth up to $24.96, but you only pay $1.99 for shipping and handling. There's no obligation to buy additional books—ever!

Save Up To 30% With Home Delivery!

Accept your FREE books and each month we'll deliver 4 brand new titles as soon as they are published. They'll be yours to examine FREE for 10 days. Then if you decide to keep the books, you'll pay the preferred subscriber's price (up to 30% off the cover price!), plus shipping and handling. Remember, you are under no obligation to buy any of these books at any time! If you are not delighted with them, simply return them and owe nothing. But if you enjoy Kensington Choice Historical Romances as much as we think you will, pay the special preferred subscriber rate and save over $8.00 off the cover price!

We have 4 FREE BOOKS for you as your
introduction to
KENSINGTON CHOICE!
To get your FREE BOOKS, worth up to $24.96, mail
the card below or call TOLL-FREE 1-800-770-1963.
Visit our website at www.kensingtonbooks.com.

Get 4 FREE Kensington Choice Historical Romances!

YES! Please send me my 4 FREE KENSINGTON CHOICE HISTORICAL ROMANCES (without obligation to purchase other books). I only pay $1.99 for shipping and handling. Unless you hear from me after I receive my 4 FREE BOOKS, you may send me 4 new novels—as soon as they are published—to preview each month FREE for 10 days. If I am not satisfied, I may return them and owe nothing. Otherwise, I will pay the money-saving preferred subscriber's price (over $8.00 off the cover price), plus shipping and handling. I may return any shipment within 10 days and owe nothing, and I may cancel any time I wish. In any case the 4 FREE books will be mine to keep.

KN054A

Name _____

Address _____ Apt. _____

City _____ State_____ Zip _____

Telephone (___) _____

Signature _____
(If under 18, parent or guardian must sign)
Offer limited to one per household and not to current subscribers. Terms, offer and prices subject to change. Orders subject to acceptance by Kensington Choice Book Club.
Offer Valid in the U.S. only.

unknowing, invariably made him tense up to avoid grabbing her.

No doubt she was safe inside that cabin now. Precisely where the confounded woman belonged. He'd ride home for the night and try to forget the troubling way she made his blood pound.

Turning his horse to leave, Stewart took one last look over his shoulder at the cabin . . . and flinched. Sukey Howard's willowy form emerged from her father's doorway. Instead of walking to Rachel Butler's adjacent cabin, she strode uphill . . . straight toward Stewart.

What in hell was she up to?

Transfixed, he willed himself to remain silently concealed in the brush. She might fail to notice him hidden amidst thick stands of pines. Most likely, before long, he could slip away undetected.

She strode to the hilltop. Shielding her eyes from the lush brilliance of a lowering sun, she twirled slowly in all directions as if looking for something.

Or someone.

Seemingly disappointed as no one appeared after awhile, she called softly into the clover-scented June evening. "Rafe? Rafe, are you here?" Sukey's gentle voice trailed off through the fragrant pine boughs as robins chirped their evening lullabies. "You promised . . ." she whispered.

Stewart gripped the leather reins in his hands so tightly that all color blanched from his knuckles. He closed his eyes against the curves of Sukey's graceful figure . . . the sweetness of her tender call. Man was not meant to be tantalized like this, he thought, and yet have to hold back. Man was built to robustly love a woman with his hands, his mouth, his—.

"Rafe?"

Bloody hell. He felt the tension everywhere in his

long body. Even his jaw ached from wanting Sukey Howard. Eyes slitted to screen out the temptation, Stewart nudged his mount forward.

"What are you doing up here, Mrs. Howard?" he grunted, glaring down at her from his saddle.

What indeed? She groped for proper words. " 'Twas . . . 'twas warm in Pa's cabin. I decided to come up here in search of fresh air." Her hand fluttered to the scarf crossed over her bodice.

Dismounting, he tied his reins to a jagged hickory limb. "So you ran up here calling my name."

Sukey stiffened. Was her desire so readily apparent? "Nonsense!" she exclaimed. Studying Stewart's glowering rough face and thick-muscled arms, she almost feared for her safety. "I saw you up here, Mr. Stewart, that was all. And . . . and I merely called out a civil greeting to you."

She stepped back from the heat of his unswerving stare. Her breathing quickened. "June brings out the blue violets, one of my favorite flowers. Aha! I see a clump of them on that next rise, so I shall bid you goodnight, Mr. Stewart, and . . ." Nervously moistening her lips, Sukey turned her back to him.

She heard his furtive footsteps. He was following her. Her breathing accelerated even more. Did the thrushes and clover-scented wind sing of love? Or did it only seem that way?

"Ah, Mr. Stewart," she called to him across her shoulder as she walked in haste. "I . . . I see you also seek the wildflowers."

"I seek you, Mrs. Howard."

She walked faster. Suddenly a gnarled root tripped her. With a lurch, she grasped the patchy bark of an ancient sycamore.

His hand was on her in an instant.

A strange energy, unfamiliar to Sukey, boiled from Stewart's every muscle, from his piercing blue eyes, from his tight-lipped mouth. A need that unsettled her with its craving intensity.

He lifted stray curls from her cheek. Still silent, he moved his hand down her face, across her throat, to the back of her neck. The touch of his coarse fingers roused hot forbidden sensations throughout Sukey's body.

He lowered his head and kissed her mouth. A long, conquering kiss. Hard, fierce, unrelenting. A kiss that made one simmering truth perfectly clear. Rafe Stewart was man. Sukey Howard was all-too-willing woman.

His crude power frightened her.

Stumbling backwards, she broke from his grasp. "Mr. Stewart!" she cried, brushing her lips with the back of her hand. "Whatever do you think you are doing?"

"I want to give you what you beg for."

"You . . . ! You are most certainly in error, sir!" She could still feel the burn of his stubbled jaw against her face. Across her mouth. That delicious sting made Sukey ache for much more.

He took one step toward her.

"You need the touch of a man, Mrs. Howard. A real man. Something you have never known. With all your being, you crave what only a true man can give you. What I want to give you."

"Get back!" she demanded. "Stay away from me."

Strong, unyielding, he stared at her. "Come here, Mrs. Howard."

"No!"

A clamor of indignant voices scolded within Sukey. She knew what Stewart offered. With every unloved fiber of her being, oh, how she yearned to receive it! But decent women who served tea in proper Lancaster drawing rooms did not make love with coarse men out on open mountaintops. They did not allow suitors wanton caresses of their delicate unclothed flesh. They never permitted . . .

Sukey's gaze returned to his somber face. She read his power, his sheer might, his masculine need. He stood defiantly with feet planted wide and arms crossed over his chest.

Stretching out her slender limbs, she reached for him.

Unmoving, he stared down at her as she slid her hands up over his thick forearms and broad chest. "Do not play with me, Mrs. Howard," he growled.

"Play? Oh, Mr. Stewart," she whispered, blushing at her confession, "I want very much to play with you." Standing on tiptoe, she planted a kiss on his sullen ruddy mouth.

A kiss that broke the last of his resolve.

Engulfing her in his strong arms, he returned her kiss. Driven by an arousing madness, he parted her reddened lips with his probing tongue. Damn! He needed to taste Sukey Howard . . . every tender part of her. Now, at last.

"Rafe!" she murmured, as his mouth found the soft flesh of her earlobe. She sank against Stewart's chest wall.

He kissed her lips, her cheek, her throat. Every touch of Sukey, every taste of her soft skin, brought more engorgement to his throbbing organ. His mouth explored the honeyed satin of her shoulder, till he reached the forbidding confines of her scarf-covered neckline.

In one determined sweep, he lifted her into his arms.

Sighing, she kissed his neck. "What are you . . . ?" she questioned.

A faint smile tugged the corner of Rafe's mouth. "Have you forgotten, sweet Sukey, what happened the last time we held one another?"

"The bear cubs!" she recalled ruefully.

"This time, milady, we shall entertain no interlopers." Still carrying Sukey, he strode off fifty feet through the tangled underbrush to a tiny abandoned Indian hut.

"Complete with a door," he announced, as he carried Sukey inside.

She blushed. Had she gone mad? Worse, did she care? All Sukey knew was that she could not bear it even for a moment when Rafe, setting her down in this quaint shelter, removed his hands from her.

"Come, Sukey. Let me love you," he said, kneeling at her side.

She tugged off the white scarf shielding her shoulders. Her silver pendant glowed in pale dusky shadows as she settled on the floor beside Stewart. With near-primitive delight, she watched him kiss the rise of her breasts bulging above her chemise drawstring. The gentle scrape of his stubbled jaw against her bosom excited her to fine madness. "Rafe, I . . ."

"Are you afraid, my love?" His hand warmed her breast.

"Yes," she answered, trembling.

"You need never fear me, Sukey." He hesitated. "But I am a man. Stop now, at once, if this is not what you want."

She glanced at the confines of this rude hut, then laced her slender arms around his neck. "I know not what I fear, Rafe Stewart. You, or . . . or what a man does to a woman. Perhaps I fear my own response."

He nodded. "Just as I thought. 'Tis time for me to show you what you have missed all these years, my girl . . . with actions, not words." He patted the floor. "Lie down here beside me, Sukey, and let me love you."

Kissing Stewart's mouth, Sukey sensed that never again would she be the same. Her inhibitions dropped away with each garment that Rafe helped her unhook and remove.

At last, she lay before him clothed only in her chemise.

He warmed her limbs with his bare hands. His kisses stimulated her breasts to swell and tingle with new demands unfamiliar to Sukey. She clawed at his leather shirt and bear's tooth necklace, not even certain what it was she wanted. Watching him strip to his loincloth, she felt like a wildcat of the forest. His masculine bulk excited her. She rubbed at his hair-matted muscles as he suckled her breasts like a man desperate for nourishment.

"Rafe!" she cried, watching him ease down her chemise and kiss her naked belly.

A strange beast inside Sukey rose to the surface. The fire of Stewart's kisses made her breath hot and fast. Helping him untie his loincloth, she caressed his glowing, swollen manhood. "Never, never have I . . . !" she whimpered. This new urgency, ah, 'twas driving her mad! Never had George Howard touched her—kissed her—in so thorough a manner! Sweet friction raged on her lips, in her breasts, and in some deep secret place between her legs. How could she be released from this torment? How?

When Stewart lay back and pulled Sukey atop him, she lunged like a creature in heat. Mewling, begging, clawing. Gently he eased her onto his probing hardness.

"Oh!" Sukey wailed, feeling the sweet pull and tug as Stewart filled her feminine hollows. "Rafe . . .!" she begged, clutching his shoulders. His arms shielded her tight and tender against his chest. She loved the feel of Stewart's powerful arms holding her close. Loved the fervor of his mouth nuzzling her breasts while she settled into a rhythmic rocking motion. What was this persistent restless need that unsettled her; drove her on; made her perspire and cry out? Everything about the feel and taste and aroma of Rafe Stewart urged her to ascend a lofty mountain. Higher, higher, till suddenly . . . !

In a cascading sea of groans, Sukey crumpled against Stewart's chest.

Gently he stroked her hair, then kissed her cheek. "You are indeed a passionate woman, my sweet," he murmured.

"Only with you, Rafe. Never before have I experienced anything . . . anything at all like this."

He held her close against his naked body. Her auburn hair, dangling loose through his fingers, still bore the scent of lavender. Rafe Stewart needed this woman in his arms forever. Sukey Howard made him realize, as no other woman ever had, that life would be unbearable without her love at his side.

An utter impossibility, at least for now.

Too much, and too many lives, depended on his mission for the British. He could not continue to lower his guard and love her as he wished. Nor would the memory of Isabel allow him to.

Yet somehow, it seemed he had lived all his life for this one stolen moment. Leaning astride Sukey, he gently nudged her legs apart with his knee.

She clutched his shaggy mane of dark hair in both her hands. "Come to me, Rafe, my darling," she urged.

He never meant to yield. Never intended to fall in love on this most vital of all missions. Never wished to . . .

Slowly, Rafe eased his throbbing organ inside Sukey. Her honeyed moist warmth drew him further within. He tasted the tang of her lips, felt her softness in too many places to resist. Drawing back, then plunging forward, he lost his will to resist. Another plunge.

He shuddered against her slender frame.

At twilight, he escorted her back to her father's cabin. "When will I see you again, Rafe?" she begged. When no answer came, she turned to see that Stewart had once more vanished into the forest.

Next morning, Sukey set out a communal breakfast for the entire family in Eli's kitchen. She hummed all the while.

Nursing little Adam, Rachel watched her sister. "Never have I seen you quite this cheerful, Sukey," she commented.

Eli studied his older daughter. "Something different about you, my girl," he added, pulling on his boots.

Dancing past her father's scrutiny, Sukey tucked a loose tendril back inside her mob cap before serving out more slabs of ham. "Nonsense, Pa. Whatever gave you such a thought? Nothing different about me at all." Busying herself at the fireplace Dutch oven, she ignored his sidewise glances.

"Never heard you sing at breakfast before, Sukey," Zeb added. "I'll wager you hope to see your 'fiancé' while paying a call at the fort today. Hm?"

Jonah chuckled. "Ah, June brings love on the air."

Hands on hips, Sukey glared at the faces assembled around Eli's breakfast table. "All of you, pay more attention to your food and less to entertaining such foolishness! I declare, can a woman not sing along with the birds on a pleasant June morn?"

Eli took a swig of cider. "The prospect of a visit with Sir Edward has not brought on your good cheer?"

"The only person I *hope* to see this day, if you inquisitive meddlers must know, is Jardine Nicolet."

Eli scowled. "A woman of child-bearing age who avoids marriage is an affront to society and—"

"Pa!" Sukey's flared temper matched her father's belligerence. "I did marry once, thanks to your insistence, and near died from the misery."

"Pa," Zeb Whitfield called, winking knowingly to his sisters as he leaned in the doorway. "Can you lend me a hand sorting out the new shipment from Philadelphia?"

Watching the three men trudge outside to Eli's storehouse, Rachel cast a sly smile at her sister. "We are alone, now, Sukey, dear. Just us girls—and little Adam, whose tiny ears count not, yet. You can be honest with me. I sense that Pa indeed winkled a kernel of truth from you."

Sukey set leftovers aside in a clay bowl destined for the springhouse. "I declare, Rachel! Are you no better than those absurd menfolk?"

"I see things only a woman would notice, Sukey. More pink in your cheeks, a brighter sparkle to your eyes, a lighter step. And that hint of a coy smile, when you think no one notices."

Sukey fanned herself with an open hand. "Indeed? Then 'tis only the result of dew-sweetened violets on a warm June morn."

"And not pleasant words whispered in your ear by our dear Sir Edward? Or the anticipation of clinging to his arm once more?"

Sukey bristled. "One fine day I shall tell you the truth about that irritating man, Rachel. At the very least, I feel certain he is a shallow, incapable excuse for a man."

"And the most?"

"If I am correct, the truth about his duplicity shall quite likely astonish you."

"But if you are not? If Sir Edward is the kind, forthright, responsible sort that I believe he is? A man ideally suited to become your husband?"

Sukey stared longingly out the kitchen window. Somewhere on that next tree-shrouded mountain was a secluded cabin where Rafe Stewart had made love to her. Sukey ached to linger in his protective arms forever.

"I have met such a man, Rachel. A handsome, rugged, robust man quite unlike Sir Edward Knowles. Someday, perhaps, I can tell you more."

"Unpleasant, Edward, to say the least! Messages Red Hawk gleans from forest runners are decidedly unpleasant." Watching her nephew apply a thick layer of white powder over his clean-shaven face, Regina Ramsey frowned.

Fitch eased a silk coat over Knowles's broad shoulders, then shook a finger in anger. "Scalps! Bloody scalps! The French and their Indians leave those ghastly reminders of their villainy dangling on trees all along Braddock's march."

Regina handed the rouge pot to her nephew. "Braddock's men are terrified of what they cannot see . . . yet know is hidden behind those trees awaiting them."

Knowles glared at his mirror reflection. His eyes deepened to calculated blue ice. "Red Hawk never errs. Time nearly runs out for us. Without fail, I must complete the sketches of Fort Duquesne's interior at once for Braddock."

"A frightfully dangerous enterprise, Edward," Regina commented. "More times than I care to count, I have observed Charlevoix Mouceau and that tedious wretch, Michel Margry, study you in a most peculiar manner. As if they struggle to recall where they previously met you." Regina gnawed anxiously on her lower lip.

Knowles reached for his powdered wig. "Have you forgotten, Aunt? I thrive on adventure! A day without risk is, for me, a day too boring to contemplate. Surely you remember my lust for danger."

His false bravado failed to convince Regina.

Or Fitch.

"I recall your lusts all too well, my bold lad," he commented, wincing. "They indeed courted danger, but I fear those lusts had more to do with provocative skirts than rescuing British armies."

Glancing in a small tortoise-rimmed hand mirror, Knowles shifted his elaborate queued wig till it clung perfectly to his scalp. "I shall ignore your skepticism about my robust appetites, Fitch. I have serious work to do, today, and I will not be hindered by any fool Frenchman."

"Or a well-turned ankle?"

Knowles spun on Fitch. "Skirts, ankles, armies. Bloody hell, Fitch! An adventurer lives constantly by his wits, no matter what manner of danger threatens him. Now, hear me out, you two scalawags. Your roles today at Fort Duquesne imperil you both."

Regina put the finishing touches to her dress. "Have I ever let you down, Edward?"

Knowles's expression softened. "Never, Aunt. But men in this wilderness live by a different code than that to which you are accustomed. And they will permit you only one opportunity to fail. If the French suspect even for a minute that you labor against them—"

"Those bloody scalps are a reminder of their backwoods brand of justice," Fitch finished, for him.

"Precisely. Now, Aunt, are you ready to accompany your 'spineless' nephew on a jaunt into the den of lions?"

Tugging on her pink satin gloves, Regina grinned at him. "Never forget, Edward, dear boy, you inherited your passion for intrigue from my side of the family. Now, gentlemen, shall we ride?"

* * *

"No need to apologize, Jardine," Sukey insisted, rising to leave the Nicolets' quarters. "I so enjoyed our afternoon chat!"

"And you will forgive me, now that I must return to my laundry chores?"

"Of course. *Adieu*, Jardine. I shall search for my father, who doubtless lingers over gun repairs."

But Sukey had no intention of seeking her father within the confines of Fort Duquesne. Strolling inside the fort's perimeter, she fought off an old dread of authority at the sight of so many uniformed French soldiers.

She ignored sweat beads forming at her forehead.

"For England," she reminded herself. "I shall learn all that I can of this evil fort, for my country. "

Just as she rounded a corner near the magazine, Sukey heard a familiar voice, though this time speaking in French.

"'Tis Knowles!" she murmured, ducking behind a wagon to avoid detection.

Sir Edward gestured in animated conversation with Corporal Allouez, who quickly led Knowles to the Commander's hut. Pretending to readjust her gloves and scarf, Sukey sidled over toward Mouceau's quarters and pressed her back against the outside wall to eavesdrop.

"Fie!" she whispered to herself. "If only I understood French."

Through a cracked chink between logs, Sukey peered in at the men. Knowles seemed altogether familiar and friendly with Mouceau. Just as she suspected! But the captain glowered intently at Knowles as they conversed. A strange camaraderie, for villains sharing British secrets. Both men seemed almost too alert, too guarded for comrades.

Suddenly, Michel Margry and Corporal Allouez entered the commander's hut.

Sukey's blood pounded with new intrigue. Squinting between logs, she watched the men interact. For brother spies, they seemed unusually tense. As if eyeing his prey, Michel Margry nervously paced around the seated Knowles. Charlevoix Mouceau glared at the pair of them, as all three conversed rapidly in French.

Annoyed, Sukey tapped her pattened foot in the Duquesne dust. "One way or another, I must force these ogres to speak in English," she murmured. It would benefit her cause to appear stupid. A dangerous stunt for Sukey. If she miscalculated, they might kill her.

Or . . . or worse.

Reluctantly pushing aside her old dread of abusive male force, she cleared her throat. "Sir Edward! Sir Edward?" she called, as if she had no notion of his whereabouts.

Rising from his seat, he met her at Mouceau's doorway.

"What are you doing *here*, Mrs. Howard?" he hissed between clenched teeth.

She quivered in triumph. Obviously, she interrupted a vital communiqué. Why else would Knowles have been so annoyed? And why did these four men, gathered in Mouceau's headquarters, seem so tense?

She had to learn more.

"Ah, Sir Edward, I thought I heard your voice! How delightful to find you at last," she burbled. Looping her arm through his, she boldly strode inside the hut.

"Gentlemen," she said, greeting Mouceau and his two cohorts. "Can you imagine my pleasant surprise? I accompanied my father to Fort Duquesne on business, only to discover that my *fiancé* arrived here simultaneously." Gazing fondly up at Knowles's tight-muscled face, she relished his subtle discomfort.

Mouceau's chair scraped against the plank floor as he

rose to acknowledge Sukey. "Madame Howard!" His gray eyes glittered with icy recognition. "The pleasure is all ours, madame."

Sukey felt Margry's cold stare rake every detail of her figure.

"Please, gentlemen, pray continue with your business," she urged. "I shall remain quietly in the shadows whilst you men labor in earnest."

To her chagrin, they conversed in French. Mouceau, she noticed, tended to moisten his lips whenever his gaze fell on her. His eyes, the color of chilled slate on a wintery day, betrayed no emotion. A man without a soul, she decided. And without a heart.

To remain alive, she would have to exercise caution around such a merciless man.

Mouceau's fleshy tongue dallied over his lower lip once more as, listening to Knowles, he leisurely contemplated the scarf tucked across Sukey's breasts.

"*Oui*, Monsieur Knowles," he assented to Knowles's comment. His gaze flickered back to Sukey. He switched to English. "But I fear we bore Madame Howard with our tedious military talk."

"Not at all, Captain Mouceau," Sukey declared, feeling much like a mouse within a circle of hungry cats. "Women manage households all the time, so I quite enjoy hearing how you resolve the many difficulties of controlling a large fort so far from your own towns. Perhaps you might continue speaking in English so I, too, could learn from your wisdom."

Too strong a compliment for such a dangerous man? Sukey feared her excess, yet it seemed the only way to pry English words from these men.

"My wisdom, madame?" A pulse throbbed at Mouceau's right temple. He quickly shoved a handful of papers into the leather carrying case on his portable desk. "Our conversation concludes for the afternoon, Monsieur Knowles. Monsieur Margry shall escort you to Sergeant Nicolet, if you care to discuss the matter further. Meanwhile, I shall chaperone Madame Howard on a proper and private tour of Fort Duquesne. *Bonjour*, Monsieur Knowles."

A mirthless smile decorated Mouceau's face as he extended his arm toward Sukey.

"You are indeed most kind, Captain," she answered, sensing dread constrict her chest in this dusty, manure-spattered fort. Mouceau, the cat, had his paw upon her throat. Would she survive his pounce in this cage of fellow Frenchmen? For silent reassurance, she flexed her thigh against the tiny sheathed knife concealed beneath her skirts . . . and reached for Mouceau's arm.

"A proper tour of the fort?" Knowles waved his ruffle-trimmed wrists in gaudy circles. "Ah, *mon Capitaine*, I, too, should find that most edifying." He edged closer to the French commander.

"Another time, perhaps, Monsieur Knowles," Mouceau insisted. "When I can devote my full energies to your exhaustive comments. Today, though—" Again he managed a brittle smile. "Today, I shall direct my attention to answering Madame Howard's queries. Madame?"

Wedging Sukey's arm tightly inside his own bent elbow, Mouceau escorted her outside.

"Most kind of you, monsieur," Sukey chirped, feeling herself all but dragged to a private, deep-shadowed corner of the magazine, which Mouceau described in tedious detail.

Mouceau clutched her arm tighter as he leaned to peer down her cleavage. "Madame, you are indeed a most lovely woman."

Sukey cleared her throat. "These . . . these guns, monsieur, tell me again where you will mount them."

"Mount?" Mouceau breathed more rapidly. "Madame, I can only think of 'mount' in terms of—"

"There you are, my good fellow!" Knowles cried, clapping his hands with glee at the sight of Mouceau. "I simply could not be so rude as to depart without thanking you for your splendid hospitality, this afternoon."

Mouceau's mouth thinned to a taut purple line as he glared at Knowles. "Somehow, monsieur, though surely it be impossible, I sense we have met before."

Stumbling backwards, Knowles kicked over a bucket of knives. Crouching on all fours, he gingerly returned the sharp items to their holding bucket. "Ah, monsieur, sadly I fear not," he replied with a titter. "Had I previously met such a fine French gentleman as yourself, I should never have forgotten your identity."

"Edward? Dear boy?" Suddenly Regina, furiously waving her painted fan, burst upon the scene. "Ah, there you are, my boy. What have we here? Another clumsy accident on your part? So typical of your style, I fear, Edward. 'Tis the heat, perhaps, but I feel strangely peaked. If you have completed your . . . mercy! Can that be our dear Sukey in the shadows?"

Michel Margry squinted suspiciously at the fort's three eccentric English guests.

Rushing to comfort Regina, Sukey clasped the older woman's arm. "You do seem pale, Regina. I shall fetch you a cup of water."

"No! That is, uh, dear Sukey . . . I find your company close at hand comforts me enormously in my indisposition."

Knowles studied Regina's flashing hazel eyes, then raised an eyebrow. "You wish to leave at once, Aunt?" he asked somberly.

"I do so hesitate to inconvenience you, Edward, but I feel a hasty departure most wise. One of my pernicious spells is upon me." Whimpering, she mopped her forehead with a lace handkerchief.

Knowles turned to Sukey. "Might I impose on you, Mrs. Howard, to accompany us back to our lodging and assist in my aunt's recuperation? I would, of course, make certain you are safely escorted home thereafter."

With Sukey Howard free of his grasp, Mouceau scowled.

"Of course, Sir Edward. I should not rest knowing Regina suffered while I denied her my assistance. But I must notify my father that—"

Regina moaned. "No! No, dear child! Please, stay by my side! Fitch will inform your father of your revised plans." She dismissed her servant with a wave of her hand.

Bewildered, Captain Charlevoix Mouceau glared first at the equally confused Michel Margry, then at his noisy guests. "But . . ." he began.

"*Adieu, adieu*, kind captain!" Regina wailed, clutching her forehead with one hand and Sukey Howard tightly with the other.

Chapter Ten

Blackened clouds surged across the last steep hill before Knowles's lodge.

Insects fussed and stung at Sukey's sweat-beaded face. "A treacherous storm brewing overhead," she called out to Regina, as the two women rode their horses single file behind Knowles's mount.

"No more dangerous than that lot we just left behind," Regina shot back.

Fitch silenced her outburst with a frown.

Puzzled, Sukey tapped her companion's arm. "What do you mean, Regina? Have you so little regard for the French? Or did they behave as less than gentlemen today?"

"Pay no attention, Mrs. Howard," Knowles scoffed, flashing Regina an unspoken scolding as fierce gusts tore at his silk coat. "Just my aunt's petulant sense of humor. Of far more pressing concern is this infernal imminent storm."

"Storms unsettle you so, Sir Edward! Be assured, I ride with you and Regina to calm you both."

Knowles's bushy black eyebrows raised above his spectacles as he gnawed his lower lip. "You have no idea, Mrs. Howard, just how reassuring is your presence by our sides."

Strange, Sukey thought, how such a large man as

Knowles could at the same time be so fearful in the face of danger. "Sir Edward, do you calculate that we might reach your lodging before the storm strikes?"

"If we hurry, madam."

Her insides tightened as Sukey appraised the furious storm bearing down on them. Even with Fitch at their beck and call, could she handle the formidable challenge of an ailing Regina alongside a hysterical Sir Edward? Lightning bolts zagged earthward. Gusts bent quivering trees horizontal as thunder exploded across the mountains. Just as they descended to the valley of Knowles's lodge, torrential rain pelted horses and riders alike.

Soaked from the downpour, Sukey tucked Regina in a wooden chair by the kitchen fire and poured a cup of tea, while Knowles helped Fitch tend the horses.

Regina gratefully accepted the steaming beverage. "Indeed, your heart is kind, Sukey."

"I could not live with myself, Regina, if I abandoned you in the throes of one of your spells! Pray tell me, just what happens when these ills seize you?"

Regina coughed quickly. "Oh, forgive me, my dear. Must have sipped the tea too hurriedly. The wretched spells do that to me, you see. Along with other maladies. But your presence comforts me immeasureably. Still, there is one other thing . . ."

"You have only to ask, Regina."

"'Tis Edward, dear." She hid her face in her hand. "Hear the thunder and lightning crash with such virulence? Edward is tending the animals in this downpour."

"Likely."

"But, Sukey, he surely is more terrified than the stabled animals themselves. Oh, if only Edward possessed greater manly traits. Could you . . . ?" Regina's lips trembled as she once more averted her face. "Dear me,

I should not ask it of you. But could you find it in your heart to calm my poor, quivering nephew? Dear Edward! Far too timid to cry out for help! I feel certain he . . . he needs your blessed assistance, Sukey."

Her speech finished, Regina sagged back into her chair with a moan, and vigorously fanned herself.

"Dear, thoughtful Regina! It pains me to see you so troubled. If it comforts you, I shall go at once and . . . and, well, tend to Sir Edward's frailties."

Regina smiled. "Thank you, my dear. Oh, I have tried to make a man out of poor Edward. Indeed I have! But despite all my labors, I failed dismally. Perhaps, dear Sukey . . . perhaps you might succeed . . . where I have failed?" She resumed fanning herself.

"I? Make a man out of Sir Edward?" Sukey shook her head till tendrils escaped her white lawn cap. "No human alive, I fear, can accomplish that feat!"

Regina seized her friend's hand. "Sukey, my dear, it takes a great woman to craft a great man. Great men do not happen by chance. They are created by stalwart women. Somehow, my dear, I feel certain you are up to the challenge."

"Pray tell me, Regina, how is it that you and Sir Edward remain so fond of one another? And why do I never hear him mention his own parents?"

Regina's smile faded. Her fan dropped to her lap. "Quite a story, that one, my dear. A tragic one. And most likely, the reason that Edward grew into such a trembling, fearful individual."

"Wha . . . What happened?" Eyes widened with wonder, Sukey refilled both their tea cups.

"The story began many years ago, when my brother, Charles, married wild-spirited, beautiful young Isabel. I knew in my heart the marriage would never last. Isabel was far too young and restless for Charles. I begged him not to marry her. But Charles was absolutely besotted with Isabel. Her laughter, her flashing blue eyes, that dazzling golden hair—oh, Isabel completely melted all his wisdom. They had two handsome little boys, Edward and Thomas. Then one day . . . " Regina closed her eyes.

Sukey gently pressed Regina's arm. "This tale distresses you, Regina. I should not have asked you to open old family wounds. Perhaps another day, when your health improves."

"No, Sukey. 'Tis better I tell you now. You might then better understand Edward's frailties." She sipped more tea and savored the beverage's warmth. "One rain-soaked autumn day, when leaves turned scarlet and hearth fires sputtered from the moldering damp, Isabel ran off with a heartless libertine—a sailor who apparently promised her an exotic life filled with adventure."

"She abandoned her children?"

"Utterly. We never heard from her again. Rumor had it that she died at sea during childbirth, though we could never be certain."

"Merciful heavens! Did your brother remarry?"

Regina set down her teacup and exhaled solemnly. "Charles never recovered from his sorrow. He died soon after of a broken heart."

"Oh, Regina! How dreadful!" Sukey clasped her hands with sympathy.

"Rupert and I raised those little boys as if they were our own. High-spirited little rascals, they were, as toddlers. But after Isabel abruptly vanished, Edward changed completely. Never again did he trust people. Most especially women."

"Or the danger of everyday life, I dare say."

"Quite. So you see, dear Sukey, that anything you

might do to bolster Edward's frail heart would . . . would be most noble indeed."

The door slammed as Fitch entered and lunged for the comfort of a sputtering fire.

From her hearthside chair, Regina eyed the servant's actions. "Clean your shoes before entering, Fitch!" she barked. "The rain creates mud, which I shall not have indoors." Turning back to Sukey, she whispered low, "I shall be quite all right, here, with Fitch to wait on me. Go now, Sukey. I implore you. Please consider Edward's plight!"

A huge sigh escaped Sukey, contemplating her colossal task. "I promise no miracles, Regina. The man defies all attempts to rebuild his spine."

"I have confidence in your abilities, Sukey. You will find a way, I feel certain." Once more, the hint of a smile crinkled Regina's mouth.

Doubting the ailing woman's misplaced confidence, nevertheless Sukey dashed across the narrow courtyard through drenching rain to the stable. She hoisted the heavy door bar and entered. Aromas of straw and the presence of animals assailed her nostrils. Reaching out to grasp a coarse-hewn wooden beam, she hesitated in the dark blue shadows.

"Fitch? That you?" a male voice inquired.

"No, Sir Edward. 'Tis I."

"Mrs. Howard," he answered with a nod, by way of acknowledgment.

She sneezed twice.

"The rain drenched you, Mrs. Howard. You should have stayed warm by the fire." He patted his horse's muzzle.

Lightning flashed thru barn slats as Sukey felt thunder shake the earth under her feet. She tiptoed toward Knowles. 'Twould not do, letting him know that Regina had mentioned his mother's perfidy. She would have to find another way to . . . to build his confidence.

"I was concerned about you, Sir Edward." Another thunder crash. She jumped, then edged closer to him. "I know how frightened you are of storms. I came out here in the rain to . . . to calm your fears." Trembling, she sneezed again.

He stared down at her.

Silently, he shrugged off his embroidered coat and draped it round her slender shoulders.

Sukey saw his cheeks suddenly flame crimson. She reached up to touch his face. "Thank you, Sir Edward. I do hope you are not feverish."

"Not in the least, madam. But 'twould not do, allowing you to catch the ague on my account."

"Sir Edward . . ." She scarcely knew how to begin. "You see, it concerns me, that is, it reflects poorly on me . . ."

She sneezed again.

Wrapping his coat tighter around her, he silently drew her closer.

"If you are to function—to pretend to function, that is—as my *fiancé*, then I must urge you to be more, well, strong and manly in your deportment." How had she gotten this close to Knowles? Such proximity made it difficult to expound on his abundant character flaws.

She pushed back against his chest. For a man who shrank from altercations, Knowles seemed unusually hard-muscled.

He studied her slender hand pressing against his waistcoat. "Strong? Pray, in what manner, Mrs. Howard?"

She reached for his hands, dangling at his sides.

"Look at the size of your fists, Sir Edward," she insisted, holding them up for his inspection. "With such strength, you have nothing to fear. Not from tumultuous thunderstorms, armies of pestilential insects, or wild animals. Why, surely you could easily crush the most dedicated villain with your might."

A shaft of light, piercing the shadowy stable, illuminated one side of Knowles's face. Puzzled, Sukey saw his blue eyes sparkle with curious emotion. Bushy black hairs of his brow twitched. Suddenly, his head drooped low.

"Ah, if only I could believe you, Mrs. Howard."

"But you can, do you not see, Sir Edward?"

"Alas, I fear I shall forever tremble before the threats of storms, or creatures, or fierce men. And women? Oh, my dear Mrs. Howard! They terrify me most of all."

Still clutching Knowles's hands, she felt his fingers slowly clasp her own.

Squaring her shoulders in frustration, Sukey cleared her throat. To make a real man out of this whimpering raw material might drive her mad, but it was her compassionate duty . . . to Regina and to Knowles.

"You must learn to trust me, Sir Edward. For the sake of your personal safety, and your manhood, you must trust me."

"My . . . manhood?" A cord tightened along Knowles's neck.

"Yes. When confronted by would-be terrors, you simply must not dissolve into a panicked litany of . . . of . . ."

"Screams?" A corner of Knowles's mouth twitched.

"Well, yes. No! I mean, sputtering helplessly about your terror can only strengthen your enemy's resolve. With each of our visits, I shall continually remind you of your own innate courage."

He leaned closer.

"And you feel our discussions will . . . embolden me?"

Something about the direct expression in his vibrant blue eyes gave her pause. "I . . . I believe so." She took a step backward.

"And strenghten my manhood?"

Sukey stared up at her male challenge. What if she succeeded? Beyond her wildest dreams? And Sir Edward became something of a raging, out-of-control beast? She gnawed at her cheek. Clearly, her imagination had run amok. Edward Knowles could likely always be controlled by a firm hand and voice.

"Of course," she responded warily. "If you listen to my instructions, we shall build you into a new man. One with courage and, yes, determination."

Abruptly shrinking back from her, Knowles leaned against a wooden stall. "No. No, 'tis more than I can believe. 'Tis not possible."

"Shame, Sir Edward! Shame!" she cried, shaking an accusatory finger at him. "Not even an hour has elapsed and already you doubt my resolve." In her anger, she edged toward him.

A booming thunderclap impelled nervous horses to whinny and stomp restlessly on the straw.

"I fear the touch of a woman, Mrs. Howard. Surely you cannot help me overcome my clumsiness on that score."

Gently she clasped his arm. "I understand your problem, Sir Edward. Regina related your past sorrow to me. I . . . I shall teach you to trust women again." She struggled to sound confident.

"My most basic fear? Ah, Mrs. Howard! You would be willing to help me overcome it?"

Additional uneasy sensations crept through Sukey. Something about this scene struck her as, perhaps, a trifle unreal. She tugged Knowles's coat closer round her shoulders. "Yes. We shall begin with your most basic fear, Sir Edward, if that one be it, then proceed to dash all your other terrors as well."

"Then kiss me."

"What?" Her chin dropped.

"I'm quite unaccustomed to the touch of a woman, Mrs. Howard. My prodigious fear of them leads me to tremble in their very presence. I . . . No. No, this simply will not work." With a shrug, he crossed his arms over his chest.

"And why not, sir?" she demanded.

"Slowly, indeed frequently, I need to be touched by a woman till I no longer cringe at the very sight of one."

"You cringe . . . ?"

"Every time. Without fail," he nodded dismally.

As rain pelted the stable, Knowles's horse shook its head and whinnied. In a calming gesture, Sukey stroked its muzzle. "Dear me," she whispered, "am I the only brave creature in this entire stable?"

Knowles clasped his hands in a supplicating gesture. "'Twould seem so, Mrs. Howard."

She sighed.

Clad in his lace and fine fabrics, Sir Edward Knowles was no more stalwart than common beasts of the field. And twice as frightened.

"Give me your hand, Sir Edward."

"You mean . . . like this?" He extended his right hand toward her.

A puzzling paradox, she noted once again. Broad, well-veined, adorned with black hair, Knowles's hand was the very emblem of a fierce, determined warrior. Yet, terror seemed daily to suffocate him.

She clasped his large hand in both hers. "Now, close your eyes, Sir Edward, and repeat after me." Watching him comply, she felt his hand pulse in her grasp. "I fear nothing. Come, come, Sir Edward, you must say the words."

"I . . . I fear nothing."

"Again, sir! This time with genuine conviction."

Opening his eyes, he gazed down at her. "Oh, Mrs. Howard, this cannot possibly help me. I tremble before storms, I tremble before—"

"Hush!" she murmured. "I shall not accept defeat, Sir Edward. Nor should you. Now, come sit down beside me on this haymound." Once seated, she clasped both his hands in a soothing gesture. "I shall stroke you till you relax." Her fingers and palms massaged his knuckles, then his wrists.

The gesture brought warmth to Knowles's arms.

His voice dropped lower. "Praise be, Mrs. Howard. When you stroke me, I do feel better." He leaned close to her. "But when you abandon me . . . ?"

"Not truly abandon you, sir, though I must depart for home shortly. But I shall stay with you till your senses calm." Her ears perked at the sound of thunder crashes.

Listening to high winds and rain thrash the small stable, Knowles widened his eyes. "Oh, dread seizes me at the thought of facing my apprehensions without your noble assistance, Mrs. Howard."

"Harm shall not befall you, Sir Edward. Repeat again, I fear nothing." She rubbed his hands . . . then his arms.

He shifted his pelvis on the straw mound. "I fear nothing."

"Nor any beasts, or insects, or man."

He watched her fingers creep along his sleeve. "Nor beasts. Or insects. Or man." His voice dropped a notch lower.

"Nor do I fear any woman."

"Nor . . . but Mrs. Howard, I fear women most of all."

Sukey struggled to make sense of Knowles's situation. A large man, quite possibly a treacherous French spy, who trembled at the presence of his own shadow? She sighed at this great tribulation. Still, her compassionate nature would not allow her to reject the terrified, quivering hulk of a man before her.

In their damp, hay-filled retreat, she tried to shut out sounds of the raging downpour.

"Poor Edward. Your tragic past continues to bedevil you. Come, lay your head in my lap while I hold your hand."

"Your lap? Oh, I do sense a ray of hope, madam. Perhaps your kindness will indeed help heal my infirmities."

Her bodice tipped near his face as he rested his head on her outstretched thighs. Abruptly, his eyes closed.

Stroking his forehead, she sang a short lullaby to Knowles. "Do you feel more relaxed now, Sir Edward?" she purred compassionately.

He clasped her hand. "In a manner of speaking, madam, though I sense these things will all take much time and reinforced effort on our part. Still, one fear continues to fill me with dread."

"We shall work on it together, Sir Edward."

"How I hoped you would say that, madam. I feel certain that were you to kiss me—oh, not a deep, passionate kiss full of longing. That, of course, would not be right. But perhaps a mere peck on the lips? Then, mayhap, the dreadful grip of fear regarding all women might loosen its paralyzing hold on me."

"A kiss?" She glared down at his wide-eyed countenance. "I fail to see . . . you truly think that would . . . would help your—?"

"Yes, madam," he agreed with a solemn nod, easing

his frame into an upright position on the straw covered barn floor. "That, I suspect, would help me a great deal. Of course, I have not forgotten your earlier admonition about your powers of discipline. I remain in awe of your ability to control mere mortals, such as myself."

Heal a man with her kiss? Sukey shifted uneasily. Was she selfish to abstain?

She contemplated Knowles's gangling body sprawled on the carpet of straw. She set her mouth in a prim, straight line. "Very well. All in the name of healing, you understand. There shall be no nonsense involved with this kiss."

"Quite so, madam," he rasped, patting the straw mound beside him to accommodate her body. "No nonsense whatsoever."

Careful to tuck her skirts primly around her ankles, Sukey knelt down on the straw. Bracing her hands against Knowles's broad outstretched shoulders, she pressed a light, delicate kiss on his mouth.

Arms at his sides, he sat motionless, without touching Sukey. "It . . . it does not seem to be working, Mrs. Howard."

"I beg your pardon?"

"I believe it will take greater effort to assuage my fear—my complete horror—of women. Perhaps if your kiss lasted just a hint longer . . . ?"

"That hardly seems likely, sir."

"Indeed you are too kind, madam. Pray, leave at once. I have imposed on your good nature. My consuming problems are far too comprehensive for a timid woman such as yourself." He waved her off with a flourish of his ruffled sleeves.

"Timid? Sir Edward, I am most assuredly not timid! And I do not abandon problems that remain unsolved."

Kneeling tight against Knowles's side, she slid her

arms around his shoulders. Her kiss, this time, would be anything but delicate, she vowed.

Sukey brushed her lips vigorously against Knowles's mouth.

He stirred.

Deepening her kiss, she pressed harder, raking his lips with fiery exploration. When she paused, she felt her own heartbeat pound. "Anything?" she asked him.

He deliberated. "Possibly. I could not be certain, the reaction was so faint. Perhaps if I might be permitted to . . . No. No, I could not ask it of you."

"Tell me, Sir Edward. I insist." Her face was only inches from his, as she knelt beside him on the barn floor.

"If I were to put my hands on your waist, like so . . ." He demonstrated. "And you were to kiss me again, as before, we might hope for a modest victory over personal frailty this day." The corner of his mouth twitched.

Clucking her tongue, she sighed with resignation. "Very well, sir."

She felt his arms tighten around her waist as she leaned into his kiss. But somehow this kiss was decidedly different from the first. Knowles . . . appeared to be returning her kiss. He pressed her backwards in the straw against a wooden beam. The heady wine of his warm mouth enflamed her own with movement ever more fast-paced. Her heartbeat leaped, pounding blood to her face, her breasts, her . . .

Appalled at her own response to Knowles's kiss, Sukey broke from his grasp.

She coughed quietly while returning several stray tendrils to her confining mobcap. "I believe . . ." She coughed again. "I believe we met our objectives for the day, Sir Edward. Therefore, I—"

He pressed her hand against his chest. "My fearful

heart flutters anxiously in my throat, Mrs. Howard. Pray, feel it. One more kiss would free it to beat normally, I feel certain. Might I impose on the merciful goodness of your nature just one more time? For medicinal purposes?"

She heard the gravel in his voice, saw the soft downturn of his mouth, breathed in the musk of his male warmth . . . and decided to offer Knowles one more brief therapeutic kiss.

But somehow, this time, when Knowles slid his arms snugly around her waist, she felt a glorious release in his kiss. A vibrant letting-go that unknotted every tense, unfulfilled tangle in her body. His mouth brushed and warmed her own into sweet hot flames. She kissed him back and could not stop.

Delicious fire danced across her limbs and licked at that dangerous hollow above her thighs. A demanding fire. Flames that urged and begged and insisted.

Holding her tight as they deepened their kiss, Knowles rolled Sukey onto her back on the hay-strewn floor. Her hands clutched at his shoulders, then clawed possessively behind his neck. She gloried in the press of his body atop her own. The kiss! It must never end. It must . . .

Suddenly horrified at the vulgarity of her actions with a man she ardently disdained, Sukey broke free from Knowles's embrace and leaped to her feet. Brushing straw wisps from her skirt, she spoke brusquely. "I believe we made progress today, Sir Edward. With . . . with your problems, that is."

His mouth remained unsmiling, though slight mirth lines fanned out from Knowles's gentled eyes. He sat upright on the floor, with his elbows propped on his bent knees. "Indeed, I think we have, Mrs. Howard."

She backed away toward the stable door. "Therefore,

you shall not be needing my services any longer. That is, my . . . my therapeutic powers of assistance."

"Oh, but Mrs. Howard, eternal vigilance is the price of liberty. Your touch—yours alone, madam—restores calm to my anguished brow. Without your persistence, I do fear I shall backslide into a morass of trembling terror."

Sukey smoothed her rumpled clothes and tidied her mobcap. She squared her shoulders. "We shall deal with that eventuality when, and if, it occurs, Sir Edward. Personally, I remain hopeful that your courage and manhood shall rise to the occasion."

Knowles choked back a sudden cough.

Jerking open the barn door, Sukey stared out into restored sunlight. "The storm has ended, Sir Edward. Now that you are calmed, I must see to poor Regina's welfare."

"A true angel, Mrs. Howard! I fancy you are an angel of mercy to us all. However, you, uh, might want to wipe that white powder from your cheeks before visiting my aunt."

In furious strokes, Sukey rubbed at her face as she stomped toward Regina's front door. Had she lost her mind? Kissing a sinister, overdressed fop who wore thick face paint and trembled at the sight of his own shadow?

Well, yes. But only to insinuate herself into the confidence of a poisonous French spy, Sukey reminded herself. Indeed, it had all been part of her clever calculations.

Did that explain why she enjoyed kissing Knowles?

Sukey shuddered. No! Impossible. That could not have been joy she experienced, nestled in Sir Edward's arms. Knowles was an inadequate caricature of a man, no more exciting to Sukey than pompous George Howard had been.

For Britain, she reminded herself. This sacrifice—shadowing a dangerous French spy—was solely for the benefit of Britain.

How she longed for Rafe Stewart's comforting embraces! A man who set her on fire with a mere glance, or the touch of his hand. Still, she was disturbed by her arousal from Knowles's kisses.

Approaching the cottage door, left open to admit cooling breezes, Sukey overheard words from inside that made her pause.

"A close call, indeed!" Regina said, hooting a victorious laugh.

"You need be more careful, my dear," Fitch growled. "Michel Margry is obviously suspicious. And though he seems a drunken fool, he has quick eyes."

"And the privilege of Mouceau's ear."

"Which makes him even more of a menace. As well, my dear, you must take care in the vicinity of Mrs. Howard. 'Tis imperative that she not learn . . ."

Their voices dropped to a mere whisper.

Sukey's breathing halted. Tiny hairs along her nape stood on end.

"No telling what Sukey might have overheard as she strolled through Fort Duquesne on Mouceau's arm, Fitch. Indeed, risks mount for us by the day. Quite clever of Edward to suggest fetching her home with us."

Hearing her name mentioned again, Sukey gulped hard. Far more was at stake here than she realized. She had stumbled upon, not just one evil spy, but a trio of them!

Perhaps even more.

Suddenly the dull shelter of her Lancaster drawing room, with its thick damask curtains and fine-crafted furniture, beckoned to Sukey. A place of refuge, comfort, and safety.

What had she done to herself?

In a rush to escape her dreary false mourning, Sukey had dashed from Lancaster's security and plunged headlong into a dangerous adventure more stunning than even she could have predicted.

Adventure? Oh, indeed! Exactly what she had craved.

But what of the grave personal danger she now faced? Was that all a disturbing part of adventure?

Terrifying childhood memories of Ezekiel Richards, the pompous church rector who had shoved her into a dark corner with his breeches undone, swept over Sukey. She recalled her own screams and frantic footsteps as she escaped the rector's planned rape. Shaking herself to refresh her courage, Sukey knew she must boldly resist danger now, just as she had then—this time posed by French threats.

If only Rafe was here to protect her!

Rafe—big and strong and wise to forest intrigue—he would understand exactly what to do next. She scanned the tree-clad slopes, desperate for any sight of Stewart. Her shoulders sagged.

Rafe was nowhere in sight.

Hearing footsteps, she turned to see dandified Sir Edward Knowles shut the stable door and stride toward her. Sukey shivered. Had Knowles seen her eavesdropping by the lodge door?

She cleared her throat and prayed for words.

Chapter Eleven

Squeezed between two anvils, with no hope of escape.

Sukey Howard cocked one ear toward Regina and Fitch's talk as she eyed Knowles's scowling approach from the courtyard. Would she be permitted to live through this day?

"You tarry, Mrs. Howard," he said, studying her actions.

"Ah, Sir Edward! The . . . The air smells marvelously cleansed after a summer storm. I paused for one more sweet breath before seeking Regina." She quickly trotted indoors to avoid his questioning gaze.

"There you are, my dear Sukey!" Regina cooed.

"Thankfully, your spirits seem revived, Regina," she replied. "A rest by the fire and a cup of mint tea has restored the color to your cheeks, for which I am most heartily grateful. And, praise be, the storm has abated. Since you have Fitch and Sir Edward to attend you, I shall be on my—"

"Dear Sukey! Surely you will sup with us before riding off? I could not, in good conscience, allow you to depart on an empty stomach."

Sukey glanced from Regina's beseeching face to Fitch's glowering countenance . . . then to Sir Edward's inquisitive frown.

No escape?

Then again, how was she to learn more of their sinister exploits without closely observing these charlatans? For England, she reminded herself once more, working up her courage.

"If you feel certain I do not presume on your hospitality."

"Nonsense, my dear. Fitch, prepare a cold platter for us, if you please."

Over biscuits and sliced meat, Sukey posed a question. "It only just occurred to me, Regina. At Fort Duquesne, I find it interesting to visit Jardine Nicolet. You, on the other hand, seem to, well, disappear. What is it you find to do at the fort?"

"Do?" Regina shook her fan at an intrusive fly and took an exceptional amount of time to swallow her biscuit as her eyes darted from Knowles back to Sukey. "Dear me! A lonely old woman like myself delights in all the people and sights in a bustling fort like Duquesne. I chatter so much, the poor dears are likely thrilled to see me leave!"

Knowles dabbed at his mouth before rising. "Forgive me, ladies, but I must excuse myself. My journal beckons."

"And I shall ride for home," Sukey announced abruptly. "Pa will fret if I fail to appear shortly."

Regina pouted. "Edward, that seems most ungentlemanly of you to abandon Sukey, our cherished guest."

Knowles gestured lavishly. "Have you forgotten, Aunt? Mrs. Howard is far more skilled at horsemanship than I. Besides, I have thrilling news. Brace yourselves, ladies! This very morning I spotted a rufous-sided towhee for the first time this summer. A towhee! Can you imagine? I must seek him out once more, to be certain, and verify the sighting in my journal."

Regina sighed. "Birds, Edward? Is that the sole source of elation in your life?"

Fluttering his fingers in a departing wave, Knowles backed out the door. "They delight me so, Aunt. Truly, can anything be more exquisite? *Adieu*, Mrs. Howard. Ride with care, madam, until we see you again."

Regina waved from the cottage threshold as Fitch led Sukey to her skittish piebald mare.

Fitch was clever, Sukey noted. A somber man, usually taciturn, with secretive dark eyes. Alone with her, however, might his tongue loosen? Even clever men made occasional mistakes.

"Your master, Fitch? Have you known him long?"

Unsmiling, the servant offered Sukey a hand up on her horse. "For close to a decade, madam."

"Then I presume you know of the tragedy surrounding his childhood."

Aha! She detected a slight flinch in the servant's demeanor.

"I have heard rumors, madam."

Liar, she thought, studying his carefully narrowed eyes. "Can it be true, Fitch? All that sorrow in his past? Or might Regina be mistaken about those troubling details?"

"A wise servant, madam, does not comment on his master's private affairs."

"Quite so, Fitch." She sighed, tugging on her riding gloves. "Still, I only wanted to learn more about him in order that I might help the poor anxious man. You understand my concern, do you not? Unless, of course . . . Sir Edward is not all that he seems." Much to Sukey's delight, her level gaze seemed to unsettle the servant. Yet if she probed further, might she risk assault from this dour charlatan?

For Britain, she reminded herself once more, dismissing her own personal safety.

"Sir Edward is consistently what he seems, madam. According to my humble observations, that is. 'Twould be improper for me to further comment on his idiosyncrasies. Now if you will excuse me, madam, I bid you safe ride home."

Watching Fitch turn away, Sukey urged her horse on.

Lush outgrowths of glossy poison ivy menaced the narrow trail where she rode. Violet-blue wild geranium blossoms threaded their way through tangled raspberry bushes. Overhead, red-tailed hawks soared on lofty air currents. Inhaling the delicate perfume of mauve phlox and yellow mustard, Sukey listened to the echo of woodpeckers assaulting decayed trees.

Suspicious.

Everywhere she turned, everyone she met these days, except for her own family, seemed suspect. As if they were not what they appeared. As if they harbored secret, perhaps menacing, lives that somehow threatened England.

"I shall uncover these mysteries," Sukey murmured, as she rode past robins poking through leaf rubble on the forest floor. "Somehow, that is. And I shall tell no one—not even Rachel or Pa—of my suspicions or designs." The truth might imperil her own safety before she could advise British authorities of her discoveries.

Fitch? Regina? Sir Edward Knowles? Which of the three was a true villain?

Or were they all?

Urging her mare on, Sukey tried to ignore faint rustling sounds. More birds, doubtless, scratching among dry leaves on the ground.

And what of Captain Charlevoix Mouceau? Was he truly the malevolent monster that Red Hawk depicted?

"Lecherous, perhaps, but scarcely a monster," she murmured half aloud.

Mouceau favored Sukey, though their countries bristled at one another. Perhaps . . . she could winkle more information from him before she approached British authorities.

"Provided I can dodge Michel Margry's wrathful intrusions!" she muttered.

The slight noises she heard frightened Sukey. Yet glancing round at the forest, she saw nothing to fear. If only she understood nature as did Rafe Stewart! He read the forest as others might read a book. Like an Indian, Rafe knew a use for every plant. He sensed the meaning of every sight, sound, or smell.

Those rustling leaves . . . was an animal creeping nearby? Or could it be a man following her? Shivering as she fingered the outline of her knife, Sukey nudged her horse on faster.

The only trustworthy man she knew, outside her family, was the mountain man, Rafe Stewart. Strong, bold, arousing Rafe! Yet more elusive than a bolt of lightning flickering across a summer sky.

"Rafe," she whispered longingly. "How I wish you were with me now . . . and forever."

She rode down the last slope leading to Eli and Zeb Whitfield's cabin. A sudden shrill birdcall made Sukey turn. One last time she scanned the high ridge she had just descended. There, Rafe Stewart stood silhouetted against the setting sun.

"My darling!" she murmured, turning her horse in Stewart's direction.

But in a flash, Stewart vanished.

Heart aching with an unfamiliar version of loneliness, Sukey trudged inside.

"You took a dangerous chance today, my friend," Red Hawk said, dousing a small campfire. "Do you think Mouceau figured out your identity?"

Rafe Stewart gnawed on a birch twig clamped between his teeth. "He tries hard, Red Hawk. I see him struggle to remember. But the truth still eludes him."

The aging Lenape shook his head. "You dance on cliff's edge, Rafe. One day soon, Mouceau will realize you are the trader he threatened to kill on sight. Then it will be too late for you."

"I have no choice. Mouceau is the devil's own spawn, Red Hawk. For the sake of England, and for Thomas—damn Mouceau's soul—I must finish this job."

"You failed to learn all you needed to know about Fort Duquesne from your visit today?"

Stewart spat derisively. "That rogue, Michel Margry, followed me around like a trained puppy. Try as I may, I could not break free. I must return under the cover of darkness tonight and ride in close for additional surveillance."

"Countless huts ring the fort, Rafe. You could easily be detected by a sentry. Or some soldier full of liquor who relieves himself in the dead of night."

"I know."

"It means no fire for you. Without fire, night insects will feast on your skin."

Stewart's teeth gleamed white in the moonlight as he grinned at Red Hawk. "You test my will, Red Hawk, but fail to frighten me. I call your bluff. Friend, will you ride with me?"

The Lenape nodded. "I will be the silent shadow at your side."

"A shadow with knife at the ready?"

Red Hawk cracked a barely perceptible smile.

Late that night, high on a southern ridge overlooking Fort Duquesne, Stewart lay on his belly to avoid creating a silhouette. The Monongahela River lapped far below as Stewart studied fort details. Danger threatened his life every minute of every day, here in the Allegheny Mountains.

Bloody hell! He had a vital mission to complete for the British Army . . . a mission critical to the balance of European power in America.

Why, then, did his thoughts continually drift to tart-tongued Susannah Whitfield Howard?

He should never have laid hands on her. He knew that, of course, from the start. Yet despite all his inner cautions, from that first minute he laid eyes on Sukey, Rafe knew he would never rest till he had her . . . at least one time.

Despite the damp night air, Stewart's throat went dry.

Once was not enough, though. Not for a man with Rafe Stewart's carnal appetite.

He found himself craving everything about Sukey Howard. The firm roundness of her limbs. The sound of her sensual voice. The feel of her soft skin. Even the smell of her drove him mad—like teasing perfume on a sultry summer evening. Day and night he longed for Sukey Howard.

Love?

Stewart spat. In his world, women did not exist for love. Cruel vixens, never to be trusted—all that could be said of women. Stewart trusted none of them, valued none of them, loved none of them. Except for his kind-hearted aunt, Regina Ramsey, who rescued Thomas and him after the death of their parents, women were to be used and discarded at will.

He had no explanation for his fascination with Sukey Howard. Except to be absolutely certain it was not love.

Marriage?

God's blood! Stewart shuddered at the very thought of marital bondage. He would play with Sukey Howard, just as he had amused himself with other women. Then one day, he would cast her off, like all the others.

In the dark, Stewart grunted. He turned his full attention back to the torches illuminating Fort Duquesne.

Rachel Butler sprinkled dry flour on her wooden kitchen table. "Pa's got that look about him again, Sukey." She warned, dumping a mound of dough atop the flour.

"Which face might that be? The one which implies no Frenchman shall ever dislodge him from these hills?"

"Worse than that, I fear." Rachel bit her cheek to keep from laughing.

"Aha! Then 'tis the one where he scolds about widows who fail to quickly remarry being an offense against society." Sukey furrowed her brow in a mock portrayal of her father's chastisements.

"I fear so, sister."

"Then I shall run into the woods and hide for the day, leaving you and little Adam to bake all the bread yourselves."

"Nay, my dear! Adam and I think you shall plant your feet right here in the kitchen and promptly begin kneading dough."

At the sound of Adam's cries, Sukey lifted him from

his rude cradle and sang to the infant. The pink-cheeked baby scrunched his fists against his face and wailed.

"He wants what only his mother can supply." Sukey handed him to Rachel, who undid her bodice and nursed her son.

"You would make a divine mother, Sukey. I see the look in your eyes whenever you hold Adam and comfort him. You long to mother a child."

Sukey pushed hard at the dough mound. "You forget one tiny detail, my dear."

Rachel laughed. "A husband? Oh, Sukey! I feel certain Sir Edward would be only too happy to comply in that matter."

"Sir Edward?" Rolling her eyes, Sukey slapped out her frustration on the bread dough. "That relentless coward? Never! Not in a lifetime of years, Rachel. He would be no better at marriage than George Howard. I shall never again marry an emasculated dandy. I want a husband who rouses unbridled passions in me, not some limp excuse for a man."

"But, Sukey dear, mayhap you . . . you could teach Sir Edward how to love a woman after you marry. In the manner you require, that is."

Images of wild, almost savage-looking Rafe Stewart flooded Sukey's mind. Rafe needed no tutors. Instinctively, he knew how to be a man . . . in every sense of the word. And how to make Sukey feel like a woman.

A sensuous shiver danced down her body.

"The right man will require no tutors," she said, repeating aloud her thoughts. She lifted the dough loaf onto a long-handled wooden peel and carried it outside to a beehive oven.

"Sukey?" Eli Whitfield bellowed.

"Oh, dear!" Sukey murmured, hearing the stern edge to her father's voice. "Yes, Pa?" she replied with forced innocence as she flipped the wooden peel to slide her loaf onto the bare oven floor.

"If Sir Edward Knowles were to come by here, today, Sukey, you might consider treating him more kindly. I suspect, with a bit more encouragement on your part, he might even offer you marriage."

"Pa!"

"See here, daughter, 'tis neither right nor proper. You're not getting any younger. Womenfolk your age should be married and having babies. They need a man to watch over them."

Her eyes narrowed with anger. "Pa, Sir Edward is *not* the man you imagine! At least I think not. And when I choose to marry again—if I ever choose to marry again—I shall select the man myself!"

"Not one of those Frenchmen you seem to fancy!"

She could not reveal even one shred of her scheme to Eli Whitfield—that she fraternized with Frenchmen merely to learn valuable army information, or that she endured Knowles's presence only to document and trap a menacing spy.

Someday, when the British army glorified Sukey Howard for her incredible bravery in the face of danger, Eli Whitfield would swell with pride over his daughter's exploits!

Provided she lived long enough to complete her plan.

The June sun, high and hot, beat down on Sukey. Sultry breezes did little to dissipate the perspiration collecting along her face and arms. Across her shoulders, she bore a large wooden pole loaded with a water bucket at either end. Her destination—a cool spring burbling with the sweetest of mountain water.

A sharp bird whistle pricked her ears.

Wishful thinking on Sukey's part. That whistle often signified Rafe Stewart's presence. She studied the surrounding hills. No sign of the elusive Stewart. She trudged forward . . . and heard the whistle again, this time much closer. Pivoting, Sukey searched in every direction.

Framed by thick wild-grape vines, Stewart's brawny frame stood outlined against an elm tree only twenty feet away.

"Rafe!" she cried.

Silently he lifted the pole from her slim shoulders.

She watched the play of shadows across his rawboned face. And felt instantly aroused. Everything about Rafe Stewart made Sukey feel urgent needs deep within her body. As if she were insatiable, miserably hollow.

And only Rafe Stewart could complete her.

Like some untamed creature, he lounged near . . . so near she could feel the warmth emanating from his bulging muscles. She knew the taste of him. Those hardened male arms. The broad chest flecked with dark curls. That surly downturned fullness of his lower lip. She knew, too, how that same mouth felt as it tasted her own willing body.

The fire of Stewart's compelling mouth! Only a few daring inches, now, from her own.

His half-unbuttoned linen shirt invited—nay, demanded—that she touch his unyielding chest. But before she could reach for him, his rumbling voice startled her.

"I must apologize for taking unfair advantage of you, Mrs. Howard. It shall not happen again." His hands remained firmly at his sides.

What? Was she never to know the gentle rasp of his calloused touch again . . . ever? A touch she yearned for, with all her being, night and day? She craved every inch of this wild mountain lion, and he was saying . . . ?

Dear God!

Sukey wanted to beg . . . to grovel before this masculine beast who had stolen her heart. But that would never do. Instead, she jutted her chin forward.

"I permit no one to take unfair advantage of me, sir. You have troubled yourself with apologies for naught. If, as you say, it shall not happen again, so be it. I could scarcely care less."

She turned aside from Stewart to hide the yearning which threatened to well up in her eyes. Was that his strong hand lifting an escaped curl from her shoulder? Sukey shivered under his touch.

"Can you, in all honesty, Mrs. Howard, say that you did not enjoy our . . . time together?" His voice, low and husky, hinted of desire.

Still avoiding his probing gaze, she swallowed hard. He stood so close, she could feel his breath across her cheek. Sukey prayed for self-restraint to keep from leaping into Rafe's burly arms.

"Enjoy?" She coughed quietly. "My, you do puff your vanity, Mr. Stewart."

He drew his hand back.

"Sunlight across your hair, Sukey, creates colors I have never seen before. Reds and golds, like fire burning out of control."

At the sound of his voice, she tried not to breathe faster. Her fingers fidgeted nervously with a slick campion stem. "Why have you come here tonight, Rafe?" She still avoided his steadfast gaze.

"To offer you an apology."

So near. She felt his breath tickle her ear. He smelled of pine branches and male musk. Aroused male musk. Sukey balled her hands into tight fists. Those rebellious fingers of hers—they must not reach for Rafe Stewart. They could not be allowed to betray her eagerness to make love with this beautiful ruffian.

"Nothing else?"

He hesitated. "What else would you like me to offer you, Sukey?"

Words caught in her throat like dry slivers of wood. "I assumed you came here with, well, a multitude of motives."

"Maybe I did."

She could not tolerate the tension. Was he playing a raw little game with her? Every particle of Sukey's body screamed out for Rafe Stewart's touch. "Then . . . then state your true purposes, sir, that we may resolve them and quickly part."

"The truth, madam? I came to see one last time how the green satin of your eyes reflects moonglow. How lavender smells when it lies next to your soft skin. How your dimples curve and taunt. How your voice rings with the sweetness of songbirds in spring."

Sukey glanced over her shoulder at Stewart. Was she a wanton harlot for aching to crawl naked into his brawny arms? Or a woman in love? Sukey no longer knew or cared. Facing him, she freed her hands to slide up over his broad chest.

He stood motionless.

Her fingers traced the chiseled curve of his jaw. Tentatively, she kissed his mouth.

He glared down at her. "Are you teasing me, Mrs. Howard?"

"Perhaps."

His eyes flared as he caught at Sukey's inquisitive hands. "I hunger for you, Mrs. Howard. Like an unrelenting bear. But a famished man does not settle for idle crumbs when a complete meal lies within his grasp."

"Perhaps it is time to eat, Mr. Stewart," she whispered.

At her implied invitation, he pulled Sukey into his arms and raked her mouth with kisses. With one hand he cradled her head as he kissed her cheek. His lips and tongue played with her ear lobe.

"Rafe, darling!" she cried, clutching his thick mane of sable-colored hair.

"Woman, I have missed you. I vowed to stay away . . . to keep my hands off you forever."

She kissed his sulky down-turned lips. "Then I shall simply have to do everything within my power to make you break that vow."

Drawing in a deep breath, he held her at arm's length. "Regarding vows, woman, have you forgotten that I am not the marrying sort?"

She stiffened. "Nor am I, Rafe. Never again shall I permit any man to imprison me in marriage!"

"My work here may force me to vanish, Sukey. On a moment's notice."

"Then we must count each moment together as if it might be our last."

A huge ballet of swaying fern fronds shielded them as they sank to the earth in heated embrace.

Later, when he had dressed, she tenderly slid his bear's tooth necklace around his neck. "Your mission, Rafe? Can you share with me the purpose?"

"No, my love. Not more than I work to halt French intrusion in the Alleghenies."

"Then let me help you! I can be quite brave and daring."

He touched her arms affectionately. "Dear Sukey, this is not some harmless parlor game. The price for error here on the frontier is death—sometimes slow and brutal in the execution."

"But, Rafe, you underestimate my capacity for guile. I can help you, and yes, England as well! Do you not see? We can be bold intriguers together!"

"My conscience rarely motivates me, Sukey. This time it does. My life is far too dangerous for you."

She stamped her foot on the mossy earth. "You sound just like Pa! He insists women are only fit to tend hearths and have babies. He continually connives to marry me off."

Stewart scowled. "And does he have someone particular in mind?"

"A spineless wretch you likely never encountered. Sir Edward Knowles."

Stewart's expresssion softened. He quirked an eyebrow. "The dandy who parades around in fine lace and silk?"

"You know him!"

A slight smile tugged at Stewart's mouth. "Only in passing. Your father speaks the truth, Sukey. Knowles could offer you a proper and serene life, complete with vows and the babies your father urges you to produce."

Inflated with rage, Sukey could scarcely speak. "I hasten to inform you, sir, that Edward Knowles is not man enough to produce babies!"

A tremor ruffled Stewart's bushy black eyebrows as he contemplated Sukey's outburst. "Is that a fact, my dear? Most interesting. How is it you know such a personal characteristic of the well-bred gentleman?"

She huffed indignantly. "I surmised as much, that is all, you wicked man. But even if he were . . . virile, I could never find it in my heart to love him." She finished wrapping her scarf around her shoulders "Now, Rafe, do not think you have distracted me. For my country, I shall gladly risk danger."

He cupped her chin.

"Not too gladly, I hope, Sukey." He gently stroked her smooth cheek. "'Tis enough that I risk life and limb for England. Knowing that you keep safe shall comfort me when guns blaze, as they assuredly will, soon."

Her chin shot forward. "Do not patronize me, Rafe Stewart! I can face danger with as much courage—yes, and useful purpose—as any man."

He kissed her lips, then fastened his shirt. "Goodbye, my lovely."

"Rafe!" She caught at his sleeve. "Where is it you go, when you leave me? Can you not tell me more about yourself?"

He hesitated. "Perhaps, Sukey, if I live through this battle, then I can tell you more. Meanwhile, tend your hearth in safety."

Abruptly, he vanished like a ghost of the forest.

Sukey stared with narrowed eyes at the entangled vines where he disappeared. Her hands tensed into tight fists.

"I have a plan, Rafe Stewart," she whispered to the silent June afternoon, as she batted at darting insects. "You, and Pa, and everyone else shall soon see. I can be as devious and quick-witted as any hulking mercenary of General Braddock's army."

Chapter Twelve

"French land, Monsieur Knowles!" Michel Margry shouted, waving his arms in a wide arc to include all that he saw. "Your cabin here on the Monongahela, these mountains, even Monsieur Whitfield's trading post on Turtle Creek—all of it lies on French land. And soon . . . we shall set matters straight with the English."

Seated on a bench before Knowles's kitchen fireplace, he glowered at the Englishman.

"Monsieur Margry, you are a man of firm convictions," Knowles declared, nodding his head assertively. "I respect that in a man. Indeed! I thought perhaps a man of your . . . your exceedingly high caliber might relish possessing this fine silver buckle."

He dangled the enticing ornament before the Frenchman.

Margry's eyes widened. He grabbed the buckle and fingered all its shining curves. "Other British traders invaded these hills earlier, monsieur. Arrogant men. Boastful in their declarations and intent. Two brothers, Thomas and Rafe Stewart, were the most obnoxious. They insisted this land was theirs." His eyes glittered full of solid hate.

A small muscle twitched in Knowles's clean-shaven jaw as he studied the unkempt Frenchman. "Is that so, monsieur? And what became of these two . . . ruffians?"

"Gone!" Margry shouted. "We drove them off, monsieur, with the sternest of warnings. If ever we should see their malicious bodies again, we shall kill them on sight."

"Indeed! A French warning of that magnitude no doubt frightened those miscreants far east of the Susquehanna River."

"One can never be sure, monsieur. The two Stewarts were capable of crafting great disturbances. Blackguards, they were, defying French authority here at every opportunity!" Margry pounded the kitchen table with his grimy fist for emphasis.

"Just imagine, monsieur! Well, surely you rest easier knowing those two villains are long gone." Rising from the opposite bench, Knowles silently beckoned Fitch.

"If only that were so. Captain Mouceau believes he shot Thomas Stewart at that pathetic British redoubt they named Fort Necessity, last year. But the other one—the more dangerous one—most likely still lives."

"That would be Rafe Stewart?"

"*Oui.*" Grunting, Michel Margry rubbed his stubbled jaw. "A man, they say, known to assume numerous disguises."

"Disguises? Just imagine!" Clicking his tongue in noisy sympathy with the Frenchman, Knowles reached for a bottle hastily supplied by Fitch. Knowles poured a dram of liquor into a small horn mug. His eyes narrowed. "May I offer you some whiskey, monsieur, to cleanse the trail's dust from your dry, thirsty mouth?"

Seizing the cup, Margry gulped its fiery amber liquid.

"Rumor has it that Rafe Stewart still lurks hereabouts." Margry wiped at his mirthless smile with the back of his hand. "If that be true, monsieur, it will be his final mistake, I can assure you. Frenchmen shall make him regret his villainy. The only question is whether we allow him to die instantly . . . or slowly amidst great pain. I suppose really it depends on which of us finds Stewart first."

"Hm. Well, I certainly respect your determination, monsieur. I should not wish to cross a man of your . . . your ferocious bravery."

Recrossing his legs, Michel Margry studied the Englishman. "You know, Monsieur Knowles, I find something puzzling."

"What might that be, sir?"

"In a certain sunlight—particularly the strong afternoon rays, mind you—you bear a slight resemblance to Stewart, himself."

Knowles blinked, then chortled. "Utterly amazing, sir! Delightful, actually! My aunt will find it quite amusing that you feel I resemble a backwoods ruffian, even for a brief moment." Tittering into his lace cuff, Knowles poured more whiskey. "Care to join me in another drink, sir?"

Margry licked his lips. He glanced from Knowles's face to the mug of fiery liquor. His fleshy tongue lingered along the rim of his lower lip. "Captain Mouceau becomes angry when I drink."

A ghost of a smile fluttered across Knowles's mouth. "But, my good fellow, Captain Mouceau is not here right now. And we gentlemen are simply having a little drink among friends—man to man, eh, monsieur? Is that so wrong? Does Captain Mouceau control every moment of your life?"

He held the refilled mug out to Michel Margry.

The Frenchman scowled. "*Non*! Of course not! I am my own man, answerable to no one." He grabbed the refilled cup and gulped its contents.

"There's a good fellow," Knowles commented. Though he pretended to join Margry in a drink, his own cup remained full. A necessary pretense, he felt. Imperative, now, for him to remain clear-headed and alert.

"Ah, *Mon Dieu*! This tastes near as good as a woman feels!" Margry whimpered, eagerly licking his mouth.

"Glad you enjoy it, *mon ami*. I wonder, my good fellow, if you can help me solve a puzzle of my own. Captain Mouceau mentioned something about requiring additional ammunition if a shipment from Montreal failed to arrive. As an influential trader, I would most cheerfully take care of this matter for the captain. However, Captain Mouceau . . . neglected to mention whether his French delivery arrived or not. And whether it included all the weaponry that he required. We both know the captain is a frightfully busy man, *mon ami*. Perhaps too busy to personally handle every business detail."

"*Bien sûr*," Margry grunted.

"Since you clearly are his most trusted aide, I thought perhaps you would know . . . what supplies, if any, recently reached Fort Duquesne from Montreal."

Knowles hooded his own eyes and poured another dram into the Frenchman's cup.

Margry switched his sluggish gaze from the refilled cup, to Knowles's face, then back to the cup. "I . . . I wonder, monsieur," he began in slurred speech, "if I should be discussing this with you, an Englishman."

"A valid concern, *mon ami*. I respect your wise and most excellent judgment. But since your own captain was about to do it anyway, you shall surely be . . . helping our poor beleaguered Mouceau resolve yet another of his many tedious problems. Eh, *mon ami*?"

"What good fortune, Sukey! Is that not your *fiancé*?" Jardine Nicolet asked, peering out the window of Captain Mouceau's hut.

Sukey swallowed hard. Please, not now, she prayed, feeling her insides constrict miserably. Not after she had ridden over rough terrain to extract vital information from sharp-eyed but amorous Charlevoix Mouceau. Clearly the captain had a weak spot for Sukey. His unguarded desire made her shiver, of course. Repulsed her, even.

But Charlevoix Mouceau's weakness would become Sukey Howard's strength . . . so long as she avoided his grasp.

Bolting up from his chair, Mouceau glowered out the same window. "*Mon Dieu!*" he raged. "Michel Margry lies like a sack across one of Knowles's horses. The fool is drunk again!"

He spun towards Jardine.

"Madame Nicolet, please be so kind as to instruct our guest to ride beyond the fort and deposit Margry in his hut. The drawbridge is down. Your husband can help. He has business to discuss with Knowles anyhow."

Jardine stared helplessly at Sukey. "But . . . ?"

Mouceau smiled, a cold, brittle twitch of the mouth. "Have no fear, Madame Nicolet. I shall not abandon Madame Howard."

With a sinking heart, Sukey watched Jardine depart. She cleared her throat quietly. "You . . . you were describing the cannon, Captain Mouceau. And the tremendous force which they possess."

Puffed and vain, Mouceau beamed at mention of his military might. "Eight cannon, my dear Madame Howard, four of which are three-pounders." He walked toward her and leaned close behind her chair.

Sukey's armpits dampened with perspiration.

She fought to blank out the horrifying childhood memory of Ezekiel Richards, church rector, with his breeches undone . . . cornering her. Sukey's heart pounded furiously now as she felt Charlevoix Mouceau's hot breath fan her neck. To accomplish her task, Sukey had to blot Ezekiel Richards, and a mounting fear of violent frontier rape, from her mind.

She took a deep breath.

"Three-pounders? Indeed! Oh, Captain Mouceau, I feel such admiration for your cleverness, for your vast responsibility. How it thrills me to hear of your exploits. Do, please, tell me more."

She knew he loved to boast. That, however, did not seem what Mouceau had in mind at the moment. She stifled a shudder as his hands rested on her shoulders. Someday England might revere Susannah Whitfield Howard for her courage at staring down a viper in his own den. For now, though, she had to concentrate on garnering secrets of Fort Duquesne's military strength . . . and manage to stay alive at the same time.

Mouceau's breath tickled Sukey's ear as he bent down close to her.

"I should like very much to teach you about my cleverness, madame. Or better yet . . . to show you." His voice dipped lower.

Springing from her camp chair, Sukey reached for the door. "Oh, monsieur! Would you indeed? I should *so* love to see those magnificent guns up close and proper. And yes, visit the magazine to see the very shells required to fire them."

Mouceau grabbed her hand and smothered it with kisses. "Later, madame. First, I must show you—"

"Darling Sukey!" Sir Edward Knowles exclaimed, suddenly rounding the doorway corner. "I could not believe my ears when Madame Nicolet announced you were here as well, today!"

Mouceau blinked.

With a black stare at Sir Edward, he abruptly dropped Sukey's hand. "Monsieur Knowles. I thought—"

Knowles waved his arm with a great flourish. "I simply could not bear the thought of attending to business when my own cherished *fiancée* sat only a short distance away. Oh, yes, so besotted with love, am I!"

Sukey glanced from the Frenchman to Knowles. Heaven help her, the English fop was trowelling it on.

She walked a fine line between two impossible men. Mouceau's cruelty was legend. She needed to pluck vital information from his unsuspecting male vanity. Yet push him too far, and all her worst fears—what frontier men did to women in lust and hate—would come true. Knowles, on the other hand, might very well be a deceitful spy, perhaps capable of turning on her as well.

Exhaling, Sukey straightened her spine.

"Sir Edward," she replied coolly to his greeting. "A pleasure, sir."

An angered Eli Whitfield paced the bare planks of his cabin floor at Turtle Creek.

"Pa! I am, after all, a grown woman. And a widow at that!" Sukey pretended to resume her mending.

Eli rolled his eyes in exasperation. "Two sins of commission, Sukey, all at the same time!" he shouted. "Fort Duquesne is a den of . . . of French scoundrels and iniquity."

"Oh, Pa! I merely went to visit Madame Nicolet."

Eli's gaze shifted toward Sir Edward Knowles, quietly slaking his thirst with a cup of water poured from a crockery pitcher, then back at his daughter. "As for your unmarried status, Sukey, 'tis no longer justifiable. All women of child-bearing age can find husbands, if they care to."

Sukey's mending basket fell from her lap and clattered to the floor.

Setting down his cup, Knowles edged toward the door. "I fear I intrude on a private family discussion, dear friends. I shall go explore your orchard. Please excuse me." He quickly vanished.

"Pa!" Rachel Butler cried, bracing her hands on her hips. "See what you have done? You embarrassed poor, gentle Sir Edward."

Eli locked his arms across his chest. "Hmph! Needed to be said. Maybe Knowles as well as Sukey needed to hear it."

"Upon my word, Pa," Sukey cried. "This is the frontier. You simply must understand . . . the time has come for your children to lead their own lives."

Rachel giggled. "Pa has this disturbing tendency to want to play Cupid with us."

"Perhaps we should turn the thing about and play Cupid with Pa," Sukey declared. "Then he would be too busy to meddle in—"

"Sukey! Your foolish prattle fails you. No matter how ridiculously you chat on, I shall not be distracted from my concerns. You court danger by visiting that God-forsaken French fort. No fit place for a single woman, I tell you. A French fort! Aye, merciful heavens!"

Rachel struggled to be helpful. "Would a French son-in-law really be so terrible, Pa? Mixed marriages happen all the time here on the frontier."

Eli's face flushed bright red. He could scarcely speak. "French? A French son-in-law? May God have mercy! They want to kill us all. No, Sukey needs to stay away from all Frenchmen. Methinks I should go out to Knowles straight away and arrange for him to marry—"

"No!" Sukey held up her hand defiantly. "I shall never enter another arranged marriage, Pa," she shouted. "Never! Most particularly not with weak and cowardly Sir Edward Knowles!"

Still fuming, Eli stomped out the door.

Rachel caught Sukey by the arm. "Find Sir Edward, Sukey. Quick! Before Pa does. Go to him and smooth the poor man's delicate senses. And remember, dear, however you feel about him, Sir Edward is a . . . a kind man. A good man."

Sukey sneered. "He might be. Though I think not."

"Encourage the poor dear, Sukey. Can you not see? He needs your dauntless strength to help him become the man God intended."

Sukey's lip curled.

"Sukey, dear! Mercy! Such an unlovely expression on your face! Now hurry, at once, before Pa corners the unsuspecting innocent with a barrage of paternal demands."

"Unsuspecting innocent! Hmmph!"

"And remember, Sukey, even if you cannot love Sir Edward, you can nevertheless help him grow as a man. 'Tis your duty, being the noble and strong woman that you are, to embolden and instruct the poor helpless dear."

Wrinkling her brow, Sukey grudgingly assented. "But only to keep Pa and all his absurd designs away from Sir Edward, mind you, Rachel!"

"Ah, what a noble sister!" Rachel hugged Sukey. "How proud I am of you, dear."

"Hmmph!" Sukey muttered through clenched teeth.

She found Knowles leaning by an apple tree in Eli's small orchard.

"Please, forgive my father's absurd outbursts, Sir Edward. He means well, I suppose, like most fathers."

Knowles examined the gleaming white petals of an ox-eye daisy held in his hand. "I both respect and admire your father's fortitude, madam. He does not offend me in the least. Though, of course, I . . . I understand your great reluctance to consider me as your swain."

Eyeing Sukey sideways, Knowles twirled the daisy in his hand.

Swain? She could speak to no one of her longing for masculine Rafe Stewart. Not yet. Or how little Knowles resembled that rugged, compelling man. "We shall have no mention of that topic, Sir Edward."

"My becoming your swain, you mean?" he asked, still contemplating the flower.

"Precisely." She cleared her throat noisily. "And while we are on the subject, sir—"

"But we are to avoid the subject, correct, madam? Oh, I do so want to avoid your scorn. A woman of your might is capable of fearful discipline." He hid his expression in his elegant handkerchief.

She caught at his coat sleeve. "Look at me, Sir Edward."

"N-no," he whimpered, still hiding his face.

She clicked her tongue in disgust. "Look at me, sir. I insist."

"Are you about to punish me for my indiscretions, madam?"

"You have no indiscretions, Sir Edward. No visible ones, anyhow. Though, God knows, it would seem a real man should possess a few."

"Then, is it time for another of our lessons, madam? Oh, I do so revere your wisdom in matters of men and women."

"Perhaps. First, though, we must clear up some pressing misconceptions. The *façade* of your appearing as my *fiancé*, in the presence of Frenchmen, is nothing but a *façade*. Done, I might add, to humor my father and lend minor credence to your . . . your masculinity."

"Oh, indeed, madam."

"I permit this . . . farce only to further both our needs."

His right eye peeked from the folds of his handkerchief. One black-winged eyebrow lifted. "How courageous of you, madam, to champion both our needs." Knowles's voice plunged deep on that last word.

Sukey wagged her index finger at him. "But you are not to carry this theatrical performance to absurd extremes, as you did today at Fort Duquesne," she scolded.

"Oh, dear heavens! I felt certain you were displeased, madam." He turned aside.

Annoyed, she tugged once more at his sleeve. "Sir Edward, I insist you look at me at once. What do you see before you? Truly! Look at me."

His gaze lingered on her hair, the full curves of her bosom, the shape of her hips. His cheek tensed. "I see a beautiful woman, madam. One I could never attain."

"A taboo subject, Sir Edward. But what you do see before you is simply a woman who stands no taller than your . . . than your chest." To demonstrate, she thumped the mid-section of his broad chest.

He leaned close. "Here, madam?" he asked, lightly touching her hair as he appeared to measure her diminutive height against his own.

Surprised at the unyielding strength of those male muscles, Sukey absentmindedly trailed her hand across Knowles's chest, to his coat sleeve. "There," she murmured in agreement. "You see, sir. You stand much taller and stronger than I. Truly, you have nothing to fear from me."

"Nothing?" he asked. His mouth seemed in search of something on her face.

She swallowed with difficulty. Knowles had been known to get foolishly bold once or twice in the past.

"Well, then again, there is the knife I carry with me at all times."

"I say! Impressive. And are you skilled in its use?"

She smiled. And took one step backward from those imposing broad shoulders. "As skilled as I need to be, sir."

"Which means you only slice selected body parts?"

"Which means I slice body parts with a selected degree of accuracy." Her smile deepened. "Now, Sir Edward, you were saying . . . 'tis time for another lesson?"

Zeb Whitfield suddenly burst upon them. "Have you heard? Indian runners just arrived from Braddock's march. They dislike Braddock's arrogance. Most natives have abandoned him. Even so, the English will drive those arrogant French braggarts out of Duquesne. And I shall be a part of it!"

Knowles grew somber. "Your womenfolk need you here, Zeb, not embroiled with the French in war," he warned.

"I am a man, Sir Edward, and as ready for war as any able-bodied frontiersman." Zeb's faced flushed red-hot with determination.

Sukey thrust back her shoulders. "Pa taught us all to shoot straight, Sir Edward. Rachel and I hit the target more often than most men. We need no one to protect us."

Knowles scowled at them both. "Neither of you ever lived through the horrors of war . . . close-up. I have. Not a pretty sight, my dears."

Abruptly relaxing, he waved his arms effeminately through the air. "The truth is, I find I simply cannot bear the sight or smell of bloodshed. Thankfully, I have no need to become a soldier. We hire mercenaries for that vulgar purpose, after all."

Sukey clicked her tongue in disgust. "Your fine clothes and suave manner fail to conceal your monumental cowardice, Sir Edward. I fear that no lessons on earth can ever replace your faint heart with that of a real man. Can you not understand? When danger threatens, we all must take a stand."

From the corner of her eye, Sukey suddenly spotted Red Hawk, quietly appearing on a wooded rise. As if he waited for someone. Rafe? Surely, he awaited Rafe Stewart! Rafe must be near! But where? she wondered, glancing in all directions.

Spotting Red Hawk as well, Knowles suddenly grew restless. He bowed low. "Oh, my dears! I have offended you with my fragile nature. Forgive me, I beg of you. I shall depart in haste while we yet remain friends."

Trembling, Sukey scarcely heard his words. Her gaze remained fixed in the shadowy direction of Red Hawk. Rafe was near! Her entire body tingled with euphoria at the knowledge. She sensed it in her very bones. But where? Why could she not see Rafe when she so strongly felt his proximity?

"*Adieu*, my friends." Knowles bowed once more and slipped away almost unnoticed.

Sukey drummed her fingers nervously on an apple tree limb. "Zeb, I need your help."

He crossed his arms over his chest. "Your plea leaves me unmoved, Sukey. The look on your face! I recall that same vexing expression invariably causes me trouble."

"Nonsense, Zeb. All that I ask is just a trifling favor. No one need ever know."

He snorted. "Your plea rings all too familiar, Sukey. And hollow! I have heard that before, usually right before Pa discovers your chicanery and tans both our hides."

"Zeb! Being grownups, now, surely we are not likely to incur Pa's wrath."

"Hah!" He snorted derisively.

"I need to track a certain man, Zeb. And your tracking skills surpass mine."

Zeb guffawed. "Why not use feminine wiles, as you usually do when hunting down some poor unsuspecting male?"

"What!" Sukey flamed with rage, just as Eli shouted for Zeb from the smithy doorway.

"I must get back to work, Sukey." He seized her by the shoulders. "Listen, sister, pay close attention to the forest, to the angle and impress of your man's foot. That will tell you the direction he takes, even if you lose sight of his footprint. But have a care, Sukey. Not every concealed man cares to be found. Nor may the story you find, at trail's end, be to your liking," he warned, before dashing off.

She would use Zeb's advice selectively, in search of Red Hawk, a Lenape who seemed to move through the forest like an elusive shade. Of a certainty, where Red Hawk appeared, Rafe Stewart lurked nearby. And, oh, how Sukey longed for even a fleeting glimpse of the man she had grown to love! Ignoring her unease over Zeb's warning, she darted to where Red Hawk last appeared. Surely if Rafe saw her, he . . . he would clasp her in his arms. The sound of his deep voice comforted her as no other. His touch, gentle yet powerful, roused every craving instinct within Sukey to a compelling peak of urgency.

She needed everything about Rafe Stewart, night and day. His reassuring touch, his laughter and teasing. His solid, comforting manner. With Rafe, Sukey could let down her guard. She could be "woman," to his "man."

Sukey trusted Rafe. Then why the curious prickle down her spine as she sought his tracks?

Tossing aside her concerns, she kneeled to study the sheen of fragrant crushed grasses. Freshly-bent laurel twigs indicated someone had just passed by. Her scrutiny led her to trail imprints of an Englishman's shoes—sturdy squared heels and pointed toes.

"Oh, bother!" she whispered. "I seek Rafe, and instead find that vexatious Sir Edward! But surely if I find the precise spot where Red Hawk last stood . . . ah! The very sycamore tree on which he leaned!" She pivoted in search of clues.

Odd. Parting tangled ferns, Sukey found in the moist earth an imprint of one set of Indian moccasins. More broken fern fronds. Then mysteriously, another set of moccasin prints. Deep ones. As if perhaps a second, notably brawny, Indian dropped from the trees overhead.

Or Rafe! Oh, it had to be!

Sukey squinched her eyes closed and smiled. "This is far easier than Zeb described," she murmured. "I shall learn to read the woods as efficiently as any native."

Then just as abruptly, the trail halted.

Frantic, yet curiously sensing she neared her goal, Sukey crawled on all fours in search of tracking clues. She found an old buffalo trail, the fine-fingered prints of a raccoon, and an occasional moccasin print.

"You shall not elude me now, Rafe Stewart!" she whispered, searching the telltale soft earth. "I shall learn to hunt you down and discover your magical hiding place."

Then, beyond a sweeping bank of jewelweed, Sukey crouched low and parted laurel branches with both hands to reveal . . . a pair of moccasined feet!

Her head jerked up.

"Red Hawk!" she gasped, seeing the huge Lenape.

"Why are you following me, madam?" he asked sternly.

"I, uh, that is—"

What was it Zeb had warned about not all hunted men wishing to be found? "My brother, you see, has begun teaching me how to track. I . . . I decided to practice his instructions today, Red Hawk. A delightful summer afternoon, would you not agree?" Sukey clasped her hands together in feigned innocence. "Truly, sir, I had no idea 'twas you who created the footprints."

Off to one side, bushes rustled.

"What was that?" she exclaimed, convinced that another man lurked nearby. "Is someone with you?"

" 'Twas nothing, madam. Only a westerly breeze from the Ohio River. You may be certain you would never have found me unless I allow it. I suggest you be more careful prowling these woods, madam. Men will soon be at war here. Should they find you alone in the forest, they will not view you with . . . proper dignity."

Another slight rustle disturbed the interwoven bushes. Sukey suspected human movement beneath those waving branches.

"Another breeze?" she asked dubiously. "Or perhaps a fox?"

Red Hawk nodded. "Just the wind, madam, I feel certain. Now, return the way you came. I shall watch to ensure that you strike the correct trail." He crossed his burly arms over his chest.

"But I . . . !"

"Now, madam."

Sukey planned to argue but Red Hawk's stern demeanor convinced her otherwise. Zeb, it appeared, was right. Not all tracked men cared to be found. Most likely Red Hawk's imposing block of a figure allowed someone else to . . . escape? Vanish into thin air?

But why?

Why would anyone deem it necessary to hide from Susannah Howard in the Allegheny forest? Was she truly at risk here? Or was Red Hawk more concerned about shielding someone else?

Testing her skirt, to be certain the dagger remained strapped to her thigh, and casting one last glance over her shoulder at the recently shimmering bushes, Sukey reluctantly turned back toward her father's trading post.

"Dear boy!" Regina exclaimed, watching her troubled nephew pace their lodge floor. "What has put you in such a state? Surely Mouceau's men have not—"

Rafe Stewart thundered his displeasure. "'Tis a woman, Aunt. Not the more predictable and manageable French."

"Ah! But of course," she smiled knowingly. "I should be willing to gamble that you crossed swords once again with the delectable Sukey Howard."

Stewart growled. "God's blood, Aunt! I vow, if I could lock that crazed woman up till this bedeviled war is over, I would."

Regina shook her head. "'Tis you who are bedeviled, Edward Rafe Stewart, far more than any war. Do you not see how much you adore Sukey?"

He shuddered. "Love? Aunt! That woman is a . . . a menace! Bloody hell, she shall have us all killed with her nonsense. She nearly stumbled upon me as I changed in the woods today."

"A clever woman, our Sukey. Are you her match, Edward?"

"And then some, Aunt!" he snarled.

"Two wild ponies, are you and Sukey Howard. A perfect match, I dare say. In your heart, Edward, you compare her to Isabel. But that is not fair to Sukey. Though beautiful and headstrong like your mother, Sukey lacks Isabel's . . . cruel insensitivity."

Staring at the kitchen fire, Stewart leaned his shoulder against the chinked-log wall. "Nay, Aunt. I disagree most vehemently. The same cold-blooded vein runs through all women. Except you, of course."

"Not true, Edward, and you know 'tis so! When your mother abandoned you, and poor Thomas and Charles as well, you lost all trust in women. But you cannot allow Isabel to poison your entire life, else you shall die a lonely, embittered man."

A harsh light glittered in Knowles's eyes. "Lonely? Nay! Always, there shall be comely women willing to share my bed."

Regina shook her head. "Oh, Edward! 'Tis not the same at all. And you fool no one with your prattle, not even your own troubled self. One day soon, you shall finally love and trust a woman enough to make her your wife. Betting woman that I am, dear boy, I wager that special woman to be Sukey Howard."

"Hypocrite!" He lit his pipe from the kitchen fireplace. "Fiercely have you guarded your single status all these years since Uncle Rupert died. Even so, you dare preach marriage to me?"

"My situation is entirely different," she sniffed.

"Quite!" He waggled his fingers at Regina. "Shall we attempt to count the number of times I flushed you and Fitch out of the bushes?"

"Different, I repeat, Edward. Besides, Fitch and I may yet surprise you one of these days."

A curl of smoke rose above his pipe. "Believe what you like about Sukey Howard and me, Aunt. It matters not one jot. More important, that audacious woman might jeopardize our entire operation. We have no more than two days at most to discover what has become of French troop reinforcements." He paced restlessly. " 'Tis vital for us to learn whether those men were called back to protect French forts along the St. Lawrence, or . . ."

"Or whether they in fact hover near Fort Duquesne even as we speak." Regina nodded in comprehension. "I have a plan, Edward."

He grimaced. "God save us all from your plans."

"I shall ignore your unwarranted—well, near-unwarranted—and contemptuous attitude, my boy. Here is my plan. You may thank me later." Regina rubbed her forehead with the back of her hand and moaned. "I feel the advent of one of my spells. In fact, the most bodaciously sinister spell ever to torment my frail constitution."

"You? Frail?" he bellowed in disbelief.

"I shall beg Sukey to come minister to me in my helpless, pain-wracked state. Meanwhile—"

Regina gestured toward her nephew.

"Ah, I see. Unburdened from the meddling Mrs. Howard, Red Hawk and I shall prowl along the Allegheny River and determine the exact position of those French troops. It might work, Aunt. If that is, you truly can keep Mrs. Howard out of our hair. My turn to ask you . . . are you indeed her match?"

Opening her painted fan to cool her perspiring brow, Regina grinned triumphantly. "Edward, dear boy, I shall not let you down."

Chapter Thirteen

"Your kindness, my dear Mrs. Howard, surpasses the most compassionate angel in all the heavens!" Sir Edward Knowles gushed, gesturing dramatically with outswept arms.

Rosy embarassment pinked Sukey's cheeks. "Your superlative praise is unnecessary, Sir Edward. How could any decent person refuse your request?" She busied herself tying up a cloth satchel.

"Poor Regina!" Rachel shook her head. "Imagine! Driven to her sick bed by one of those dreadfully malevolent attacks. And at the very same time Sir Edward and Fitch need urgently to travel upriver on trading business."

Wringing his hands, Knowles sighed audibly. "Quite! The very thought of abandoning dear Aunt in her desperate hour of need filled me with lamentation, I can assure you, ladies."

"Calm yourself, Sir Edward," Sukey chided. "I shall be assiduous in my attentions to Regina." She fought back a smile. Sukey welcomed this unexpected opportunity to explore Knowles's den of spies. With judicious scrutiny, she might discover a clue carelessly dropped by Knowles, or Fitch, or even Regina.

"Ah! Doubtless you ladies surmise my intense relief that Mrs. Howard has so graciously agreed to hover by

Aunt's side and rescue us both . . . as she has so frequently done in the past, I might add."

Sukey tucked dried sprigs of ginseng and pennyroyal in her satchel, tied her bonnet strings, and kissed Rachel goodbye. Rachel, she noted, seemed to smile more broadly than necessary.

With Adam snuggled in her arms, Rachel escorted her sister to the door. "You must not worry about a thing, Sukey. We shall all manage quite well. I beg of you, take all the time you need with poor ailing Regina!" She beamed at Knowles, busy outside harnessing Sukey's horse.

"Contain your joy, Rachel, I beg of you. 'Tis nothing more than a mission of mercy."

"Pa will be so pleased, Sukey! That you rendered assistance to Sir Edward's aunt, that is," Rachel called out, waving goodbye.

Settling into her saddle, Sukey comprehended Rachel's intent and glared back at her sister. "Will my family," she muttered under her breath, "never desist from their foolish attempts to marry me off?"

Towering white pines quivered in the morning air as Knowles, on horseback, led Sukey up the first incline west of Turtle Creek.

"Your . . . urgent business upriver, Sir Edward," she called to him. "Might you share some details with me about such an imperative venture?"

His unsmiling face darkened. "I could not bear to weary your amiable self with tiresome details of trade, madam."

A ruse! It had to be, she reasoned. Knowles was no more meeting with tradesman than with the King of England! He was about to reconnoiter with French officers streaming down the Allegheny Valley. A stunning opportunity for him to tell them everything he knew about British army plans!

He had not counted on Regina's illness to complicate his ill-conceived plans, though. Now Knowles relied on Sukey to save the day. "I shall save the day, all right," she whispered to herself, "but not in the same fashion that ogre imagines."

Spy, or fop, the despicable Sir Edward Knowles would never lie in Sukey Howard's bed, despite Eli Whitfield's ham-fisted prompts. Of that much she was certain!

Loose stones cobbled the next hill's descent. One of them caught in the hoof of Knowles's stallion. Halting to examine his mount, Knowles frowned.

"I fear my horse is lame, Mrs. Howard. He cannot be ridden." Knowles strode over toward Sukey's mount.

Sukey's eyes widened. "Sir! Surely you do not think. . . !"

"My horse is lame, Mrs. Howard." He reached for her saddle.

"Then walk, sir! I assure you, we cannot ride together on the same horse. It . . . it would not be proper."

"You mean that in such close quarters you cannot control yourself, madam?"

Astonished, she stared open-mouthed at Knowles. His expression betrayed nothing but apparent innocence.

"A saddle is scarcely a marital bed, madam."

Sukey clutched her reins tightly. "Bed or saddle— you shall share neither with me, sir!"

Knowles's left eyebrow arched. "Since we first met, madam, you stoutly proclaimed you have nothing to fear from me. Would you now condemn a weak, harmless wretch like myself to walk several miles over these hills on a hot summer day . . . while you ride in relative comfort?"

Something about Knowles's enigmatic expression gave her pause. No, he bore no smile. But . . . did she only imagine it? A sparkle of amusement seemed to lurk deep within his blue eyes. She patted the knife bulge at her thigh, then nervously readjusted her straw hat.

"Very well. But I shall control the horse, you understand, Sir Edward?"

"Oh, quite, madam. And you shall control me as well, for I live in daily fear of your temper and rigid sense of discipline." He swung his leg up over her horse and settled behind Sukey in the saddle.

They rode in silence for a quarter of a mile.

Somehow, Sukey noticed, the red trilliums were more showy this day, the sweet cicely more fragrant. Tiny, needle-beaked hummingbirds darted into welcoming folds of campion and cardinals flashed their ebullient red from hickory limbs.

Despite her concentration on forest drama, Sukey sensed the growing warmth of Knowles's chest and strong legs pressed around her own stern figure. His large hands covered hers as he caught at the reins. The cove of his chest felt almost comforting.

Dear God! A repulsive fop at best, was Edward Knowles, she scolded herself! At worst, a treacherous spy. She wanted no part of the ogre. None whatsoever.

Suddenly she felt his mouth lightly brush her nape. "I beg your pardon!" she exclaimed.

"And I, yours, madam." His voice was deeper than usual. "But an insect lay poised ready to sting your delicate throat. Since my hands were already occupied—fearfully clinging to your reins that is, madam—I was forced to use my mouth. Only to protect your delicate skin, you understand."

"I understand nothing of the sort! Do not force me to teach you an ugly lesson, Sir Edward."

She heard his sudden intake of breath as he tightened his arms around her.

"Mrs. Howard, in truth, I relish each and every lesson you teach me. The cultured ones, and yes . . . even the ugly ones."

An unexplained urgency tinged Knowles's voice, now lower tuned and noticeably bolder.

Sukey stirred inside his arms. An unwilling prisoner of sorts, she was! Still, she felt her mutinous heart begin to race. Warmth suffused her cheeks. Moisture beads formed at her hairline.

"Mercy!" Sukey exclaimed, fanning the sticky air with her hand. "This June sun seems far hotter than usual."

"Quite right, madam. I, too, feel unusually warm." Knowles's mouth lingered scarcely a hair's breath from Sukey's ear. His arms drew tighter around her waist.

For one brief moment, she allowed herself to luxuriously lean back against his chest. No! At the very least, the man was a self-absorbed dandy who lived only for his next set of elegant clothes. More likely, Knowles maintained a secret treacherous life meant to undo England's American stronghold.

She sat bolt upright.

"Sir, a gentleman does not grip a lady so tightly."

"No?" Knowles whistled softly. "I beg of you, madam, to educate me in the ways of men and women. Pray, then, how should a gentleman grip a lady?"

She pushed against the knuckles of his hand, wrapped tightly around her waist. "A gentleman does not grip a lady at all, sir! Not a proper gentleman."

"I see. Most enlightening, madam. But . . ."

"There are no 'buts,' sir."

"Oh, madam, I cannot thank you enough for teaching me the proper manner in which men and women should, well, touch one another. Still, only suppose that the woman was not . . . a proper lady."

Additional heat flamed Sukey's cheeks. A sultry suggestion lurked somewhere in Knowles's husky voice, she was convinced. "I could not possibly know, sir, as I am at all times a proper lady." Her spine stiffened despite the horse's jounce.

Knowles shifted his hips. "Perhaps we should dismount, madam, to allow our horses a drink from that stream, yonder."

She glanced over at a setting far too romantic for her inner warnings. A graceful waterfall, framed by delicate fern sprays, tumbled from a rock face speckled with lush miniature wildflowers. Secretive trees shielded the entire scene. Just what amorous intentions, she wondered, did Knowles have in mind? Worse, in such a glorious setting, was there a chance she might succumb to the treacherous ogre?

She tipped her chin upward. "My horse can quite adequately drink while we remain mounted, sir. We must not dally. Your poor infirm aunt awaits us."

As they approached Knowles's lodge, Sukey noticed unfamiliar horses tethered to the porch railing.

" 'Twould appear you and Regina have visitors, Sir Edward."

Knowles dismounted. His eyes became wary slits as he eased Sukey off her horse and approached his own front door.

"Monsieur Knowles! Always a pleasure, *mon ami*," a French-accented male voice bellowed from within. "Monsieur Margry and I were passing by and decided to pay you and your amiable aunt a social call. To our delight, we have the added reward of seeing Madame Howard as well."

At the sight of Sukey, Charlevoix Mouceau stood taller and flicked imaginary road dust from his shirt front.

Regina's gaze travelled rapidly from Mouceau's eager, shining face, to that of Knowles. She shared a silent nod with her nephew.

"Sukey, my dear, you have no idea how glad I am to see you!" Regina exclaimed. "Do come sit by my side and comfort me with your presence." She made a show of re-arranging chairs, in the process distancing Mouceau from Sukey.

Knowles, Sukey noted, appeared strained.

"Sir Edward," she began, pretending to be helpful, "I feel certain you long to embark on your business journey upriver. You need not tarry one moment longer here. I shall devote my full attention to restoring Regina's good health."

"Eh?" Mouceau asked, raising his eyebrow. "You . . . have business upriver, Monsieur Knowles?" He rubbed his chin. "'Tis not wise at this time for Englishmen to be . . . visible along the Allegheny River."

Knowles hesitated. Suddenly his lace sleeve cuffs fluttered in the afternoon air as he waved dramatically and tittered. "Ah, Captain Mouceau, you misunderstand, my dear fellow. I have a social call to pay, north of here. That is all, I assure you. Just a gentleman's call. You know how I do so love to pass a day in cordial conversation with high-born gentlemen, such as yourself."

Sukey gaped. "But you said . . . ?"

Instantly, Regina reached for Sukey's hand and moaned. "Oh! The pain returns! A blessing that you choose to stay close by my side, dear child. Even with my affliction, however, I could not possibly permit Edward to be so rude as to depart while our valued French guests are here, Sukey. You understand, my dear."

But Sukey did not.

She glanced from stern French faces to Sir Edward's tight expression, then to Regina's pinched jollity. Something was happening here in this lodge that mightily perplexed Sukey. Somehow, she intended to learn the truth underlying it all.

When, late in the afternoon, Mouceau and Margry at last departed, Knowles abruptly reached for his satchel.

"Poor dear Regina!" Sukey exclaimed. "Surely the afternoon's events have exhausted you. Come, I shall assist you back into bed."

"Most kind of you, Sukey. Let me kiss my dear nephew goodbye, while . . . while you turn down the bedcovers."

Tidying Regina's bedding, Sukey overheard low whispers.

"Do be careful, Edward. Each additional day here places you in ever greater danger."

Knowles's voice dropped to an unintelligible buzz.

So! She was right!

Sir Edward Knowles—and Regina—were not what they seemed! But no Englishman would believe Sukey without evidence. Perhaps here, in the snakes' very own den, she would find what she needed to prove their guilt.

At considerable risk to her own life!

Leaning against the doorjamb, where she stood eavesdropping, Sukey exhaled. For England, she reminded herself. For . . .

"Sukey? You wish something?" quizzed a suddenly appearing Regina. "Perhaps a farewell to Edward?"

"Uh, yes. Yes, as a matter of fact." Sukey quickly collected her thoughts.

"Sweet of you, my dear. But Edward has dashed off in somewhat of a hurry, I fear. The dear boy has always been a bit hasty and impetuous."

"So it would seem. Are you ready, Regina?"

The plump-hipped woman blinked. "Ready? For what, child?"

"For your nap. I turned down your bedcovers."

"My nap? Oh, yes! Yes, of course. How thoughtful of you, Sukey, dear."

"I shall make you some mountain tea to soothe your weary nerves."

"Mountain tea?" Mulling over the term, Regina deliberated a moment as she approached her bed. "Unfamiliar to me, I fear. Pray, what constitutes 'mountain tea?'"

Sukey assumed an expression of total innocence. "Er, in fact, I do not know, Regina. But a Mingo squaw once taught Rachel how to gather the appropriate leaves, known to induce a state of supreme relaxation akin to sleep. Rachel gave me a sack of the dried mix, some of which I brought along today."

"I see. Most gracious of your dear sister, Sukey. However, I really do not feel the need for—"

Tipping Regina down in bed, Sukey patted her shoulder while plumping two pillows. "Tut, tut. Under my care, Regina, your dreadful malady shall vanish. In no time, I assure you, you shall rejoice with new found health and vigor."

She returned shortly with a steaming mug of herbal tea. And held it out for her "patient."

Regina's dubious gaze switched from Sukey's face, to the steaming cup of pale tea, then back to her caregiver's smiling visage. "Somehow, I feel better already," she murmured, raising the cup to her mouth.

"Shall I hold the cup for you, Regina?"

"No! I mean . . . I shall savor this delicious tea while you go out to the kitchen and pour yourself a cup."

"Can I do anything to make you more comfortable?"

"I believe you have done quite enough already, dear Sukey. Ah, yes. Only a few sips of your marvelous mountain tea and already I feel encroaching sleep. I shall simply lie back on these down pillows, close my eyes, and allow delicious rest to overcome me."

With one last pat to Regina's arm, Sukey tiptoed from the bedroom, which adjoined the lodge's kitchen. She waited until soft snoring sounds emanated from her apparently sleeping patient.

'Tis here somewhere in this cottage, she thought, glancing high and low. The precise piece of evidence she needed to prove Sir Edward Knowles's identity as a French spy. Most likely, Regina's and Fitch's, as well. A heaven-blessed opportunity to search now, she thought, with Knowles and Fitch absent and Regina drugged into a deep sleep.

She prowled the oblong room which served as both kitchen and parlor. Nothing! Not so much as a shred of paper or article of clothing to betray its occupants. Knowles was clever and careful, as well as dangerous.

Sighing, Sukey nibbled anxiously on her lower lip. No one would believe her bizarre accusations without some semblance of proof.

She studied the kitchen once more. Only one additional room adjoined this area—Regina's cramped bedroom. Knowles and Fitch slept on rope beds at the kitchen's far end.

Her eyes narrowed.

Knowles's sleeping area. It had to be!

Gliding noiselessly toward Sir Edward's cot, she studied the immediate area. Between the two crude beds was a small table with basin and a water jug. A trace of

Knowles's cologne lingered on an embroidered frock coat folded neatly atop a rough chest of drawers.

Cautiously, Sukey pulled open the thin top drawer.

Inside lay pots of his thick white face powder and red cheek-rouge. Strange, she thought, touching them, that he would not have taken all this with him. Perhaps he forgot them.

She froze at the sound of a slight noise!

Nothing. Must have been her imagination.

Sukey reached for the second drawer of the maple chest, just as a shriek and clatter arose from the next room. She dashed over to find her patient sprawled on the floor.

"Regina! Whatever has—!"

Clutching her forehead, Regina wailed. "A dream, dear Sukey! A dreadful dream that fair frightened me with its menacing intensity."

"Oh, poor Regina! Here, let me help you back into bed."

The older woman clung to Sukey's arm with both hands. "This malady plays such naughty tricks with my mind, dear child. Oh, promise me you will not leave me, even for a moment, till it fully subsides."

"Well, I—"

"Promise, Sukey!" Regina's hands trembled as she spoke. "Drag Fitch's cot in here, in my own room, and stay with me even as I sleep. Your gracious presence will stave off the demons of my dreams, I feel certain."

"You are convinced that will calm you?"

"Oh, yes! More than you can possibly know, my child. Just until Edward returns, which hopefully shall be in a day. Or two. Surely my malady will abate by then, under your tender ministrations."

Next evening, they shared a cold supper of venison pie and cider outdoors.

"Regina, it pleases me so to see your health improving. The fresh outdoor air does justice to your complexion."

Regina took another bite of meat pie. "Splendid idea of yours to picnic out here, my dear. Bear in mind, however, that I am prone to relapses, so I must beg of you—what is it, my dear? What do you see that alarms you so?"

Sukey stared hard at a high ridge choked with staghorn sumac and witch hazel. Her eyes widened. "Upon my word, Regina! 'Tis Fitch, on horseback!"

"Delightful! Edward returns even earlier than anticipated."

Sukey peered more intently. "No. It does not appear to be Sir Edward in discussion with Fitch. 'Tis a man clad in buckskins. He—" Rising from the fallen tree which served as her bench, Sukey took several tentative steps toward the distant men.

A faint cry escaped her lips. "Rafe! But why ever would he be chatting with Fitch?" She took another step forward.

"Rafe!" She cried, waving her arms to attract his attention.

Watching this reaction, Regina abruptly clutched at her own bodice. "My breathing grows labored! Sukey, please, I beg of you, come help me back to the lodge."

Moments later, Fitch appeared at the door, followed closely by Rafe Stewart.

"Madam," the servant announced, "his business completed, your nephew remains upriver on a social call. He sent me back with instructions to stay close by your side, to render aid as needed." Turning his head aside, the servant seemed overwhelmed by a strangely sudden coughing fit.

"And, uh, who might this stranger be?" Regina inquired, nodding in Stewart's direction.

Balling her hands into fists, Sukey fought to keep from touching Rafe's thick-muscled arms. "Regina, may I present Mr. Rafe Stewart? An old friend. An old family friend, that is," she hastened to add, beaming with joy at seeing Stewart once again. "But, Fitch, how did you . . . ?"

Recovered from his coughing attack, Fitch composed himself long enough to explain. "My, ah, horse shied at the scent of a bear and tossed me. Mr. Stewart kindly fetched my wretched runaway animal and assisted me back here."

"Remarkably kind of you, Mr. Stewart," Regina commented, her smile a bit more sly than usual. "Sukey, might I presume on you to set out a cold supper for the gentlemen?"

"Cold ham and cheese remains in the springhouse, Regina. I shall fetch some."

Stewart's mouth twitched. "I shall help, Mrs. Howard."

Regina raised an eyebrow. "Quite thoughtful of you, indeed, Mr. Stewart. But perhaps you ought to rest from your . . ."

"My arms are a tad weary, Regina," Sukey interjected, wide-eyed with feigned innocence. "Indeed, I welcome Mr. Stewart's able assistance. This way, sir. The springhouse lies down below the next hill."

Straight-faced, Sukey walked outdoors alongside the rough, buckskin-clad frontiersman. "I have missed you, Mr. Stewart," she whispered playfully, scarcely able to conceal her emotions. "Mr. Stewart?"

He spoke not a word as he strolled briskly.

She glanced sidewise at him. "Mr. Stewart? Have you nothing at all to say for yourself?" She caught at his large hand with her own slender fingers.

He jolted at her touch. Dark-faced, tense-mouthed, he

remained silent as his long strides picked up speed ahead of her.

Annoyed at Stewart's reticence, Sukey thrust her chin skyward. "I understand your hunger after spending a long day on the trail, Rafe Stewart. But you and I are scarcely strangers. Would it pain you so to affect even a modicum of civility towards me?"

Scowling, he glared briefly at her before ducking beneath a huge sycamore limb and continuing on toward the springhouse. A grass-covered knoll led downhill. He descended five stone steps to the springhouse doorway, then turned to await Sukey.

"Rude man!" she fumed, menacing him with an angry stare as she tiptoed down the limestone steps. "Uncouth, rude, barbaric, unpleasant, surly, vulgar, coarse . . . !"

He leaned one arm against the doorjamb while enduring her tirade. "Are you quite finished blathering, Mrs. Howard?"

"Blathering?" Her eyes flashed with fury.

"Or can we now expand your discussion about hunger, and include all its various forms?" A faint smile teased his lips.

She shook her fist at him. "You are a beast! Get your own damned supper, and never darken my doorstep again!" She turned to leave.

"Never, Sukey?"

She paused. A gravelled catch in that low male voice made her squeeze her eyes shut and tremble.

Suddenly he swung her up into his arms and carried her inside the cool, damp springhouse.

"Fie on you, Rafe Stewart, you wretched creature!" she shouted, thumping her fist against his chest while flailing her legs.

Still carrying Sukey, he secured her mouth with a lingering kiss.

Her body softened. "Fie on you . . ." she murmured.

He set her down. Pressing her slender frame against the smooth slab walls with his own brawn, Stewart cradled her head in his hands.

"Woman, I have missed you."

She waited, disbelieving, with her hands pressed to her sides.

He kissed her mouth. Sensuously, his tongue tasted her lips. "Each day, darling Sukey, I find it more difficult to live without you."

Eyes wide, she stared up at him. "Fie . . ." she whispered, her voice nearly inaudible.

Parting her lips with his tongue, he revelled in being inside her. His kiss deepened. His breathing accelerated. "I love you, Sukey. Though God knows, you are more ferocious and troublesome than any she-bear with young."

Fighting back a smile at his confession, she slid her arms upward across his chest. Her hands lingered on the breadth of Stewart's shoulders before threading up through his coarse dark hair.

"'Tis cool in here," she murmured. "A welcome relief from the stifling heat outside."

"Nay, Sukey, love. My passion for you rages red hot." His mouth explored the silken curve of her cheek. "It can never be quelled by the chill of a springhouse." His lips teased her ear lobe. At the sound of her moan, he bent down and kissed her mouth again.

She leaned back. "I tremble for your safety, Rafe. Why will you not allow me to help you?"

"Safety? 'Tis the very reason, my delicate feminine angel."

"Rafe! I am not delicate."

His hands moved gently down across Sukey's breasts before resting on her waist. "But you are a woman. Sukey, I shall be fortunate, indeed, to live through this month. I have no intention of placing your life in danger, as well as mine."

She tuggedd impatiently on the fringes of his soft leather hunting shirt. "Why must you risk your life, Rafe? Surely nothing can be that important."

Eyes suddenly blazing, Stewart tensed his jaw. "I have a personal score to settle with Charlevoix Mouceau. And a job to do for the British army."

"I could not bear it, Rafe, if you were to be harmed. I . . . I love you."

Silently, he stared down at her.

"'Tis true, my darling, though you be a heartless, mysterious wretch who vanishes from my sight at every opportunity." She stood on her bare toes and kissed the corners of his mouth. "Please let me help you, Rafe."

He remained adament. "Stay out of this, Sukey. A beautiful woman like yourself would be torn to pieces by those French jackals."

Batting her eyes fetchingly at him, she kissed him full on the mouth. Her tongue traced a light path across his lips.

Stewart grunted. "This will buy you precisely nothing, my girl."

Her dimples deepened. "For shame, Mr. Stewart! Whatever makes you think I have ulterior motives?"

"Wicked wench. I know your game," he growled. "You mean to play on a man's fondness for feminine affection. You shall fail, I assure you." Still, his hands tightened their grasp of Sukey's waist.

She tickled his lower lip with her tongue. "Nay, Mr. Stewart. Men are weak. Easily conquered by a determined woman."

He felt her stir restlessly within his arms. His breathing came faster. "Madam, you play foolish games with a grown man. 'Tis men who conquer women. Or resist wenches, should a man choose."

Slipping her arms around his neck, Sukey nibbled Stewart's ear lobe. She pressed her hips firmly against the bulge of his manhood. "Resist? Is that what you shall choose this lovely July evening, Mr. Stewart?"

His tongue snaked across his parched mouth.

Exhaling a protracted sigh, Stewart suddenly lifted Sukey onto a flat stone ledge inside the springhouse. Now she stood eye to eye with him. Kissing her as he moved, Stewart hoisted Sukey's linen skirt and shift up to her hips.

She deftly reached inside his leather breeches and freed his engorged manhood.

"Ah, Sukey!" he growled, closing his eyes to the pleasure of her touch. He buried his face in her soft cleavage. One at a time, he savored the sweet rosiness of her nipples, till her escalating cries begged for satisfaction.

In searching thrusts, he eased into her moistness as Sukey leaned back against a cool stone wall.

Standing upright, she rode his masculinity. In delicious waves of squeezing and relaxing, she journeyed to a paradise of light and sound and body nectar that made her heart pound unbearably fast.

Till she cried out with sweet release as Stewart exploded inside her.

They clung to each other, still standing upright, as he kissed her throat. With her arms still laced around Stewart's neck, she nestled her face into his chest. "I have never . . . Ah, Rafe, you teach me new and wonderful things all the time."

Cupping her cheek with his hand, Stewart nuzzled

Sukey's pale throat. "The lessons, my sweet, have only just begun. And to achieve excellence, they require devoted practice." He playfully tugged at her ear lobe with his teeth. "But for now, I fear those two very proper English—Regina and Fitch—will wonder what became of us."

Sukey made an effort to smooth her rumpled skirt. "They really are quite pleasant, Rafe. Except—"

Tucking his shirt back inside his breeches, Stewart studied her frown. "Except what, my girl?"

"Promise you will not laugh."

He hesitated. "I promise nothing of the kind."

Sukey bent to fill an earthenware bowl with cheese and sliced ham from the springhouse for Stewart's supper. "Then I shall not reveal my suspicions." She turned to leave.

He caught her arm. "Sukey? What troubles you about those two straitlaced English?"

"I . . I think they might be spies."

A gargled sound emerged from Stewart's throat. "Spies? Those two dolts?"

She nodded. "And Sir Edward Knowles, Regina's nephew."

Stewart's eyes widened. "British spies?"

"No. Not that easy. I believe they are skillful, treacherous French spies."

Goggle-eyed, he struggled to mouth the words. And failed.

"I think they meet with the French and share details of General Braddock's troop movement up from Cumberland."

"Have you told anyone of these suspicions?"

"No. Do you think it time I should?"

He held up his hands in a defensive gesture. "No, my love!" he bellowed. "Most definitely not. 'Twould only imperil your safety. Besides, quite possibly you are mistaken. Keep these thoughts to yourself till I can locate a proper British soldier for you to contact."

He took the bowl from her hands.

"Now, my love . . . er, Mrs. Howard, shall we rejoin the flighty Mrs. Ramsey and her humorless servant? By now, they likely distrust our actions far more than we do theirs." Stewart paused on a stone step leading from the springhouse. "One last reminder, Mrs. Howard. Be cautious at every turn. These are treacherous times in which we live."

Chapter Fourteen

Rafe Stewart wiped vestiges of the cold ham from his mouth with the back of his hand.

"Most gracious of you to offer me hospitality, Mrs. Ramsey," he commented, rising from a wooden kitchen bench. "I understand you are ailing, ma'am, so I shall trouble you no further."

Sukey lurched from her seat to follow him outside, but Fitch quickly intervened, blocking Sukey's exit.

"With your consent, Mrs. Ramsey," the servant intoned, "I shall escort Mr. Stewart to a comfortable niche in the barn for the night."

"Certainly, Fitch," Regina agreed with a nod.

Stewart ambled toward the door. "Thank you again, ladies, for your tender kindness to me this evening." He glanced first at Regina, then a more lingering silent salute to Sukey. "I bid you leave, now, as I shall ride off early tomorrow morning, likely before you rise."

Sukey's eyes flared.

Regina glanced at Sukey, poised anxiously by the door, before viewing unspoken signals from Stewart.

"Ah, my dear Sukey!" she burst out suddenly. "I fear another frightful episode bears down upon my frail constitution. I shall be exquisitely grateful for your calming presence close by my side every minute of this night."

"But . . . !" Sukey choked back her intended words.

"No need to inconvenience yourself on Mr. Stewart's account, madam," Fitch insisted, gently steering Sukey back from the front door.

"Nor would I wish to trouble Mrs. Howard," Stewart concurred, grinning as he stepped outside. "She has done quite enough already."

Fitch's expression darkened. "I shall assist our guest in bedding down for the night, Mrs. Howard. Thus, you may feel completely free to attend Madam Ramsey's needs."

Sukey's shoulders sagged.

"Dear child!" Regina exclaimed, clapping her pudgy hands together. "You possess a healing touch. Surely you were sent down to earth to nurse the infirm. None could be more grateful than I. Come, Sukey, let us retire to my bedroom. I feel certain your reading to me will calm my ravaged nerves."

Forlorn, Sukey watched Rafe disappear out the door with Fitch. The very minute Regina lapsed into sleep, Sukey vowed, she would slink off to Rafe Stewart's bedchamber of straw and snuggle against his warm, burly body.

Night shadows crept over Sukey's shoulder as she turned another page of "*Dr. Virgil Slugbetter's Essays on Women's Proper Decorum.*"

"One more chapter, I beg of you, Sukey, dear," Regina pleaded. "The knots of pain in my weary back loosen, one by one, with every page you read."

"More?" Sukey yawned again.

"Only one more chapter, please! Like soothing medicine to the infirm is your gentle-voiced reading, my dear."

Sukey's eyelids felt heavy.

The very minute . . . she vowed once more with yet another yawn. If only poor frightened, ailing Regina would lapse into a deep slumber. For some reason though, this particular night, Regina seemed unable to sleep.

Or unwilling.

Still reading aloud, Sukey crept onto her own cot, lined up beside Regina's bed.

"Another page, please, Sukey! Just . . . just one more."

Waking to the sound of a noisy rooster, Sukey jolted upright. Morning sunlight peeped across the cramped bedroom she shared with Regina. The plump woman's still-sleeping form lay sprawled and snoring on her own tick-covered straw mattress bed.

"Perhaps he is still . . . !" Sukey murmured under her breath. In her bare feet, and still fully dressed from last evening, she slipped out to the barn.

"Rafe!" she called softly, wishing for another embrace from the man she loved. But a hasty perusal of the barn's stalls and loft revealed nothing. Nothing, that is, till she discovered the lone empty stall, with its telltale sculpted-out straw mound, where Rafe Stewart had apparently spent the night.

Sukey needed to touch that same straw. Needed to feel Rafe's lingering warmth. Had to breathe in any trace of his stimulating male aroma and share the earth with his vital presence just one brief moment before it vanished again.

She knelt into the straw mound, scooped a pile of it in her hands, and inhaled. In the process, a small hard object in the golden straw scraped her palm.

Brushing back clipped hollow strands, Sukey sought the offending article.

"A ring!" she exclaimed. And not just any ring. Nor was it a ring she had ever seen Rafe Stewart wear. "I have seen someone wear the very same ring."

She pondered a moment.

"Of course! It belongs to Sir Edward Knowles!"

"Madam!" Fitch's stern voice sliced through the dawn mists.

His unannounced arrival startled Sukey into a stutter. "G-good morning, Fitch. I . . . I wanted to see if our guest cared for . . . for breakfast. But apparently he has already departed."

"You found something, madam?"

"Found something? Ah, yes! Indeed." She opened her clenched fist to reveal the masculine ring. "Though truly I think it must belong to Sir Edward, and not to Mr. Stewart."

Fitch studied it. "Indeed, madam. The master's signet ring. He will be most grateful you found it. Thank you. Now, madam, Mrs. Ramsey has sent me to fetch you for breakfast."

To her dismay, that morning Sukey found nothing to indictate the activities of Sir Edward, Regina, or Fitch. She chafed under the close scrutiny of Fitch and Regina . . . until the surprise appearance of late-afternoon guests.

"Madame Howard!" Captain Charlevoix Mouceau gushed, as he flicked imaginary lint from the shoulder of his pearl-grey uniform. "Monsieur Margry and I could no longer restrain our concern over poor ailing Madame Ramsey. And of course, you, Madame Howard!" The tips of Mouceau's greasy moustache twitched as he focused hard on Sukey. "Here all alone, without Sir Edward to properly protect you. Tsk. How this troubles us!"

Regina waved her embroidered handkerchief at the Frenchmen. "Ah, dear Captain Mouceau! You, sir, are entirely too kind. You may be comforted to learn that my servant, Fitch, returned to watch over us."

Mouceau's moustache drooped. "*Oui*, madame. To be

sure." His eyes darted nervously toward Fitch, then back to contemplate Sukey's ample bosom.

Thumbs thrust into his leather belt, Margry stomped boldly into the center of Regina's long kitchen. "We hear that the ruffian, Rafe Stewart, has been sighted near here. Perhaps even emerging from your own lodge."

For a brief instant, fire blazed from Regina's eyes. Her good humor quickly returned. "Why, my dear sirs, is it possible? Can my poor humble household merit French surveillance?"

Grabbing Margry by the sleeve, Mouceau scowled. "I shall handle this, Margry, you dolt! *Non*, madame," he announced, turning toward Regina. "Your lodge is not under French surveillance."

"But Rafe Stewart is?" Sukey asked.

Mouceau's eyelids narrowed to slits. "A dangerous man is Rafe Stewart, Madame Howard, to be avoided at all costs." He leaned tight against Sukey's side. His gaze travelled from her face to the trim laces restraining her bodice. "But then, madame, you have naught to fear. I have come here to . . . protect you from that swine."

"Mrs. Howard is a fortunate woman, indeed, Captain Mouceau," a male voice boomed from the doorway.

"Sir Edward!" the French commander exclaimed, blinking nervously. "A pleasure to see you again, monsieur," he added contemptuously, chewing back a sneer.

With a flourish of his ruffled sleeve, Knowles bowed low. "My dear Captain Mouceau! It cheers me so to know that, in my absence, you took it upon yourself to guard my beloved *fiancée* and aunt. All this, despite your busy schedule of military affairs."

Sukey swept back from Mouceau. Puzzled, she studied Knowles and the French commander. An apparent air of tension sizzled between the two men. But why?

Surely not because of her!

Perhaps Sir Edward Knowles, in his role as a French spy, had provoked Mouceau's ire by not delivering sufficient information to the French.

Knowles reached for his snuff box and took a pinch, before turning to Mouceau. "This villain, Stewart, monsieur, what has he done to so arouse your ire?"

An agitated Margry could scarcely contain himself. "Displayed uncommon arrogance in the face of French edicts, Monsieur Knowles! Rafe Stewart and his brother, Thomas, two braggart British traders, claimed French lands along the Allegheny River for their own."

"Just two lone men, monsieur?" Sukey asked. "Surely a mere two men could not pose any threat to the French army."

"The Stewarts are no ordinary men," Margry insisted. "Born trouble-makers, more like it. Mean-spirited wretches! They foment resistance wherever they travel. Thomas is likely dead, but that scoundrel, Rafe . . . ! He has been spotted in this vicinity."

Mouceau stared hard at a French soldier waiting outside, then slowly circled Knowles. "Monsieur Stewart is known to assume a variety of disguises. Curiously enough, Monsieur Knowles, Margry feels at times, and in certain light, that you bear something of a resemblance to Rafe Stewart."

Hearing Mouceau's words, Regina suddenly exploded with laughter. "Oh, my dear sirs! Today you cheered an infirm old woman with your blessed merriment. Only imagine! Confusing my poor effeminate, easily frightened nephew with a fierce mountain man!" She laughed heartily again.

"A gross miscalculation," Sukey agreed. "I can assure you from past experience, messieurs, that Sir Edward possesses not one fierce bone in his entire body. Why, he even trembles at the sight of spiders!"

Tittering, Knowles concurred, before exploding into a series of sneezes.

"God only knows, I have always tried to embolden Edward," Regina continued. "Alas, he . . . he will always be a weakling. A beautiful individual, of course. But a weakling, all the same."

Sukey nervously fingered her muslin apron. "Tell me, *messieurs*, what do you plan to do with Stewart should you find him?"

"Cut off his head!" Margry shouted.

Sukey flinched. "His head? Well, we shall indeed keep an eye out for the blackguard."

"Most wise, Madame Howard," Captain Mouceau advised her. "And pray, in the future, dear ladies, do not entertain strangers with your gracious hospitality."

Knowles sneezed again.

"Dear boy!" Regina cried. "You are ill! Let me have a look at you."

Mouceau, preparing to depart, managed to corner Sukey alone just outside the doorway. His fingers pecked at her sleeve in a would-be tickle.

"I despair that you have not paid me, er, us a visit at Fort Duquesne of late, Madame Howard."

Sukey swallowed hard. A fine line she traversed, in her effort to gain French information for England. Visit a French soldier she detested inside Fort Duquesne? An ogre who had lascivious plans for her body? Or remain safely tucked in her father's cabin?

The obvious answer unsettled Sukey.

Only inside Fort Duquesne—at great personal risk to herself—could Sukey glean vital reconnaissance information for General Braddock's approaching British army.

Too late to turn back now.

Once and for all, she would prove to Pa—and all of England—that a woman could equal any man in bravery. The added risk for a woman would only make Sukey's accomplishment more commendable. Her childhood terror? Those wretched flashing images of Ezekiel Richards's fumbling rape attempt in Lancaster? Sukey dare not think of that horror now.

She forced a smile at Charlevoix Mouceau.

"Monsieur, how kind of you to invite me. Since Mrs. Ramsey's health seems improved, I shall take you up on your offer tomorrow. Properly chaperoned, of course."

Mouceau's cold gray eyes narrowed. "But of course, madame. I shall see to it, myself. No need for you to trouble Sir Edward, especially since the poor man seems indisposed at the moment."

"I quite agree, monsieur."

"*Bonjour*, madame . . . until tomorrow." Once more, his fingers brushed her sleeve.

Sukey returned inside Knowles's lodge. She would say nothing to him and Regina about her plans with Mouceau. Something did not add up properly. She meant to find out why. To that end, she needed to keep silent about her plans.

Inside, Knowles sat by the kitchen fire while Regina applied a cool compress to his forehead. "Poor Edward!" she exclaimed to Sukey. "Seems to have incurred the ague while on his recent travels."

"A shame, indeed, Regina. But your own renewed spirits cheer me. Since you now seem fit to tend Sir Edward, I shall leave here on the morrow."

Knowles and his aunt glanced at one another, then stared at Sukey.

Knowles slid the cloth off his forehead. "Do you really think that wise, my dear Mrs. Howard?"

"Most certainly. You can regale us with tales of your travels tonight—that is, if you feel up to it, Sir Edward.

Then I shall return to my dear father's house tomorrow. Poor Pa likely misses me dreadfully."

Listening to Sukey's sugared inflection, Knowles shifted uneasily in his chair.

When she stepped outside, later, Knowles muttered to Regina, "The wench is up to another of her tricks, Aunt. But which one?"

Regina smiled. "Sukey Howard is your responsibility, Edward. And your abiding love, if you be honest."

He groaned. "This cannot be love, Aunt. 'Tis far too painful."

With a hearty laugh, Regina patted her nephew. "Then for absolute certainty, 'tis true love, my boy."

Sukey returned just in time to hear Regina laugh. "Ah, 'tis wonderful to hear your mirth again, Regina. Mercy, Sir Edward! Your . . . your face powder and rouge stains the cloth!"

He quickly replaced the cloth over much of his face.

"I fetched you some broth, Sir Edward, to tame your innards."

"Broth? To tame my . . . ah, Mrs. Howard! How thoughtful of you. Aunt mentioned your wondrous curative powers. I beg of you, madam, please hold my hand. I find it soothes the savage beast of this illness within me." His mouth twitched.

"Lie back in your chair, sir, and rest. You need warm broth far more than someone to hold your hand. Besides, I shall require both my hands to spoon the broth into your mouth."

Holding the cloth over his face, Knowles whimpered. "My dear *fiancée*, how shall I manage without your tender ministrations when you depart?"

Her green eyes flashed, before she offered another spoonful of broth. "I am not your *fiancée*, Sir Edward— now, or ever in the future! Drink your broth, at once!"

Impatiently, she tipped another spoonful into his mouth.

Knowles cringed. "Oh, fie! Once again I have angered you, Mrs. Howard. Pray tell me you will not discipline me. I do so dread your discipline, madam."

Sukey gritted her teeth. "You, sir, are a morbid coward!" Pausing to breathe deeply, she regained her composure. "Forgive me, Sir Edward. I should not have assailed you so. But truly, you must learn not to fear me—or any woman."

He sipped the broth. "You . . . You have not lost patience with me?"

"No," she answered, unsmiling.

"And you will stay on another day or two?"

"No."

Moaning, he clutched his head, then sneezed. "Ah, the misery!"

Sukey frowned in disgust. "Regina loves you dearly, sir. She can nurse you back to full health."

"But dear Mrs. Howard! 'Tis you who soothes me best of all." With his left hand, he raised the cloth above his forehead to peek at her.

His signet ring! The sight of Knowles's hand jogged Sukey's memory about the ring. "Tell me, Sir Edward, do you often frequent your stable?"

"Only to retrieve my horse. Fitch customarily performs stable chores."

"Hm. So I thought."

"Why do you ask?"

Just then, Fitch entered the kitchen with an armload of firewood. "I neglected to inform you, sir, that Mrs. Howard found your signet ring in the stable, this morning."

Knowles clicked his tongue. "Careless of me! Doubtless I dropped it when fetching my mount."

"But Sir Edward," Sukey pressed on, "the ring was buried deep in the straw of a stall not used for days. Except, that is, last night when Rafe—"

"The master is weary!" Fitch interrupted, suddenly appearing at her elbow. "Allow me to assist Sir Edward in preparing for bed."

Jolted by the servant's brusqueness, Sukey stepped back. "Quite," she responded.

Returning milk and butter to the springhouse that evening, she recalled Rafe Stewart's passionate and spontaneous lovemaking. She touched the cool stones where he'd stood . . . where he held her close. How she yearned for Stewart's warmth now!

And some answers. Her puzzled mind fretted over deepening intrigue.

Did Rafe steal Sir Edward's signet ring? What was the mysterious connection between Fitch and Rafe? Who could she trust . . . if anyone?

All she knew for certain was that she loved the evasive Rafe Stewart with all her heart. That she died of loneliness whenever he vanished.

Gathering her belongings to depart Knowles's lodge next morning, Sukey repeatedly fought with her auburn hair as she adjusted her mob cap. Turning, she caught Knowles studying her.

"You seem . . . uneasy, this morning, Mrs. Howard," he commented, before lapsing into a coughing spell. "Might it be that you dread returning to your father?"

She shook off his query. "Nonsense, Sir Edward. You completely misread my emotional state. I . . . I am eager to return home."

"Then perhaps you fear French encroachment on your ride. If that be the case, Mrs. Howard, I shall gladly accompany you to Eli's cabin." He blew his nose into a large handkerchief and coughed again.

She braced the air with her hands in a stern gesture. "I would not hear of it, Sir Edward. The current state of your health prevents you from leaving this lodge. And have you forgotten, sir, that you yourself have frequently stated I am fearless?"

"So I did," he answered grudgingly. "And so you are."

"The journey to my father's cabin holds no terror for me whatsoever. None!" She tied the ribbons of her straw hat under her chin.

Regina clasped Sukey's hand. "Then we must reluctantly bid you *adieu*, my dear, and send you on your way. Truly you were an angel of mercy, coming here to aid me in my needy hour."

After hugging Regina, Sukey shook Knowles's hand—less limp than usual, she thought—and hurriedly urged her horse beyond Knowles's dooryard.

Inside, he leaned by the cottage window and watched her ride off.

Regina made her own observations. "She switched course, Edward."

Fighting back a cough, he shook his head. "Fool woman. She rides into the face of disaster at every blasted opportunity."

"So it would seem, my boy. Then you agree she is headed straight for Fort Duquesne?"

" 'Twas written all over her beautiful, determined, dimpled face." His jaw tensed.

A sly smile puckered Regina's lips. "And why should this bother you, Edward?"

" 'Tis not love, Aunt, if that is what you are thinking!" he spat out. "The fool wench will not stop till she gets herself killed by those French devils. Or worse!" Knowles's expression darkened at the thought of those tortured images. He coughed again.

"You are an ill man, Edward. If you do not rest, you might be a dead one."

Knowles glared out the window where Sukey had vanished from his sight. "She rides straight into their waiting jaws, Aunt. I . . . must try to save her."

"As Sir Edward Knowles?"

He nodded. "Rafe Stewart would be shot on sight. And neither you nor Fitch have a plausible reason to visit Duquesne."

"They might be on to you, Edward. One way or another, this trip is incredibly dangerous for you."

"General Braddock is quite close. Perhaps within a day or two's march. I have done all I could for his army . . . except join them to fight, which I shall do shortly. I just dispatched Fitch with our last message to Braddock."

Regina caught his sleeve. "Only you cannot see how much you love Sukey Howard, Edward."

"Not love, Aunt. 'Tis a man's duty to watch over helpless women, 'tis all."

"Edward, do not allow Isabel's sins to poison your life. Your mother was weak and selfish. An untrustworthy creature. But Sukey Howard is brave, loyal, and . . . fiercely devoted to Rafe Stewart."

"I know."

In silence, he slipped into Knowles's clothing and coughed as he applied thick powder and rouge to his face.

Regina hugged Knowles, then wiped tears from her ruddy cheeks. "May God preserve you, dear Edward," she murmured as he strode out the door.

"*Bonjour*, Sergeant Nicolet!" Sukey called out, dismounting alongside Fort Duquesne's parade grounds. "Your wife, monsieur, is she hereabouts?"

"*Non*, madame." Nicolet tended Sukey's horse. "She went upriver this morning to help a trader's wife give birth."

Sukey clicked her tongue. "How disappointing! I mean, 'twas good of Madame Nicolet to go help another woman. But I had so hoped to visit with her."

A guttural male voice emerging from a barracks doorway interrupted them. "We shall just have to find ways to entertain you, Madame Howard, without Madame Nicolet's presence. Eh?"

Sukey spun around to face the speaker. Even with her eyes closed, she knew the man's identity. And cringed at his proximity.

"*Bonjour*, Monsieur Margry. We meet again."

"This way, Madame Howard," Margry insisted, pointing to a shadowy open doorway. "Captain Mouceau will be . . . cheered by your arrival."

Sukey took a moment to fortify her spirit.

Old memories consumed her. Terrifying memories. Threatening words . . . from a man in authority whom the Lancaster community respected. And tiny Susannah Whitfield feared.

Now, with trembling legs, she faced another man in authority who had evil designs on her body. A man from whom Sukey could learn vital French information for General Braddock's army. She needed to go directly to the source—no matter how fearsome or threatening.

Or dangerous.

The only way Sukey Howard could prove her bravery to Pa and Rafe Stewart and all of England—and most of all to herself—was to walk boldly into the lion's den and not flinch at his roar.

Squaring her shoulders, Sukey strode into Charlevoix Mouceau's headquarters in time to hear his tirade.

"You dolt, Allouez!" Mouceau screamed at one of

two sergeants standing before him. "And you, Bellestre! Can you do nothing right? One more accident such as this and . . . !" Suddenly he glanced up and leered at Sukey's feminine form.

"*Bonjour*, Captain," she began, "Forgive my intrusion. I shall—"

Standing at the doorway, Margry blocked her retreat.

"Sergeants," Mouceau barked, rising from his desk chair, "I shall deal with you later. Dismissed!" He lunged for Sukey's hand. "Dear Madame Howard, your presence gladdens us as always . . . does it not, Michel?"

Alone, now, with Margry and Mouceau, Sukey smelled the stench of whiskey and unwashed clothes. "*Messieurs*, I did not wish to interrupt your business. In fact, I can sit quietly in the background whilst you complete—"

Nervously fingering his stained breeches, Mouceau jerked his head toward the door. "Margry, wait outside! *Understood*?"

Smirking, and with a nod to Mouceau, Margry yanked the door closed behind him.

Oily-voiced Charlevoix Mouceau bore down on Sukey. "Your fetching attire, madame, seems excessive for such a warm July day. Why not remove your scarf to grant you greater comfort?"

As he fumbled at Sukey's shoulders, she touched the knife outline on her thigh and stepped back. "Monsieur, surely my scarf cannot concern you nearly so much as a large British army approaching your fort."

Mouceau licked his sun-cracked lips. "Madame, I . . . I can wait no longer. This very moment I must have—"

A noisy thump and a boisterous high-pitched voice, just outside the door, halted his words.

Chapter Fifteen

"My dear Monsieur Margry!" Sir Edward Knowles intoned, "I feel certain dear Captain Mouceau would wish to hear my jolly news at once!"

"Faith! 'Tis my own dear *fiancé*!" Sukey exclaimed, assuming the crafty Knowles had arrived to relay his latest spy information to Mouceau.

The door suddenly jerked open. A beaming Knowles stuck his head inside Mouceau's hut. "My dear Captain! Ah, and . . . and Madame Howard!"

"What the devil are you . . . er, *bonjour*, monsieur," Mouceau answered, in a tight-lipped greeting.

"Indeed, I cannot imagine a more pleasant surprise!" Knowles exclaimed, clattering inside the muddy office to reach for the French commander's hand.

Mouceau scowled. "Why have you come here, sir? This precise afternoon, I mean. I thought you were . . . too ill to travel."

"My dear captain, I felt the need of some beneficial fresh air. And I simply had to share some truly superb news with you." A brief coughing attack broke his speech.

Grateful for Knowles's absurd appearance, whatever his motives, Sukey slipped her hand through the crook of his arm. "Edward, my love, what possible news could raise you from your sick bed?"

At her unusually gentle touch and kind demeanor toward him, Knowles peaked an eyebrow. "Why, the very finest! I spotted not one, but three, mind you, belted kingfishers! With the captain being a man who appreciates nature, I knew at once he must be informed."

"Captain!" Appearing in the doorway, Corporal Allouez saluted smartly. "Sir, the Quartermaster requests your approval on a new order of salt pork at once, sir!"

Knowles resumed coughing.

Mouceau glared at him with clenched jaw and balled fists. "I shall return shortly," he bellowed.

Alone with Knowles in the office, Sukey tugged at his sleeve. "Do sit down, Sir Edward. You are unwell. And unwise. I cannot comprehend why you went birding while waylaid by such a malignant humor. I shall fetch you a cup of cool water to allay your coughing."

"Madam, I am touched by your tenderness to your 'fiancé.' Also, by your ability to ride in one direction, then magically appear in the opposite direction."

Sukey blinked. "You pay closer attention to my 'directions,' sir, than you ought. As for my perceived tenderness, do not be too touched, sir. 'Tis only an act which suits my purposes as well as yours."

"An additional favor, madam? Aunt sent along some medicinal cherry bark, which I tucked in my saddle bag." He resumed coughing.

"I shall fetch it at once, while you rest here quietly, sir."

Out of Knowles's sight, Sukey found his roan stallion tied to a barracks railing. Regina Ramsey's cherry bark offering lay tied across the saddle horn. But the temptation of Knowles' bulging leather saddle bag haunted Sukey. She glanced in both directions, then standing on tiptoe, lifted the worn flap to Knowles's saddle bag and peered inside.

"At last!" she whispered. This smooth leather sack

surely contained secret documents that would establish Sir Edward Knowles's identity as a traitorous French spy.

What Sukey found shocked her.

Granted, she had to look past a half dozen small articles—tiny leather sacks of Knowles's white powder and rouge, a tin snuff cup, a horn mug, a broken silver buckle. But at the bottom of his saddle bag lay an intriguing item. A man's necklace made of three bear's teeth linked by a rawhide string. Primitive jewelry. Something Sir Edward Knowles would never wear.

A necklace that Sukey Howard knew belonged to Rafe Stewart.

Stunned, she fingered the forbidden item. What possible reason could Knowles have for possessing Stewart's crude ornament? Had he stolen it from Rafe? Had Rafe given it to the English fop? Were the two dead-opposite men actually colleagues in crime—two clever French spies outfoxing every Englishman on the frontier with their roguish charade?

In an effort to make sense of this odd discovery, Sukey shook her head. Quickly she repacked Knowles's saddle bag before being discovered.

"Never have I seen Knowles and Stewart together," she murmured. She assumed the two men had never met.

Perhaps she was wrong.

Clutching the cherry bark in her left hand and a cup of water in her right, Sukey glided back inside Mouceau's hut.

"Tell me, Sir Edward, while we remain alone, the true reason you roused yourself from your sick bed and rode all the way over here." She soaked the bark in Knowles's water cup and offered the drink to him.

"Why, to relate my joy upon hearing—"

"The truth, Sir Edward! The actual reason."

He gnawed at a corner of his mouth. "You . . . do not believe me, madam?"

"I certainly do not."

"Will you accept that I chose to watch over my tempestuous *fiancée*? An exhilarating woman who appears to be in two places at once?"

Sukey stamped her foot impatiently. "Indeed not! I am no more your *fiancée* than—"

His expression turned solemn as he lowered his voice and caught at her arm. "I beg of you, Mrs. Howard, be careful with these games you play. Mouceau and all his men are far too dangerous to toy with. They would not hesitate to dispatch a curious interloper with a knife to the throat. Or worse, to a woman."

She shrugged off his warning. And his touch.

"Men! All of you with greedy fingers and lascivious thoughts."

"Monsieur Knowles!" Michel Margry called from the dusty courtyard. "I have a handsome new foal you must see. The finest horse on the entire frontier! You need not concern yourself over Madame Howard. Captain Mouceau has arranged a repast for her of biscuits and tea in that hut over there with the open doorway."

Knowles's glance darted from Margry's wrinkled, tobacco-spattered face to Sukey's defiant expression. He coughed. And hesitated.

"A new foal!" Sukey gushed. "How charming! I shall come join you men for a look at the little darling, after I finish tea with Captain Mouceau. Be off with you now, Sir Edward."

She watched Knowles trudge after Margry, then whisked off to join the Captain.

Striding past the storehouse, Sukey overheard loud French voices. She halted. Snatches of words, some intelligible, caught her ears. She looked up to see Mouceau glaring at her.

"Eavesdropping, Madame Howard?" he sneered.

"Certainly not, monsieur! I, a mere woman? What possible interest would I have in French military business?" She readjusted the ribbons of her straw hat. "No, monsieur, I was merely about to fix my *chapeau*."

Seizing her by the arm, Mouceau dragged Sukey inside a dark, empty hut. "I am a busy man, madame, with no further time to play at polite parlor intrigues."

"Oh, then please forgive my interruption, Captain. I shall leave you to your—"

Abruptly, he glued his spittle-flecked mouth onto Sukey's scarlet lips as he pulled her into his perspiring arms. "You are a lovely woman, madame," he declared, breathing in rapid heaves, "and I need you at once."

With all her might, Sukey slapped Mouceau's face.

He tipped backwards.

Rubbing the bright red imprint of Sukey's hand on his stubbled cheek, Mouceau squinted his eyes at her. "I am sorry you did that, Madame Howard. And in a short while, you shall be heartily sorry as well."

In a frenzied dash, Sukey fled from this shadowy enclave into a sea of Indians and French soldiers. Her breath came in painful gulps as she searched for Knowles.

At Fort Duquesne, Sukey's situation lay in smoldering, dangerous ruins. Granted, in self-defense she could stab the fort's commander to death with her knife, a move that would scarcely win her any future French confidence. Her chances to glean information for the British Army were now doomed.

She rushed up to Knowles as he returned from the stable.

"Ah, Sir Edward!" she cried, slipping her hand round

his arm. "I feel a bit peaked. Might you perhaps consent to escort me home?"

"Now?" He peered at her quizzically.

"Yes. That is, if your business here is completed, sir."

" 'Twould be my pleasure, madam."

With a short bow to Sukey, Knowles turned back to Margry. "Monsieur, I commend you on owning the finest horseflesh this side of the Susquehanna." He clapped Margry on the shoulder one last time before assisting Sukey onto her piebald mare.

In silence, Knowles rode beside her for the first mile. Past aromatic sassafras and elderberries and hawthorns. Under towering sycamores loaded with orioles in song. Alongside rockcliff springs that dampened the air with a haunting fragrance of sweet violets and ferns.

Finally he peered sideways at her. "Mrs. Howard, you seem . . . chastened, somehow."

She sniffed. "You are mistaken, sir, as usual."

Knowles sighed. "Ah, there's the pity. My foolish heart somehow supposed that you felt more kindly, perhaps even a bit tender, toward me."

"Wrong, again." She urged her mount in front of his.

Knowles coughed. "Doubtless your ailment renders you peevish."

"My ailment?"

"Yes. You said—"

"Oh, quite. And I do thank you, sir, for escorting me back to Pa's cabin." She nervously adjusted a nosegay on her bodice.

He tossed her a sly sideways smile. "Which is where I thought you were headed when you left my lodge this morning."

She ignored his caustic comment. And rode faster.

"Madam, you ride quite rapidly. For an enfeebled woman, that is."

His calculating tone annoyed her. "I am certainly not enfeebled, Sir Edward. Only just a bit . . ."

"Madam, are you . . . in love with Charlevoix Mouceau?"

Sukey gaped at him. She hesitated a moment while her mind raced with assorted possibilities. Perhaps this scenario might work for her after all. "Why . . . why yes! How did you divine my secret?" Let Knowles believe such nonsense, she reasoned. 'Twould suit her purposes perfectly and allow him to explain away her cunning actions.

"I merely hazarded a guess. So 'love' is why you rode alone to the fort?"

"Y-yes. Sadly, though, d-dear Charlevoix would not have me."

He clucked his tongue. "Poor innocent Mrs. Howard. Were you not aware that the captain has a French wife back in Montreal?"

She feigned a gasp. "Dear me! He never mentioned—"

"Alas, my dear. Men can be such cads."

"Oh, indeed, Sir Edward! In far too many ways to count!"

At her reaction, Knowles managed a slim smile. "Your zealous response surprises me, madam." He edged his mount closer to hers. "Might you be feeling too weak to ride alone, Mrs. Howard? That is, your ailment and broken heart might have rendered you unstable in the saddle. Perhaps you should . . . ride with me."

She flashed him a wily smile in the July sun. "You, sir, are entirely too kind. But I shall remain in my own saddle. And you shall remain in yours."

* * *

Captain Charlevoix Mouceau paced anxiously along Fort Duquesne's ramparts. "Braddock's army will not come by water," he muttered to Sergeant Nicolet, who lingered at his side.

The two French soldiers scrutinized their fort's location on the land point created by the Monongahela and Allegheny Rivers.

Michel Margry lurked in shadows behind both men.

"The bastions, the picket walls, the entrenchments— on a small fort thrown up so hurriedly," Nicolet fretted. "Will they be enough to hold off the British?"

"*Mon Dieu*! Nothing I see or hear pleases me!" Captain Mouceau growled, glaring down below at the cramped parade ground.

Atop a tall flagpole, a *fleur-de-lis* fluttered above crowds of French backwoodsmen and soldiers mingled closely with Indians.

"Throngs of natives, Nicolet. Ojibway, Ottawa, Pottawatamie, Shawnee. Perhaps a thousand Indians, compared to only a handful linked to Braddock. That part is good. But the pathetic few troops we've been sent number far fewer than the British. And likely in three or four days, those huge British guns will be lobbing fire at our drawbridge."

"We could surrender with honor, *Capitaine*. In the face of such firepower, that is." Nicolet fidgeted nervously. "More lives might be spared in that manner."

Mouceau's face flushed purple. "Surrender? Honor?" he snorted. His greasy moustache twitched in rage. "I have a better idea. We can ride out, in advance, and ambush Braddock's army."

Nicolet blinked. "Sir, most likely we shall fail. In that case, we could . . . could expect no quarter from the British."

"Fool, Nicolet! I am the captain here, and you shall do as I say! Dismissed!"

Michel Margry advanced from the shadows as Nicolet slunk off. He licked his lips anxiously. "The woman, Charlevoix, what are we to do about her? You promised, remember? You would have a turn first, of course, but . . . but I was to . . . to—"

Mouceau glared at his perspiring diminutive friend. "Madame Howard? Ah, *oui*!" A smile eased out across his tobacco-stained face.

"She would feel good, *mon ami*, especially before a battle when you need her comfort. That soft skin, the long sparkling hair, those breasts that invite a hungry man to . . ."

Mouceau shifted his groin. "*Oui*, Michel! Madame Howard is precisely what I need now to release my tensions over the impending battle. But I have already approached her, and she will not . . . will not go willingly."

"You approached her?"

"She slapped my face and rebuffed my offer. I intend to make her pay for that."

"A woman of fire. Yes, yes!" Margry cried, slapping his hands together with glee. His tongue snaked across his lips once more. "Then if she has rebuffed your affections, *mon ami*, you must take her by force."

"Out in the woods?" Mouceau's eyelids blinked in spasms as he studied the surrounding trees.

"*Non*! I know just the place, Charlevoix." Margry giggled nervously. "Several hundred yards from the fort lies an abandoned Indian hut. We could have her taken there as our . . . our prisoner. We could take turns, *mon ami*. You first, of course, since you are the commander, and must give the order to have her taken there. Then I . . . ah, I shall have my turn."

Mouceau beamed. "Michel, *mon ami*, when you are

near-sober, some of your ideas actually please me. 'Twill not be easy, though. Madame Howard just rode off in the company of that simpleton, Sir Edward Knowles."

"Charlevoix, that man troubles me. I sense, somehow, that he is not the dolt he pretends to be."

With a guffaw, Mouceau clapped his hand on Margry's shoulder. "You still suspect him of being that blackguard, Rafe Stewart, eh? Ha, ha!"

Suddenly Margry seized his friend by the waistcoat till Mouceau's pewter buttons jangled. "Finally, Charlevoix! The mists clear. Edward Knowles is definitely the scoundrel, Rafe Stewart, and I shall tell you how I know."

Approaching Eli Whitfield's Turtle Creek Post, Knowles drew his mount closer to Sukey's.

" 'Tis no use, Sir Edward. I have already informed you, I shall remain on my own—"

"My dear Mrs. Howard," he said, seizing her reins, "I do not wish to alarm you, but I sense that we no longer ride alone."

Sukey's eyes widened. "Surely you do not think we are in danger, sir?"

"Perhaps at least one of us, madam."

"But why? And which of us?" Suddenly she recalled Charlevoix Mouceau's veiled warning.

Keeping his head still, Knowles cautiously scanned his forested surroundings. "Immaterial, madam," he replied. "All the same, we are followed."

"I have a knife, Sir Edward. And I am quite capable of putting it to good use!"

"Blessings on you, Mrs. Howard. I so hoped you would say that."

She eyed his firm grip on her reins. "I shall endeavor

to protect you, Sir Edward. But do you really need to ride so . . . so close to me?"

"Forgive me, madam, but I feel so much safer close in your shadow." Knowles bit on his lower lip.

"Tsk!" she muttered. "Truly, Sir Edward, I do wish you would become proficient in the use of guns. Do you not understand? A real man simply *must* handle weapons accurately."

Knowles scanned the tree-lined hills. "All that you say is true, madam. If only I could live up to your expectations." His left hand slid to a bulge under his coat flap.

He cocked his ears in the direction of muffled twig snappings.

"Ah, at last! Pa's cabin is just over that ridge, Sir Edward. Then you can stop breathing down my neck. And I declare, sir, within the next day or two, you positively must practice handling guns."

"Madam, I have the distinct impression you are absolutely correct."

Next day, Rafe Stewart squinted his eyes and leaned forward in his saddle. In silent scrutiny of General Braddock's army, camped two miles from the Monongahela River, Stewart grunted with dissatisfaction.

"All too perfect," he muttered to Red Hawk.

With a sly smile, the Lenape agreed. "Nothing amiss. The men are even well-fed, for a change. Those hundred oxen Dunbar sent filled every man's belly with fresh beef."

Stewart shook his head. "Even so, the hairs on my neck prickle with alarm."

"Braddock knows all that you have seen?"

"Fitch dispatched the last runner to Braddock this

morning." Stewart shifted uneasily in his saddle. "Maybe 'tis the odd numbers that give me pause."

Red Hawk grimaced. "Men?"

Nodding, Stewart jerked a thumb toward the British camp. "A formal army that size clomping through the American wilderness, yet the Indians with them number no more than, say, eight?" He spat contemptuously.

"Runners claim that over a thousand men from many tribes hover around the French at Duquesne."

Stewart shook his head. "Bad medicine, Red Hawk. All wrong."

"No foreigner understands these hills like the men who prowl them every day of their lives. British men have trouble learning that."

"Ah, Red Hawk, my friend! They may pay a fearsome price for their arrogance. Look at them! They seem almost happy. Men before a major battle should not look so contented."

"Their long march from Fort Cumberland is over, Rafe. Somehow they hauled those mammoth guns over the mountains. They seem relieved."

"Hear their foolish shouts of celebration? Those Britsh soldiers think tomorrow they shall drink French wine inside Fort Duquesne."

The aging Lenape contemplated Stewart. "But you do not agree, eh?"

"Something feels amiss, my friend. I shall ride with them, of course. But I wonder . . ."

"You fear they might not understand the rigors of frontier fighting?" The Lenape's greased scalp lock shimmered in the afternoon sun as he swatted an aggressive fly.

Gathering reins, Stewart drew himself up tall in the saddle. "I know so," he growled, then spat once more before riding away.

Cautiously he approached Sir Edward Knowles's lodge, then dismounted and crept inside.

"Edward, dear boy!" Regina Ramsey exclaimed, clutching her chest in surprise. "You near startled the life out of me! Have you come to switch clothes?"

He snatched a warm scone from the kitchen table. "Sir Edward Knowles is finished, Aunt."

"You mean your work is done?"

"No. I fear not. But Knowles's work is. The British army will likely attack Fort Duquesne tomorrow. As for the French, I feel certain that weasel, Margry, finally pierced my identity today. From now on, I must ride as myself."

"But Edward, if your work is completed, we can immediately begin our journey back to Philadelphia for our next set of orders." She paused. "That scowl of yours, dear boy, what can it mean?"

"The battle is tomorrow, Aunt."

"Edward! Surely you do not plan to . . ."

"I plan to mete out justice, on my brother's behalf, to Charlevoix Mouceau. And help the British at the same time."

"Far too dangerous, Edward!"

He guffawed. "I nearly got my backside shot off as that nosy fop, Knowles. Now you say it gets dangerous? And what of this new-found eagerness to revisit Philadelphia, Aunt?"

She twisted her fingers anxiously. "Fitch says he has a surprise for me there."

"That old turkey?" he bellowed. "Probably the same surprise he has given you out here, on a fairly regular basis, I might add."

She sniffed. "If I did not love you like my own son, dear boy, your impertinence would be offensive. Besides, what will you do about the adorable Sukey Howard?"

"Do?"

"Well of course, Edward. Surely you will not leave her out here on the frontier to fend for herself . . . loving her as you do." She studied him slyly.

He nearly choked on the last of his scone. "That woman? Bloody hell, Aunt! That woman is more dangerous than all the British and French armies rolled together! You think that I . . . ?" He stomped out of the lodge and disappeared.

Regina smiled. "That, dear boy, is precisely what I think," she murmured to herself.

Rafe Stewart found a quiet kink of Turtle Creek. A soothing site, cool in the summer heat, branched over by tall, gracious sycamores and oaks, serenaded by a thrush's trill. Here, he could calm himself before battle.

Warriors needed that, he reminded himself.

Suddenly, he glimpsed a pink-fleshed woman delicately splashing stream water over her bared arms.

Stewart groaned.

'Twas none other than Sukey Howard. She had loosened her shift drawstrings to expose her throat . . . and shoulders. Sweet, soft skin that Stewart knew so well by touch and taste.

He felt himself instantly harden. Warriors did not need this, he reminded himself. They . . .

He stood up and advanced a dozen feet toward her, before halting behind a tree to control his powerful urges.

In a delicate feminine voice, Sukey began humming a song.

Stewart licked his lips. He could stand it no more. He bolted through the trees toward her.

"Who is it?" she gasped, clutching her loosened

bodice, which now failed to conceal the rise of her bosom.

"Bloody hell, woman!" he scolded, stomping up to her. "Any overheated male, riding by, could . . ."

"Rafe! I was properly concealed from all but the most inquisitive eye!" Glaring at him, she quickly redid her bodice strings. "Rafe, have you heard? Braddock's army is camped so near the Monongahela that surely they will attack Fort Duquesne on the morrow!"

His tone softened. " 'Tis likely."

"I have decided . . . I have decided that I shall be with them."

"What?" His dark eyebrows formed astonished wings. "In spirit, you mean. 'Tis commendable of you, madam."

"In body. I can be as fierce as any man. And I am determined that Captain Charlevoix Mouceau and all his sneering evil men shall be banished back to Montreal from whence they came."

Stewart propped his fists on his hips. "Quite a speech for a woman who only stands chest-high." He touched her hair where it brushed against his leather shirt.

"Mock me if you will. But I carry a knife, and I can be ferocious."

His hand slid back toward her nape. "Sukey, stay at your pa's cabin tomorrow. I insist. The fighting will be ugly, I have no doubt. Not as easy as some cavalier redcoats might assume." Now both his hands tipped her face up toward his. "After the battle, I shall leave here."

"For good?"

Swallowing hard, he struggled for words. "Yes."

"Then . . . then I might never see you again? Tell me now, Rafe, why you shroud yourself in so much mystery? Why?" Her green eyes brimmed with tears.

Those delicate tears unhinged Stewart. He bent down

and gently kissed the curve of her dimples. "I cannot, Sukey, for serious reasons. Not yet."

"You have a wife in Philadelphia?"

"No."

"In Montreal?"

"No."

"In London? Or anywhere?"

He lightly kissed her mouth. "Not anywhere. A wife and children would never fit in my life."

"So you are not the marrying sort. And this . . . this might be the last time I shall ever see you again." She stood on bare tiptoes and looped her slender arms around his chest.

He breathed out, heavy and slow. "Sukey, warriors do not do this. Not before a battle." Grasping her shoulders, he intended to push her back.

"But I am a warrior for my country, too, Rafe Stewart. And I need this before the battle." She squirmed against his warm, hard-muscled body.

"Sukey, this is good-bye, luv. Forever. I must leave and . . ."

She slid her hands up over his shoulders. Her fingers teased the coal-black strands of his long hair. "You were saying?"

He swallowed, but no words emerged. He tried again . . . while his arms reached to enclose her waist. "I am a man, Sukey. If you tease me this way . . ."

Delicately she kissed his mouth. "Yes? What then shall happen, Rafe?"

Stewart groaned. "This, you cunning wench."

Chapter Sixteen

Thrusting Sukey toward the trunk of a long, straight oak, Stewart wedged his bulk tight against her body. "You, Mrs. Howard, are my prisoner," he growled, wrapping his arms around the tree to further entrap her.

She slid her arms around his waist. And smiled. "But what if I do not wish to escape, Mr. Stewart?"

"Run, my beauty, while you still can. If you can."

Her expression sobered. "I never want to leave you, Rafe. Ever!" Clutching his tanned face, she let her fingers explore each craggy curve and line. "Ah!" she murmured, stirred by the arousal of Stewart's touch. So precious to her, this rough-hewn face she knew so well.

And . . . and oddly familiar in some unknown way.

Stewart pulled her inside his arms. "Sukey . . ." His voice broke. "This goodbye . . . aye, 'tis much harder than I anticipated."

"My darling! It need not be! Why can I not stay with you?"

"There are reasons."

"Share them with me. The pain of holding those secrets is too heavy a burden for you, Rafe. I see that on your face."

"Someday."

"*Now*, Rafe! Tell me *now*!"

He shook his head. "Leaving you, my love, is the

heaviest burden of all. My heart and soul remain with you." He kissed her, in a lingering deep coupling. "Forever I shall yearn to be with you, Sukey, my love. And in you," he whispered.

His tongue probed the delicate recesses of her mouth, then tasted the sweetness of her silken cheek and ear.

She moaned with greedy pleasure at his advances. Her impatient fingers tugged at his dark hair. "Love me, my darling, this one last time."

" 'Twould not be fair to you, Sukey, luv. I cannot die in battle or slink off like some varmint and leave you pregnant."

"I can listen to none of your valorous words, Rafe Stewart! Fill me with your life and love, my darling. I shall manage the consequences." Kissing him, she allowed her probing tongue to twirl with his in a sensuous mating dance of need.

A demanding kiss that drove Stewart to shift restlessly.

The gentle rasp of his tongue maddened her with desire. He buried his face in her throat and kissed her wolfishly. She felt her knees buckle.

He caught her sagging frame and laid her down on a pillowy bed of moss. With fumbling fingers, he eased her shift down from her shoulders.

"Ah, luv!" he exclaimed, at the sight of her soft, bare breasts. "No woman on earth was ever so beautiful as you. And no other woman ever seized my very soul as have you." He greedily kissed her breasts as if fearing he might die in battle and never taste this feast again. His mouth caressed every curve of her breasts.

"Rafe!" she begged, groping for his breeches.

"Let me love you more, sweet," he replied, kissing and licking every inch of her exposed skin. His fingers and mouth teased her nipples into warm demanding peaks. His large hands moved across her body in gentle massage. At last, pulling up her chemise, he probed her damp recesses with his warm hand.

Releasing his male organ from his breeches, he eased in between her moist thighs. In. In further.

Then deep inside.

She felt his warm, engorged flesh fill her with his need. Deep inside, then pulling back, then in. That sweet delicious tug tortured Sukey with desire. She clamped her thighs round his thick male torso and savored the rocking passion of love . . . till she could stand it no more. Clinging to his neck, she wailed with a pleasure that seized and demanded and soared and . . .

On a fluttered cry, she collapsed into his arms as she felt his warmth explode within her.

Limp, they clung to each other.

At last, he stroked her wild, loosened mane of chestnut hair. "Know, my Sukey, that if I die in battle tomorrow, I . . . love you more than I have ever loved any woman."

Tears welled in her eyes. "You shall not die, Rafe Stewart! I . . . I will not allow it."

"Aye?" Kissing Sukey's cheek, he smiled ruefully. "And just how do you propose to guarantee my fate?"

"I shall accompany you into battle."

"Sukey, luv," he growled, "promise me you shall attempt no such thing."

Fingering her silver pendant, she sat bolt upright. "This necklace, Rafe, have you forgotten its legend? Rachel was told by Old Eliza that the life of its wearer will be saved from death. At least once, anyhow, so goes the legend."

"Surely you do not believe—"

"I do indeed, Rafe! Rachel told me stories of its former owners, including Old Eliza. And Rachel, herself, was saved from capture and certain death when she wore the pendant. The shiny silver sparkled in sunlight, alerting Jonah to her perilous location. Afterwards, she passed the pendant on to me."

He gently knuckled her chin upward, then met her gaze. "Hear me, Sukey Howard," he thundered. "No sparkling pendant can protect you from stray French bullets or an attacker's knife. Stay indoors tomorrow, safe within your pa's protection."

She glared hard at Stewart's broad back as he mounted his horse and rode off. George Howard, her former husband, was dead. No man would ever again dictate her actions. No man! Not her blustery pa, Eli Whitfield. Certainly not the preposterous, effeminate Sir Edward Knowles. And try though he may, not even burly Rafe Stewart.

Fixing a determined stare in the direction of Stewart's vanishing figure, Sukey plotted her next move.

Rachel Butler propped her hands on her trim hips in disgust. "Sukey! That green wood simply will not do for a cooking fire! Whatever was Zeb thinking when he brought it inside?"

"Thinking? Ah, Rachel, the same as every man hereabouts, it would seem."

"The battle for Fort Duquesne?"

"Precisely. Even your Jonah, I wager."

"True enough." Rachel heaved a sigh. "I wish 'twas all over now. Merciful heavens, I cannot bear the thought of even one hair on Jonah's head harmed." Rachel shivered. "Or . . . or worse."

Sukey patted her sister's arm. "You love him so, Rachel. 'Tis beautiful to behold, a love such as yours."

"Ah, how I wish you had been blessed with such a lover, Sukey."

Lowering her gaze, Sukey turned aside. She fussed unnecessarily over a brace of ducks roasting in a reflector oven.

Rachel's eyes widened. "Mercy! I guessed right weeks ago! You never could hide things from me, Sukey. You *do* have a lover! And not just any man, either. 'Tis a man you love with all your heart!"

Eli Whitfield stomped across the kitchen threshold. "Aye, leave two women alone for a morning, and what happens? They set up a chatter about love and affected hearts. Well, daughter," he insisted, scrutinizing Sukey, "have you finally come to your senses about Sir Edward Knowles?"

Sukey huffed indignantly. "The man is a coward, Pa! Can you not see? And worse, I tell you!"

Eli lit his pipe with a rush taper from the kitchen fire. "A fine Englishman is Knowles, I tell you, Sukey. A fitting husband for a widow in need of a man and children." A fair hint of a twinkle lit Eli's pale green eyes.

Angered, Sukey stamped her foot. "Pa, can you not see? Not only is the man a likely coward, he . . . well, I feel certain he is a spy as well."

Eli sputtered into a cough. "A spy?"

"A French spy, Pa."

"Oh surely, Sukey, you cannot believe such a heinous thing about gentle Sir Edward!" Rachel gasped.

"I do, indeed. And I fear he is calculating some form of devilment against General Braddock's troops as they approach Fort Duquesne."

Tapping his pipe, Eli stared at his daughter. "'Tis a serious accusation you make, Sukey. And likely a mistaken one. I urge you to remain silent lest you damage a good man's repu- —"

"Pa?" Sukey darted to the open kitchen door. "Three British officers just emerged from your smithy."

"Aye. Jonah and Zeb repaired their rifles."

Unspoken determination flashed across Sukey's flame-cheeked face. She edged out across the threshold.

Eli guessed the message imprinted on his daughter's earnest face. "Sukey!" he bellowed after her.

In a mad dash, Sukey raced toward the soldiers.

"Afternoon, miss," a squat lieutenant nodded in response to her approach.

"Gentleman, I have vital news you must convey to your superiors this very day!" she insisted, gasping for breath.

The three officers exchanged startled stares.

She gulped air before continuing. "A French spy huddles in your midst."

"Ma'am?" Their mouths hung agape.

"Conniving, unpredictable, misleading, this treacherous man—at least, I believe him to be treacherous—attempts to undermine General Braddock's efforts to capture Fort Duquesne."

The thickset lieutenant squinted at her. "Just who might this charlatan be, miss?"

"His name is . . . is Sir Edward Knowles."

The three men noisily cleared their throats. "A serious accusation, miss," one of them growled.

"I shall lead you to his temporary abode, gentlemen. You can question him for yourself," she insisted.

"Ah!" Regina Ramsey cried, fanning herself with a handkerchief as she leaned out the top half of the Dutch door of her kitchen. "This breeze is a blessed relief from the—"

Abruptly she halted mid-sentence, leaving her mouth agape.

"Aunt? You all right?" Rafe Stewart looked up from the Pennsylvania rifle he carefully cleaned.

Fitch chortled. "Regina merely finds it necessary to rest her mouth on occasion. After all, no woman can prattle on forever, though Regina tries her best."

Regina clicked her tongue in annoyance. "Wretched miscreant! I shall administer unto you the discipline you particularly deserve, Fitch . . . later. Now, however, we have something far more pressing to resolve."

Rising from his chores, Fitch peered over Regina's shoulder at a narrow footpath leading to their lodge. "God's blood!" he muttered.

"'Tis Sukey Howard, Nephew, leading three British officers straight to your front door."

"Bloody hell!" Stewart exclaimed, bolting to the door for a look, before quickly ducking out of sight.

"The woman is relentless, I must admit," Fitch commented.

Regina resumed fanning herself, this time more rapidly. "She appears to be on a mission of some sort, Nephew. And I feel certain she expects to find, not Edward Rafe Stewart, but Sir Edward Knowles."

Darting into a cramped back room, Stewart lunged for the requisite spectacles, make-up, and clothing. "Detain her, Aunt, with your gift of gab while I change," he urged. Struggling into his sophisticated garb, Stewart uttered a string of heated oaths.

Wooden hinges squeaked as Regina flung open the Dutch door and stepped outside. "Sukey, my dear!" she cried exuberantly, arms outstretched. "A pleasure to see you again! And what gentlemen friends have you brought for us to meet?"

Sukey swallowed hard. "Regina, I . . . these officers have come to ask Sir Edward some questions. Some . . . important questions."

Regina clapped her hands together in apparent delight. "Edward will rejoice at the chance to visit with these British officers. You know Edward, my dear! He so loves the company of true gentlemen." Hands clasped and still smiling, Regina remained rooted to the spot as Fitch emerged from the cabin.

Indulging in some minor throat-clearing, Sukey shifted from one foot to the other. "Then where is he, Regina?"

Regina blinked twice. "Who, my dear? Fitch? Oh, ever-faithful servant that he is, Fitch can always be found right at my—"

"Sir Edward, Regina."

"Oh, but of course! The forgetfullness of advancing age, my dear. Such a torment!" She broke off to laugh. "Why I remember once when I—"

"Is Sir Edward at home, Regina?" Sukey probed persistently.

"Yes, dear, of course. I informed him of your approach. Edward does labor so on his appearance, though. Mercy! If his make-up and wig are not vibrantly fresh-looking, Edward despairs to the point of—"

The door squeaked on its hinges once more as Knowles clattered outside. "Dear, dear, Mrs. Howard! A confection for us all to behold on this hot summer afternoon!" He covered Sukey's hand with a theatrical kiss. "Pray, whom have you brought to converse with us, my dear?"

She met his whimsical gaze with a fierce stare of her

own. "British officers, Sir Edward. Men with pointed questions to ask of you."

With a flourish, Knowles tucked her hand inside his elbow to escort her inside. "Gentlemen! I am delighted that my fiancée brought you all here this afternoon."

"Your fiancée?" The diminutive lieutenant, puzzled, glanced from Knowles to Sukey and back again.

"Really, Sir Edward!" Sukey burst out impatiently.

Regina quickly stepped forward with a fond pat to Sukey's arm. "No need to be shy about it, Sukey dear. We are all so happy for you two."

"I shall need to speak with you at once, Sir Edward," the stern-faced lieutenant barked.

"Of course, my good man," Knowles replied.

Sukey watched the exchange with smug satisfaction. Hallelujah! At last, the truth about Sir Edward Knowles was about to unfold! The villain would finally receive his just punishment. And she, Sukey Howard, had played a vital role in his capture.

She smiled.

"In private, sir, if you will."

Sukey's eyes widened. "In private? But . . . ?" Her hands curled into fists as she contemplated Knowles and the three British officers before her. Something seemed out of balance. Inappropriate. The looks exchanged among those four men, perhaps? Their controlled responses to one another?

"Of course, gentlemen," Knowles responded politely to their request. "My aunt will entertain my dear *fiancée* while I excuse myself into your company."

Inside, Sukey paced the cabin nervously as the four men withdrew to a secluded section of woods.

"You seem on edge, dear Sukey," Regina commented. "Might I offer you a cup of, er, mountain tea?" A half-smile tugged at Regina's lips.

"I intended to be included!" Sukey burst out, pivoting on the worn plank floor as she resumed pacing.

"Of course you did, dear. But they assuredly will entertain themselves with 'men talk.'" Regina shielded her mouth with upraised fingers in a show of modesty. "And you know how offensive men can be when they chatter on with loosened inhibitions! Mercy! Enough to make a grown woman blush." Regina fanned herself vigorously.

"Surely not Sir Edward!" Sukey scoffed.

"Oh, my dear Sukey! Scratch the surface of any man, my dear, any man, and what do you find? A beast, I tell you! A beast! Take it from a woman with a long record of such tawdry recollections."

An emerging smile disappeared beneath Regina's covering fingers.

"Oh!"

"What is it, my dear?"

"Another man approaches, Regina."

"Perhaps you mistake Fitch for—"

"No. 'Tis another British soldier, heading straight for the lieutenant." Leaning on the half-opened Dutch door, Sukey watched the men closely. "He seems quite animated, the new man. He . . . I cannot believe it!"

Regina halted her mending. "What is it, Sukey? What do you see that astonishes you so?"

"They have all ridden away! The four British soldiers . . . they are gone!"

"And Edward?"

"They did not take him with them."

"Did you expect them to, Sukey?"

"Well, I . . . yes! I did! Why have they not . . . ?" Fuming, Sukey yanked open the door's bottom half and stomped toward Knowles.

He smiled at her sudden approach as he leaned

against a smooth gray beech trunk. "Delightful of you to join me, my dear."

"Why did the soldiers leave so abruptly?" she demanded.

"Pressing business, I suppose, m'dear."

"The man who just arrived?"

"A courier of some sort."

"With news of General Braddock's encampment?"

"Indeed. But the mention of imminent bloodshed can scarcely interest you, m'dear. Or me, for that matter. Ghastly business, war." He sniffed disdainfully.

"But . . . surely they—! Did they not ask you pointed questions?"

"We had a most amiable conversation. Delightful chaps, actually. However, they had to scamper off to resolve a military difficulty of some sort or other. Come, my dear *fiancée*, let us enjoy a cup of tea—or what passes for tea in these parts."

Sukey did not budge. A placid July breeze, rich with the scent of sweet flag, teased her arms and pressed her linen skirt against her legs. Overhead, warblers and chickadees offered a lavish serenade to the busy forest floor scamperings of gray squirrels probing through leaf litter.

Sukey breathed in giant huffs. "Sir, your cowardice, and your complicity with the French enemy, is despicable!"

"My dear lady!" He viewed her with astonishment.

"No, Sir Edward! I am not, nor have I ever been, your dear lady. Or your *fiancée*!"

He reached for her. "Mrs. Howard, surely the July heat has made you overwrought with—"

She jerked back. "Not the summer heat, Sir Edward! Your unmanly behavior! Especially at a time when bravery is so desperately called for by every decent British man and woman."

Knowles grimaced at her outburst. "Perhaps you do not know all pertinent details."

"I know enough, sir! Brave colonists will die soon, to rid these hills of the arrogant French. And you mock their efforts!"

He caught her by the hand. "My dear . . ."

Shaking free of his grasp, she ignored tears that welled in her eyes. "I shall never be your 'dear.' My heart belongs to only one man, and he is far more courageous and heroic than you could ever dream of being."

Knowles cocked one eyebrow. "Who might this valiant soul be?"

She glared at him. "Since I shall likely never see you again, I will divulge his name. Rafe Stewart. The finest, most courageous man I have ever met. And if he dies attacking Fort Duquesne, Sir Edward, then I shall despise you and your offensive cowardice even more."

At the sight of unchecked tears spilling down Sukey's cheeks, a somber Knowles pulled her inside his arms. "Sukey, darling," he whispered, before bending to kiss her mouth.

Enraged, she struggled against his chest, then slapped his face. "Do not ever touch me again, Sir Edward, for any reason, or I shall stab you to death! My knife is small, sir, but altogether deadly."

Knowles watched, mournfully, as Sukey ran toward her horse. He could stop her, of course. Easy, that, for a man of his might and speed. But as Rafe Stewart, he had already said goodbye to Sukey Howard, the woman he loved—ached for—with every ounce of his being.

A woman he could never have.

Best, then, to let her go. Let her despise him. That made his departure easier. On the morrow, he would either die fighting the French at Duquesne, or hail the conquering British and leave shortly thereafter for

Philadelphia. New orders would await him there. Orders that required him to undertake another dangerous new mission against the French.

Knowles propped one arm against the beech trunk and watched Sukey Howard ride out of his life forever.

He hated deceiving her. Bloody hell! His gut clenched at the thought of losing her, the first woman he'd begun to trust. But no woman—other than Regina—belonged in his dangerous life of espionage. No woman could endure that peril.

Danger? The threat of an enemy hand at his throat?

Rafe Stewart could live no other way.

With the toe of his leather boot, he scuffed at the dainty foot imprints where Sukey had just stood. He could still feel the softness of her arms against his hands, and smell the lingering lavender from her skirt folds, see her sad green eyes brimming with tears.

"God's blood!" he raged, pounding a fist into his open palm.

Fate had spun him in an unforeseen direction. He intended Sukey Howard to be nothing more than an amusing little diversion. Saucy fun. Merely another woman to satisfy his physical needs.

Scowling, Knowles yanked off his sham spectacles and rubbed his jaw with the back of his hand.

Somehow, when he was not looking, Sukey Howard had stolen his heart, blast it! By day, he longed for even a glimpse of her. At night, she taunted his lonely dreams till he moaned with restless need. Odd urges daily threatened to overcome him. A sense that he needed to watch over Sukey, to protect her at all cost to his own personal safety.

"Madness!" he growled, balling his hands into tight fists.

His own mother had taught Edward Rafe Stewart

well that no woman could be trusted. A man who fancied himself in love with a woman was weak. Vulnerable. On a downslide to self-destruction. Stewart would never allow himself to be that defenseless.

Glancing over his shoulder one last time at the narrow trail where Sukey Howard had vanished, Sir Edward Knowles hastened inside to once again shuck his dapper identity.

Fleshy half-moons rose alongside Captain Charlevoix Mouceau's bitten fingernails.

"Not one piece of good news!" he shouted to his officers. "Not one! The long drought has slowed supplies coming from Presqu'Isle. Now Braddock, his army—and those monstrous howitzers and 12-pounders he hauled over the mountains—are less than two days' march from Duquesne. Unless something is done at once . . . *Mon Dieu*!" he cried.

"We shall suffer a British shelling, sir," Sergeant Nicolet advised.

Mouceau nervously bit his lip. "We have two choices, gentlemen. Surrender the fort. Or ride out and attack Braddock's column with all that we can muster, before those English demons reach the fort."

"Perhaps, *Capitaine*, we should—"

Tugging at his soiled mustache, Mouceau held up his hand for silence. Then smiled. "Gentlemen, we shall select the second option."

Nicolet's eyes widened. "Sir? Ride out and ambush the British?"

Mouceau's cold gray eyes glittered. "Sergeant, make the necessary preparations at once."

As the officers shuffled out of the commander's headquarters, a dark form emerged from shadows to address Mouceau. "Hsst! Charlevoix! Have you forgotten?" Michel Margry whispered.

"What is it, you drunken fool?" Mouceau demanded.

"The woman, Charlevoix! Ah, this time, *mon ami*, this time I am not drunk! I found the perfect place to . . . to detain her, *mon ami*. An abandoned Indian hut to the north, not far from here."

Scratching his furrowed brow, Mouceau hesitated. "I have much on my mind right now, Margry. The war intensifies and—"

Crouching, Margry licked his lips till spittle formed at the corners. "But Charlevoix, a man who satisfies himself before battle with a fine woman will . . . will hone in on the enemy with inconceivable fortitude. You first, of course, *mon ami*. Then . . . then it will be my turn!" At the thought of his potential conquest, Margry clapped his dusty hands together with glee.

Mouceau stroked his groin. "You will get Madame Howard to the hut?"

"I shall take care of everything at once, Charlevoix. Two men will assist me in capturing her. I know where she wanders alone. But Charlevoix . . . ?" He tapped his friend's shoulder nervously.

"*Oui?*"

"When I send a messenger to you, with word that we . . . we have her, come to us at once, *mon ami*! Here, I shall draw you directions to the hut."

Hauling water buckets toward a mountain spring, Sukey watched a yellow butterfly flutter its black-edged wings on cool morning air currents. It was the last thing she remembered before her world went dark.

She awoke to a sensation of constraint and pain.

Wide-eyed, Sukey stared through dangling cobwebs

at her surroundings. On a packed earthen floor of a small, smoke-scarred cabin, she lay propped against a coarse grain sack. Her arms were pinioned behind her back. A foul-smelling rag, covering her mouth, seemed knotted at her nape. Even her ankles were bound together by rope.

Struggling to focus on a candle burning on a makeshift table, she saw a hand, missing half a little finger, reach to touch her hair.

"Ah, my beautiful woman awakes!"

Sukey grimaced at the sound of Michel Margry's rasping voice.

"A fine widow like yourself needs men to love you, Madame Howard. In many ways." He stroked the curve of her bosom.

She wrenched backwards with a muffled warning.

"'Twill do you no good, my lovely. Soon, we shall all take turns caressing your sweet body. All four of us." He turned impatiently toward two hunched figures in the shadows. "Damn Charlevoix! Where can he be? Does he not appreciate how urgent the need?"

"Listen! I hear guns in the distance!" the taller of them barked, as he slunk toward the open doorway.

Cocking her ear sideways, Sukey heard the distant commotion as well. Booming guns and cannon. Frenzied Indian whoops. Men bellowing. Terrified horses screaming.

War! The battle for control of trade throughout the Ohio Valley and down the Mississippi River. The battle for Fort Duquesne itself.

"It has begun!" the younger man shouted. "Captain Mouceau will not appear for hours."

"If ever." Turning toward Sukey, Margry's mouth crooked into a grin. "A man can wait only so long," he murmured, pulling at his breeches as he studied Sukey, then paced the floor.

Hours later, Sukey twisted her shoulders to listen as war cries waned. Suddenly she realized, no cool metal tickled her throat. The pendant! For the first time, Sukey realized her silver pendant had vanished, perhaps torn from her throat as the villains carried her into this rude cabin.

Sukey's heart sank.

The beautiful etched silver pendant, which reputedly saved the life of its wearers at least once, was nowhere to be seen. Hemp bound her arms and legs, so that she could not reach for her knife. And now, these three grimy Frenchmen who visually feasted on her with naked lust . . . walked toward her with brutish determination.

Sukey frantically gulped air through the dirt-encrusted gag. All hope was gone. Watching the three Frenchmen approach her, Sukey prayed for a speedy death.

Suddenly, a shadow flickered across one of the paper-sealed windows.

Chapter Seventeen

"What was that?"

Michel Margry's eyes blazed with fear and guilt as his hand rested on his knife scabbard. Listening to a red-tailed hawk scream somewhere outside, the Frenchman shuddered.

" 'Twas nothing, you fool!" a tall Frenchman chided him. "Just some damned hawk in search of food."

A second shadow flashed by the cabin window.

"Charlevoix? Is that you?" Margry shouted. The echoing silence unnerved him. He coughed fitfully. "I tell you, Jacques, I feel uneasy. Something . . . something does not seem right."

Sneering, the tall man held up his hands in a placating gesture.

"Go outside and look anyhow, Jacques!" Margry insisted. "I am the master here for now, not you!"

Hearing the hawk scream again, Sukey felt her heart pound. Rafe Stewart knew how to imitate birdcries to perfection. But surely he was not here now! Most likely he was wounded, or dead, outside Duquesne. Or perhaps he had ridden elsewhere with glorious news of a British victory.

Regardless, he would have no way of knowing her current shabby location. And he would not care. His goodbye to her sounded final.

Suddenly, two large men swept into the open doorway and smacked their fists into the jaws of Margry's accomplices.

Wide-eyed, Sukey sat bolt upright.

"Rafe! And Zeb!" she muttered through her gag. She watched dumbfounded as her two rescuers held an even match with the three Frenchmen. Fists thudded into solid flesh. Men grunted in conflict. Slowly, Rafe Stewart and Zeb Whitfield gained the upper hand.

Jerking his glittering gaze from one thrashed Frenchman to another, Margry slunk backward from the scene and shook his head.

Surveying the skirmish, Sukey grew frantic. Margry could never be trusted, under any circumstances. Somehow, she had to intervene! But, trussed up like some roasting fowl, how could she possibly help?

She glanced around her. A broken metal axe head in a dusty corner might prove useful. On her backside, Sukey slithered back toward the jagged metal. Cautiously she slid her bound wrists up and down the fractured implement.

As she labored, she saw Margry withdraw something shiny from his hip scabbard. A knife!

Frantic, she worked furiously to free herself.

At last!

Flipping up her skirt, she retrieved her own knife from its dainty thigh sheath and sliced the ropes binding her ankles.

"Rafe!" she screamed, as Margry crouched behind Stewart's back. The treacherous knife gleamed in the Frenchman's fist as he drew his arm back to strike.

With a cry, Sukey lunged for Margry with her knife. In a desperate thrust, she struck just below the villain's left shoulder blade. She stepped back in horror as Margry crumpled to the dirt floor.

Rafe and Zeb dispatched their foes with a final round of punches. The two Frenchmen sagged earthward.

Stewart faced Sukey with a stunned expression. "You . . . you risked your own life, Sukey, to save mine."

"I love you, Rafe. Would you have expected less from me?"

At last, Sukey could allow herself to let go. Clenching her fists to her lips, she began to cry. Great sobs shook her slender frame.

Zeb reached for his sister while Stewart disarmed the three fallen Frenchmen. "Did they . . . ? Sukey, did those men . . . ?" Zeb demanded.

Stewart watched her carefully for the reply.

"No. They did not rape me, Zeb. But they taunted me with their would-be power. They said Charlevoix Mouceau was to have me first. Then . . . then they would each take turns." Sukey dabbed at her tear-stained cheeks with her dirty knuckles.

Stewart exchanged stern glances with Zeb.

"What is it, you two?" she insisted.

Zeb released her. "Rafe will fill you in, on the ride back. Meanwhile, I shall let Pa and the others know you're safe."

"Wait! How did you two know? How to find me, I mean."

Grim-faced, Stewart explained. "At the battle, I stumbled on Zeb."

"I told Rafe you were missing, that Pa and I suspected the French had grabbed you."

"Afterwards—" Stewart dragged the back of his fist across his mouth. "Afterwards, we combed the hills for you. No clues of your whereabouts. Until, that is . . ."

"Until what?" she begged.

Stewart slung his hands from his leather belt. "A

sparkle of silver in the sun, just outside this cabin, led us here."

"Your necklace," Zeb added, dangling the gleaming pendant from his index finger. "We found it tangled in the bushes over there by the cabin's front door."

Her hand fluttered to her naked throat. "Then 'tis true!" she exclaimed. "'Twas true all along! The silver pendant saves the life of its wearer once. Then it must be passed on to someone else. The very words of Old Eliza!"

"Let's get you out of here," Stewart growled, steering her by the arm.

Sukey covered her nose. "Not a minute too soon. The smell of blood and filth clogs my nostrils. Thankfully, you two arrived here in time, before Mouceau."

Again, Rafe exchanged silent glances with Zeb.

"Charlevoix Mouceau is dead, Sukey," the turbulent mountaineer informed her.

"Dead?" She looked quizzically at both men. "The battle! You have not told me the outcome."

A somber Zeb untied his bay mare and swung up into the saddle. "I must ride home and let the others know you and I are unhurt, Sukey. Meanwhile, Stewart will tell you the news, and take you to Knowles."

"Knowles? But why?" Sukey demanded.

"You owe Sir Edward an apology, sister, for sullying the man's reputation." He rode off before she could besiege him with more questions.

Sukey glared at Stewart. "Zeb's tone, and yours, Rafe, is grim. What has happened? And why must I apologize to that troublesome dandy, Sir Edward?"

"Not here," he warned. "We shall talk further at Knowles's cabin." He hoisted her atop his stallion, then settled himself in the saddle, behind her.

Stewart rode in silence over three miles of rough-hilled terrain.

Unnerved by the quiet, and her ordeal, Sukey fidgeted. Even the warmth of Stewart's strong arms around her failed to calm Sukey.

"Rafe! I beg of you! Speak to me!"

The only reply was a harsh July wind, as Stewart tightened his grip on the reins.

Her fingers stroked his firm knuckles. Closing her eyes in fear of his response, she called his name softly. "Rafe? Dearest, do you not love me as before?"

His somber silence frightened Sukey even more than French captivity. She leaned back against the cove of his chest. The bear-tooth necklace! She could feel its impress against her back.

"Rafe, I found that necklace in Sir Edward's saddle bag. Now 'tis in your possession once more!"

"Lots of frontiersmen wear such animal necklaces," he scoffed.

Unconvinced, she shook her head. "Not with the same tooth striations. You and Sir Edward share some mysterious sort of relationship! I mean to learn what it is. Are you his servant?"

Stewart guffawed. "Ask Knowles," he rasped, before nudging his mount into a gallop. He rode hard for Knowles's lodge.

Dismounting in front of the familiar cottage, Stewart lifted Sukey down to her feet. "Go inside," he ordered.

"But . . . but I am indeed a filthy sight! What am I to say to these people?"

At the spectacle of Sukey's wide-eyed fearful wonder, Stewart hesitated briefly, almost as if he was about to comfort her. Apparently changing his mind, he walked his horse toward the stable. "You will know, Mrs. Howard," he called over his shoulder, "when the time is right."

Alone, Sukey glanced down at her appearance. Dirty

feet peeked at her from beneath a soiled homespun linen skirt. Caked mud and flecks of blood streaked her once-clean apron. Margry had yanked off her mob cap and thrown it away before strewing her hair loose across her shoulders.

She sighed.

Her fate was now in God's hands. Even her own brother had cast her off to the discretion of Rafe Stewart and Sir Edward Knowles.

With a shudder, Sukey mounted the step leading to the front door and knocked gently.

A tense Regina responded at once. "Sukey, come in. Oh, poor dear, you need attending to, as well. I shall be with you shortly." She resumed dabbing at wounds on Fitch's arms and scalp with a moist rag.

"You . . . you were in the battle, Fitch?"

"Yes, ma'am."

"Then please, I beg of you, tell me what has happened!"

"Braddock's army," Regina began, "has been ambushed and defeated by the French, outside of Fort Duquesne. Braddock is near death, if he has not already died on the trail."

Sukey clutched her chest in horror. "Defeated? 'Tis not possible, not with all his manpower and guns! I suppose you and Sir Edward played a role in this defeat! Most likely you shall all cheer the French victory at last!" Angry tears stung Sukey's eyes at the thought.

Regina finished binding Fitch's flesh wounds, then rose. "'Tis time, Sukey, that you know the truth. All of it. Yes, Edward played a valuable role in this battle, and all the days leading up to it. A role that nearly cost him his life too many times to count."

"I suppose he sits rejoicing somewhere!" Sukey spat

out. She pivoted to seek him and scorn his very breath. "Where is Sir Edward?"

Regina hesitated. "Edward . . . knows you are here, Sukey. He . . . he is freshening his appearance for you, in my room. So fastidious, is our Edward. He will be with you shortly."

She eyed Sukey's own disheveled garments, hair, and skin.

"This bodes ill, Sukey. Tell me what has happened to you."

"I was captured by three of Mouceau's evil henchmen—Michel Margry, and two other villains. They . . . they intended to rape me, all of them."

"My poor Sukey! And did they?"

"No. Mouceau was to be the first, but he never arrived, thank God! I was bravely rescued by Rafe Stewart and my brother, Zeb."

Fitch sat up on his pallet. "Charlevoix Mouceau never arrived because he is dead, madam," he announced. "Rafe Stewart intended to kill him, but as Rafe drew his rifle, another frontiersman shot Mouceau first."

"I see our news stuns you, my dear." Regina fetched a basin of clean water. "Now, let us refresh you after your own horrible ordeal. Did those wretches starve you, or have you been fed?"

Sukey gratefully took the basin from Regina and made an effort to tidy herself. "A biscuit or two. A mug of cider."

Regina shook her head. "Not nearly enough. We can do much better than that, my dear. Here." Reaching toward an iron pot in the fireplace, she ladled out a bowl of venison stew. "And I feel certain my biscuits are far superior to Michel Margry's," she added, setting a plate of fresh biscuits and a cup of tea before Sukey.

When she had finished the last of her stew, Sukey heard a clattering noise announce Sir Edward's arrival in the kitchen.

"Mrs. Howard, dear lady!" he gushed, reaching to kiss her hand with affected attention. "I understand, from Rafe Stewart, that you have, ah, something to say to me. An apology of some sort?"

Mouth clenched into a pout, Sukey studied lanky Sir Edward Knowles with palpable resentment. His white wig, a bit askew, framed a heavily made-up face and his spectacles. Contemplating him, Sukey shifted nervously from one bare foot to the other.

"My brother, Zeb, seems to feel that I have sullied your reputation. That I owe you an apology."

"For what reason, madam?"

"For . . . well, 'tis because I believed you were a French spy." She crossed her arms defiantly over her chest.

Knowles probed further. "And you still believe it, Mrs. Howard?"

She nodded. "Yes! Unlike Rafe Stewart, who bravely risked his life to help the British, you, sir, aided and abetted the French. Despicable!"

He tapped his forehead with an index finger. "Permit me to clarify the situation, Mrs. Howard. You believe Rafe Stewart has behaved heroically?"

"Yes. Most definitely."

"I see.

"Though admittedly, your odd association with Rafe Stewart puzzles me. I discovered your signet ring where Rafe had slept, and his bear-tooth necklace in your saddlebag." Loathe to verbalize her conclusion, she winced. "Is he, perhaps, your . . . your servant?"

"I could not possibly hope to command Rafe Stewart,

madam. No man can. The rogue does as he pleases. More likely, I am his servant."

Mouth agape, Sukey stepped back. "His . . . ? But I do not understand."

From the corner of her eyes, she saw Regina and Fitch close in on either side of her. Something dramatic was about to unfold, judging from the expressions those two wore.

But what could it be?

Astonished, Sukey focused again on Knowles.

The tall dapper fop carefully removed his gloves and felt black tricorne trimmed with silver cords, and laid them on a wooden kitchen bench. Next, he shrugged off his elaborately embroidered frock coat, and handed it to Regina. He unbuttoned his silver lace-edged waistcoat.

"Sir Edward! What are you doing?" Sukey begged.

He smiled. " 'Tis time, madam, for you to see what lies beneath my apparel."

"Are you mad?" she demanded.

"Altogether possible, madam." He lifted his spectacles and powdered cadogan wig with looped-up queue from his head.

Eyes bulging, Sukey gulped at the newly-exposed lustrous mane of raven-black hair. "It . . . it cannot be!" she cried, clasping her hands to her mouth. Tentatively, she touched the ruffle of Knowles's fine linen shirt as if it might bite her.

"So you see, madam," he announced, "Sir Edward Knowles was never a French spy. He worked in disguise as a spy for the British government."

"As did we!" Regina chimed in, pointing to weak but bandaged Fitch.

Knowles placed one hand on Sukey's shoulder. "Sir Edward Knowles is—"

"Is actually my darling Rafe Stewart!" Suddenly she leaped into his waiting arms.

His embrace engulfed her. He kissed her full on the mouth for what seemed an eternity. Finally he paused.

"Marry me, Sukey. Without you, there is no sunrise or sunset for me. Truly, I never wanted to love or trust any woman again in my life. But I learned there can be no life for me without you at my side."

With her arms looped around his broad neck, she grinned. "And shall my husband be the spineless dandy, Sir Edward Knowles? Or the ferociously rugged Rafe Stewart?"

"That question requires a two-part answer, my love. Here, then, is Part One." He tightened his arms round Sukey's waist and pressed her lips with a lengthy, deepened kiss.

"And . . . and Part Two?" she murmured, when he drew back.

"That, my dear," he replied, glancing over at Regina and Fitch, "shall be delivered behind closed doors when no witnesses are present."

"Ye have not shared the entire story, Edward," Fitch warned, between sips of mint tea. "Best be open about everything."

"'Tis true. Come sit on my knee, Sukey, while I explain."

Sukey snuggled close against Stewart's chest while he cradled her on his lap.

"Our work for the British government," he began, "is dangerous. 'Tis about to become more so. Today's French victory means the French government now controls a string of forts from Canada into the Ohio frontier. And all the trade that flows down the Mississippi River."

Brushing biscuit crumbs from her skirt, Regina

shook her head. "England will not stand for that, luv. Today we stand bloodied and beaten. Tomorrow, England will search for a new way to overthrow the French scoundrels entrenched along the Allegheny River."

Stewart gently brushed Sukey's soft cheek with his fingers. "And we shall be part of that effort, luv. Regina and Fitch and I. 'Tis in our blood. We can live no other way. Charlevoix Mouceau, who killed my brother, is dead. But there will be other villains that we must stop. And a new British offensive that we must assist."

"Perhaps in disguise—always great adventure and fun!" Regina added.

Sukey traced her finger across Stewart's craggy eyebrows and aside his temple. "Sir, you ask me to join you in a life of danger? And adventure?"

Stewart's breathing halted for a moment. "Yes, luv. Am I selfish in hoping you will join me forever? Perhaps 'tis too much to ask of a cultivated woman such as yourself." He hung his head.

Still cuddled on Stewart's lap, she cradled his tanned face. "My darling, how could you know? Adventure with the man I love is precisely what I hoped for when I left my fine Lancaster drawing room. When shall we marry?"

Fitch cleared his throat to get attention. "Begging your pardon, you two lovebirds, but Regina, here, and me—we have some news of our own."

Regina's eyes twinkled. "Fitch, the old devil, has finally decided to make an honest woman of me."

"About time, you old scoundrel!" Stewart chided, with a hoot. "You two have been chasing one another for a dozen years."

"I had no choice this time," Fitch mocked. "She threatened to brand me with her rolling pin."

"Then 'tis settled. A double wedding it shall be!"

Stewart announced. "Now, we must ride at once to visit Eli Whitfield."

"Pa?" Sukey asked. "To ask his blessing?"

"Nay, luv," Stewart told her, as he tenderly stroked her hair. "To save his life."

"Leave here, now?" Rachel Butler could scarcely believe her ears. "But . . . !" She hugged her infant son before handing him to her husband, Jonah.

"Aye," Stewart warned, with a nod. "You have only a matter of days. The French and their Indian allies are drunk with bloody victory from today's battle. I expect the bastards will fan eastward and push every living Englishman back across the Susquehanna."

"Or murder those who refuse to budge," Zeb Whitfield added, absentmindedly touching his knife scabbard.

"My house in Lancaster!" Sukey suddenly remembered. "All of you—Rachel and Jonah and the baby, and Pa. Yes, and even Zeb, can stay there. Surely you will be safe there."

"Eh?" His eyes twinkling, Eli puffed on his clay pipe before good-naturedly thumping Stewart on the back. "And just where will you be, daughter?"

Sukey's eyes narrowed. "Pa! You crafty old Cupid! You knew all the time!"

"Well, almost from the beginning."

"But how?" she begged.

"A father's responsibility, Sukey, my girl. I met Edward Rafe Stewart years ago when he and his brother, Thomas, traded out here on the frontier. Finer men I never met. Rafe swore me to secrecy, last month, in exchange for some smithing help he needed on his horses."

Stewart draped his arm over Sukey's shoulder. "Well you know, Eli, I shall protect her with my life, if need be." He winked. "Though next time you see her, you might not recognize even your own daughter."

Clapping her hands with anticipation, Rachel laughed. "Our own dear Sukey! Shall she be round with child? Or hidden under one of your clever disguises?"

Stewart revealed nothing, only smiled.

"The preacher!" Eli thundered. "Sukey shall not gallivant about in Rafe's disguises till the preacher says his words over the two of them."

"And us, as well," Fitch informed them.

"That settles it, then," Stewart commented. "We shall leave—"

"I will not be going with you." Zeb's solemn words came as he knocked ash from his pipe.

Sukey frowned. "But why, Zeb? 'Tis far too dangerous for you out here now!"

Zeb's face darkened. "I have a score to settle with the French. The scars they left on my back, two years ago, remind me of that fact every day."

Patting her brother's arm, Sukey thought a moment. Her fingers flitted to the silver pendant dangling from her own throat. She untied the rawhide string holding the charm.

"You shall have this, Zeb," she said, handing him the pendant. "'Tis your turn. It saved Rachel's life, and mine. Now you shall need protection."

Zeb backed away. "'Tis nonsense, Sukey. Just mere happenstance, is all. I am not deceived by such gibberish."

Undeterred, Sukey held the pendant against her brother's chest. "Then wear it as a handsome piece of jewelry, Zeb. I insist. 'Twill look fine against your dark complexion."

" 'Tis your turn, brother," Rachel agreed.

Rafe laughed at the two sisters. "They conspire against you, Zeb. You have no chance against two such determined women."

Reluctantly, Zeb allowed his sisters to slip the pendant around his neck. "All nonsense," he repeated. "You shall see." He joined Eli and Jonah, busy packing their most valued belongings, while Rachel sat down to nurse Adam.

Rafe caught Sukey's hand and led her toward the stable for a brief kiss.

"You naughty man!" she whispered, eyes shining with joy. "All those shameless kisses you stole from me dressed as obnoxious Sir Edward . . . here in the stable and elsewhere."

"I fell in love with you the first moment I saw you, my darling. And knew I could never rest till I kissed you."

She giggled. "We had delightful escapades, Rafe, did we not?" She draped her arms around his lean-muscled mid-section.

He tipped her face up toward his. "We shall have many more escapades on behalf of the British government, love . . . if you're game for it. A life full of costumes and adventures."

"And abundant lovemaking, Rafe? Ah, my darling, I can no longer abide life without your touch."

He pulled her close within his arms. "I shall touch you whenever you wish, my love. Though, with your hawk-eyed father watching, I suspect we shall have to wait till we locate a preacher."

The words played across her tongue. "Rafe Stewart . . . my husband. Oh, Rafe! That day cannot come too soon!"

AUTHOR'S NOTE

Marilyn Herr is published in both historical and contemporary fiction. She's happiest when immersed in nature. Gardening is a joy so long as she can contemplate flowers, listen to songbirds, and ignore weeds. A former nurse, she finds that writing is a magic door leading to a kingdom of surprises, where her imagination can roam freely. She loves hearing from readers and can be contacted at: mherr@ccis.net